GUE   Guerard, Albert J.
           (Albert Joseph),
           1914-

           The hotel in the
           jungle.

GUE   Guerard, Albert
           J. (Albert
           Joseph),

           The hotel in the
           jungle.

$23.00 SEP 27   Z 3740

DATE	BORROWER'S NAME	

The Hotel in the Jungle

Also by Albert J. Guerard

Novels
THE PAST MUST ALTER
THE HUNTED
MAQUISARD
NIGHT JOURNEY
THE BYSTANDER
THE EXILES
CHRISTINE/ANNETTE
GABRIELLE

Literary Criticism
ROBERT BRIDGES
JOSEPH CONRAD
THOMAS HARDY
ANDRE GIDE
CONRAD THE NOVELIST
THE TRIUMPH OF THE NOVEL:
Dickens, Dostoevsky, Faulkner

Personal Experience
THE TOUCH OF TIME: MYTH, MEMORY AND THE SELF

The Hotel in the Jungle

a Novel by

Albert J. Guerard

64,940

BASKERVILLE
PUBLISHERS, INC.

All rights reserved under International and Pan-American Copyright Conventions. Published in the United States by Baskerville Publishers, Inc., 7616 LBJ Freeway, Suite 220, Dallas, Texas 75251-1008

Library of Congress Cataloging-in-publication data

Guerard, Albert J. (Albert Joseph), 1914-
    The hotel in the jungle: a novel / by Albert J. Guerard
    p.   cm.
    ISBN 1-880909-45-6
    1. Americans--Travel--Mexico--Fiction. 2. Missing persons--
    Mexico--Fiction. 3. Hotels--Mexico--Fiction.
    I. Title.
PS3513.U353H6   1996
813'.52--dc20   96-7746
                                                        CIP

All rights reserved
First printing, 1996
Manufactured in the United States of America

For Sabrina
blithe spirit

THE INHABITANTS

Adivina Alicia (dates unknown), fortuneteller
Angelita Braciano (born 1903), Mexican dancer
Cyrus Cranfield (1906-1982), entrepreneur, owner of hotel
Artemio Angel de la Cruz (born 1900), guide and interpreter
Delphine Deslonde (1834-1901), friend of Rosellen Maurepas
Eloise Deslonde (born 1959), graduate student, Tulane University
Brian Desmond (1874-disappeared 1918), poet, heavyweight boxer
Hippolyte Dupoint (1811-1872), French solitary
Nicanor Díaz (1890-1932), bandit and guerilla leader
Juan and Juanito (dates unknown), Rosellen's Indian guides
Dolores Inocencia, Lupita, Consuela, Suzy (all born ca. 1964),
    starlets
"Marita" (born ca. 1856), Zoque friend of Charles Stanfield
Rosellen Maurepas (born 1834), met William Walker in 1848
"Hap" O'Brien (dates unknown), 49er, drifter
Pascualito (dates unknown), Mexican curandero, caring for Cranfield
Roberto Rodriguez (born 1944), lawyer, entrepreneur, bon vivant
Monica Swift (1878-1966), English poet, married to Brian Desmond
Charles Stanfield (1850-1922) engineer, teacher
Papa Jack (1878-1946), former heavyweight champion
William Walker (born 1824-1860?), filibuster, statesman
Unnamed amateur archeologist (dates unknown), possibly
    B. F. Traven
Antonio Vinalva (born 1893), concierge, later hotel manager
Ramón Vinalva (1860?-disappeared 1916), Antonio's father, hotel
    manager
Jimmy Wilding (born ca. 1900), English boxer, companion of Papa
    Jack

GRAN HOTEL BALNEARIO CHIMALAPA

JUNGLE ADVENTURE AND EXPLORATION

NIGHT CLUB CASINO FREE MOVIES

FAMOUS HOT SPRINGS FOR ARTERITIS ASTHMAS

45 ROUND FIGHTS

ALL MASSAGES INDIANS CURES AND HERBS

SALON DE BELLEZA

"AN EROTIC PARADISE!" TROPICS TRAVEL

Gran Hotel Balneario Chimalapa

The first hotel was built in 1890 and was destroyed the next year.

The second hotel was open 1908-1915, 1922-1943, 1946-1968. Reopened 1982.

The hotels were built on the outskirts of the Zoque Indian village of Santa Rosalia, in the Isthmus of Tehuantepec in southern Mexico, at the edge of an unexplored jungle.

PROEM: The Hotel in the Jungle

IN A JUNGLE in southern Mexico, in the wild region known as the Chimalapas, are the ruins of two small cities abandoned more than two hundred years ago. They are on the Isthmus of Tehuantepec in the province of Oaxaca. One of the two cities, Chimalapilla, has long since disappeared beneath jungle growth, although the foundations of a church and a ball court have been found. But the second, Casas Grandes, a few miles farther up the Rio Corte, remained remarkably free of vegetation, like the Biblical rock city of Edom or the solid monolith of Gibraltar. The two cities, inhabited by Zoque Indians, were abandoned after the plague known as the mehualtha reached them in 1757. Many of the inhabitants fled down the river and settled in the villages of Santa Rosalia and Santa Maria Chimalapa. The fugitives left the bodies of the victims untouched. Years later a few Indians ventured to Casas Grandes out of curiosity or for loot. They were terrified to see on the plaza the unburied bones and staring skulls of the dead.

Since then Casas Grandes has been a dreaded and forbidden place for the Zoques of Santa Rosalia and Santa Maria, not least because of the stone city's occult resistance to jungle growth. An immense flat monolith extended from a row of stone habitations, caves really, to and across the bed of the small river, leaving an unencumbered space or plaza some hundred yards in depth. Trees sprouted in crevices between the stone houses but did not flourish. Above and behind them the jungle took command, although a ball court remained remarkably free. The covered ruins extended another hundred yards beyond the ball court and ended in a small pyramid.

It is an area of many earthquakes and the two great historical eruptions of the volcano El Chichón; perhaps the smooth monolith was caused by a natural disaster. But some Indians believed the plaza had been kept clear of jungle by the supernatural labor of *moyós,* savage dwarfs who inhabited the caves of the region, not only those of Casas Grandes. Others thought it was the work of wild men, descendants of Spanish soldiers of Cortés who fled into the jungle to save themselves from further combat. They sought to escape by an ancient *camino secreto* leading south into Chiapas, a network of streams and paths and stone causeways. The first generation of deserters didn't dare emerge to face their officers. Their descendants were said to have accepted the free life of the wilderness, although a few retained memories of the old civilizing ways of conquest. It was they who cleared away the jungle growth and cast spells to prevent its return.

There were also stories of gringo miners returning disappointed from California, who went up the Rio Corte in search of gold. One of them, who seems to have had a truly charmed life, was on a number of occasions seen floating down the Rio Corte on a balsa raft. In time his hair turned white. But no one ever saw him go back up. There were also stories, about the time of the opening of the first hotel, of a tall white woman whose long blonde hair hung in serpentine coils, a belated companion, it would seem, for the lonely miner.

The location of the *camino secreto* remains unknown to this day, and many fugitives have lost their lives trying to find it, among them soldiers of Almazán and Felix Díaz in 1916. As for the rock city of Casas Grandes, it has been from time to time a place of refuge for smugglers, filibusters, revolutionaries, bandits, deserters. The Indians, who know better, keep away.

There were also three imaginative American adventurers, two of them women, who went on expeditions to Casas Grandes in search of people who had disappeared long before. They too were curious concerning the secret of its white stone houses miraculously free of encroaching jungle, as though the city had been periodically washed by flood or, even, existed outside chronological time. Two of the three seem to have discovered another of the stone city's secrets: that to free oneself from time, in such a visiting of the past, is to experience eternity here and now, and, incidentally, to be freed of their mortal envelope.

The first, in 1870, was Rosellen Maurepas. The second was Charles Stanfield, who met Rosellen in 1870, and who returned to the area after fifty-two years. The third, Eloise Deslonde, was a graduate student in history and she was motivated by curiosity concerning the others. She went there in 1982.

Such was Casas Grandes. It was in Santa Rosalia, some fifteen miles downriver, that the first Gran Hotel Balneario Chimalapa was built in 1890. Here the weary traveler could pause between his Atlantic and Pacific sea journeys, and for a few days enjoy the exotic experiences of a remote tropical jungle and an unspoiled Indian village. But few travelers had a chance to see the new hotel's gaudy Victorian furnishings. For it was literally washed away in 1891 in a flood that followed on an earthquake. The earthquake struck in the midst of wild summer rains. The new road almost instantly disappeared beneath fallen trees and jungle ooze. Everything that could float went down the river between its crumbling banks. The imperturbable Indians watched chairs and beds and an entire mahogany bar with brass fittings rush past, banisters and stairs, even a large fragment of wooden ceiling to which a chandelier remained firmly attached. What was left of the hotel, scattered over a half mile of fallen trees and uprooted garden, was abandoned over the summer, and by October, when the rains slackened, very little remained.

The second hotel was erected in the same place, in 1908, five stories of solid limestone, a column of white towering above the nearest trees.

This was the hotel Charles Stanfield visited in 1922 and Eloise Deslonde, the biographer of Rosellen Maurepas, sixty years later.

Eloise Deslonde

IN THE HOT dying New Orleans afternoon Eloise Deslonde, dressed only in bermuda shorts and a T-shirt celebrating a Delta Queen cruise, listened with mounting irritation to the chatter of tourists standing beneath her wrought iron balcony. Above her, above her typewriter with its blank page, the wistful yet commanding eyes of Rosellen Maurepas in daguerreotype looked out from an ornate Victorian frame. It was a Rosellen about her own age, in her early twenties, who had already lost her family in the plague of 1853. And who had not yet married the husband she would lose in the War Between the States. Attached to each side of Rosellen's were studio portraits of Charles Stanfield, one as a young man of twenty, the other as a pensive man in his sixties. Beneath them Eloise had affixed a large Hallmark valentine as in honor of their 1870 encounter in Mexico.

They met in Minatitlán on the Isthmus of Tehuantepec, Rosellen on her quixotic journey in search of the possibly surviving William Walker, Stanfield a very young civilian engineer attached to the Navy expedition surveying for a transisthmus canal. She was nearly twice his age and had had many suitors; she detected at once both his shyness and his interest in herself. *He moves with great ease, as though his lithe body had no bones. He pretends to look in the other*

direction, but his beautiful brown eyes roll back to seek mine.
So she would note in the journal of her trip. And, only a few
days later, *Why have I never had such a lover as my brave
young engineer?*

She had begun her diary at thirteen. *I will faithfully write
in this Book all my Adventures and my Sentiments both good
and evil. Today ordered a straw hat of full satin merveilleux.*
A diary that would describe her fateful meeting at fourteen
with William Walker, not yet the notorious filibuster and conqueror of Nicaragua, at a cotillion at the St. Charles Hotel.
And that twenty-two years after that would record her belief
that Walker had survived execution. The soldiers had fired
blanks.

All about Eloise, in her small room in the French Quar-
ter, were the books and notes for her Tulane thesis on Rosellen
Maurepas as a "Liberated Woman in Antebellum and Postbellum New Orleans." Near the open window and balcony
was a newspaper portrait of the once famous poet Monica
Swift, who died in 1966. She too belonged in the thesis. Did
Monica, who had so many lovers on two continents, entice
the seventy-two-year-old Stanfield to her bed in that jungle
hotel in Santa Rosalia? Probably not, to judge from his journal and hers. Eloise kept the most precious of her materials
in a small steel box: photographs, letters and journals inher-
ited from her great grandmother Delphine Deslonde, and the
water-stained but still legible journal of Rosellen Maurepas
herself. There too were the 1870 and 1922 journals and numerous family photographs of Charles Stanfield.

All the essentials for a good Ph.D. thesis, one which would
plausibly relate Rosellen's two obsessions: the Isthmus of
Tehuantepec and William Walker. *The Isthmus of
Tehuantepec.* Rosellen was nine when she first heard the rolling sound of words that would weave in and out of her daydreams. She heard them because she was huddled only a few
feet from the open living room door. The rich masculine odor
of cigars gave authority to the subdued voices of men ex-

changing secrets. Beyond the door her father and several important men, one of them the Mayor, were discussing the building of a railroad in far-off Mexico. They spoke of shares and loans and grants. But also of Aztecs and Zoques and Zapotecs, jaguars and iguanas, great limestone cliffs to quarry. Far up the Rio Corte were the mysterious ruins of Casas Grandes. The wild Indians were strong enough to move mountains, though "their love of liquor is inordinate." The railroad born in this drawing room, in their own house, would "carry coal to the steamers of the Pacific" and "return bone and oil from the whaling ships."

Her father found her studying the map of the region affixed to a living room wall. Small black dots to indicate the ruins of Chimalapilla and Casas Grandes.

"I want to go there some day. Casas Grandes."

"It is a haunted place. The Indians sacrificed maidens. They threw them into a sacred well."

"But not now?"

"Not now."

For many days Rosellen could not get the beautiful phrases out of her mind, and skipped to their rhythm on the sidewalk. *Isthmus of Tehuantepec, their love of liquor is inordinate, bone and oil from the whaling ships.*

Rosellen had always been adventurous. At nine she rode uninvited on the ceremonial first trip of the suburban Carrollton Railroad, in the car nearest the engine as it puffed its way, all gleaming brass boiler and high thin smokestack, along the route followed by the St. Charles Avenue streetcar today. In this year, 1843, with a genial father who dispensed silver dollars as readily as pennies, she became an inveterate shopper, and liked to buy desirable objects by mail. All the doll petticoats, bodices, skirts and corsets arrived as promised. She bought at the French Market a canary that refused to sing, so her next mail order was for a bird organ designed to teach birds "to sing and whistle popular airs." Her mother was a bedridden somnolent invalid for whom she ordered

Ozone Paper to relieve spasmodic asthma. At eleven she bought gris-gris ankle bracelets for Delphine and the black slave Sarah. That year she also bought *The Facts of Mesmerism*, and made her first efforts to hypnotize her companions. The nuns at the Ursuline convent school made her remove the ankle bracelet. Only here was there any discipline in her life. During recess she managed whispered conversations with a favorite nun, and told her what she had learned about magnetic fluid.

"You are flirting with the Devil," the young nun said.

An oil portrait of Rosellen at twelve has a pink-cheeked Romney innocence except for an odd twist at one corner of the mouth, as though her tongue were rooted there. The dark brown eyes are mischievous but kind, the brown hair falls in ringlets on bare shoulders. In a daguerreotype of Rosellen in her twenties, with the whole family dead from the plague of 1853, she has the porcelain pallor and otherworldly dreaming expression of a Pre-Raphaelite victim or saint. There are also surviving photographs of the friend Delphine from the time of her marriage until her death, and one of Edward Lyndon, to whom Rosellen was engaged off and on for years, and married at last, and who died in the war. It is faded so badly that the eyes do not glare, as in so many pictures of that time, but instead seem utterly vacant, as though a dead man's head had been attached to the confederate uniform of a photographer's backdrop.

Eloise had more than enough material for a thesis that should neatly end with 1870. So her thesis adviser urged, a tired fatherly professor who always wore a Borsalino hat to cover his bald head. It should end with Rosellen disappearing without a trace in the ruins of Casas Grandes. Yet was she not still alive in 1922, if only in the memory of the young engineer now old, returning to the area in an act of erotic faith? *Erotic faith:* it appealed to Eloise as a nice title for a chapter, one devoted to the life of Charles Stanfield, who also found his way to Casas Grandes. How could she leave

9

out his later life? And how could she omit the Gran Hotel Balneario Chimalapa and the events of 1922? The poet Monica Swift there, looking for traces of her lost husband Brian Desmond. And the former heavyweight champion Papa Jack, enlisted to publicize the hotel, with his diminutive sparring partner Jimmy Wilding, a young British bantamweight. And Charles Stanfield, now a retired school teacher, returning to the scenes of two youthful adventures, one chaste, the other evidently not. To sleep together after only a few days acquaintance would have been unheard of in 1870, even for a Liberated Woman. But was there nothing at all between Rosellen and Stanfield, not even a few passionate kisses in their short time together, since it seems to have been love at first sight for him and for her at least a bemused longing, a hint that the dead Edward Lyndon had not been much of a husband? Again the haunting phrase: *"Why have I never had such a lover as my young engineer?"* And did Stanfield really expect to find the other one, the Zoque girl Marita, when he returned to the village after fifty-two years?

Eloise acquired the Stanfield papers after only a short interview with Charles' grandson, an aged stockbroker in Nashville. He was amused by this interest in an ancestor who had led such an unprofitable life and who acquired nothing of value on his return to southern Mexico in 1922, fifty-two years after his first excursion.

"He had no business going back. So many Americans simply vanish down there. What was the use? There were oil rights to be had for the asking in 1922, but he apparently did no asking. He bought nothing and sold nothing, he extracted nothing from the earth. His papers? I have only glanced at them. You are welcome to anything I can find in the attic. The papers have no monetary value." So now she had Charles Stanfield's diary too for that 1870 romance, not only Rosellen's. *A quiet enchantment unspoiled by stirrings of lust,* he wrote, *We were two children touching hands, she much over thirty, I only twenty. From our first hours in Minatitlán, and how much more on the* Allegheny Belle, *we were drawn together in spiritual kinship, though I share none of her delusions regarding General Walker.*

The true kinship, Eloise surmised, was between Rosellen and William Walker, felt even at their first meeting in the grand rotunda where every day slaves were bought and sold, she fourteen—*in my pink tarletan with wreaths of small white roses, three skirts one over the other*—Walker twenty-four and the editor of *The Crescent*, not yet the filibuster General of the 58 Immortals and conqueror of Nicaragua. He was accompanied by his deaf-mute fiancée Ellen Martin, who carried a pencil and little pad to be used with those who did not know sign language or could not read lips. At five-foot-six Rosellen was a good inch taller than Walker: a thin freckled man, towheaded, whose *"gray eyes appeared to look through me inattentively."* He was entirely in black, except for a plain lace shirt, with skintight trousers strapped under his shoes. A sombre figure among the dandies in their flowered waistcoats. *"But then his eyes changed, I could see behind them, a hidden being had swum to the surface and was moving toward me."* And now Eloise the sober historian could see and hear the exchange reported in the diary.

Rosellen curtsied, William Walker bowed.

"Miss Rosellen. It is my pleasure, although I am told your father disapproves of me."

"Disapproves?"

"Of what I have written about foolish expeditions to Cuba."

"Perhaps someone else's father, not mine."

"Is there more than one Gilles Maurepas in the city? I am convinced the extension of slavery to Cuba or any new territory would be a mistake. I am opposed to drunken filibusters who violate the neutrality laws. We have no right to interfere abroad. This is not a popular opinion in New Orleans."

"I have read your articles, I admire them. I do not intend to own slaves, Mr Walker."

"I commend you for that. You are a surprising young lady."

She could think of nothing further to say about slavery.

"Do you know the Isthmus of Tehuantepec, Mr Walker?"

"You are thinking of your father's plans for a railroad?"

"It is a romantic place. The railroad will provide a short-cut to the Pacific bringing bone and oil from the whaling ships. The Indians are strong enough to move mountains. Their love of liquor is inordinate."

"No doubt," Walker replied, much surprised. The gray eyes appeared to move toward her as with a purpose to draw her deep inside. She fancied she could see herself reflected in the tiny pupils.

The words *Casas Grandes* came to her unbidden, as though dictated by the staring man.

"There are remarkable ruins on the Isthmus of Tehuantepec. I particularly wish to visit Casas Grandes."

"You are an adventurous young lady, Miss Rosellen. Like father, like daughter. Be sure you are well armed."

She wrote in her journal for that day, October 28, 1848: *His fingers dance nimbly as he and Ellen "talk." There is occult communication when their eyes meet, but also when his eyes meet mine. To think his whole life will be devoted to poor Ellen's happiness! And there will never be raised voices in anger or scorn between them. She will lie silently in the softest of Spiritual Embraces, as did Psyche in the arms of Cupid before her fatal mistake. If Ellen were also blind his fingers would speak by touching her lips.*

After that there were only two meetings in the twelve years that took Walker to fame and ruin, and at those meetings no words were exchanged. In April 1849 Ellen Martin died of cholera. At the cemetery service Rosellen stood behind the other mourners with her face well hidden by a black rain cape. She did not want to be teased or asked questions. But as the service ended the stricken Walker appeared to look directly at her and for some moments did not look away. *He saw me! He knew I was there! I am more than ever convinced of magnetic communication between kindred minds. I now also believe it may exist between the quick and the dead. Mr Walker and I are destined to meet again and know each other's minds and hearts.*

And she felt it, the magnetic communication, even during the years when there were no meetings, even during the solitary months in a silent house during the worst of the plague, her mother and father soon to be dead, and still *a precious current flows into me, if only from a damaged soul.* She would feel it from time to time, during the eight years of Walker's flamboyant career, the short-lived conquest of Baja California, then the triumphs in Nicaragua, the Indians' gray-eyed man of destiny now President, June 29, 1856. On August 12 she wrote: *They say Nicaragua is a gracious place of old Spanish times. I would like secretly to visit that country, to watch unseen the President about his ceremonies. Then one day he might espy my white face in the crowd of dusky natives at the gate to the palace. "Have we not met before? Was it not in New Orleans, at a cotillion in the St. Charles?"* But then came the startling news that Walker, once the idealistic reporter, had reinstituted slavery by decree.

He has betrayed his highest principles to win the support of the new landowners who need cheap slave labor. From this day I put him out of mind.

But that she could not do. And then the third and last meeting as Walker was leaving the court in New Orleans, charged with planning still another expedition in violation of the neutrality laws. His skin was now brown and leathery, almost Indian, the cheekbones higher than she remembered. And again their eyes met: *I try to look back with cool reason on our silent encounter. He turned as in response to my thoughts. His hands rose to his face, his fingers moved in sign language as with his beloved Ellen. The glare in his eyes was that of a damned soul and for a night and a day I dreamed of sharing his damnation.*

13

And that was all. There were two more Walker expeditions and two more ludicrous failures. It was only with Walker's last invasion attempt, at Trujillo in Honduras, and with his execution there, that he reappeared in Rosellen's journal and in her daydreams, still wearing the black suit of the St. Charles cotillion, but sometimes with no clothes at all, since the ruffian firing squad had stolen them. He fell on a sandy beach, near a small abandoned adobe house and beside the crude hole that had been previously prepared, in which he was buried in a ten-peso casket. So the newspapers reported, September 21, 1860. *"He is dead. His eyes were not bandaged, he faced fearlessly the murderers. Requiescat in pace. And yet I cannot truly believe he is dead."*

On the 25th came news that he had been "on the eve of being shot," and on the 27th people arriving on the schooner *Taylor* said the story of an execution was false. But two days later came a detailed report. The firing squad had turned away from the fallen body in scorn, leaving everything to the foreigners present. But in the next ten years (all her family dead from the plague, the war lost, a husband disappeared or dead in the furnace of war) Rosellen continued to feel it, the magnetic current flowing into her from an unseen but living source. And so she was ready to believe the stories of survival. The firing squad had fired blanks, the bribed executioners had walked away from the body already thrown into an open grave. Or a common criminal had been executed in Walker's place.

One story told of falangist veterans who claimed to have seen their leader years after his supposed death. A Louis Jeffry saw Walker in a bar in Panama, dressed as a common sailor, drunkenly singing a confederate marching song. At the jeers of young sailors nearby he broke off his song and shouted *"I have killed many! I will kill again!"* Another old falangist found him lounging in a ship-chandler's office in Havana. The familiar gray eyes were unseeing. *"It might have been a dead man in the chair, with the burnt out stub of a cigar in his hand.*" A third veteran almost ran him down on a dingy back street in Whitechapel, London, in a heavy rain. The ravaged face glared, "*Look out where you're going, matey!*" But this apparition turned and ran at the sound of his shocked exclamation: "*Mr Walker! General!*" Hearing these stories, Rosellen believed and did not believe. In the end it may have been a poem by the California poet Joaquin Miller, "At the Grave of Walker," that decided her.

> He lies low in the leveled sand,
> Unsheltered from the tropic sun,
> And now of all he knew not one
> Will speak him fair in that far land,
> Perhaps 'twas this that made me seek,
> Disguised, his grave one winter-tide.

She too would go to Trujillo, if only to rid herself of her obsession that Walker had survived.

November 7, 1870. I will not let his ghost haunt me any longer. I will put an end to this uncertainty once and for all.

And Eloise Deslonde, the unconventional graduate student of history, holding the water-stained page up to the light, still seemed to share Rosellen's uncertainty, even though she had found no modern historian who subscribed to the story of a false execution. There were times when, pondering the last entries in Rosellen's journal before she left New Orleans, she Eloise seemed to be living in the past she was supposed to be coolly examining. She was stifling in Rosellen's cramped quarters aboard the *Confluencia*, she could see the miserable Indians standing in a Nicaraguan hotel courtyard under the rain, she was there with Stanfield and Rosellen in the moonlight, under the hill where the Malinche was buried. But at other times she was with Stanfield and Monica in 1922 as they talked on the terrace of the Gran Hotel Balneario, with the four Indian pilgrims camped a few feet away, incorrigibly believing there was something sacred on the third floor of the hotel.

Questions that occurred to Eloise at odd moments were scrawled on yellow notes affixed to a bulletin board beside grocery lists and admonitions to get up earlier, write letters, pay bills:

Ask geology prof. about rock city of Casas Grandes. Like Gibraltar?
Anything in Santa Rosalia now? Just ruins of hotel?
What happened to Brian Desmond?
Did he really fight Papa Jack in Barcelona?
Hard to get to Santa Rosalia now?

The last question was not a serious one. It was good party talk, when no one had anything to say, to bring up her strange thesis subject Rosellen, and the lonely retired teacher who went back to see what his indiscretion had sown, and the romantic bandit Nicanor Díaz, an instant victim of Monica Swift's notorious seductiveness. And the hulking black champion Papa Jack, no doubt more comfortable in Mexico than at home after his year's imprisonment in Leavenworth thanks to the intolerance of the time.

"I wonder if there's a road now to Casas Grandes? That's where Rosellen disappeared."

There were other graduate students who thought Eloise's speculations frivolous. What business had she writing about boxers and bandits and a jungle hotel in 1922 when her nominal subject had disappeared in 1870?

One of these students challenged her now.

"Is there a road? Well why don't you go down and see? Not just talk about it."

"Maybe I will."

But she really hadn't a serious intention of going until she came upon a travel page story about Santa Rosalia and its newly reopened hotel, now owned by Cyrus Cranfield, a reclusive and eccentric millionaire. The hotel had been closed for many years. Deep in a steaming Mexican jungle Cranfield dreamed of making movies! The article gave a short history of the hotel, much of it probably misinformed. It noted that Papa Jack the former heavyweight champion had been there in 1922. No mention of Monica Swift, of course no mention of Charles Stanfield. Elderly and infirm people came there in the dry season for the waters of a remarkable hot spring and to enjoy oil baths. There were a few permanent residents, one "an aged English boxer who claims to have been a sparring partner of the black champion."

An aged English boxer! Why shouldn't this be the Jimmy Wilding whose antics so amused Charles Stanfield and who from time to time appeared in his 1922 journal? *A pied piper, Jimmy skips rope in the village, a boxer's shuffle round and round the plaza, followed by half a school of chirping children in rags.*

At the end of the article was the travel writer's succinct comment:

Access difficult, 30 rooms with bath, some air-conditioned, inexpensive, unspoiled jungle, mosquitoes and other predators in rainy season. Not recommended.

Not recommended indeed! She telephoned her adviser for an appointment, then rushed to a small travel agency in the next block. Nothing to learn there, and nothing at the Monteleone. Any resort not in the Red Book or in their files was not worth considering. But on the third try she found an idle agent who was willing to go through a box of brochures for Mexico and the Caribbean. And here it was, a badly printed flier.

GRAN HOTEL BALNEARIO CHIMALAPA

JUNGLE ADVENTURE AND EXPLORATION

NIGHTCLUB CASINO FREE MOVIES

FAMOUS HOT SPRINGS FOR ARTERITIS ASTHMAS

45 ROUND FIGHTS

ALL MASSAGES INDIANS CURES AND HERBS

SALON DE BELLEZA

"AN EROTIC PARADISE!" TROPICS TRAVEL

On the back of the flier was a grainy photograph of a white five-story building. There were tourists in white as for tennis, and a number of smiling Indians, the women naked to the waist. The agent suspected these women were imported from another photograph, perhaps an old *National Geographic*. Guests could take a "luxury train" from Mexico City, air-conditioned sleeping cars. A hotel bus would meet all trains at Chivela.

"It looks terrible to me," the friendly agent said. "I wouldn't think of going to the Isthmus of Tehuantepec."

"I am going," Eloise announced firmly. "How do I get there?"

And so it was, five mornings later, she found herself on a Mexican train. A long noisy night after Mexico City, with a number of snoring Mexicans hidden behind the green curtains which hung, exactly as in Charles Stanfield's 1922 journal, all the way to the floor. But early in the morning the

18

snorers got off at Córdoba. Here she bought coffee, a sugary bun and several bananas from a trainside vendor. Between Córdoba and Tres Valles she was the only occupant of the old sixteen-section sleeping car, although several hundred Mexicans were crowded into the two other passenger cars.

So now she was riding alone in a sleeping car much older than she, maybe older than her parents. The fan at one end of the car was broken; the one at the other end was missing. There was no wooden or other seat in the tiny cubicle containing the toilet next the women's dressing room. Minutes before leaving Mexico City the announced air-conditioned roomette car, still bearing the name *Wichita Falls*, had been detached before her eyes, and this older one substituted, perhaps because there were so few sleeping car passengers. The substituted car had the anomalous name *Progreso*. Near the unusable drinking fountain, a tiny spigot beneath a tubular tank, a small brass plaque gave the builder's name, also the words *Missouri Pacific 1912*. Could it conceivably be the very car Charles Stanfield took on his 1922 journey into the past? Then the only other passenger was the voluble trouser salesman Silvestre Aguilar. Now there was nobody.

Eloise looked out on the bright morning. For some time the train had been creeping through the rundown suburbs of Córdoba, but now it was moving slowly in open country. Yet still a few desperate vendors trotted beside the train, tapping at her window, and offering pineapples, fruit drinks, straw hats, even a stuffed iguana, exactly as in Charles Stanfield's time. She had only to close her eyes to half believe it was on his train she was riding, in 1922, and that she would encounter him before the end of the day.

Or, better still, that she was about to join Rosellen on her voyage in search of William Walker, on board an old steamship with a slight starboard list, about to enter the Gulf.

1870

The Tehuantepec Journey

NOVEMBER 2, 1870. On board the *Alabama*, a wretched steamer, the captain a ruffian whose soiled jacket hangs open over linens no less soiled. All afternoon the paddles slapped and churned as we crept past old Mississippi's marshy shores and plantations sadly in need of renewal. In the first hour the soot covered me and I was pervaded by foul odors from below. But now we enter the Gulf. Perched at the very front of this soiled aquatic animal, I breathe the clear ear and watch dolphins at play. I long for their innocent freedom. So slowly do we move I hardly believe in less than three days we will have arrived in Honduras. No matter if Mr Walker is quick or dead. I am filled with joy to leave the *futility* of my life. "A rich widow of good family." What fun if I were to return with a fiery Spanish Creole or even a mysterious *Mayan* husband! How the tongues would wag!

Suppose Mathilde Deslonde had married Mr Walker not General Beauregard?

November 3, 1870. As the only first class lady passenger I have special privileges, with a long key to be used for excluding unwelcome visitors.

The words *Ladies Only* have been roughly chalked on the door. And at dinner I sit at the Portuguese captain's right

23

hand. On his left an oily Honduran man of business who rolled off with relish his many names, of which Vasquez was the last. His long hair is dyed an improbable black. With us too is a bold young Yankee, a Mr Hunter, who rudely stared when I said I was traveling for "curiosity and pleasure," then put a finger to his lips as to give me the lie. This Mr Hunter has the look of a man who has known all the vices and depravities. He has the fevered eye of a gambler, the goatee of Mephistopheles.

"For the pleasure of a husband? He has gone ahead to scout out the terrain?"

"My husband is dead. I hope to write a book of my travels and am much interested in the history of General William Walker."

"He too is dead," Señor Vasquez said. "A scoundrel who thought he could unite all the Americas from Panama to Honduras. He did not understand our ways."

"He understood ours," Mr Hunter replied. "Divide and conquer. After that, rule."

"Instead he died in a ditch."

"Not true!" I said. "He died on the beach of a town I intend to visit. Trujillo. He is said to have died bravely facing the firing squad. But others say he still lives."

"A cat has nine lives."

Might not the bold Mr Hunter be speaking of himself? If this were a longer journey I wager he would invite me to join the gentlemen in their smoking room for a game of cards. I think several purses will be lighter before we reach Puerto Cortés.

November 12, 1870. En route Puerto Cortés to Trujillo. *La Confluencia* is a "worthy bark" of fifty tons with a single cabin, a storeroom really, where they have slung a hammock for me while all others remain on deck. For the purposes of nature there is only a chamber pot whose contents I throw overboard myself.

There is heated discussion on the deck, which has to do with Roatán Island. In his last futile venture Mr Walker lingered several days in this very portion of the sea, hoping to take Roatán as a stepping off place for a more substantial invasion. Instead he proceeded to Trujillo and defeat.

An island has appeared to the "port side," with the inviting name of Cochinos. Did he once set foot there?

November 14, Trujillo. I have seen the small stone sunk in the sandy soil where William Walker lies. A laughing almost naked half-breed child held the stub of a cigar in his left hand while he pried at the caked mud and swept until the indistinct lettering appeared. A sombre gray sky, sultry waters lazily slapped the shore. *Sic transit gloria mundi.*

I have said here that I write a book of my travels. But the degenerate American who dogs my steps wonders why a book of travels should include Trujillo. He calls himself "the Sergeant" and has left behind any other name with whatever misdeeds of his life. I remind him that the great Cortés landed here in quest of further empire, and established this grassy and crumbling fortress Castillo where lizards and horrible green creatures lurk. He dreamed of a city that would be a thriving capital with a towering cathedral. Mr Walker too saw this miserable place as his last hope and stepping stone to revenge if not conquest.

"The Sergeant" claims to have known "the President," who was called "Uncle Billy" by some of his men. But I think he is lying. He says there are other veterans of the Walker falange in Greytown in Nicaragua. I will certainly go there.

November 15, Trujillo. An apocalyptic rain in this dry season, so I cannot leave the filth of the hotel. In the bar are traders from the interior regions who bring their motley goods by mule back: hides, deerskins, tobacco, and precious gold washed from streams. Some are coloured men whose race is indeterminate, and it is most strange to hear English words interspersed in their Spanish. There is another bar that is only a thatched roof extended from the hotel into the street. Here are a number of the shiftless and thieving Sambos but also Carib men who keep their own society. They are proud and handsome, some more yellow than black. They wear red bands around their middle and long trousers and white shirts as though dressed for a great affair. One majestic Carib man spoke the Creole French of home. Where could he have acquired that?

After the rain I plod through the mud to the bleak shore where Mr Walker died and is buried. With a fallen palm branch I sweep the windblown detritus aside. I entertain a fearful nightmare of surreptitiously hiring a native to lift the small stone and to disinter and break open the ten-peso casket. The small skeleton stirs, a bony hand rises and falls back, the eyeballs are alive. And I sense behind me a presence, the dead man's ghost, watching.

But no: it is "The Sergeant." He has followed in his slinking way.

"You can look your fill, Miss. There ain't nothing to see."

"What do you mean?"

"He ain't there. They dug him up and out long ago."

"Someone robbed the grave?"

"Could be."

"You don't really know?"

"I heard tell."

I must have been perceptibly moved, since he responded with a horrible grin. I was confused and embarrassed, though this creature had no way to know what was in my mind, or that I had often dreamed Mr Walker still lived.

At supper "The Sergeant" hovered above me intolerably. He says the story of Mr Walker's disinterment is common knowledge. Yet he shrugs when I ask him to bring other informants to me.

He rolls a wad of tobacco from one cheek to the other and spits.

"Why don't you talk to the Indians, miss? The fools don't think he's dead."

November 16, Trujillo. An appalling rain, which abated in mid-morning. I sat at a table scribbling in this journal and watched the denizens of this miserable place emerge from their holes to pick their way through the mud. Who would ever surmise that two great nations, the English and our own, would be ready to go to war for Trujillo? Or that some of these people had witnessed Walker's occupation of the town and desperate surrender? Perhaps eyes that met mine this morning witnessed the execution, and would know whether it is true the soldiers despoiled him of his clothing and tumbled him naked into the shallow grave. Or the other tale that they walked away from him without word or ceremony, to leave him unburied and at the mercy of the wind and rain?

This afternoon "the Sergeant," plied with more liquor, told me that the "Jefe Político" of the province had ordered the body exhumed, but this transaction took place secretly and at night, and that few townspeople were aware. I was ready to believe this until he said (after I had offered another whiskey) that Walker's head had been cut off and was now preserved in vinegar in a secret place in the nation's capital.

His bloodshot eyes rolled toward me warily as to measure whether I believed him.

November 17. The surly proprietor, hearing of my enquiries, this morning sought me out. Proprietor of the Hotel Castillo and of much else. He says I am not the first American to come to Trujillo with questions about Walker. He rolled his eyes when I mentioned the Indians' faith in the gray-eyed man of destiny's immortality. He says the Payas and Towkas are very superstitious, and still practice ceremonies of the times when they were all-powerful.

He pointed to several Indians standing beside a hitching-post. They had been there for some time, unmoving in the rain, their long black hair hanging down over broad faces of a most melancholy cast.

I would have liked to ask them whether they still believed their gray-eyed savior would return.

November 20, Greytown (San Juan del Norte). Nicaragua at last, though I was not sure I would live to put my foot on land. Not dry land, for the torrential rains continue unabated. The notorious breakers at the sand bar where many have drowned were scarcely visible through the rain. An hour of manoeuvering in a heavy sea to board us on the lighter, with four strong arms to lift me down. We then shot over the bar as nimbly as a frail skiff over river rapids. The lagoon was calm with a sickly smell. In the intense heat swarms of mosquitoes welcomed us.

Here Cortés dreamed of golden cities, and William Walker of a triumphal return to power. And here the miserable, sick and wounded remnant of the falange troops ended their march in 1857. It is said several of his men left that straggling band at the outskirts of Greytown, resolved to remain in the country. I surmise they preferred the demoralized ease of languishing in this heat and rain to a winter of begging in the snowy streets of New York. There is everywhere abandonment and desolate decay. A river steamboat lies on its side in the mud above the first rapids. Rusting rails tell where a little baggage train carried the effects of travelers past the rapids from one river conveyance to the next.

A mestizo approached me shortly after my arrival with powders and a flask of some dark liquid to protect me from the fevers and the "disorders of the stomach." He shook his head sadly when I informed him I had no need of these, having lived through these diseases in New Orleans and the several summer plagues.

November 22, Greytown. I have talked with one of Walker's falangists! An intrepid soldier only ten years past, one of the "58 Immortals," now a demoralized drunkard. The half-breed who guided me through trackless mud turned to me with an evil grin, patting his head as to indicate that my quarry had lost his wits. His name is Slipper Burke.

His habitation was one of several on a mud bank a good two miles from the town, between the still lagoon and a tidal stream. His windowless shack leans crazily on a sloping bank of mud at certain hours, much like an abandoned or beached ship. But at other hours it floats with the incoming tide. A few planks end to end were my avenue to him at this steaming afternoon hour.

He did not rise from his hammock when I entered. A seedy decrepit skeleton, his ribs and tattooed arms bare, he wore only shreds of trouser. The ends of his filthy beard and unkempt moustache were much chewed. I think it was beyond his physical powers to rise from the hammock. It was as though he were held down by the fat and motherly Companion, more Indian than Negro, who stood behind him unsmiling and protective. She wore only a kind of sailcloth garment wrapped around and leaving bare her large and leathery breasts. Such is often the custom with the Indian women in their own homes. Now and then, grunting, she gave the hammock a gentle push. This degenerate American has his native slave. She is all that is left of his dreams of conquest.

I told him that I had known Mr Walker, though not well, more than twenty years before. The Mr Walker I had talked with did not seem cut from the mould of the filibuster or pirate or ruthless general.

Hee hee hee was his only reply.

"He was gentle and kind. He cared for his dying mother. Later he cared for the woman he loved, who was a deaf mute."

"I need a bottle if I am to talk. Or money."

I fished in my pocket and held up a silver piece to catch the light.

A filthy claw seized it. He bit the coin, then handed it to his fat companion. She would know what he wanted.

29

"And mind you bring me full change." He twisted in the hammock, seemed about to rise, then fell back. "What is it you're after?"

"Only your memories of Mr Walker. Anything you remember."

"You want to hear good or evil?"

"The truth."

"He rode on fine horses to take ship while we his men made our way on foot. We walked and crawled here, most without boots or even strips of canvas. Our feet were torn by stones. In this country the boots do not last."

"Did his men turn against him?"

"He was a devil could make men rejoice in their own ruin and death. I have seen men volunteer to make a dash for it just to draw fire. Knew they would be wounded or killed. But I did not think he would leave us. I did not think he would ride off on a fine horse with the enemy commander at his side."

I reminded him that Walker paid the full price, though that was three years later at Trujillo.

"He faced the firing squad with no bandage for his eyes. He stood unflinching. Before dying he begged that his men be spared."

"That is a lie."

"It's not true he begged for compassion for his men?"

His skeletal ribs stirred. He peered into the darkness behind him.

"The firing squad! For another dollar I will tell you what I know."

I held a coin up to the feeble light of the doorway but did not let him have it yet.

"Go ahead, please."

"It was a fraud. The soldiers fired blanks. They were well paid for their little game."

"What makes you think that?"

"It's a secret many men share."

It was a thought that had crossed my mind many times in the first days, when the first denial of execution came. Such things happened more than once in Napoleonic times. And there were the three falangists who had claimed to see him.

"I read the report of the American who assisted at his burial. He came to New Orleans, he gave many details. Mr Walker's face was quite shot away by the commander of the firing squad, even after he had fallen."

Another obscene laugh: *he he he...*

"Women will believe anything. Newspaper fools too. Old devil Uncle Billy didn't die. He got away, it was a trumped-up affair. Slipped away to live in hiding with the Indians. They knew he couldn't die."

"He is living with Indians now?"

"Don't say he's living anywhere. But if he's dead he's dead in Mexico. He was on board a ship from Bluefields, headed for Mexico. Don't know how he got to Bluefields, the Indians must have helped him. He was on board the *Libertad*. A fancy ship of the Atlas Line. Goes to Minatitlán, Tampico, Vera Cruz. I know well the man who saw him on that ship. Was as close to the old devil as you are to me. The General didn't answer his greeting, just stared at him with his gray eyes of a jungle cat. So the man kept his peace. For three days on the same ship with that devil. He knew Walker would kill him if he told. Three days with him hiding on that ship, keeping out of the devil's way. Then the General was gone."

"So you say he is in Mexico now?"

"Don't say anything. Must have got off at Minatitlán because my pal stayed on to Tampico but there was no more sign of the General after Minatitlán. Don't say he's in Mexico or anywhere but Hell. Just know they didn't get him with that firing squad. They shot blanks."

November 23, Greytown. I thought I had not slept, but

must have since I did not hear the beginning of this appalling rain. And waking had a distinct vision of a man in a few shreds of uniform and wildly neglected hair in a jungle clearing, almost naked in fact, seated on the trunk of a fallen tree. And then a daydream of Mr Walker himself still alive. The Isthmus of Tehuantepec would indeed be a place for a fugitive to go, not the cities, not Tampico or Vera Cruz. I can well imagine a man who in self-disgust seeks an Edenic wilderness for the transformation of his soul. Or a Cain hiding from the truth of all those he has abused.

Tehuantepec! I think this wild tale is an omen and invitation to go there at last. I shall see Minatitlán and the Isthmus and with my own steps follow the line of the railroad that is still not built. In this dreadful heat and incessant rain I long for the "salubrious climate" of the Isthmus. Others make the Grand Tour of old England and the European cities, cared for by polished couriers and living in luxurious apartments. I am more adventurous. I shall wander alone along forest picaduras and up rivers to their source, Walker or no Walker. Even to those ruined cities up the Rio Corte.

What motive would this Slipper Burke have for telling me a lie?

November 27, Mexico at last. Up the wide river Coatzacoalcos toward Minatitlán. Under a glorious sun our gliding ship has shed its filth and left behind the horrid mosquitoes of the night at anchor. An earthly Paradise surrounds us, more verdurous and more colorful than any Eden of our children's Bible. We moved past marshy lagoons where long-legged golden herons are poised over their prey and fiery flamingos rise at our coming. And hide themselves in mangroves more exuberant than those of our Bayous. Golden birds high in the trees, parrots and whole hordes of paroquets. We left behind marsh and prairie, shining tributaries and lagoons, to enter great forests where for the first time I see sportive monkeys leaping unafraid among the squirrels of home. Yet such a multitude of squirrels! Red-eyed caymans, great evil creatures, scuttle away silently at our approach, but one long monster remains to stare us down. There is more than one serpent in this Eden, but only the alligator is foul.

A few habitations, but they do not mar this prehistoric landscape where wild horses cavort at the sound of our coming. A veteran of this region informed me of a French colony established nearby, forty years ago or more. But they selected a poor spot and were overcome by marsh fevers and other tribulations, and all are dead, the last one by suicide.

November 28, Minatitlán, Republic of Mexico. A straggling miserable place no better than Trujillo or Greytown. Salubrious climate indeed! Two of our naval warships are anchored here, with many men deathly ill on board. In their first nights, unprepared for the mosquito assault, the sleepless men climbed into the rigging, rendered lunatic by the heat and the stings. Two men have died. The hotel where some of the ship's officers stay, and I am the only female visitor, is larger than the "posada" in Greytown, but even filthier. The refuse from the kitchen and dining room is a steaming mound of horror.

Even the Consulate of the United States has the high thatched roof of the region. Were it not for the great seal over the door and the flag this might be the house of a prosperous shopkeeper. It is raised on stilts against the great floods, as are all the dwellings.

The Naval officers, who speak disparagingly of the railroad project, are here to survey the line for a ship canal to the Pacific. They will follow some of the same routes chosen for the planned railroad. They are fine officers and true gentlemen, though weakened by illness, and solicitous for my comfort and health. I assure them I never come down with the fevers, having survived the worst plagues.

With them are two shy young men, civilian engineers. One of them, a Mr Charles Stanfield, is young enough to be the son I never had. He moves with great ease, as though his lithe body had no bones. He pretends to look in the other direction, but his beautiful brown eyes roll back to seek mine. Long blonde hair fine as gossamer, falling in gracious translucent folds. No moustache, no beard. He might have been too young to grow them!

Last night after dinner he got up his nerve to approach me in the lounge which is also a bar. I indicated the empty chair at my side. And soon he was pouring out his history. His name is Charles Stanfield. He is from Boston and has just finished his studies. So many are sick that he has been deputized to go ahead of the others to explore the upper regions of the Coatzacoalcos and its tributaries, to determine the volume of waters. Also to learn how many Indian laborers can be enlisted for the building of locks and a dam for waters to feed the canal. Other members would join him in a place called Suchyl, which is as far as the river steamers go. After that on horseback or by carriage to a place called La Chivela. That is the rendezvous for the navy party.

"My particular destination is the meeting of two rivers, the Corte and the Milagro."

"The Rio Corte!" I said. "In my book it tells of two ruined places on the Rio Corte. Chimalapilla and Casas Grandes. I long to see those places."

I explained that I intended to follow the traces of the famous William Walker. And told him the rumor of the false execution.

"You think this rumor true?"

"With my sober reason I think it false. That is my morning opinion, when the faculties of reason prevail. But in the evening I believe the story true. I feel it in my bones. Whether he is alive or not is another matter. But I do believe he came here to the Isthmus of Tehuantepec. All my life I have been fascinated by stories of this region. So I would come even if I knew Mr Walker dead."

"And you intend to go on this expedition alone?"

"I am sure there will be parties I can join after Suchyl. At the least a public carriage conveyance. But even if I had to go alone, yes. I long to go into a true jungle on lateral reconnaissances."

"Lateral reconnaissances!"

"A phrase I learned as a child, out of a book on this region. Did you know that the Indians have an inordinate love of liquor?"

He looked at me with astonishment.

"You speak as though reciting a poem."

"Those words are from the same beautiful book. I said them to General Walker when I met him and he was as surprised as you."

"You knew Walker!"

My young admirer, for I know he is already that, stared with his mouth open. How beautiful his teeth, how red his tongue!

"For moments only. But he left an impression I can't lose. I am determined to learn the truth."

December 1, Minatitlán. I have seen the Consul. A miserable wretch who shuffles papers as I talk. He knows the broad details of General Walker's career, but doubts the story of a sham execution and flight. Two of the Walker falangists *are* living in the interior, and he surmises they are men who deserted Walker in 1857 after he was driven from the Presidency. One of them, who calls himself Doctor Rush, offers lodging to travelers to the Pacific in a village beyond the town of Suchyl.

"Do you know, sir, the village of Santa Maria Chimalapa? Or Santa Rosalia?"

"By name. Very isolated places."

"And the ruins of Casas Grandes on the Rio Corte? That is a place I would like to visit."

"I strongly advise against visiting any ruins, especially in a remote location. Some of those ruins are infested by ban-

35

dits and revolutionaries and refugees from crime and deserters from the armies. Everyone knows that is true for the ruins of Guiengola. I am told there are even degenerate creatures whose ancestors were deserters from the army of Cortés who took refuge in the jungle. Drifters who still have a trace of white blood in their veins. Still know a few words of Spanish passed on from father to son. They drift into the outlying towns to trade skins for ammunition. They too prowl the ruined cities, in search of what? Some white man's half-remembered lust? This is a lawless country. I cannot command you, but I urge you to give up your quest."

December 2, Minatitlán. The youthful Mr Stanfield is excited by the prospect of going ahead of the main canal survey expedition, even alone since so many of the others are sick. Why should I not accompany him?

Seventeen years have passed since I read of the explorer who for no given reason stopped short of Casas Grandes. I long to ascend where only natives have been.

December 3, Minatitlán. I boldly asked my shy new friend to accompany me, and by yesterday's bright moonlight, to the village of Jáltipan to see the hill of the Malinche, under which Dona Marina the loved one of Cortés is buried. On such moonlit nights, the Indians believe, she appears at the top of the hill in all her finery. Their Dona Marina the Malinche is alive for them, and is still the great Cortés's companion, and one day will shake herself free from this encumbering mound of earth and return to protect her people. So too do they believe of William Walker, their gray-eyed man of destiny.

The village itself was like a place of the dead. The thatched-roof dwellings were dark, only an occasional candle. Dim unmoving human shapes stood by the door openings and dogs silently prowled. We descended from the carriage, and Charles—I will no longer say Mr Stanfield—waited in pa-

36

tient good humor, smoking, while I silently contemplated this small hill which for the Indians remains sacred.

"How strange you look, Miss Rosellen! How the moonlight shines on your face. In your eyes. One might think you too expected her to appear."

I was startled. For it is true I did indeed, until he spoke, half believe there would be some sign. I had been watching intently for the earth to stir!

"Perhaps tonight is not the night for her, Mr Stanfield. Wouldn't you too like to see her there at the top of the hill?"

"I am a man of science. If someone were to appear I would know it to be some fraudulent native acting her part."

"Know? I don't like the disagreeable sound of that word. Don't you believe at all in powers that transcend mere common sense? I do. Perhaps no one is immortal in the flesh. But still I have unshaken faith in occult communication between the quick and the dead."

"And between the living?"

"With the living too. I have had few words with William Walker and that only once. He had no reason to remember me. Yet years later when I saw him at a distance, among his friends and besieging journalists, he looked up at me and at once stopped talking. Ours eyes met, there was a bond between us, there was communication beyond the need of words."

"So now you believe General Walker is still alive and waiting to be found? The story of an execution was concocted."

"Tonight I more than half believe. Perhaps tomorrow I will not."

We rode back to the hotel in silence, a silence broken only by the soft clatter of the horse's hooves and the faint jingle of the reins. But in that silence I felt a communication with the handsome young engineer beside me.

The women of Jáltipan are said to be of surpassing beauty and, moreover, to be exceedingly liberal in the gift of their person, even to passersby. And had I been born an Indian woman of Jáltipan? Or born to poverty in a squalid street at home? Or a beautiful quadroon offered to the arms of a rich protector, and educated to unusual pleasures of the night? The young poet Keats one day wandered in a forest and saw two fair creatures couched side by side, who lay calm breathing on the bedded grass. I am ready to weep with old longings, thinking of their happiness. Why have I never had such a lover as my brave young engineer? In another life, if another life could be, I would want him to hold me. The Indian maiden lay without protest in the rough arms of the Spanish conqueror. Did they speak of love in the words people in our time use? Nearby is an island in the river once granted by Cortés to the Malinche, and on it is a society of people who cannot speak. *Rancho de los mudos.* Why were they stricken? Why was the innocent and pure Ellen Martin?

When we reached the miserable hotel the silence was further disturbed by the laughter of men in the bar. I did not want to surrender Charles to them. I did not want to leave him.

"Thank you for your kindness in accompanying me."

"It was a pleasure, Miss Rosellen."

"I will be very bold and ask you to let me join you on your journey to Suchyl. The Consul says I should not go there alone."

"I would be delighted."

December 5, on board the Allegheny Belle. And accompanied by Mr Stanfield, for to call him thus is to make him seem older, a fitter companion for my advanced age! In Suchyl he will make a list of provisions (some of which belonged to the railroad company) and then go ahead alone. All the long glorious day we have watched the strange and wonderful landscapes move by. We glide in and out of dark bowers erected by overarching trees whose higher branches delicately touch. We saw many pirogues propelled by natives with poles.

Near the back is a little "casa" roofed with vines where two passengers may recline, protected from the sun. Much depends on the state of the waters as to how far the *Allegheny Belle* can go. It is possible we will go the last miles to Suchyl in such sleek pirogue canoes, the passengers embarking two by two, in one canoe my young admirer and I. I long to lay my hand on his.

December 6, Suchyl. All is coarseness and demoralization in this place that calls itself a "Chamberlain's Hotel." The men standing in the bar (which is also the dining saloon) shouted "Hurrah!" when they saw us enter, for I am the only white woman to have stopped here in weeks. Foul salt pork and sardines for dinner, and stale biscuit in place of bread. Mr Stanfield is embarrassed by the coarse stares and whispered jests that come my way.

The adjacent cottage intended for women travelers cannot be used. Why, the proprietor did not say. Nothing for it but to sleep on a table in the dining saloon or in a dormitory with the men. There is no door between the two rooms and I could see the long row of beds under their mosquito nettings.

In a storeroom or warehouse are relics of the old Louisiana Company in which I have worthless shares. Boxes of provisions split open and pilfered without accounting. Boilers, rusted wheels, a handcar, the nameplate SUCHYL for a station that was never built. The dark room ticks and rustles with the furtive sounds of small animals at work, gnawing and grinding away. Near the door are corroded rails vanishing into deep grass.

"Papa dreamed so many fine dreams, and all have come to this. The railroad was to bring so much! The example of progress and enterprise to the Indians and other natives. And the comforts of civilization for travelers crossing the Isthmus to catch steamers on the other side. Moreover, it was to make us all rich."

"And your father has given up?"

"My father is dead. All my family died in the epidemic of 1853, all but my little brother Philippe, who has gone off to live his life among the Yankees. Not so little any more."

"You have been married, I think."

"My husband died in the war between the states. There is no one to restrain me from pursuing my fantasies."

December 7, Suchyl. How strange to lie within the hearing of twenty rough men stirring and snoring in a moonlit chamber, each in his mosquito net sarcophagus. With much delicacy Charles erected a screen of blankets and a dusty black cloth to separate us from the men in the sleeping room, who lay naked as savages. I longed to tell him there would be no harm if he were to remove his own clothing in this heat, or even I mine. But of course I did not. I cannot tell from his soft breathing whether he sleeps or no. Through eyes almost closed I sought to discern his youthful form through the netting. I longed to reach across the short space that divides us. He is the soul of kindness.

December 9. A substantial party of respectable men is leaving tomorrow by horseback to cross the Isthmus. I must avail myself of this opportunity for a safe escort, although Charles is not yet free to go. I am most curious to talk with the two men who had been with the falange and to have their impressions. I must rid myself of this obsession that the terrible Mr Walker still wanders on and over the earth, a Cain who has killed not his brother but his own better self.

Strengthened by my first experience of the wilds under safe escort, I will venture alone on winding picaduras, or with sure-footed Indians as guides, go up the river and its rapids by canoe, even beyond Chimalapilla to Casas Grandes. The name tumbles and reverberates in my brain. Already forgotten is my languid and useless life of home.

It is agreed I will meet Charles at the surveying headquarters in a place called La Chivela. Who knows what will come of this, in spite of our disparity of age?

December 10. The fine carriage and provision road of twenty years past is now in extreme decay, with all bridges gone, so it is necessary to ford the slack streams which during the great rains would be torrents. Only oxcarts at most can pass where once were carriages transporting the railroad surveyors, and before them the forty-niners en route to Ventosa.

The landscape is of surpassing beauty. In and out we go of dense forests with foliage of many hues and innumerable vines reaching to the tops of the trees. Off the main road I glimpsed the winding *picaduras* of my dreams, vanishing into deep woods.

In our party are two grand Spanish ranchers owning land they refer to as the *marquesadas.* Their pallor is startling in this country of so many shades of brown. They are excessive in their politeness but have little to say. Their ladies remain hidden behind veils and speak not a word of English. Their attendants are dark mestizos who speak a dialect among themselves and a hesitant broken Spanish with their masters. Also a number of sad Indians, beasts of burden who trot along on foot.

Spent the night at "Ladd's Hotel," a far more miserable place than "Chamberlain's Hotel" in Suchyl. I am offered only a hammock in the public room, and there are holes in the mosquito netting.

The half-breed proprietor stands behind the bar and guards his bottles as if they were the jewels of a Spanish queen. He shrugs at the name of General William Walker. The region, he says, is rich in adventurers, thieves, pirates, filibusters, politicos. And disillusioned miners who long ago returned empty-handed from California. It seems a solitary American miner or outlaw lives in the upper regions of the Rio Corte. For some reason he remains, living far into the mountains beyond any community of Indians, though there is little evidence of gold to be found in the washings. He has been there for years. Once or twice a year he floats down the river on a balsa raft, a light conveyance which can be carried around the rapids. He glides alone down the river, his long beard white as chalk, looking neither to left nor right. And simply vanishes. No one has seen him go up the river he is seen to float down! That is certainly not William Walker.

And the story of descendants of the great Cortés's army, living in the jungle?

"The soldiers came and they raped our women and in time they were given the best land by the general. But these others went into the jungle to escape the anger of their officers. Or they did not like the hard army life. My uncle Raúl saw one. He came into a village near San Juan to trade skins for ammunition. He still had a shred of uniform, part of a sleeve sewn onto his blouse. He did not look like other *mestizos* and my uncle could not understand the few words he said."

December 11, Sanderson's "hotel." Only one public room and a storeroom that is also a sleeping place with a few planks over the dirt floor. I have now seen with my own eyes "Doctor" Rush, of whom many stories are told. He appeared at the door, silent and without expression, to look in on our party of ten men and three women. His trousers were cut off at the knees and he was barefoot. A soiled white blouse hung open to reveal disgusting hairs. He turned away without speaking.

Mr Sanderson will arrange a meeting, and has sold me the good bottle I am to offer him. He confirms that Dr Rush was one of Walker's men.

December 12. We sat at a rough table in his shack which is also a dispensing place for the sick. Dirty bottles line the wall, and on the table is the whiskey I have brought as a gift. He is, though sober at this morning hour, deeply distrustful of my purposes.

"Uncle Billy was an unforgiving devil," he began. "In Baja he banished one of his soldiers for daring to question his plans. Sent him out into the desert without arms or provisions for his bones to be picked by the vultures. With us the General would permit no looting in the hour of triumph or when all was lost. And no touching of little maids. A man who fought through the valley of death could not enjoy it afterwards, it was not permitted. First there was Masaya. Three days and nights of blood and little food or drink as we fought toward the plaza, cutting our way through the inside walls house by house because the enemy controlled the streets. That was Masaya. Granada? Walker was not there when all were drunk in Granada and set the city on fire. Henningsen was in command in Granada, a real man, and we were all drunk on the fine wines and liquors of each house. Walker was not there. It was Henningsen who led, while Walker was safe on an island in the lake where he had taken the sick and the wounded. Not as though we in Granada were not sick and wounded!"

As though impelled by these thoughts he poured himself half of a large glass. He held the bottle in his hand, affectionately, anticipating its pleasures to come. He emptied the glass.

"So you were disaffected?"

"What are you saying?"

"You disagreed with the General's policies and so you left?"

"Policies! Let me tell you of Granada before we sacked it. The wounded were side by side in a room they called a hospital and across the room were the dead lying stiff and unburied. The living lay in their muck and the vermin crawled in their hair. There were flies feasting on our wounds. No change of bandage and precious little water to drink. At least there was liquor after Walker left for his island in the lake."

"This other general ordered you to sack the city?"

"Uncle Billy gives the orders. Destroy the city house by

house and block by block, and I was on a squad to do it until I stumbled drunk into a hole. Then I was three days in the hospital and after that the city was on fire and I got away. I saw my chance with Walker off safe on his island."

I assured him I understood his good reasons for desertion. I told him of my interview in Greytown with the man named Burke, and his belief that Walker had escaped to Mexico and had disembarked in Minititlán. There had been no execution.

"Doctor" Rush was at first speechless. When he spoke his voice had changed.

"No execution! Slipper Burke told you that?"

"I don't mean to say I believed him."

"And why should you not believe him? Slipper is no fool, even though he stuck with the General too long. He would know. That devil Uncle Billy is not human like the rest of us, he has no forgiveness. In all the battles he had only one wound. A scratch. I will tell you what the Indians said. They said he could not die."

"Do you believe he is alive?"

"I cannot imagine him dead. Never could."

He poured himself another half glass and drank it at one swallow. He would soon be drunk.

"Had you not heard this story of his coming to Mexico?"

"There is no wild story of the General I haven't heard. Some say his head is in a jar of vinegar in the office of the president of Nicaragua. I would pay to see it even if the eyes were open and staring. Gray cat's eyes and a cat has nine lives. And there are them that say he lives like a king among the Indians in one of the ruined cities in the mountains. Oh yes, I can believe too well he might have come here to find me since if alive he would not rest till he punished me."

I tried to reassure him. He had begun to tremble from the drink and from his fear.

"But all this was ten years ago or more."

"It is thirteen years, which is no more than a day. Thirteen years since we set the city on fire after all and I got away to a place where I knew they would protect me."

December 14. Still at Sanderson's, but on my way tomorrow. I have made arrangements for an escort to San Miguel, and from there will engage the necessary Indian guides for the ascent of the river Corte. Mr Sanderson speaks of the deserted city of Casas Grandes I first read of the year of the plague and all my loss. 1853, seventeen years already! Twenty-seven since I first heard the name. More than a hundred years ago Casas Grandes was abandoned by Zoque Indians at the issue of some devastating plague. The terrified Indians, leaving their companions unburied, migrated to the villages of Santa Maria, Santa Rosalia and San Miguel, where their descendants remain today. This spectral Casas Grandes is an object of veneration and dread for the superstitious Indians, and few have gone near it. Even from a safe distance across a fissure or ravine whole skeletons are visible, propped against the white limestone walls of unfallen buildings. The "city," which is perhaps only a large village, has apparently escaped the jungle growth that normally covers old ruins in this climate.
"You have seen Casas Grandes yourself?"
"I am not such a fool as that."
I am all the more determined to go. I have not come this far only to be turned back by a tale of skeletons.

December 16, San Miguel. A most unexpected European recluse, a Frenchman named Dupoint, is my host, a man of indeterminate age, though his hair is white and his face worn by many disappointments or many passions spent. He has provided me with two good men from the village of San Miguel, Indians of the Zoque tribe. They have a balsa for the river journey. This is a raft of very light logs ten feet or so in length and tied together with wooden joints. One of the Indians I am to call Juan and the other Juanito—Juan's fifteen-year-old son, who is as tall and sturdy as he. Monsieur Dupoint assured me I can have the fullest confidence in his Indians, though their shaved crowns and blue scars give them an idiotic countenance. It appears many of the Indians of this region have these scars.

"And do you really expect to find this terrible fugitive William Walker? If you do, will he not gobble you up?"

"I think he was always considerate of the weaker sex. I have read that his soldiers were ordered not to abuse native women. An old falangist only yesterday told me the same thing. But no, I do not really expect to find Mr Walker, neither quick nor dead."

"And then?" said with exactly the intonation of the French *Et alors?*

"I must nevertheless make the journey."

"Then I am to understand you are, like me, devoted to enterprises that are doomed to fail?"

"I am devoted to one of my dreams."

Monsieur Dupoint lives in a quite isolated spot more than a mile from the village. An avenue of banana trees lines a long neglected path to his adobe hut. Half of the roof is tiled, the rest the usual palm thatch. A chair and table near the door are shaded by a tamarind tree, but I think he does little work at this table or anywhere else. Inside he has kept some semblance of his past life. On the shelves are volumes of French poets, finely bound in red leather embossed with gold lettering, and a bust of the famous writer Voltaire. With much ceremony he poured a small amount of Cognac into two cups, one of fine cut glass for me, and toasted my journey. Then without further ado he took down a volume of the poet Racine, and standing above me read with many gestures a long tirade. His eyes filled with tears when I responded with a few lines from the play *Phèdre*, learned by heart at the convent. He was amused by my accent, the French of New Orleans not Paris.

Surely, I ventured, he must miss his beloved Paris. How

had he come so far?

There followed a long and melancholy tale. As a young schoolteacher in Paris he was intoxicated by the eloquence of the poet Lamartine. A poet President of the Republic! But his hopes of regeneration and the religion of humanity were shaken by the turmoil and defeat of 1848. He escaped from the Tuileries with a wound in the shoulder and went into exile in England, where he nearly starved. Most vividly he remembered the weary philosopher of liberty and reason Stuart Mill, preaching on a streetcorner in the rain. Nobody listened to his discourse. From London he found his way to one of the Fourierist communities in Texas, where even the humblest labor was to be shared by all. This small town was destroyed by a tornado. He then went to Haiti, where he thought to resume his teaching of the French language and Condorcet's ideas of progress. The noble liberator Toussaint l'Ouverture had been one of the heroes of his childhood. On his second day in the capital he spoke glowingly of Toussaint to an innkeeper, and found himself hours later in an unlighted prison cell. It was during several months in prison that his hair turned white and he lost a number of his teeth. From Haiti he traveled to Cuba, where he joined a troupe of Spanish actors en route to Mérida, and from there came eventually to San Miguel. Here he had hoped to bring the principles of enlightenment to the miserable Indians, but was defeated by their incessant quarreling and their drunkenness. Some years had passed since he withdrew to his isolated hut. Sometimes he has as many as a dozen Indians who listen to his discourses on liberty and reason, and on ways of keeping the person healthy. Other times only four or five. Among them is always the young guide Juanito, for whom he has a fatherly affection.

But how, I asked, did he make whatever money he needed? I assumed his Indian pupils would not pay.

"I will show you," he said in a voice that conveyed much scorn of himself. "You will hear. I have a most exceptional

47

embouchure. By whistling I imitate successfully the music of birds. To this the Indians will listen with fascination, although not to my lessons. They employ me for their fiestas and their marriage and funeral celebrations. Ask for a bird, I will give you its voice."

His performance, which did indeed produce most beautiful trillings, was accompanied by a mandolin. It was now my eyes that filled with tears to see humiliated so a man who had once had such high hopes.

"I have made doomed efforts to give my Indians a little taste of French, if only to hear myself use it. Alas, they do not imitate me as well as I imitate the birds. Permit me to read a few scenes from the superb *Andromaque*."

He assured me that much remains visible of the town of Casas Grandes, although it was abandoned long ago. The jungle has yet to swallow it up. He raised his hands in a gesture of amused skepticism when I asked whether anyone lived there now.

"Monsters, my dear lady! Dwarfs who turn into scorpions! Serpents with scaly bosoms and the heads of beautiful sirens! Banshees with dreadful tails! The old Gods whose names no one can pronounce! One can very well understand why the Indians will not venture there."

"But your Juan and Juanito will?"

"Perhaps. Or perhaps they will lead you within sight of the place, and let you go on by yourself. The Indians are afraid of old ruins as they are afraid of all caves. At night the crumbled statues and bas-relief sculpture of the walls come to life. So they believe. Even Juan and Juanito, who will take good care of you and provide you with food and who will carry the balsa over the rapids, and who will protect you from jaguars and wild boars and alligators. I think even they will refuse to go into the ruins."

December 17. I think Juan and his tall son are most amused to undertake this mission, since I am if not the first gringo lady to come their way, at least the first to travel alone. Juan insists that for payment they want only the odd necklace and the earrings I purchased in the French Market for less than a dollar. I will leave with Monsieur Dupoint a reasonable sum to give them in a time of need.

Juanito has as good a command of Spanish as I, which is not very much. The father has almost none. The fine grave face of Juanito is marred by a few blue almost leprous spots, and his hair is shaved close to leave an ugly crown. The father also, it is a custom of the Zoque tribe. I believe they are Indians of the finest breed, and for that reason chosen to accompany me.

December 19, second day on the Rio Corte. Last night I was too tired to write, though I had only to hold tight as our raft swung in rushing waters, or caught in snags and had to be freed by Juanito wading. I could only stare uselessly, a mere woman, as they lifted the raft out of the water and carried it sure-footed up rocks and around the rapids to clear water above. Their bodies move with great ease to their tasks. They have removed their loose blouses but this almost nakedness does not embarrass them. It will not embarrass me.

They worked with admirable swiftness, arranging my hammock, and preparing fish caught earlier in the day. Through all the strange night I twisted and turned, but knew that one or the other of my guides was awake and watchful. Soft whispering sounds from the forest offered a most soothing antiphon to the rush of water over rocks. I knew well the croaking of frogs, but there were many sounds I did not know.

December 20, the Rio Corte. This morning a larger craft called a bongo rushed past us downstream. Juanito on our side and a tall Indian on theirs, poled skillfully to keep us apart. The craft was laden with oranges.

Later: I slept in the sun and awoke in a daze. My eyes smarted from the glaring reflection of sunlight on the high limestone cliffs that rose hundreds of feet above our now narrow channel. One great rock protruded with the very long corrugated head and open jaw of an alligator. Our raft seemed to be spinning, a sickening motion repeated many times, though I knew from the unchanging cliffs that we were advancing on a straight course. The spinning of our sturdy raft was within me.

Late afternoon: The spinning has continued, my hands and forehead and ribs are hot and cold, there is an odd buzzing in my ears. I dread the night, though I know I will be safe in the camp so quickly erected by my guides. All through the night one will sleep while the other is on guard.

Tonight I vomited my food for the first time in years. I rushed into the forest and relieved myself there several times. This pervasive sickness is most odd.

Juan says we are only a few miles from the town of Santa Maria Chimalapa, where I could rest comfortably and be given herbs for my sickness. But I feel a commanding need to push on, though my half belief in a surviving William Walker has diminished. My destination is Casas Grandes, and some revelation that awaits me there.

I relieve my fever by wading in the river, but for the next hour shiver with clammy cold. I will write down in my bewilderment everything I experience.

December 21. All the endless night I lay between a fevered waking and troubled sleep. The sounds of the forest were like sounds of the sea, my fevered body was tumbling in the waves. The hovering fireflies floated in still air, as though curious to inspect the intruders. Once when I awoke there was a horrid flapping of wings. The jungle was filled with the chorus of croaking frogs. Then they would fall silent as by command. Each time I woke one or the other of my two friends was close by and watchful. In the firelight their bodies are quite beautiful.

And now in the morning all is bathed in unnatural and

dazzling light. The bed of the river is only a few feet below, but the quartz rocks glitter as though on the surface, and the black rocks are slimy jasper. Then the river bed vanishes in swirling light. It is only light that disturbs me, this morning my fever seems gone. And I feel it is most imperative to take stock of my changing state. In my excited vertigo Juan sometimes seems far away from me, sometimes very near. And his sturdy son now looks much older, as though he had miraculously grown in three days. The sinews of his long legs move as though they had their separate existence freed from his guiding will.

I vomited immediately after eating the oranges, vomited into the limpid stream and thought I saw my own entrails swirl and dance on the shining rocks which are now far far down. Only hours more and Casas Grandes.

Juan hovers over me like a father, and the son watches me with troubled eyes.

December 22, Casas Grandes. Or possibly the 23rd, as I have the ominous impression that a day and night have been lost along the way. I must write with circumspection of this first visit to the ruins. A glaring and silent afternoon as we left the Rio Corte to enter the small tributary with its still waters. Rounding a promontory covered with pines we saw the white ruins immediately before and above us, built above a gentle slope of unbroken granite where no earth or verdure was to be seen. The first low buildings for human habitation are a hundred feet or so inland, cut out of solid blocks of white stone without windows, but with dark apertures which must have served as doors, large and rounded as the mouth of a cave. Above are larger houses of a smoother stone, as of white marble streaked with blue. There were none of the adobe huts or thatched roofs which had now become so familiar. Only silent and glaring stone caught in the declining sun.

When the sun was momentarily obscured the white ruins

seemed covered with verdure and strong lianas coiled about a solitary stone column. The sun reappeared and the whiteness returned.

Juan looked at me searchingly, perhaps hoping I was now satisfied, and would give him the command to turn back. But I insisted on our landing, and the two of them watchfully accompanied me.

The level area at the river bank could perhaps have been used for purposes of shipping and storage. We found no skeletons propped erect against the first walls, only two crude statues of granite or hard limestone, featureless men face down and greater than life size.

I determined to climb past the first rough houses or caves, and was not displeased when Juan and Juanito refused to accompany me with the pretext that they must make preparations for the night. I wandered for more than an hour in a labyrinth of alleys and broken walls that resembled pictures of Herculaneum and Pompeii. Most strangely in the failing light the white stone again seemed covered with jungle growth, as though long years had passed in these seconds, and in this silence I now distinctly heard a scurrying and other forest sounds, and also, but more distant, the sound of a waterfall. It could be only that, since the river itself was calm. These sounds appeared to come from beyond the highest row of stone houses. I climbed toward them with an ease that surprised me and looked down on a vast area of low ruins almost hidden by thick verdure. Among them, however, was a long rectangular field paved with stone, with gently terraced walls on three sides. It might have been cleared by human hands in the not too distant past. This had to be the court for the old ball games that could mean death to the losers. Stone hoops protruded from two of the walls. And even as I watched the declining sun threw a most disturbing shadow on the ball court, the shadow of a great dark animal, perhaps even the jaguar so dreaded by the natives. The shadow lay on the stone without motion, yet when I momentarily looked away the shadow had moved to the far end of the court and appeared to be watching me. Far in the distance I heard again the sounds of falling water. Near a small green grove of tall trees stood a small pyramid of reddish stone, a pyramid not more than twenty or thirty feet high. For a moment I believed I heard voices, the voices of women, and believed too that a real jaguar was watching me.

My head was spinning, nausea pervaded me, I turned back to rejoin my guides. But I had apparently lost the track by which I had come, and had to take another. Most strange too that whatever turnings I took found me back at the same cluster of caves that now seemed to enfold me like a closing hand. I looked in a dark doorway to see in the musty and foul darkness a crude table or stone workbench, and beneath it a scatter of papers I was reluctant to examine, although they were the only sign that someone had lived there, and perhaps not long before. A rounded object lay in the corner, white with two dark openings as for eyes and the black idiot hole of a mouth.

I did not go in, and eventually found my way back to the river bank, where my two friends were at work over a fire.

I must have slept without knowing, and woke to late afternoon, not on shore but on the raft, lying on a bed of my spread-out clothing and with a cushion made of folded blanket. My hands were cold and my face was burning. The raft was tethered to a large circular stone column. It now seemed unfortunate that I had not entered the house where I had seen the papers and the skull.

And just then the preternatural silence was broken in a most alarming way. As in response to the setting of the sun black creatures swarmed out of the first caves, and circled above us with their foul bat wings, a horrid and eerie whistling. Juan and Juanito were on the raft beside me, which was now detached from the shore and circling round and round, although the darkening city seemed not to move. A naked man, old and very white of skin, and with long nails visible even at this distance, was standing at the mouth of one of the caves. He had a rifle in his hands, he was waving it above his head. In another light he would perhaps seem to be a skeleton propped against the wall, and at another time a fallen statue.

I will put aside such visions, surely there was no naked old man. Tomorrow I will venture beyond the stone houses and the ball court. I will not be deterred by fevered hallucinations. I have not dreamed all these years of Casas Grandes, only to turn away now.

The journal here abruptly ended.

The Assistant Engineer

CHARLES STANFIELD was one of three civilian scientists attached to the canal surveying expedition. He was twenty, had just completed his Harvard College studies, and could be more accurately called an apprentice engineer. And here he was, thanks to so much illness among his elders in Minatitlán, about to embark alone on one of those "lateral reconnaissances" that had bemused Rosellen in her book on the Isthmus of Tehuantepec. His mission was to determine the volume of waters of the Rio Corte at its confluence with the Rio Milagro near Santa Rosalia. He was further to note the quantity of limestone and other materials that could be used in building the transisthmus canal. He was also to assess the availability of native labor. An older engineer would come along in due time to visit Santa Rosalia and verify his findings.

So he arrived alone at the hacienda of La Chivela, where the rest of the party would eventually join him. The large whitewashed building, the only one in the village to have a tiled not thatched roof, was the headquarters for the vast estate of the *marquesadas*, land granted in perpetuity to high officers of Cortés more than three centuries before. Thus his aristocratic host Don Alvarado, who had many additional names, was known officially as the *garda de marquesadas*.

"You are very young to be an engineer. However, my honored ancestor came to New Spain when he was only sixteen. There he is, directly above the fireplace."

The young grandee and officer of Cortés looked closer to thirty. His sickly scornful face appeared squashed between the high white collar and white wig of the time. His was one of six dark portraits staring down from the white wall. To Stanfield the stern gaze of all six ancestors seemed fixed on himself. One ancestor had but a single good eye, which shone with silver malevolence. The socket of the other eye looked to be filled with soiled cotton. The portraits were the most prominent feature of a gloomy, windy room large enough to serve as a convent refectory or lobby of a small provincial hotel. Above the large fireplace were crossed swords.

"Your canal will never be built," Don Alvarado said decisively, as though making an official declaration of a Viceroy. "I say it to you as I said it to the men planning a railroad twenty years ago. The *canaille* of the Mexican Congress tear up one day the treaty they signed the day before. A young man of New Orleans sat where you are sitting now, he was full of dreams of progress. *C'était un jeune homme très sympathique.* You speak French?"

"Not as well as Spanish."

"Your Spanish is not very good. The Indians of Santa Rosalia will not understand your Spanish. You will not understand theirs. You will need an interpreter who understands English, also the Zoque dialect. Will your railroad be an imperishable monument?"

"Imperishable?"

"Those were the words of Don José de Garay in petition to the President of the Republic. And Mexico? Mexico with this railroad was to become 'the emperor of the commerce of the world.' That was twenty years ago."

"Eighteen," Stanfield replied. "I have read the chronicles of the railroad."

"Garay promised the railroad would be completed in a

very short time. Nothing here is accomplished in a very short time. You will waste your youth making plans for a canal that will not be built. 'Il ne faut pas perdre sa jeunesse.' That is what a sick Frenchman said who alone survived a colony near Minatitlán. They built their houses too near stagnant water and they died of the fevers one by one. Pouf!"

Don Alvarado went on intolerably, as though numbering the dead, blowing into his outspread fingers with each breath. 'Pouf! Pouf! Pouf!' But the junior engineer was too young to worry about the loss of his youth. He was concerned rather about the fate of Rosellen, from whom he had separated four days before. He explained her double mission, to follow the traces of William Walker and to visit the abandoned city Casas Grandes. There were rumors Walker had not been executed and had fled to the Isthmus of Tehuantepec.

"She will never get to Casas Grandes, Walker or no Walker," Alvarado said. "None of the Indians will take her there, the place has a curse on it."

"You have heard these rumors of Walker?"

"There are stories of many criminals disappearing in the jungle. I don't listen to them. I have heard there is a gringo somewhere up the Rio Corte who has been there for many years, he is now an old man with white hair down to here." Alvarado ran his hands over this thighs. "I have not seen him myself. As for Walker, anything is possible in these degenerate times. If he went to Casas Grandes his bones are lying in the street."

Don Alvarado made a slow reflective sign of the cross, then turned up the palms of his hands as to acknowledge the wisdom of a universal futility.

"I recommend you go back to Minatitlán to rejoin your comrades. You must all return to where you came from. In Mexico there is no El Dorado and no fountain of youth."

But the Assistant Engineer was not to be deterred.

"She has been misled by mesmerists and charlatans, and by the drunken ravings of an old falangist." So Stanfield wrote

in his diary on the night of his arrival at La Chivela. A journal usually quite sparse, except when filled with hydrographic, botanic or geologic detail, and sometimes curiously confessional. He would not, he wrote, forget the moonlit visit to the artificial hill created above the Malinche's tomb.

For almost an hour she was silent, staring at the top of the crude earth monument, while I stood by, smoking to ward off the mosquitoes and other predators. A spectral figure herself in her white dress and black veil. But whenever she lifted the veil her eyes glittered in the moonlight. The look of a beautiful and misguided witch.

"Tonight I do believe men and women rise in person from the dead," she said, in the same matter-of-fact tones as "Each time the cheese woman came in her cart I bought a picayune with the cream poured over it" or "I am sure you have heard of General Beauregard."

Later, she had talked and talked through their long day on the boat from Minatitlán to Suchyl. The assistant engineer, whose Boston childhood and adolescence had been remarkably uneventful, listened enthralled to her stories of theaters on Mississippi steamboats and balls in great hotels where slaves were sold at auction, and of terrible fever plagues and the plague of the Yankee occupation. Negro priests of secret cults and quadroon balls where young dandies would look for new mistresses. Of her own power to hypnotize. Of William Walker's commanding presence, in spite of his small size. But hardly a word of her marriage to one Edward Lyndon, who did not return from the war. "Our marriage was not made in heaven, we were of a quite different temperament."

So are our temperaments, the Assistant Engineer noted in his journal.

She is a dreamer and mystic, I am a man of science. And yet I felt a deep kinship unspoiled by stirrings of lust, even as we lay side by side in Chamberlain's Hotel, separated only by her mosquito netting and mine. I have made a serious mistake not to protest more vigorously when she went on her way toward unknown dangers. At the last moment, already on horseback, she turned to me with a wistful smile. Was it also an inviting smile? Her lips moved silently, leaving me to fill in what words I would. Then she was gone, hidden from me by the horses of her haughty Spanish escorts and their silent wives. Will I ever see her again?

Thus Charles Stanfield the Assistant Engineer, writing in the cavernous public room of the hacienda at La Chivela, before turning to study his maps of the region. Late the next afternoon he went by rented mule to San Miguel Chimalapa, a night in a noisy posada there, and the next morning set out for Santa Rosalia, accompanied by a sullen Indian youth who rarely spoke, the two of them on bony but sturdy mules. The Indian would return both mules.

The Assistant Engineer's journal, some probably written while jolting along on his mule, alternated sparse technical notes on the natural products of the region and a few longer meditative comments, these written doubtless during rest stops demanded every hour or so by his guide.

Splendid forest of pines as we climb to a sharp winding ridge. Clay-slate and limestone rock, veins of quartz and feldspar. Crystals of quartz in the granite. Sandstone, porphyry, jasper upon slate. Large number of India rubber trees. Is there anywhere else such a profusion as of a still unfallen and uninhabited world?

And a long entry written once he had been settled in the small hut in Santa Rosalia shared for one night by a half-crazed "gringo."

December 14. The interminable path from San Miguel to

59

Santa Rosalia, endlessly climbing and descending, required the better part of a long day, with my stupid guide twice hacking with his machete at overhanging vines. And I a lank Don Quixote on a bony mule. Scarcely had we entered the jungle when a crested lizard, fully eighteen inches long, stood on its hind legs as to challenge us. Soon after two buzzards in the middle of the path, reluctant to fly. We are intruders in a wilderness world of orchids and butterflies, of screaming parrots and mocking birds reciting melodies never heard in our New England woods. Black birds, hawks, orioles, fly-catchers, thrush. We hear the chattering of monkeys long before we see one. A wild pig, a javelina, raced across our way. Who would have dreamed such a profusion of many-colored vegetation still dripping as from morning mist or the mists of the first days? On the shaded path the dark green and sinister rodadors attacked incessantly, more grievously the raw bellies of the mules. But not a single serpent to cross our path often sunk in ooze. And this a dry month! The sun glimpsed but rarely, being hidden by tall trees entwined and interwoven with vines, some more than a foot in diameter, overgrown with orchids blooming on the limbs. Butterflies fluttering near the orchids, then indistinguishable from them. My silent guide extracted a large amount of water from one of these vines and urged me to drink. The water was pure and sweet. Up we climbed to the crest of the cordillera amid a forest of tall pines. Then down down, fording streams where the remains of log bridges lay in the water, with turtles resting on the logs. Then up again and at last a sharp climb to the considerable village of Santa Maria Chimalapa and from there down to Santa Rosalia, which is nearer the confluence and hence more to my purpose.

But before that, midway from San Miguel in this steaming Eden, I was astonished to come upon a tiny thatched-roof cantina, only a rude table and roof supported by four poles. Can there be enough travelers to support even its modest trade? It offered only an undistilled aguardiente, hideous in color and taste. I took but a sip, but my guide drank deeply and at once became quite affable, muttering in what I assumed to be a friendly fashion. Nearby was a cleared pyramid of stone and a tall limestone slab protected by a crude fence, as though there would ever be vandals to violate what must have been a sacred place in the olden times. A repulsive peculiarity I have not seen recorded by any explorer: a stone mask of a serpent with human mouth, as though that was all that remained of our human frailty succumbing to darkness. An aged cripple was sleeping near this fence, put there to guard it. Crutches lay on the ground beside him.

It was nearly dark when they reached Santa Rosalia, with only the white tower of a Spanish church distinctly visible above the dark huts. At the edge of the village two surprising events occurred. The first was the shrill sound and beating wings of a flight of bats that rushed out of a grove of tall trees as though to welcome their arrival. The bats may have had their mules as intended prey, but Stanfield's guide beat them off. The second was the emaciated figure of a disheveled gringo who rose from a rough bench to greet them, though it was more his American voice than his lean ravaged face that identified him. He pulled himself to his feet and put a hand on the bridle of Stanfield's mule, then leaned slightly forward as though uncertain whether to bow to a visiting dignitary.

"You are late," he said in a complaining tone.

The face upturned yet unable to look Stanfield in the eye was that of a man who had known all the abominations. The right eye was screwed shut, as though he had been blinded in some awful fray. But then the eye opened and shut and opened again. Stanfield realized this was a deliberate wink. An obscene winking as to a familiar. Only sparse threads of dirty brown hair covered the creature's tanned skull.

"What do you mean, late?"

"I have been waiting for two hours."

61

"You're making a mistake. You don't know me."

"I knew you were coming. Everyone knew. I will arrange for your needs." A filthy hand reached for his, the bones were like blunted knives. "Hap O'Brien, at your service. I am the indispensable man." Obscenely the winking resumed. The teeth protruded in a skeletal grin. "You can tell me in confidence what you came for. Without me you can do nothing in Rosalia. Nothing. All I ask is a small share."

"There will be nothing to share. I'm surveying for a canal."

What O'Brien had come for was gold, he was not sure how many years before, either nine or ten. What had kept him were dreams of finding the *camino secreto*, an ancient and forgotten way through the jungle to Chiapas, a combination of small rivers, stone causeways and forest paths. The Spaniards had come to Santa Rosalia, built the church, and improved the secret way. Most of the soldiers in time withdrew to the north since there were easier ways to get to Chiapas. But a number of deserters stayed. They had found rivers shining with gold and rich veins near the surface of a small volcano. There were ruined cities along the secret way and in one of these the lucky deserters hid their findings. But most did not live to enjoy their riches. They died in the jungle.

"You believe all this?"

"I have seen a man who laid his hands on the gold. He sold me a map of the camino. But I was defrauded. The map did not go far enough to the south."

"And you followed it as far as it went?"

"Ask me no questions, I tell you no lies. We will become friends, right? Then I'll tell you what I know. All I ask is a share of what you're after."

All this he told as they walked to the center of the village and to his small hut. A deserted plaza. A dilapidated Spanish church brooded over a desolation. From the other end of the village raucous voices. On the way they could look into the huts of the villagers. There was only the light cast by the small fires where bare-breasted women were patting tortillas. In one hut three men were squatting beside a fire and the flickering light shone on their bare torsos and the shaved crowns of their heads.

O'Brien offered aguardiente from a large bottle hanging from a rafter. A filthy glass. Stanfield asked him about Casas Grandes, but did not mention Rosellen. There would be time for that when he found a more likely informant.

"Don't tell me about Casas Grandes. There's skeletons piled up in the street from the plague. I been that close to it, Casas Grandes, maybe a mile. The Indians won't go that mile and I ain't about to go in alone. I'm not a fool. Indians got me up the river that far but they won't go into Casas Grandes. And won't go much higher up. That was the first time I looked for the camino secreto but they wouldn't go on. That's what you're looking for, the camino secreto. Right? Stick with me and we'll find it. Just put in a hundred dollars real money."

"I'm not interested in Casas Grandes or the secret road. I'm just here for a canal survey. See what materials are available and how much native labor. I'm told the Zoques are hard workers."

"I'm the man for you if you want native labor. I am indispensable." He rolled out the word slowly and with relish. "I'm the one for your comforts. First thing in the morning I'll have a little girl for you, could be she's never been fucked. Clean your house and comb your hair."

"I won't be here long enough for all that. Just a few days."

"How long's it take you to wrestle? Have in mind a little girl, says her name is Marita. Maybe thirteen, fourteen. My girl is fat, looks forty. They go bad young what with the shit they eat. Should have seen her ten years ago."

"You've been in Santa Rosalia all that time?"

"I'm staying till I find the gold left by the deserters. Conquistadors! Conquistadors my ass. Deserters couldn't take the discipline. They went into the jungle and they lived and died there. But they had progeny, no mistake, fucked something that's for sure. And the progeny stayed with the savages. Now and then one of the savages comes out and sells a Spanish musket. You know what's left of the Conquistadors? Buzquitas, that's what's left. Dwarfs, skin almost as white as mine. You want to measure the flow of the waters? Just hang around the Rio Milagro you'll see the dwarfs come out after sunset to grub for snails. Crack the shells and eat them raw."

"I have a friend believes William Walker the filibuster wasn't shot and survived to come to Mexico and might be here in the mountains. Did you ever hear that?"

"Walker not dead!"

"A common rumor he's somewhere on the Isthmus. You know much about him?"

An extraordinary change came over O'Brien's features. He cleared his throat noisily and spat.

"Do I not! Am I not the man to tell you about Walker!" The name was pronounced with a vicious bitterness that was beyond hatred. He babbled incoherently, a string of badly pronounced Spanish names, then went into a narrative he must have recited to himself many times. "I was one of only three were with him in Baja and stuck with him all the way to Managua. Don't tell me about Baja. Ever had a horse shot out from under you? Ever suck cactus in the desert? Drink your own piss? Baja ain't worth losing your life for. I was right there at the General's side when we drug across the border at Tijuana to surrender. 'Neutrality laws' for Christ's sake. So back I am in Frisco, traveling the saloons for a free lunch and the General finds me in a saloon, not much left in my pockets to drink with. 'I need you, O'Brien,' he says. 'There's a fortune to be made.' So I suck it in again. And here we go, only fifty-seven on a leaking ship. Don't tell me about Nicaragua. And where was Hap O'Brien when General Walker was the President drinking champagne? A measly little casa with a big hole blown in the wall where we fought our way through and a grubby little thing my only servant. Holed up there trying to protect my loot. Not much loot at that, that Concha not big enough to warm a man under the sheets, not that I had any sheets. So I force my way into the President's office, tell a guard I'm one of the General's chums. And there he is sitting at a big desk with a silver dagger to cut pages and an inkwell of gold and silver. 'What are you doing in my office, O'Brien?' he says. Oh he was a cool one, thought he could stare me down. And I says, 'Where is the gold and silver and the señoritas? When do I get mine?' And he says, 'What are you doing here? Get out of my office and never come back. You are a disgrace to your country. If you ever come back you will be court-martialed and shot. Articles of war.'"

"And you've heard nothing of him being in Mexico?"

"General Walker is in hell." We stopped in front of one of the small huts. "Here is my humble dwelling. Tonight you are my guest. Tomorrow I will find you a good hut and I will give you candles and a young girl to fetch water and cater to your needs. Fifty cents a day will do it. God's money."

December 15. An intolerable night, as I held my breath, listening to the stirrings. Rats, scorpions, God knows what. And O'Brien snoring. I wanted to hold my nose for the smell. Slept in a hammock for the second time in my life. I could not face sleeping on a filthy mat on the earth floor. O'Brien was proud of his hut because he had two real chairs and a cook stove. And candles. "There's not many have candles, only a few mestizos and a couple of the Ancients. I'll arrange your rental with the Council of Ancients. But mind it's to me you pay. Fifty cents a day, two bits for the girl. God's money."

A beautiful morning, with O'Brien gone and an iguana staring at me from the ceiling. But he was soon back and took me around the village. Scarcely a hundred huts with thatched roofs and wattled walls wrought with mud, although there is the one small Spanish church and one ruined one. Where have the conquistadors not been in their search for riches over three hundred years ago?

The natives are as hideous as reported. The men are short and stocky and strong, but inebriated even in the morning, and the tonsure left by their shaved crowns gives their sullen faces a sinister gloom and idiotic stare. The pinta appears to affect more than half of the inhabitants, and in many the copper complexion is flecked with white, purple and blue. The spots are more than an inch in diameter.

An old woman was exhibited to me whose mere rags of clothing could not conceal arms and legs as rough and corrugated as an alligator's hide. The younger women seem little affected. Two worked naked to the waist at their eternal beating of the corn, and their flesh was unspoiled. They cast shy glances in my direction. The women do not appear to drink as much in this village of drunkards. All of the women go barefoot. In the street they wear white cotton blouses called huipils over a skirt. The young girls with the huipil reaching only to the knees, with roughly cut openings for the head and arms.

The water of the famous spring, to which I was led with pride, has a foul but remedial taste. Small fish light of color dart about. O'Brien feigns scorn for the Zoques but I think he has found here his final earthly home. He in turn is held in contempt by them. The natives look at me with unfeigned interest. But they respond with sullen grunts to O'Brien's greetings. He has become accustomed to their manners.

The hut assigned to me is somewhat better than the rest, though only one room and a lean-to 'kitchen' with a water jar and a grate for cooking.

One wall is solid adobe, so too the remains of a second wall. The rest are of wattled vines supported by many poles.

I had scarcely looked about me when O'Brien was back with the young girl Marita he had chosen to serve me. He led her to me, grinning his foolish grin, winking his obscene wink. The girl looked at me with a singular boldness as to enquire whether I will beat her at my first displeasure. At first she pretended not to understand when I asked her age, although she knows a good many Spanish words, perhaps as many as I. 'Catorce' she acknowledged at last. A boy of five or six followed her and squatted nearby, perhaps her brother. Or a youthful admirer of this village beauty? I think he resents my coming.

Her skin is relatively untouched by the pinta, only a few small spots. She wears the huipil over a plain skirt but one can still detect that her youthful body is shapely and firm. A large broad nose and full mouth, her black hair parted in the middle and looped over the ears. She stares at me with the impassiveness of a Mayan mask but I detect in the dark eyes a secret playfulness.

I intended to explore the village alone, free from O'Brien, but several native boys followed me from a distance. South of the village are springs very different from the limpid curative one frequented by natives and domestic animals. I found one of the purest petroleum, ten feet in diameter, the ground surrounding it spongy and soft. The boys skipped around the spring, then beckoned for me to advance. But they knew what ground was firm, I did not. A young boy pointed at what appeared to be solid earth, then laughed as my feet slowly sank into the oozy mess. I could not be angry for the novelty of seeing natives laugh so merrily, as I struggled to free my feet.

The petroleum, when extracted from its coverture of earth and leaves, is exceedingly rich. Beside the stream are the tracks of animals who come to bathe themselves in this green and black viscous substance. Thus they free themselves from annoying insects. So O'Brien tells me, and that the trick played on me is regularly tried on strangers who visit Santa Rosalia.

A long siesta during which I dreamed of the gentle Rosellen, her soft languid voice and lovely features. In this dream she was a mesmerist beguiling me with her hypnotic gaze. And I was her willing victim. I found myself reclined on a bed of extraordinary softness, and wanted her to lie beside me.

I awoke to the extraordinary spectacle of two large iguanas just outside my open door in playful or perhaps mortal
combat. They were holding each other by the mouth. One
would circle to the left without letting go, trying to get at the
soft skin of the abdomen, the other circling with it. I stood
up and at once they separated and stared at me, then resumed their combat.

December 16. Only sullen stares when, with Marita my
interpreter, I ask to be taken higher up the Rio Corte. Aided
by much sign language she tells of dangerous caves and tunnels and of the haunted ruins of Casas Grandes, where monsters with human faces roam by night but are always hidden
by day. And has Rosellen really tried to go there?

O'Brien says the people of Santa Maria and Santa Rosalia
deserted Casas Grandes long ago, leaving unburied the dead,
and for no amount of money would any native take me that
far. He talks again of the "camino secreto" supposedly leading to the Zoque villages in Chiapas. He has in fact found
several trails. One vanishes at the point a few hundred yards
south of the ruined town where a child was found crucified
not long ago. Such is the appalling story. The cross perhaps
goes back to the days of the Spanish conquerors or at least to
the lessons they taught. In the forest, the natives say, are caves
where "demons" and savages still live. It is evident I can go
no higher on the river, nor will Rosellen have been able to.

There is an abundance of fine wood in the region, all of
which could be floated down the Corte and Coatzacoalcos.
But who will cut it? Clearly there will be no labor available
here for arduous canal construction. The natives are beyond
redemption.

December 17. A curious fever and vertigo. Through the
afternoon I share my hut with a small iguana and several
almost translucent lizards and Marita tends to my needs, with

cool cloths on my forehead. Here the iguanas are both house-
hold pets and a favorite food for days of celebration. In a
shaft of sunlight through the doorway (for I have no window) the lizard's body has a lovely green silkiness. The body
shines. But my iguana remains in his darkness. I stifle under
my muslin netting during the hour of the siesta. And I have
more daydreams of the pure Rosellen. Yet already I find it
hard to remember her features. My naval colleagues too might
be inhabiting another planet.

In a second notebook I will record my findings concerning the waters. But I have not yet been able to summon my
accustomed energy. Tomorrow I must be at work with the
dawn.

December 18. This morning Marita watched me for more
than an hour, while I worked at the rough table. She extended
herself on my hammock, leaning on her elbow in a manner
that would seem insolent if it were not innocent. Her skin is
of a pleasing copper color lighter than most. She speaks with
her youthful still not fully formed body. Once intercepting
my glance she extended a bare foot toward me and wiggled
the toes as though inviting me to touch.

The boy whom she calls "Mon" or "Moan" continues
to hover nearby, watching. Ramón? He is evidently a mestizo, with the sharper Latin features. Certainly not her brother.
He looks aggrieved when I wave him away.

O'Brien tells me of the American miner returned from
California who continued to prospect in this region for gold.
His companions left, since the quantity was small. But he is
said to have gone up the river, far above any community of
Indians, and obstinately clung to his expectations for many
years. The story I had heard before of his having been seen
several times floating serenely down the river on a balsa raft,
alone, with no native palenqueros. But no one has seen him
return up the river. Along the banks of the Rio Corte O'Brien
has found only traces of yellow mica.

"The real gold is that stolen by the Spanish deserters and hidden in one of the ruins along the camino secreto. Don't waste your time panning."

Late afternoon: I have now experienced an earthquake more violent than any tornado or hurricane. I had just stepped outside to walk to the river with Marita. I heard a loud rumbling that came from the east and moved to the west, and turned in time to see my hut shaking itself violently like a wet dog. I thought I would fall to the ground. A small section of the wall broke off, as well as a segment of the thatched roof. The vibrations continued with the regularity of pulse. Marita did not throw herself into my arms. But she came near enough for me to hear her heavy breathing and to experience that peculiar odor which in another young woman might have been repulsive. Is her virginal charm that of an impenetrable and mysterious mental life? My body responds in a most embarrassing way. I could perhaps avail myself of her person, encircle her body and hold both small breasts in my hands, feel her heart beating as rapidly as my own.

She has for me the affection and dumb patience of a dog watching her master. It would be dishonorable to take advantage of such a young and untutored native.

Her face is perfectly shaped of its kind, and might have been fashioned by an ancient Mayan artisan. The sickle curve of the pinta seems tissue thin as though removable by a fine knife. On the first days she tried to conceal the spots. But today she exhibited one large purplish place on her shoulder and looked at me appealingly. Every strange white man in these areas is thought to have a knowledge of medicine.

It is said the Lacandons copulate in the open, as the mood seizes them, in full daylight and without embarrassment. I have seen nothing of the kind here. Again I feel the stirrings of lust.

December 19. I have made it clear to her that I prefer the tortillas baked brown and served hot with my coffee. Today when she reached through the mosquito netting to wake me I held tight to her arm and then most impulsively began to stroke it. She did not pull away. For long moments afterward the flesh of my forearm lay against hers like two bodies in embrace. Then all unintentionally I pressed my lips to her shoulder, and the salt taste was as of a wild and bitter herb. My body was tense with desire.

And the boy "Mon" was watching at the door! This afternoon I gave him the harmonica I had intended for some more important interlocutor, and at the same time indicated by gestures that I did not want him nearby. Marita reinforced my desires with a few sharp words. From not far off came the first wailing sounds of his attempts to play.

What would Captain Lewes think if he came upon my Journal and read of such frivolities? I must give myself no more than four more days, and must give all my attention to measuring the Deliveries of the Waters. Breadth and Velocity, not tortillas and lost cities of the uplands or the superstitions of drunken Zoques. Not the squirming body of a nubile princess scarred by pinta, or the manner of her staring at me while I work, a recumbent odalisk.

A report this evening that a white woman was seen to mount the river on a balsa raft with several natives. Can this be true? Or have they invented this story to please me? It must be Rosellen if anyone. And no one here will dare take me! I am haunted by misgivings.

December 20. My brief visitation of intermittent fever is gone. Again I tried to engage the sturdiest of the village men, those not already sodden by midday, to conduct me up the river. I know the tributaries of the maps are false or not existing. But there is a common dread of unknown waters and the unexplored jungle and the abandoned Casa Grandes. From the pictures drawn by Marita I surmise the ferocious festooned beasts are old legends of the village, if not her own childish fancies, and that her story of ruined structures not

71

overgrown by vegetation are perhaps as spurious. Yet the fear of the higher zones, where a number of villagers have disappeared, is insurmountable.

Today we ventured into the woods a few hundred yards. Marita led me, for all her fears of demons in the jungle. I am now armed with my own machete, with which I am more than likely to cut off my own limbs. Marita darted ahead, taunting me to follow. We came upon a small hut singularly free from the wild jungle growth. She beckoned for me to look inside, but would not look herself. Did she want me to urge her to go inside? I put my arm around her waist and her small breasts were free under the loose huipil blouse. I did not know whether to push her back or draw her in. I was overcome by confusion and tormented with desire.

We were not bothered by insects, or so I thought. But on returning to the village I found myself plagued with the miserable ticks known as garraputas. At her urging we took large containers of aguardiente to the banks of the river and rubbed each other's arms and ankles with the liquor prior to my bathing in the cold river. Alas she would not bathe. A delicious tingling of the flesh, which becomes singularly taut with the application of the rum, this followed by the healing and rushing water. My whole person longs to immerse itself until I am one with the river in an uninterrupted flowing. After the bath Marita playfully rubbed my back and shoulders. She removed her blouse and pointed to several small pinta spots as though to ask once again that I use my educated Yankee skill to remove them. I caress the flesh encircling the spots, one just below the rose nipple, and she urges me with a wagging finger to caress and even kiss it.

She is at times most modest. But at other times would willingly run naked with the small boys of the village. Today she appeared in a finely woven skirt but above the waist only a bandana looped over the shoulders and falling to beneath her necklace of beads and its pendant cross. Her small breasts were quite free of clothing.

The boy "Mon" like an incubus hovers nearby. He stares at me over his harmonica playing. He too perhaps longs for my affection.

And why do I no longer dream of Rosellen? She too was mischievous, but not in the same way. I am obsessed with this winsome child.

December 21. It is not all idleness and dream. For two long days I have worked beside the river with my instruments. And I have drunk three times each day from the spring, as the natives advise, one cup only and after at least an hour's fasting. I cannot deny the spring has important properties. Or perhaps I am only becoming attuned to the oddities of the climate. Already I no longer feel the same disgust when I see whole families squatting at their food, and tearing at the broiled fish spitted and stained with charcoal. The loamy white and sandy clay is for some of the Zoques a delectable repast. The supply of their fiery aguardiente is inexhaustible, however much they drink, since virtually every miserable house has its still. It is indeed strange that they are not violent or quarrelsome when drunk. They live in a pathetic stupor harvesting the ixtle and laboring dully at the hemp, their main product.

The female form of the young Indian woman, whether scarred or unscarred, is undeniably among the most beautiful on earth. With good reason was the Malinche revered. In all the time since Minatitlán I have scarcely seen a deformed or hobbled body of any adolescent female creature. The older women, alas, have lost it all. The naked boys are of surpassing litheness and beauty, but their bodies soon take on a visible corruption in tune with the encroaching dullness of spirit.

Still December 21. She appeared proudly by my bedside in all the finery of a costume for the fiesta, with even the ornate huipil and snowy headdress affected by the Zapotecs. Did some predecessor from the mysterious outside world bring this gift, as another might a necklace or even a watch, hoping to enjoy her favors? I remain mystified by the freedom and wildness she is permitted. Beneath the coarse rustling finery her body seemed to move even when she is still. I longed to tear at her fancy garment and tell her how far more beautiful she is in her loose huipil or with her small breasts exposed. I like to cover them with my hands and she looks down at my hands in amusement.

I am resolved to leave this place. Moreover not even the intermittent fever can explain such delay. I will take with me one man to carry samples of the spring water and another for samples of the petroleum.

Tomorrow will be the last day.

December 22. I will write the following unstintingly, for my everlasting shame or delight. I wonder does she dream that I might replace some drunken native suitor and remain here forever? I put all questions aside, telling myself this is only a last innocent walk into the forest. She took the machete from me and held my hand with her small hot one, then led me impishly to the hut we had seen before. But she did not, as I expected, invite me to go inside. Instead she lay on the needled and biting forest floor and motioned for me to lie beside her. Through a clear place in the tree tops the sun burned down on us like a judgment and I found myself without clothes yet had no intention to undress.

She too was naked. I had not moved, I had not yet touched her. And suddenly she was in my arms thrashing with an animal strength, a beautiful striped body, though the animal stripes were not to be seen on her copper and silk skin.

Then all was quietness. Unashamed I lay with her on a forest bed, unafraid of insects or crawling things. A delicious bruising of the grasses and needles, while the wild birdsong continued and the mysterious chattering of unseen innocent creatures.

It was an hour I will carry with me to my dying day.

December 23. Rejoined the party at headquarters in La Chivela, where there is much talk of Christmas festivities. But no word of Rosellen.

December 26. All my fears are realized. Two brutal Indians hired to guide her up the Rio Corte, even to the ruins of Casas Grandes, have returned without her and have disappeared. It seems they came to the hut of the degenerate Frenchman who hired them, came at night while he slept, leaving at his door a few of her belongings, valueless to them. This Frenchman claims not to have seen the two Indians again. They left also a bulky package containing papers, which should be returned to her relatives when found. It is incumbent upon me to volunteer.

I want to write something, and am struck dumb.

I am covered with a shame intermingled with my innocent love longing for the dead Rosellen. And also, alas, with ineradicable memories of Santa Rosalia. At the thought of Marita's fierce brown flesh, even of the scars of the pinta, my body incorrigibly responds.

1922

Charles Stanfield

THE ANNOUNCEMENT that a Gran Hotel Balneario had been reopened in Santa Rosalia, deep in a jungle of southern Mexico, came to the retired high school teacher Charles Stanfield as an event as preposterous as if such a hotel were about to be opened on the moon. But there it was in the travel pages, the five-story white building rising out of a dim jungle background, together with the news that the disgraced black heavyweight ex-champion Papa Jack, still The Champion to real aficionados, would transfer there his Academy of Boxing from Mexico City and sponsor 45-round fights, by 1922 illegal everywhere else. There were the added attractions of a casino and nightclub.

Stanfield had somehow missed the story of the first hotel of 1890, so soon destroyed by earthquake and ensuing flood. He did read about a Gran Hotel Balneario built in 1908, an optimistic afterthought to the transisthmus railroad opened the year before. But at fifty-eight, a busy high school teacher of biology with a family to support, he had allowed himself only a few whimsical hours of nostalgia. A long and gently ironic story appeared in the *Boston Evening Transcript*. The hotel was real enough, five stories of solid stone. The writer said the native Zoque Indians "watched astonished as steel shafts, then massive blocks of stone rose implacably, a column of white towering above the nearest trees." The fittings for the hotel arrived by bongos, dugout canoes, oxcarts, mule trains. The reports of the gringo hotel, "for the natives thought only gringos would attempt such things," followed jungle paths to distant communities. Even before its completion Indian pilgrims came to Santa Rosalia, not so much for its healing spring waters as for the mysterious hotel. They camped near it, staring up at the third story. Evidently they believed, "in their night of superstition," that some sacred object was housed there. As for the healing spring that alone justified the hotel's obscure existence, it was said to guarantee cures for scrofula, syphilis, rheumatism, arthritis, etc. "Especially the etc.," the facetious writer concluded.

The existence of this hotel was indeed obscure. Tourists and vacationers were discouraged by the long carriage ride from La Chivela, and by 1912 most of the customers were impoverished losers in the turmoil of the revolution. The world took little note, and Stanfield none at all, when the hotel closed in 1915, and the deteriorating road once again became a mule path. The natives of the region still revered the hotel and its sacred third story burden, but did not dare intervene as the jungle at the eastern edge of the village crept toward it. Only rodents and birds and monkeys inhabited its five stories.

The good limestone building nevertheless survived for the reopening of 1922. A flier designed for travel agents promised the ex-champion Papa Jack would arrive any day to set up the Academia de Boxeo. The tables for gambling were already installed as well as two splendid elevators.

Through the years, under the calm, useful New England existence of the young engineer Charles Stanfield, in due time no longer young, there flowed unevenly the quiet current of his half-remembered stay in southern Mexico in 1870. He gave up, reluctantly, the career of engineer, and taught general science in the Cambridge Latin School. Married and had two children, read the *Transcript* and the Sunday *New York*

Times, had a good house on Kirkland Street, and on spring evenings liked to walk along the Charles with his children. Now and then over the years a fourteen-year-old's sullen stare, a birthmark resembling a pinta scar, even an olive-skinned hand resting on his desk, would take him back to the girl Marita who had brought him his coffee, reaching through the mosquito netting. A waking dream of an iguana alertly watching him from the schoolroom wall while snow fell outside.

There were times too, at the movies, when the languorous prolonged stare and mysterious silence of some lovely innocent, a Blanche Sweet or Vilma Banky in diaphanous white, brought to mind Rosellen Maurepas beside him on the *Allegheny Belle* or gazing at the moonlit hill of the Malinche. Then he would feel with quiet anguish the old sense of loss that he experienced in San Miguel, in the Frenchman Dupoint's small house, reading the diary the Indian guides had brought back from the doomed expedition, together with her clothes and a small amount of money. They left these at the door to Dupoint's house, but without waking him. And disappeared, evidently fearing punishment. Charles was allowed to read the diary, but only under Dupoint's watchful eye. The Frenchman had undertaken to see that her possessions were delivered to a still unknown relative. This had become for him a sacred duty, he would surrender it to no one. "I assure you that I am covered with shame, it was the mistake of a life of many mistakes. Ce serait, monsieur, mon tourment éternel." The young engineer thought this language extravagant. But he too was acutely aware that he might have done something to deter Rosellen from her folly. He was sure he too would never forget.

And yet forget he did, in a way, since both Rosellen and Marita came in time to be mythical beings, not quite real and at times almost indistinguishable, intruding on his reveries for a few minutes then gone. Now and then he thought of going to New Orleans to find the Delphine Deslonde mentioned in the diary, but this intention too faded into the busy background of his life. Of his two loves, Marita remained the most vivid, since he made up stories about her for the bedtime pleasure of his small children. He omitted the wriggling toe extended to him in invitation and the salt taste of her shoulder. Marita's history was embellished with adventures in caves among dwarfs and jungle demons. "Tell us about the Indian maiden!" the children would cry.

So the teacher's quiet life passed, until his great adventure on the Isthmus came to seem something he had read not lived. He walked more slowly, took to wearing a heavy sweater under his jacket, also wore a scarf. His last Cambridge Latin students saw a kindly and absentminded man who might quote poems in the middle of a biology class, though no one could see the connection, and who held the door open for the girl students and might pick up the books even a boy had dropped. In due time his placid wife quietly died, the children grew up and went away, and at sixty-five he retired, moving to an apartment on Memorial Drive. In his solitude the memories of Santa Rosalia came strangely to life. No one would have known that on hot summer evenings when discreet lovers came to the river bank, and mosquitoes abounded, he might have a prolonged reverie of the Coatzacoalcos flowing serenely past islands with tall grasses and sleeping alligators and herons delicately poised. And on lazy summer afternoons he would turn from whatever book he was reading to the large illustrated volume of *Explorations and Surveys For a Ship-Canal Isthmus of Tehuantepec* (Washington, Government Printing Office, 1872) to which he had contributed. "In the neighborhood of Petapa a greenish slate was often met with, and on the road I picked up a piece of blue and green malachite." A true observation. But not so true the one that explained a rather long delay, which had to be accounted for when he returned to headquarters: "From San Miguel Pass and Cofradia I went to Santa Rosalia in the Chimalapas, where, after suffering many hardships, I was obliged to return to Chivela." Not so many hardships! He felt a twinge of envy because three older engineers had visited his village later in the winter, and stayed for two weeks, though they too failed to go higher up the river. There was no mention of Marita in their official report. Rosellen had gone farther than any of them. She had even reached the ruins of Casas Grandes.

Timetables, maps and railroad journals accumulated, as from the career of engineer he had given up. They were his favorite evening occupation. He studied engine designs, the mutations of sleeping cars, the composition of all well-known limiteds and made time tables for imaginary long-distance trains. He knew about the many problems of railroads in Mexico, and read in *Railroad Times* of the first transisthmus railway completed in 1896 but not used (its poor roadbed was due to construction fraud). And read of the line opened in 1907 and inaugurated with much fanfare, though somehow he missed news of the opening of the hotel in Santa Rosalia the following year. In one wartime map, eight or nine years later, he found San Miguel and Santa Rosalia with a secondary road between them. But in later maps there was only a thin line to indicate a jungle path for mules and people on foot. The narrowing Rio Corte still lost itself in blank space, with the words *Unexplored Area Zona Inexplorada*.

Even his remote part of southern Mexico was not exempt from revolutionary turmoil, although the Isthmus of Tehuantepec rarely appeared in the news. Dissident generals with interchangeable names led raids on small towns, captured other generals, and in due time were themselves executed. Occasionally an American businessman or tourist was kidnapped and ransomed or shot. By 1922 the revolutionary violence was subsiding. But even then Stanfield did not think to revisit the region, or to imagine any other New Englander reaching his lost and steaming village. Nothing would ever happen there.

So he was all the more astonished to read in the travel

pages of a Gran Hotel Balneario in Santa Rosalia, a resort hotel near a small but famous spring whose waters were said to cure many diseases. A unique jungle location, and a community of unspoiled Zoque Indians, as well as a chance to meet the notorious ex-champion Papa Jack. A picture of the hotel was rather blurred. But a solid white building unmistakably rose five stories, with smiling guests dressed as for tennis or a garden party standing near its entrance.

And why shouldn't he too stand there? It took him only minutes to decide to go, and to turn to his timetables, although he knew at once what trains he would take. *The Spirit of Saint Louis*, then *The St. Louis-Mexico City Limited*, with a time change in Laredo. A through standard sleeping car as far as Mexico City, another to Córdoba, a third to Chivela, with some still unknown conveyance from Chivela to the hotel. He even knew how long the train was scheduled to wait in Tierra Blanca. For he now realized he had known all along, in some dark dreaming corner of his mind, that he would some day return. Without this journey his life, and its long underflow of dreaming, would not be complete.

Papa Jack, Monica Swift, Jimmy Wilding

WHEN THE EX-CHAMPION Papa Jack climbed aboard a sleeping car in Vera Cruz, with his diminished entourage, March 22, 1922, it was with no clear idea where Santa Rosalia was, or how long it would take to get there. The entourage, in its heyday a good score of sycophants, now consisted of the poet Monica Swift, once again looking for her lost husband Brian Desmond, the young English bantamweight Jimmy Wilding (discovered by Papa Jack bloody and victorious after a London street fight fought for pennies and shillings in 1914), and two Mexicans who had volunteered their services, Artemio Angel de la Cruz and Angelita Braciano.

The lost husband Desmond (poet, amateur boxer, aristocrat, vagabond) met and almost came to blows with Papa Jack in a Paris nightclub in 1914, actually faced him in the ring in 1916, then preceded him to Mexico City two years later, and there set up an Academy of Boxing. The two arrogant exiles were good friends. Desmond had refused service in the British army, Papa Jack had served his year in Leavenworth for violation of the Mann Act (the white woman transported across state lines was in fact his wife), but he was still widely ostracized in the United States and unable to get fights. It was in Mexico that Desmond and Monica Swift were married and nearly starved, and that Desmond disappeared. Some were sure he had been killed in a cantina fight, others that he was murdered by bandits, still others that he had insulted the Mexican police once too often. Monica Swift had looked for him in prisons from the Rio Grande to Guatemala. In Santa Rosalia she hoped, incidentally, to get orders from the hotel for the lamp shades she had designed. They were applauded even by French decorators. If Desmond were alive, and read announcements of a Papa Jack exhibition, he would find his way to the Gran Hotel Balneario.

The towering Champion and his four small companions were the only occupants of the old sleeping car. Angelita Braciano, a dancer in the chorus of a Vera Cruz nightclub, had given up her Tropicana job after one strenuous night in Papa Jack's bed, and looked forward to continuing her career at the Gran Hotel Balneario, noted for its casino and healing waters. A resourceful and cheerful entrepreneur, Artemio Angel de la Cruz, a former boyfriend of Angelita Braciano, had already helped the Champion as an unpaid interpreter. He persuaded the Champion he would be indispensable in the still tumultuous southern Mexico of 1922. He would always be on hand, ready to placate bandits and swindlers and police and supply the *mordida* tactfully. He had a way of tilting his head back, as though to look at a much taller person. His small waxed beard, thus pointed at his interlocutor, made him look alert and inquisitive.

Artemio Angel de la Cruz was a patriot, and liked to read aloud from Terry's *Guide to Mexico* flattering commentaries on the beauties of everything they saw and on the pleasures to come.

"Numerous parrot-beaked blackbirds enliven the jungle hereabout," he read, though in fact they were still sweltering in the Vera Cruz station. "Here also thrive the vanilla bean, rubber, rice, sugarcane, cochineal, indigo, dyewoods, balsams, resins, and many varnish-making gums."

"I can hardly wait," Jack said.

To accompany the Champion was the culminating triumph of Artemio's career as entrepreneur, guide, Mexican. He could explain to anyone who seemed hostile the honor done to the nation when the Champion (still the "real" Champion seven years after the much-debated loss in Havana) chose to return to Mexico. In 1919 and early 1920, prior to his surrender at the border in Tijuana, he had been regarded as a hero in Mexico, praised for his attacks on racism in the United States. He was even befriended by President Venustiano Carranza, and postcards showed the two shaking hands, each giving the impression that he was conferring honor on the other. A deep inclination of Papa Jack's beaming black face brings his chin within reach, so to speak, of the President's famous white beard. But Carranza was shot in May 1920, after the capture of the "Golden Train," and on July 20, 1920 Jack stepped across the border to accept his year of prison.

One of Artemio's delicate tasks was to determine when the Carranza connection would be useful, and when it should be concealed, since there were still many factions.

"Venustiano Carranza was the noble and idealistic father of the 1917 Constitution," Artemio would explain to whoever would listen. "However, no Mexican idealist was more corrupt than Venustiano Carranza. Those he appointed were even more corrupt. Who hasn't heard of the Golden Train? In their last days in power Carranza and his followers despoiled and pillaged enough treasures to fill a train that was supposed to bring them to this very station of Vera Cruz where we are sitting. Even the chandeliers from the National Palace! The President's train stood waiting for days, and behind it waited more trains for the corrupt political associates and their families. However, no train reached Vera Cruz. The tracks were torn up, the locomotives lacked water, there was also no water for the political associates. His enemies pursued him on horseback. The President ended his days in a miserable hut. He died under a horse blanket. He was shot. Everything was taken by his assassins, even his leggings, his eyeglasses and his horsewhip."

The Champion knew all this as well as he knew his own record in the ring.

"Carranza was my friend," Papa Jack said, "He respected me."

"He was an idealist. He defied the United States government and insisted on our Mexican independence. However, he was corrupt. We do not know who still admires Venustiano Carranza, so I advise you to hide the photograph."

They were still the only passengers, though several other cars were crowded with Mexicans. The old twelve-section sleeping car, which bore the name of *Galveston,* was of the highest 1890 mahogany and brass elegance, and had served for many years on the Southern Pacific, gliding over west Texas plains. Epicene nude figures writhed in green and golden arabesques of Tiffany glass, framed by ebony and ivory marquetry. The brass spittoon beneath each window had a rich medicinal odor, less sickening than the smells of charcoal and burnt chocolate coming from the tiny buffet that adjoined the men's toilet and dressing room. There was no air, although the porter (who subsequently disappeared) had turned on the tiny fans at both ends of the car. The fading and rising whir had a lulling sound, but the metal strips of the armrests still burned. Green cushions and the center carpet were badly worn, and springs protruded from the seats.

The drawing room, however, had been splendidly restored, and was reserved for government officials. A large chain, with a warning notice not to trespass, blocked the door. But this all the more invited one to look in on the spotless room and its polished mirror. The mirror reflected a toilet and metal sink and two gleaming spittoons. The facing window seats had been made into a double berth for the night, and a small fold-down table offered an unopened bottle of tequila and a basket of fruit. All this had the effect of a museum display. But to the Champion the chain and warning evoked unpleasant memories of segregation. He stepped over the chain, removed his Palm Beach coat but not his shoes and, still wearing his straw hat, lay down on the forbidden berth.

"Take a picture of me, Jimmy. Lying on the governor's bed."

"There ain't any film."

"Take it anyway."

It was hot. Artemio Angel de la Cruz, who had unbuttoned his white shirt to the waist, assured them it would be much cooler once the train was underway. But there was no indication it would ever be underway.

"We play cards to pass the time. Also we discuss your plans. When we pass famous and beautiful spots I will read about them from the guide."

The poet Monica Swift, who had changed to a silk gown, withdrew to the women's dressing room for a nap on its leather bench. Angelita Braciano followed her, but returned wearing only a teddy and a loose blouse. Silver stars painted over the nipples for her nightclub performances were visible beneath it. Jimmy Wilding had stripped to his shorts.

Two hours later, and without warning, the train jolted forward with an angry lash of slipping locomotive wheels. The train stopped, then moved slowly out from under the glass overhang of the station and onto a crowded street. Vendors looked up from the street market and waved. But it was hard to imagine the train ever arriving anywhere, let alone a distant place named Chivela far to the south, since it appeared not to be gaining on a newsboy who trotted beside them. He was holding up a stack of newspapers and magazines, and shouting headlines.

They played bridge as the train crept through ragged suburbs, stopping frequently, Papa Jack and Angelita as partners, Monica Swift with Jimmy Wilding, while Artemio Angel de la Cruz read aloud from the guidebook. He read about the banana plantations they would soon see.

"These rich alluvial plains, which bask in the never-failing, all-vivifying sun, know no agricultural repose." He relished the more difficult sentences, and wanted the poetess

Monica Swift to correct his accent. "In these tropical woodlands there dwell also the collared peccary, the Mexican deer, the black-faced brocket, tapir, Mexican spermophile, jaguar, tiger-cat or ocelot."

"Tiger, tiger burning bright," the Champion put in. "I want to see a collared peccary."

"I have seen these animals in the Jardín Zoológico in the city of Mexico," Angelita Braciano said.

"The Yaguarondi cat, the nine-banded armadillo, the white-nosed coatamundi. In flight the birds flash like brilliant sprites through the jungle."

Monica Swift laughed. Her musical voice blended the teasing irony of wealth and privilege, a British schooling and British first husband, two years in Greenwich village, several lovers of different nationalities. And the soft slow chant of a true poet. The recent years of poverty had left no mark.

"Flight and sprites! I'm sure your Mr Terry was proud of that sentence. But I do believe birds enjoy the rhythms of their songs, don't you? Even if they don't know what they mean. Who shall say what powers of intuition are not possessed by birds?" She closed her eyes, summoning memory:

"I shall not ask Jean Jacques Rousseau
If birds confabulate or no."

"Thou wert not born for death, immortal bird," Papa Jack intoned, shuffling the cards. "Don't you know any poems, Jimmy?"

Wilding recited Kipling's poem "If," not missing a line.

There were still no other passengers, though a second sleeping car had filled with raucous young men, possibly army recruits, and behind it trailed several crowded coaches.

The sweltering afternoon deepened. The train crawled through banana plantations, giving off torrents of smoke and soot. Shortly after two o'clock it stopped at a small station where soldiers were sleeping with their backs to a wall covered with proclamations. There was no town in sight. A swarthy officer with many medals rushed into the car, shouting orders to the porter, though in fact there had been no sign of a porter since the train was underway. He was followed by two barefoot Indian girls who might have been twins. They were carrying baskets and disappeared into the drawing room with the officer. An angry tirade came from behind the closed door because the bed had been mussed.

"Probably a military aide of the governor," Artemio explained. "There will be a small delay in this rural station."

"Anything can happen with these brutes," Angelita said. "Every general is a bandit, every bandit is a general. The military aides are worse. I think I will go to the ladies' rest room. I do not wish to be insulted. Please tell me when the military aide leaves."

"You're with me," the Champion said. "I'm the one who would be insulted. Jimmy will tie his hands behind his back and stuff him into an upper berth and close it. If necessary I will help."

"Nevertheless I do not feel safe."

"It's a good thing Brian isn't here," Monica Swift said. "He would already have started a fight and been arrested."

The next half hour was punctuated by giggles and screams.

"It is just good natured fun, the military must be the military," Artemio said, returning to his guidebook. "Cane-fields stretch away as far as the eye can reach, and great quantities of sugar are produced."

Presently the aide to the governor left, followed by the two barefoot Indian girls. More than ever they looked like twins. The conductor standing outside their window at once blew his whistle. The whistle of the locomotive responded, the conductor whistled in confirmation, and the train resumed its journey.

At Tierra Blanca, it appeared, there would be a delay of several hours, while they waited for the connecting train from Córdoba. Posters announced a Grand Circus, and in fact a large tent had been erected across from the station. Artemio reconnoitered, accompanied by Monica Swift, and returned to say that the manager would have been honored by a Papa Jack exhibition, whether of boxing or dancing, but there was no afternoon performance. Moreover, he had no money. Monica Swift went with him to show photographs of Brian Desmond. For Desmond loved circuses, and if penniless might turn up even at a circus possessing only a tame bear, a mangy lion, a dancing girl, a clown. He could earn his keep as the Strong Man. But the circus manager had seen no sign of an Englishman of Desmond's size and aristocratic mien.

A favorite vaudeville act was for Wilding, who still weighed under 120 pounds, to challenge the Champion, now over 230, fat with adulation and alcohol. He would hold the dancing Wilding at arm's length for a round or two, then flatten him with one blow. Wilding would not move; someone would call for a doctor or nurse. But as soon as Papa Jack's back was turned Wilding would come to life, leap onto his shoulders and wave his arms as in victory.

After Tierra Blanca, soldiers rode on the locomotive, one on the cowcatcher and one with the engineer, two more on the roof. There were several tunnels before the junction with the transisthmus railroad, and these were inviting to bandits, whether real bandits or idealistic guerilleros. The train might be held up inside the tunnel, or when it emerged. A locomotive had been blown to pieces as it entered one of these very tunnels by explosives laid on the track. The holdup of trains was an everyday occurrence in 1919, but was not unknown in 1922 in the more peaceful aftermath of the revolution.

It was on a long bridge over the Papaloapam river that the train stopped unexpectedly. In the late afternoon heat the water far beneath looked cool and inviting. So too had the great white peak of Orizaba far behind them. Artemio had told them about the volcano lovers towering over the Valley of Mexico. In the remote past Popocatepetl had lain upon Iztaccihuatl, the Sleeping Woman, in the posture of a romantic lover, and had erupted, pouring volcanic ash into her.

"That is ridiculous," Angelita Braciano said.

"This river," Artemio read, "is the most important stream in the state of Veracruz. It is a picturesque waterway."

"I wonder why we're stopped," Monica Swift said. "It's getting even hotter."

Two soldiers appeared, accompanying the engineer, who saluted them in a friendly manner. All three were smoking expensive cigars, which they must have just acquired.

"It is a strike," Artemio explained after a long exchange in Spanish.

"The employees of the union have not received satisfaction."

"Why are they striking in the middle of a bridge?"

"They are asking for money to compensate for the legitimate increase in wages they have not received. Otherwise the train will remain on the bridge."

"Asking us for money?"

"Asking all the passengers for a patriotic contribution. But more from us, since we are in a sleeping car. If we do not pay they will uncouple the locomotive and leave us on the bridge."

"It's absurd," Monica Swift said. "On the other hand it's not the first time it's happened."

"How much do they want?"

"I will explain who you are," Artemio said. "That may help."

He took several postcards of the Champion from his hip pocket and showed them, though not the card shaking hands with Carranza. A discussion ensued. The men asked to be photographed with Papa Jack, who also autographed a timetable. In the end they settled for twenty American dollars.

It was already dark when the train reached Santa Lucrecia, and they had had nothing to eat. But here they were surprised to learn that a dining car would be attached to the train. A good thing! At each long stop through the afternoon passengers got down from the other cars, surrounding the vendors who offered tortillas, fruit, even chickens. Nothing was left by the time the vendors reached their sleeping car. Some of the passengers built fires by the side of the tracks to warm the food they had bought.

The shiny dining car, green with bordering strips of yellow, had been newly painted but was of an old-fashioned design. It stood on a siding directly opposite their own car. Its name, *Boca Chica,* meaning small mouth, seemed an odd one to give a dining car. Men with flashlights were hammering at the bright, almost silvery wheels while other workmen watched and smoked. Above them, in the dining car itself, two waiters were moving smartly, setting the tables, while an encouraging plume of smoke rose from the area of the kitchen.

The conductor, who had remained out of sight since the brief strike, informed them that it would be possible to cross over to the dining car and have their dinner now, although it might be another hour before it was attached to the train. The shunting engine was for the moment busy elsewhere.

They were welcomed with much bowing by a maître d'hôtel in a thready and soiled white jacket. He insisted on seating each of them, with special gestures for the two women. Since they were five, and the tables had only four places, Artemio sat across the aisle. The word had reached the dining car that the famous Champion was in the party, and the chef and two waiters at once asked for autographs.

"We have the best cuisine of any train in southern Mexico," the chef said. It was an English sentence he had memorized. He said it would be useless to see the menu, since many items were unavailable. They should put themselves in his hands. He would produce a typical meal of the region, with embellishments from northern cuisine.

Artemio translated, and offered to explain the dishes as they came, and to read appropriate descriptions from the Guide's section on food.

"Tell him I want fried chicken and mashed potatoes," Jack said.

"He wants you to put yourself in his hands."

"I'll tell him myself. Pollo con puré de papa."

They had ample time to inspect the beautiful car, while workmen continued to hammer at the wheels. The Tiffany glass clerestory and half-moon windows were of turn-of-the-century design, also the large brass spittoons. Yet all might have been installed only recently, so spotless and polished was it. The marquetry was of several fine woods, with lozenges of ivory. The most extraordinary feature of the dining car was an immense mirror nearly filling the wall that divided the dining area from the kitchen. The mirror was so designed as to bring the whole car into view, but much lengthened, so that Artemio at his table and the four at theirs were clearly visible yet seemed to be seated at a long corridor of tables. Papa Jack and Jimmy Wilding, who had their backs to the mirror, appeared to Angelita and Monica to be behind them, and thus farther from the reflecting glass. But when Monica pointed this out to the men, who turned to look, their real position was restored.

The first dish was served from a large silver tureen still bearing the words *Missouri Pacific*. There were imbedded pieces of gray gelatinous meat and shreds of onion and chile. Artemio leafed through the guide until he found the section on Mexican dishes.

"This is pozzole, also pronounced possole, a favored dish of the Indians. It is deliciously flavored with oregano."

"What is that meat?"

"Pig's head."

While the others hesitated, Artemio took several tortillas from the shared dish.

"I will show you how the peon eats his pozzole. But first I will show you how the peon keeps his tortillas fresh and warm. I will read from the Guide. 'They are the staff of life to the peon, who often carries a stack of them tucked in his shirt, above the belt, next to his hide.' Artemio unbuttoned his shirt, wedged the tortillas under his belt and continued to read. 'If this unwashed pellejo imparts a saline flavor to them he minds it not, for it is thus that they keep moist. The tortilla may also be used as a spoon.' He removed the tortillas from his waist, putting two back on the plate and doubled the third, pinching a bit off the end. This he dipped in Angelita's plate of pozzole and tasted it.

"That's disgusting," Jimmy Wilding said.

"Disgusting is in the eye of the beholder," Monica Swift contributed. "I think I'd prefer a spoon. A silver spoon."

"Listen to the guidebook. I was only following instructions. It says to dip both tortilla and meat into chile sauce as hot as a scorpion's tail."

Before the others could follow his example, the waiter appeared and swept away the dishes of pozzole. On the next track where their own train was stationed a noisy switching of cars had begun.

A broiled fish followed. It was ringed by eggs on a platter that the waiter deftly displayed before each diner. On a side dish were Tamales de Muerto, which contained small chunks of musty cheese. These, Artemio explained, were ritually placed in coffins for the benefit of the dead. But before they could make much progress with the tamales a new delicacy arrived in a bucket carried by an old Indian woman in a flowered skirt. Evidently the waiter understood the Champion's longing for chicken and had gone out among the vendors swarming over the station platform. The dish consisted of fat moist pieces of chicken swimming in a rich sauce of chocolate mole, almost a soup, also chiles and garlic.

They were still at their dessert—a corn meal mush with molasses—when they were startled by a conductor's whistle, followed by the repeated wailing of their train, the train they had left, the train containing their baggage. It was now gliding, after only a few moments of slipping wheels, in the direction of Chivela, Tehuantepec, Salina Cruz. It had apparently forgotten them.

They reached Chivela at noon the next day on a mixed train, five clattering freight cars and two second class coaches

with hard benches. The Champion and his friends had been
honored with brandy and a long speech by the manager of
the miserable hotel in Santa Lucrecia, but this did not protect them from fleas during the night. In Chivela a cold wind
blew across the plain past huts with thatched roofs and several adobe houses in ruins. Here they were met by a short,
wiry and enthusiastic young Indian who had a tumpline richly
lettered with the word *Pepe*. He gesticulated happily in the
direction of a large hotel autobus with five rows of seats,
brightly painted and open at the sides, with the streamer *Gran
Hotel Balneario Chimalapa*. Beside it were their suitcases.
The conductor, remembering their destination, had put them
off with a florid pencilled note of apology.

But first, the driver explained, they must stop at the Casa
Blanca Hotel in Chivela itself to pick up several passengers.
In fact, there would be time there for a leisurely comida, since
the bus would not proceed to Santa Rosalia before three
o'clock. The hotel, moreover was of historic interest for travelers, since it had been owned for centuries by descendants
of Cortés. They would see, in the salon where meals were
served, portraits of famous persons who had ruled the Isthmus in the past.

One of these, the driver said, laughing as he pointed to
his own left eye and making a motion as to scoop it out, was
blind. Only the socket remained.

Long before the handsome yet eccentric hotel bus reached
Santa Rosalia Papa Jack knew coming was a mistake. Near a
small ruin, where unexpectedly they were offered a vile drink
of raspberry color, the bus was disabled for more than half
an hour. An old cripple with the crinkled leathery countenance of a mummy appeared to be guarding the ruin. He
pointed a crutch at them menacingly, then went back to sleep.
A wild wind that shook the forest above them, and sent
branches crashing, gave way to cold torrential rain. They
huddled together on the floor of the bus, which was open at
the sides the better to permit sightseeing, no windows or

doors. Minutes later the rain had stopped, the jungle was steaming again, and the raucous cries of birds had resumed. Brown furry creatures swung from tree to tree as though pursued by the already distant roaring of the storm.

It was dark when they reached the hotel, exhausted, and much bitten by unseen insects. Maddened horses, three abreast, rushed toward them near the first dark huts of the village, pursued apparently by bats. The five stories of the hotel, with lights only on the ground floor, was a black gloom. There was no one at the desk to welcome them. The driver, who had long since removed his chauffeur's hotel uniform, and was wearing only tattered shorts, pointed to a cavernous room off the bare and uninteresting lobby. It was the bar, casino, nightclub and theater combined. In the very center of the room two men in guayaberas were seated at a roulette table, while a croupier in a tuxedo, but with no tie, called out his commands. On a raised stage, under a weak and unshaded light that hung from the ceiling, was a boxing ring. One of the four posts had fallen and on two sides the lower rope almost touched the floor.

A bartender, who introduced himself as José, at once offered them milky cocktails from a glass beaker. The drinks were warm.

"You are very late," he said. "You are too late for the dinner. However, I offer you gratis a speciality of the hotel, our welcome Margarita made from the excellent sugar cane aguardiente of the Chimalapas."

The drinks were also sticky.

"Where is everybody?" Papa Jack said. "There's nobody at the desk."

"You have a reservation?"

"I'm Papa Jack, for Christ's sake. These are my friends."

"Of course. You will create the Academia de Boxeo."

"That I sure as hell won't. We'll be out of here first thing tomorrow. What time does the bus go back?"

"Tomorrow it does not go back. Why would you go

back?"

"I want to see the owner right away."

"The owner lives in retirement in Cuernevaca."

"The manager, then."

"The manager has withdrawn for the night. I myself will take you to your rooms." He reached quickly for one of Monica's hands and held it close to his eyes. "You poor lady, you have been bitten. I think also there are pinolillos under the skin. Ticks. Why did you not wear gloves? For the pinolillos you will bathe the hands in aguardiente."

"We've all been bitten," Artemio said. "This Gran Hotel is a disgrace to the Mexican hotel industry."

The next morning, however, things looked brighter under a warm sun that glittered in the pine trees of a hill behind the village. In another direction the jungle was a wall of dark green. Wild flowers were everywhere, blending with those planted in front of the hotel. Near the terrace were a few metal tables and chairs. Just beyond the terrace five or six miserable Indians, it was hard to tell how many, were sleeping hunched over. Filthy robes covered them, although the bare feet protruded.

A message in faded blue typing had been slipped under each door.

Desayuno (Breakfast) in bar or on terrace or Beside the Pool at your choice. Beside the Pool recommended.
Antonio Vinalva, manager.

It was signed with a flourish.

The several poolside tables were shaded by a tall tamarind tree from which hung bunches of red and yellow flowers and russet pods of fruit. Nearby a papaya tree spread a canopy of broad leaves, with clusters of melons near the trunk. On one of the stiff ribs, half hidden by the leaves, a monkey, apparently domesticated, looked down. Orchids grew in wild profusion near rusted machinery at one end of the pool.

Albert J. Guerard

A young iguana, dark green and shiny, rested watchfully beneath a tree bearing blossoms of white bells.

Jimmy Wilding, Monica Swift and Artemio were already at a poolside table when Papa Jack came down. Angelita remained in bed.

"This is an earthly paradise, Papa Jack," Artemio said. "For breakfast you will have native fruits."

Small Indian girls were standing silently a few feet away, offering stuffed iguanas for sale. There were leprous spots on their faces and hands. Artemio explained these spots.

"This is the disease of the pinta, common to the Zoque Indians of the Chimalapas. Nothing to give alarm. The Zoques believe it is a visitation for the evil behavior of their ancestors."

"What evil behavior?"

"It is not specified. However, the pinta protected them from the recruiting of the bandits and the generals during the Revolution. Nobody wanted men with these spots. I assure you the spots are harmless."

Two barefoot waitresses arrived with pungent coffee and platters of sliced papaya, pineapple and mango, and red and golden pomegranate split open to reveal many seeds. There were plantains larger than the largest banana. Other platters offered strangely colored eggs, purplish and small, as well as tortillas and beans. Bees were immediately attracted.

"The bees are harmless," Artemio said. "These fruits have the highest medicinal qualities. The seeds of the papaya are a vermifuge. This is true also of the seeds of the mammee apple."

"What is a vermifuge?" Jimmy Wilding asked.

"Worms. To cure the worms. The alligator pear or avocado is also a vermifuge. It is shaped like a sheep's testicle and is therefore said to provoke sexual excitement."

The small Indians with the iguanas watched them gravely.

"Tell them we don't want any iguanas this morning," Papa Jack said.

"What a strange pool," Monica Swift said. "Quite beautiful in its perverse and subtle way. Do take a close look at the water."

The pool was fed from a tower that collected rain, but also from some underground source, possibly a conduit from the famous medicinal spring, since the water was very warm. Small fish moved lazily, sometimes in clear water, sometimes in water that was green and nearly opaque. It was doubtful whether the pool's bottom and sides had been recently cleaned, if ever, but an Indian with a net at the end of a long pole was occupied in scooping up leaves, dead insects and yellow fragments from the floating gardenias and pads of water lilies at the hotel end of the pool. A large frog sat on a raft of serpentine green fronds and palm branches, as though a permanent resident there. Its throat ballooned obscenely, a bulging thin tissue of silky green. Nearby, a single humming bird whirred and darted among hibiscus plants and overarching bougainvillea.

The two small girls with the trays of iguanas had not gone away. One of them turned an iguana on its side and lifted the tail to permit closer inspection. The iguana, when righted, had an even more malevolent expression than before. The small living iguana was edging closer to their table.

"The flesh of the iguana is as tender as the tenderest chicken," Artemio said. "Any real traveller should give it a try, and enjoy what the Zoques enjoy."

"Not this morning," Papa Jack said. "Not even for lunch or dinner."

The quiet scene was suddenly charged with life as three young Mexican women in strange bathing suits appeared at the pool, and tried the water with their toes. The suits were even longer than those seen on American beaches, with frilled yet drab and sagging knickers that reached almost to the knees. Black silk stockings were rolled just beneath the knees, which were thus left provocatively bare. The upper portions of the bathingsuits were quite audacious and revealing, since

101

the silky cloth fit tightly over every curve and protuberant bone and valley, all dominated by nipples thrust out like hard and swollen peas.

"Those are bathing beauties," Artemio explained. "I think they are also prostitutes who come here to entertain the big gamblers. Some gamblers believe it brings luck to have a beautiful prostitute beside him."

"I haven't seen many big gamblers," Papa Jack said. "Just those two at the roulette table. They were asleep on their feet."

"Wait for the weekend."

"Yes, friends, wait for the weekend!" It was the enthusiastic voice of the bartender José, who stood over them rubbing his hands. "On Friday night the hotel comes to life. Gamblers rush to us from far away, even Tampico and Vera Cruz. Also reliable customers from nearby Tehuantepec, and rich invalids who come for the waters and for the benefits of the petroleum pit. The best spring in southern Mexico, both for men and women. There will also be coming the Royal Jazz Band, six pieces and sexy singer. The hula dancers have already arrived."

Papa Jack nodded to the three bathers who with interlocked arms were floating near the water lilies, and casting friendly glances at the breakfasters.

"Are those the hula dancers?"

"No, no. They are paying customers enjoying a tropical holiday. Naturally they expect to make friends."

"That must make six or seven."

"Six or seven?"

"Paying customers."

José laughed.

"Wait till you meet our manager Antonio Vinalva. He will tell you of the many interesting guests. There is even one of your compatriots coming from Boston, Massachusetts, who visited Santa Rosalia Chimalapa before there was any hotel. fifty-two years ago in fact. Mr Charles Stanfield, teacher. He will come tomorrow or the next day. You will also meet the famous Nicanor Díaz."

"Nicanor Díaz the bandit!" Artemio exclaimed.

"Call him the general, although he disdains that title. A hero the authorities will never touch. Maybe you know the story of Robin Hood who lived in the forest and robbed the rich to give to the poor? Nicanor Díaz is our Robin Hood of southern Mexico. He would be eager to meet the famous Papa Jack."

"I can't see enough trade here to pay our way," Papa Jack said. "Not even for an exhibition fight, let alone the Boxing Academy. Or Monica's lamp shades."

"The money will come from the gamblers. They are generous men, also they like to bet on the fights. Señor Vinalva the manager will explain."

"You can't bet on an exhibition fight," Papa Jack said. "Besides, who would bet against me?"

"They can bet on the fights of your young companion Mr Wilding. He is to take on all comers. That was the agreement."

"The agreement didn't say this hotel was the ass end of nowhere. We're leaving."

"You will talk to Señor Vinalva. Now I offer you a complimentary breakfast drink. What do you say to a garapina? A blissful drink made of the skin and pulp of the pineapple. For a stronger drink I recommend the chica, which is made from the pineapple's rind. Or a simple mescal from the bottle."

"I'm not leaving," Monica Swift said. "I love this place, even the stuffed iguanas and pineapple pulp. I'm certainly not leaving until I've given Brian a chance to find us."

"Here comes Señor Vinalva," José said. "He will welcome you officially."

A young man in white flannels and immaculate tennis shoes and short-sleeved embroidered guayabera approached, bowing. A sunshade such as tennis players wear all but concealed his black hair cut short. Only the tennis racket was

103

missing. His features were Hispanic, except for the cheek-bones, his dark brown eyes were alert and friendly. They appeared to acknowledge the others, even as he bent to kiss Monica Swift's hand.

A graceful little speech welcomed them. The Gran Hotel Balneario was honored by the presence of the Champion, truly the greatest champion in the history of boxing. And to welcome his friends, including a true poet and maker of lamp shades.

"I love your accent," Monica Swift said. "I can't quite place it."

"I was exposed to both British and American teachers during the construction of the transisthmus interoceanic railroad. Your own voice interests me, Miss Swift."

"Mrs Desmond, though I write with my maiden name. I'm British, I suppose, but I've been around so much I don't think I'm really anything."

"Mrs Desmond. Yes, of course. The hotel looks with the greatest sympathy on your efforts to find your husband. So do I."

"Do sit down, Señor Vinalva. José is bringing us some pineapple pulp and mescal. Please join us."

"Pineapple pulp! I think you mean garapinas."

Papa Jack offered Vinalva a cigar, which the manager at first declined, then unwrapped and contemplated with relish. The finest Havana, a cigar worthy of the Hotel Genève in the capital or the cafe La Vie Parisienne or a dinner of political leaders at the San Angel Inn! As Antonio Vinalva talked, praising the cigar, both the curious monkey in the papaya tree and the iguana near the white bell flowers appeared to be listening. The monkey now hung by its tail.

Papa Jack, whose own speech was measured and poetic, also listened with appreciation to the flow of geniality.

"I'm sure you will have a nice little place here some day, Mr Vinalva. I estimate eighty or a hundred thousand for sprucing up. Get the road from Chivela repaired. Then I guess you would have a resort worthy of the adventurous carriage trade. But not now. There's no way I can see it for us now. The money just isn't here."

"It will be, sir, it will be! What do you say to a Papa Jack fight with an opponent of international renown, preferably from South America? People will flock to Santa Rosalia. Gamblers from Havana, from Rio and Buenos Aires, yes even from New York! Not to mention our own millionaire gamblers. Even from Chicago, sir! A syndicate of international sportsmen and aficionados will guarantee your purse. No need for a big crowd."

"I wasn't thinking big, Mr Vinalva. I just want a thousand and expenses for a three-round exhibition, and two hundred for Jimmy taking on all comers. Then we'll start the Academy and take orders for this lady's fancy lamp shades and be on our way."

Antonio Vinalva gave Monica Swift a speculative glance.

"An exhibition would not put Santa Rosalia on the map. But one international fight would. Only one. The owner might arrange to have it approved as a world championship. By the Mexican Boxing Federation if no one else."

"What do you have in mind?"

Antonio Vinalva hesitated. He turned aside, as though embarrassed, and caught the attentive stare of the monkey hanging from the papaya tree. This first conversation with the champion had gone faster than he planned.

"An Argentine heavyweight. The Wild Bull of the Pampas, to be precise. Luís Angel Firpo."

"Firpo!"

"Exactly. A Papa Jack-Firpo match, forty-five rounds or even twenty, would be the event of the year. The Gran Hotel Balneario would become overnight the most famous resort hotel and casino in Mexico."

Papa Jack stared.

"Do I look in condition to fight someone like Firpo?" He stood up, towering above Vinalva. "Put your hands there, feel a little of that fat."

Vinalva drew back, embarrassed, but at last did as he was told.

"Firpo is also out of condition," he said. "Everyone knows that. In his photographs there is even more fat than on you."

"Sure. And who would put up the purse for a fight like that? Even at two hundred dollars a seat you wouldn't begin to make it. Unless you built an arena."

"No, no. It must be more private, held in our theater-restaurant, just like the sporting clubs of old England, where only club members attended, always in tuxedo. In Mexico the guayabera is sufficient. The gate receipts are unimportant. The proprietor could mortgage the hotel for the great renown given by Papa Jack vs Firpo. There are also the gamblers."

Papa Jack frowned. He did not like talk of gamblers, with its reminders of the 26th round in Havana and allegations that he had thrown the fight. He took in the pool, the huddled Indians, and the five stories of the hotel in one long scornful glance. Even the splashing bathing beauties participated in his scorn.

"Why don't you put Jimmy in with Firpo, all a hundred and eighteen pounds? What does Firpo weigh now, two-seventy? That might make an interesting fight for your gamblers. They could bet on how many seconds it would last. Or maybe Firpo would never catch him."

Vinalva shrugged.

"Perhaps this fight will never happen. In fact we could agree strictly among friends that it will never happen. It would still be possible to discuss plans. Even discussion in the newspapers of such a fight would call attention to our attractive hotel. In fact I propose that you sign an agreement to fight Firpo. Photographers will come for the signing."

"How much do I get to sign for a fight that won't come off?"

"An interesting question. However, I cannot answer it

myself. I will have to consult the owner. For the moment I suggest you enjoy our last days of quietness. Visit the spring and taste the waters, two cups after each meal. Go to the edge of the jungle, but do not go in without a guide. Look at the life of the village and our friendly and interesting Zoques. Enjoy our pool! Swim among the lilies and gardenias! Now I leave you to your Mexican breakfast."

The Blue Notebook of Charles Stanfield: 1922

TWO NIGHTS AND DAYS of calm joy on the serene *St. Louis-Mexico City Limited*, magazines and ice tea, and a diner with gleaming silver and tablecloths of the finest linen, sliced oranges on ice in a cut glass and a silver bowl. The black faces of the waiters shone. By day the porter was expert in timing the moments when the train would stop and start, a royal sentinel on the dirt platforms of the lost towns where the train paused for coal or water. Here Stanfield could walk to the front of the train and admire the locomotive, an almost new 4-6-2 Pacific with a Delta trailer truck. The hiss of steam and the green shine of dripping oil, and high above him the ruddy engineer and a glimpse of polished brass. He was a child again, and regretted all the many train trips not taken.

Late at night the porter polished the passengers' shoes in the men's lounge, oblivious of the salesmen's conversations. On waking Stanfield found his shoes under his berth with a richer mahogany shine. The passengers exchanged pleasantries in soft tones punctuated by the soft whirr of the fans and sipped ice tea in the club car. He spent the last hours before Laredo staring from the observation car at the disappearing west Texas plains in the company of a corset salesman who was also a poet. This salesman spoke of the lonely water towers as "pensive" and "austere." He sold Stanfield typed copies of three poems.

After Laredo, where the salesman poet got off, the train stopped for two broiling hours on the International Bridge. Then Nuevo Laredo and Mexico in a smoky dust, and the absurdities he had expected and almost hoped for began. His through sleeping car to Mexico City was detached without warning some time after midnight in Monterey, and left outside the station proper in a dark desolation of many tracks. The porter had forgotten that one of the lower berths was actually occupied by a sleeper. So it was necessary to rush, still in pyjamas, down the dark tracks and across a crowded platform to rejoin his train. The porter preceded him, carrying his two bags. Disheveled soldiers lounged against the wall, laughing at his plight. He had the impression whole families were living on the platform, with many children hidden under serapes and blankets.

His new car was a "tourist" sleeper of the late 1890's, such a car as belonged with the old Southern Pacific "Argonaut" and its burden of modest families moving west. But he was not displeased, since this journey south was a journey into the past. The car had sixteen small sections not ten ample ones, and upper berths that lacked the standard Pullman's graceful mahogany curve. The sheets had a different smell, his window would not budge, and the buttonholes of the green curtains closing him in his lower berth were in shreds. Several buttons were missing. A thief's hand could rummage without waking him.

Four of the sections had been made up, with the curtains open over lower berths and turned-down sheets. But there was only one other passenger, a tall thin man in a bright red nightgown that reached his ankles and bare feet. A mestizo? He was slumped in one of the unmade sections with a newspaper covering his face and snoring. Why had he not gone to bed?

Stanfield could not have been asleep more than an hour

before a flashlight thrust through the curtains woke him. It was the new porter, a Mexican, who asked to see his ticket. He studied it at length, as though he were examining such a ticket for the first time, then turned the light on the face of the man standing next to him. It was the Mexican of the red nightgown. The newcomer smiled apologetically, displaying many teeth and a grainy black stubble. He would need to shave twice a day. He introduced himself as Silvestre Aguilar, and reached in to shake hands. Both of them had been assigned the same section 6 lower berth, but Aguilar had the better title since he got on at Monterey, whereas Stanfield's section 6 was in the car they had left behind. The explanations were lengthy and good-natured in Spanish, somewhat different in English. In the end, and although this was clearly illegal, the porter agreed to let Silvestre Aguilar use one of the other sections. It was three o'clock in the morning and more passengers could hardly be expected.

He awoke to a stifling morning, with the toothy face of Aguilar thrust in between the curtains. The overnight beard reached his cleft chin in two black sickle curves.

"Silvestre Aguilar," he said. Had he forgotten the introductions of the night before? "We must get to the dining car before it closes."

Stanfield had hoped for coffee brought to his berth by the porter, then lazy ablutions. But the Mexican's tone was peremptory. He pulled trousers and sweater on over his pyjamas, regretting his lost sleep. On the other hand, he was glad to make a Mexican acquaintance so soon, even this rather pushful one. They walked through three swaying coaches filled with sprawled Mexicans, some wearing only undershirt and shorts. Two women were suckling babies while several grown men were wrestling in the aisle. Other passengers cheered them on. In the third car a band was playing, two trumpets and a drum, as three small children in faded yellow tights and green jackets danced up and down the aisle. Could they be triplets? The trumpeters had identical handlebar moustaches, and their cheeks bulged and shone.

"Gymnastics stars for the theater," Silvestre Aguilar explained.

He nodded to a lean yet muscular woman who was standing at the end of the car, smoking a cigar. "Perhaps a gymnastics family." She too was wearing yellow tights and a green jacket, and appeared to be blocking their way. The tights were patched in several places. A bandana, also green, bound her peroxide blonde hair. She measured Stanfield and his gray hairs coolly before moving aside.

They were alone in the diner. In fact, there were no waiters. But one of the tables had been set with silverware and paper napkins and a bottle of mineral water "gaseosa." The train was moving leisurely across a brown emptiness. Dry arroyos curved away and lost themselves in the sage and cactus plain. Stanfield longed to be back in his lower berth.

"I am a lover of your country," Aguilar said. "No need to make excuses for the thieves in Washington. There is enough oil in the oil fields for us all."

"And I am a lover of Mexico, though it's over fifty years since I was here."

"Fifty years!"

"Fifty-two. I was in the Isthmus of Tehuantepec. We were surveying for a canal."

"I do not believe you. Fifty years ago there was nothing on the Isthmus of Tehuantepec. Certainly not a canal."

"No, no we were just surveying for a canal. They built the canal in Panama."

"Of course, everyone knows that. I could have told you a canal in the Isthmus of Tehuantepec was not possible." Aguilar clapped his hands sharply, hoping to rouse a waiter. "I am a traveler salesman. In the U.S. you say 'drummer.'"

"Traveling salesman, not traveler salesman." Stanfield said. Now and then, years after retirement, he slipped unwittingly into the habits of the classroom.

"Thank you for correcting me."

"What are you selling?"

"The best pants. I will show you the pants when we return to the sleeping car, two for the price of one. You will try them on and choose. Also I take orders for motorcycles, watches, and refrigerators. In addition I am a travel agent representing the great Mr Foster of 'Ask Mr Foster.' Where would you like to go?"

"I am going to Santa Rosalia in the Isthmus. The Gran Hotel Balneario Chimalapa."

"I suggest Vera Cruz instead. In Vera Cruz you have the pleasures of the sea and the pleasures of a great city. Women and music. Do you like to zig-zig? The best whores are in Vera Cruz. Why go to the Isthmus?"

"I was there fifty-two years ago, and I want to see it again. Santa Rosalia is a village of Zoque Indians. And there's a good hotel that has just reopened."

"That's impossible," Aguilar said. "Fifty-two years ago I was not alive. I don't think there was a hotel then."

"No, just a village, deep in the jungle. The hotel is now."

"I recommend Vera Cruz."

A waiter arrived with lukewarm coffee and sweet rolls thickly crusted with sugar. He explained there would be nothing else available before San Luís Potosí, if then. The bleak landscape studded with cactus slid past. In the distance were smoky mountains, hostile mountains where prospecting miners and fugitives would starve. The train was already several hours late.

They returned to their car, and found the woman with the yellow tights and green jacket seated and in animated conversation with the conductor, who was perched on the armrest beside her. The conductor's right hand was only an inch from the knot holding the bandana at the back of woman's head. He wanted to untie it. The three children had climbed to upper berths, two on one side of the aisle, one on the other. Pillows flew back and forth. The children in the upper berth of section 4 began swinging on the curtain rail, then leaped across the aisle in unison. Now all three were in section 5. They began to chant in unison a song that imitated the sounds of animals. A barking, moos, a donkey's bray.

The conductor frowned but made no protest. Stanfield watched with fascination as he played with the bandana's knot. His fingers moved rapidly but gently, like a tentative pianist's. The woman too did not protest. Perhaps the children were simply rehearsing their act.

"Let us retire to the men's lounge," Aguilar said. "We will try on trousers. As a friend of your country I will give you a special price."

"I'm sorry but I just don't need trousers."

He nevertheless found himself being led to the men's lounge. On the leather settee two Mexicans in gray undershirts were smoking cigars, while a third was shaving. The shaver appeared to be using two of the shiny metal basins at the same time, cleaning his razor first in one, then in the other. The mirror in front of him was flecked with lather. Where had the three come from? Intruders from the coaches, no doubt, but they seemed to be friendly. A witchhazel odor hung in the air, and even more pungent perfume.

"How do you like our Mexican train?" one of the men asked, addressing Stanfield. He took a cigar from the coat hanging behind him, and offered it, but in a way that indicated a smiling refusal would be welcome.

"I like all trains," Stanfield said. "Especially Mexican ones."

"But your American trains are faster?"

"Not always. The locomotive on this train is a fine old American Tenwheeler, 4-6-0."

"How do you know that? What is 4-6-0?"

"The wheel configuration. I saw the engine when we were taking a broad curve. A Tenwheeler, probably a Baldwin."

"I think the locomotive is Mexican," Silvestre Aguilar said.

He opened his suitcase of samples, considered several pairs

of trousers, held them up to measure Stanfield's girth, then selected shiny gray ones made of some heavy material, possibly sailcloth. The trousers had thick blue stripes, and florid material folded over the fly to make a heavy waistband, almost a charro's or torero's. The belt loops were studded with embroidered red dots. A dashing youthful pair of trousers. What would his Cambridge Latin colleagues have thought? What would he wear in the Gran Hotel Balneario in Santa Rosalia?

"Try these on, Mr Stanfield. No obligation."

"Have you something a little simpler? And not so heavy. It's pretty hot where I'm going."

"Just try these on for size."

He reached for Stanfield's belt, and with a quick deft move flipped its end free of the buckle. Would he even go after his buttons?

"Do you have any plain blue? Or white?"

"This pair will be better for your vacation in Vera Cruz."

Later that morning Stanfield made his first Mexican entry in the large blue notebook that would record his journey. He thought of it as *the* Blue Notebook, recording a new phase of his life. He wrote on the little table brought by the porter. It fitted into slots beneath the window. He wrote with the sturdy gold Parker given him on his retirement, enjoying the freedom of a blank page and the many blank pages to come. At seventy-two he was ready for a new life.

My garrulous trouser salesman companion has gone back to bed, and the bouncy little gymnasts and their florid but bony mother are also asleep, or at least in bed, having persuaded the conductor to let them use a section. So here I am alone in this worn but beautiful tourist car, still unshaved and quite hungry, but in a state of elation that is like drunkenness. Who knows when we will reach Mexico City, not to mention Chivela? Certainly not Mexico City before midnight, yet I find myself welcoming all delays, savoring the surprises to come. For two hours we stayed on a siding, not a house or tree in sight, while a "military train" of twenty freight cars was stopped on the through track. As many as thirty men on the roof of each car, smoking and laughing. Their rifles and tin pans glittered in the sun. A few have ragged uniforms, most look like ordinary campesinos. The door of the nearest freight car was open. Several ragged women were seated there with their trousered legs and bare feet dangling outside. They saw me and waved. Held up a tin cup as though offering me a drink or a friendly toast.

How odd to see Falstaffian soldiers on the roof of a New York Central freight car! Nearby are boxcars from Missouri Pacific, United Fruit, Santa Fe, as well as Nacionales de Mexico. I wanted to get out and walk up for a closer inspection of the engine, but a man with a better uniform than the rest pointed his rifle at my knees in warning. When I asked Silvestre where the soldiers were going or what they were up to, he shrugged.

"They go to fight the revolutionaries. Unless they are themselves the revolutionaries."

Two hours later the train resumed its slow progress south. At San Luís Potosí the family of gymnasts left the train, but a woman evangelist from El Paso got on. She was more Mexican than not, appeared to be in her forties, had flaming red hair, and a white gown that reached her ankles and high-heeled gold shoes. A belt drew the gown tight below her prominent breasts. She gave tracts in Spanish to Sylvestre Aguilar, and one in English to Stanfield entitled *The Whore of Babylon.*

"Read it!" She had the rasping voice of one who could command crowds. Her perfume and lipstick were overpowering.

"Thank you. I will."

"Are you saved, mister? Have you been washed clean?" She scrutinized Aguilar appraisingly. "In Mexico you will be beset by temptation. Do you know this man?"

"I am Silvestre Aguilar. I too know English. I will understand what you say."

She looked at Aguilar sternly, then addressed Stanfield again.

"Do you pray on your knees or standing up?"

For the next hour she talked without interruption, passing easily from one language to the other, fanning herself with a tract. She gave them the story of her life. Her father had taken her virginity, a priest had touched her while she prayed. As a virgin she was Elena Consuela Ortíz. Before her Protestant conversion she had been a medium, La Atrevida, an innocent vessel through whom a French psychiatrist who died many years before communicated medical advice. From a famous cemetery in Paris, the body there that is, all the way to her in Queretaro, Mexico! Now, saved, she was Prudencia Luz del Mundo, and accomplished healing by prayer and faith.

She got off the train in Queretaro, home of the heroine of the 1810 war of independence, La Corregidora. She wanted Aguilar and Stanfield to take her to dinner, spend the night in the city, and in the morning visit the Palacio Municipal where La Corregidora had whispered warnings to the insurgents through a keyhole, thus saving Hidalgo.

"It would be interesting and patriotic," Aguilar said. "However, there will perhaps be a strike of the Ferrocarril any day. I must get to the capital, my friend must get to the Isthmus of Tehuantepec. Tomorrow there may be no train."

They were even afraid to leave the station, since there was no way of knowing when the train would leave. The blackboard recording arrivals and departures was almost illegible because of the many erasures. So they had dinner in the station cantina. Here they could keep an eye on the shunting of their train's cars, some destined for Guadalajara, some for Mexico City.

Three mornings later, and on the Isthmus at last, he wrote in the Blue Notebook:

March 26. We have now been four hours at Santa Lucrecia, waiting for the connecting train from Mérida. Had I only known I could have hired a car or carriage to Suchyl and back, only seven miles. Suchyl so near, and my two nights and days there with Rosellen Maurepas! The thirty bunks under their mosquito netting like so many white tombs. Yet I would have perhaps recognized nothing. Certainly that Chamberlain's "hotel" will have sunk to the center of the earth. All the same I remember it fondly.

Much regret to have had only a glimpse of Mexico City, paralyzed by tram and bus strikes. The fine Buenevista station was filled with strikers preparing a Gran Manifestación. An inexhaustible orator waved a red and black flag in time with his flowing words. A beautiful winding journey, then, but not much to see of Popo and its volcano companion, their summits lost in clouds. In Córdoba I did see the snow-topped Orizaba flecked with gold as the sun set, before a miserable night in a hotel which once boasted colonial splendors. A man in a splendid hotel uniform seized my bags and hustled me into a horse-drawn bus before I could make inquiries. Roaches and fleas through the night, rather than the rodadors and mosquitoes of the Isthmus.

Then a fine morning journey. Wide plantations of pineapple and plantain and sugar cane, and Orizaba slowly fading behind us. In Tierra Blanca, where we awaited the train from Vera Cruz, three "officers" spent an hour in the drawing room drinking and noisily playing cards, then got off and never reappeared. One paused to stare at me and the two other passengers, Guatemalan businessmen, as though debating whether to demand a contribution. Then passed on with a friendly salute. Twice since then floridly courteous officers came on board to ask for "destination taxes" while horseback brigands with rifles waited outside. No possibility of separating the legal and the illegal. Another long stop at the great bridge over the Papaloapam. Far below Indians in dugout canoes with high prows, all but naked as they paddle along. It seems that here, several days ago, and on the bridge itself, the train was held for ransom by bandits who claimed to be railroad employees demanding their back pay.

At each stop after Tierra Blanca Indian women came to the side of the train offering oranges and lemons, papayas, mangoes, watermelons. And always cold ears of boiled corn. At one stop, with no village or station in sight, a woman held a chicken in one hand and an iguana in the other, with a wide decorated gourd on the top of her head, it too for sale. The faces were ever darker as we moved south, more truly Indian, and I catch even fewer Spanish words interspersed in their bright chatter offering their wares. They smoke small black cigars.

And I learn with delight that the jungle is not entirely gone. For many miles, before Santa Lucrecia, it seemed ready to swallow the tracks. The wall of jungle had been burned off in many places to protect the right of way. Swamp and seepage and fallen trees below, a matted undergrowth no doubt harboring much reptile life. Foulness in the oozy earth, but serpentine lianas above, and delicate flowers in the highest branches. Our train crawled as slowly as if exploring an uncharted way between the green walls. And I saw with delight a true jungle path branching off, two Indian men carrying machetes. I pretend to follow them in a speculative daydream, and sink still deeper into lost time.

Santa Lucrecia, and a dozen or so houses raised on stilts against the rainy season floods. Pigs rooting in a mound of refuse not far from a two story shack calling itself "Imperial Hotel." Here in Santa Lucrecia for the first time I cross my path of fifty-two years ago, while workmen probe with their flashlights, hammering at the car's wheels. Or almost cross my path. I doubt there was more than a decaying rancho in Santa Lucrecia then. If I had a photograph of Rosellen, or of my little Indian friend Marita, would my two daydreams dissolve before reality? I see them only as they were then.

The train from Mérida has still not arrived. Flat cars and oil cars move back and forth as though unsure where to attach themselves, shepherded by a shunting engine that gives off much steam and many whistles. The engine with its neat little drivers and its high stack is a Baldwin of the early 1880's. Why should it ever die? Our locomotive from Córdoba was a handsome 2-6-2 Prairie of around 1900. At Tierra Blanca saw a splendid Vulcan Compound 2-8-0 with still faintly visible its *M. and N. G.* Marietta and North Georgia! How many avatars has it experienced before reaching Mexico? And now (I can hardly believe my eyes) a Class D *woodburner* has appeared at the head of our small train of four cars, ready to be attached. I thought the last such woodburning locomotive had been scrapped six or seven years ago. Still older, but on a siding and presumably abandoned, is a rusted diamond stack of the early Santa Fe vintage, a 4-4-0 with immense wheels and a cab still elegant though the faded green paint is all but gone. I would give a month of my life to ride a train pulled by a diamond stack.

Our cars are shunted back and forth for no reason I can discern. According to the timetable we should have arrived at Chivela long since, but the station blackboard tells another story. Here a man in a soiled white suit and mud-caked high boots, but wearing a florid tie and wide sombrero, sidled up, offering a cigar.

"I think you look for entertainment, sir? A good hotel? A fine comida with Mexican beer? Welcome to Santa Lucrecia. I know all the ropes. You want a woman, ask me. Fat or thin."

I could not help from laughing, and told him I was getting back on the train, and hoped to reach Chivela tonight. Did he know of a good hotel in Chivela?

"You will never get to Chivela, not tonight. I tell you why. Every night in Rincón Antonio your train stops for repairs. The engineer, the conductor they all go to the cantina. You are in the luxury sleeping car?"

"Yes."

"Then go to sleep with confidence. Tomorrow morning you are in Chivela, if no more repairs. The Hotel Casa Blanca, use my name, Señor Padilla, licenciado."

Two hours later, still Santa Lucrecia. But now I write in splendid comfort as the only occupant of a curious, ornate diner, with the promise that a good "typical" evening meal will be served. *Boca Chica*, which appears to be the work of several improvisers altering, not entirely for the worse, a fine American diner of around 1900. The marquetry and Tiffany glass are a joy.

No indication of such luxury in the timetable, which had promised only a sleeping car buffet from Córdoba. But also there is no sign of life in the kitchen, though a smiling chef welcomed me, saying the maître d'hôtel and waiters would soon be back. Mañana perhaps? A good bottle of tequila appeared unasked, however, a tray of lemons, a dish of unpeeled shrimp, and a menu for almuerzo not dinner. I look up from my writing to see myself, pen poised and quizzical, as from a far distance in a distorting mirror such as one might find in a Revere Beach fun house, but going almost to the ceiling. My image in the mirror changes as I stare. I seem to recede farther and farther from the mirror yet also to be sinking imprisoned into it, as my poor worn face fades. Will my twenty-year-old's face of Santa Rosalia appear in its place?

But no matter: I continue in a state of almost drunken elation that could well be a fever. Will I again succumb in Santa Rosalia, though now safely inoculated? Would there be a young Marita to hold my hand?

And here is the maître d'hôtel full of apologies, buttoning his dirty jacket, and asking if I wish to see the menu. It is for breakfast, though it is now past dark. *Huevos y Tortillas de Huevo, Platillos a la Parilla, Bollos Pan Tostada. Arenque Ahumado,* which an almost effaced pencilling says is Kippered Herring. A friendly gesture suggests that the offering is pro forma. A diner should have a menu however ancient and frayed. He advises me to put myself in the chef's hands.

March 26, long past midnight. I write lying in my lower bunk. A strange experience I must immediately record. Only this year have the trains again regularly run at night, and ours should be the only one between Santa Lucrecia and Rincón Antonio in either direction. A single track, so no other train can pass. I lay blissfully awake in my lower berth, thinking of my childhood reverie of the first western trains—blissfully, though the window would not entirely close and dust and soot poured in. But then I heard a sharp whistle, followed by the banshee wail of a train coming fast from the other direction. My heart beat fast, I waited for its thundering approach, the expanding then blinding light that would appear in a few seconds, the sucking rush and shuddering draft and pull of passing cars. But nothing for a long minute. Then the receding wail of a spectral train now far behind us on its way east.

Impossible, there could have been no train. And I know I was wide awake!

March 27. La Chivela, still the barren plain I remember, and miserable huts with palm-thatched roofs. A cheerful young Indian porter tied my two bags and strapped them to his forehead with a tumpline, then led me across an empty field to the once-white building that been our headquarters in 1870. So I do indeed loop back, and it is here I learned of Rosellen's disappearance! The Casa Blanca of the marquesadas, now a miserable hotel of rotting doors and stained white walls much cracked from recent earthquakes. And now I write in the same gloomy and cold vault of fifty-two years ago, since the Gran Hotel Balneario bus is delayed. A man who looks a hundred years old, and who holds his mug in both hands, eyes me steadily from a rocking chair near the bare fireplace. His guyabera unbuttoned over a brown and bony skeleton. Could he be the scornful young administrator of that earlier time who said all projects to cross the Isthmus, whether by railroad or canal, were doomed? Familiar too are the grandees on the wall, their portraits even darker after fifty-two years of soot, and the haughty descendent with one blind sunken eye and the other eye fixed upon me malevolently. After a long wait I am served cold coffee, a fried egg with a morsel of fish, a crumbly pan dulce.

And screw up my courage to approach the old man. I tell him I was here, even in this very room, fifty-two years before. Had he always lived in La Chivela?

But he only stares and says nothing.

Still March 27, Santa Rosalia and the Gran Hotel Balneario. I will recount in order the events of this exciting day. My first of many surprises was the splendid bus, a fifteen-passenger Stanley Steamer only two years old, with the sides open for five rows of seats. A dream of appropriate glory for whatever consortium or rich man owning the hotel? The driver has a smart hotel cap and jacket, but removes both the moment we are underway. A silent ghostly gliding after the long premonitory hiss.

The village of La Chivela is not much larger after the fifty-two years, still the palm-thatched roofs of one-story huts, though San Miguel (where the driver stopped for half an hour, disappearing into the only cantina) now has an ugly new church. The oxcarts move lumberingly over broken roads.

Poorly tended fields shared by maize and tobacco, not the rich wet milpas of the Santa Rosalia I remember as from a dream. Then the jungle wall, and a scarcely visible road winding into an unspoiled prehistoric wilderness. No oxcarts here, as the bus picks its silent way in a green gloom, between limestone outcroppings, huge boulders, and around and over the enormous roots of fallen trees. Even in this dry season the jungle floor is a seeping mass of rotten leaves,

while above serpentine growths and conical masses like giant nests reach toward the sun. Screechings and chatterings
up there, though I have not yet seen any monkeys. The
rustlings of unseen life as mysterious as unseen winds. I know
so much more of this natural world, from my classroom charts
and texts. Yet I no longer see with the dazzled eyes of my
twenty-year-old self. Live oak, cypress, white cedar, pine,
tamarind, rosewood, ebony, how many more I cannot name,
and a wild profusion and variety of palms. We climb sturdily,
always winding, then down and down. There are more small
streams than ever to be crossed with bridges of sturdy logs
laid side by side.

The streams and the road itself must be impassable at the
height of the rains, but now the sturdy Stanley can surmount
any obstacle. At one crossing a green snake four or five feet
long, a maize snake I think, almost as deadly as the red
coralina. The snake did not move. A stillness as I watched,
which was broken by a chattering in the trees, then a wild
clamor.

All, all a dream. For we came around a bend, and I saw
what I was sure I had seen before: a meagre fence protecting
a grassed-over small ruin, even a sleeping guardian. He had
covered himself with a poncho, so I could not see his features. I called to the driver to stop, but he shook his head as
though to say no time could be lost, or that there was something in that ruin to be feared. So on we went, the road no
better, I think, than the road of fifty-two years ago, but our
Stanley Steamer is undeterred. We climbed toward Santa
Maria Chimalapa on its ridge, but bypassed it, and descended
to Santa Rosalia and the river.

Seeing the small church tower, then the first thatched-
roof huts, I was tempted to get out and run ahead.

And here are the first villagers, who do not look up as we
pass, some of the men still with the crown of the head shaved,
but otherwise much the same as the peons seen at every stop
since Tierra Blanca, and the barefoot women in drab shape-

less sacks that trail to the ground. Is it only my own weariness of age, or have the Indians lost what little fire they showed in that old time? At least these first ones did not appear to be drunk.

Then the Gran Hotel Balneario, rising most improbably from the clearing, five stories with two stubby chimneys, a truly solid building of white limestone, wide balconies, a terrace with chairs and tables. All in all more durable in appearance than anything I have seen on the Isthmus or since Córdoba. No tourists in white trousers or silken dresses, however. Just off the lobby there is a large salon, and half a dozen men were engaged in roulette, while a croupier in tuxedo, but with no tie, called out his commands. At the desk two employees engaged in some kind of game played with matchsticks, from which they did not look up.

When I said in my best Spanish that I wanted to register, and would like a room with a view of the village, they told me to go to the bar and ask for "José." But the bar was empty, so I went outside for a first timid look. A group of five Indians were camped in front of the hotel, and beyond them was the spring. But it does not seem in the right place. Or has the modern structure of the hotel distorted everything? I will venture toward the first row of huts, I will dare look into the faces of women who appear to be in their sixties, I will let them look at me. But not this first afternoon.

It will be still another hour before dinner. I write in my room at a table that already shows the ravages of ants, and my chair seems likely to lose a leg. But I was ready to weep to find a friendly green lizard fixedly watching me from the very center of my wall. The chair and table will be consumed before long, no doubt, to be replaced by others as vulnerable. But I could see at a first rapid look that the hotel proper has been built to survive the humidity and summer rains, the many small earthquakes, even Biblical inundations. The staircase is of the famous guapaque wood that can lie in water for centuries. Mahogany here, cedar there, cypress, pine, splendid hardwood floors though unvarnished. It seems odd that a few thousand more were not spent for the furnishings of the rooms. The plaster of one of my walls is cracked and peeling, but solid wood and steel lie beneath.

March 28. Last night the hotel came alive at dark, the bar filled, a solitary guitar player looked down on us from an elevated stage. There were two more tables for gambling now, with several men in business suits, as though they had stepped only moments since from a Mexico City office. Others might be gamblers from nearby towns, wearing their straw hats back in a reflective manner. The bartender says there will be a floor show later and a "Gran Bal" on Saturday. Is the floor show the three much painted young women in hula skirts and flowery leis over ample brassieres who sit disconsolately at the back of the stage?

I recognized the famous Papa Jack at once. Palm Beach suit tight over powerful shoulders, the bow tie of so many photographs, intense wary eyes and the whites very large, a rounded face that is haughty in repose but full of warmth when he smiles. The bartender led me to him and to his companions, as though demonstrating the hotel's amenities. Papa Jack is patronizing with an elaborate courtesy and shakes hands with a politician's brisk but perfunctory grasp. But his deep voice is pleasing and musical. With him is a peppy young cockney, he too a boxer, friendly, telling a joke I did not understand. Also two young Mexicans such as one might find in a hotel with gambling, full of eagerness and enterprise, the woman writhing even when she sits still. Artemio and Angelita. The ex-champion's hangers-on.

With them most surprisingly is a woman of strange and delicate beauty, a face in an ivory cameo, she also English, but with the voice of an educated aristocrat. Restless pale eyes of blue and gray that measure everything, an inquiring chin and nose, a mysterious perhaps deceptive gentleness. Her soft silks move as she moves, a bizarre dress the color of

125

her eyes that reaches almost to the ground. She is, Papa Jack says, a poet. He adds that so too is he. It appears this woman, Monica Swift, lives in Paris and has left small children there, having come to Mexico to look for a husband who disappeared nearly four years ago, the husband both a boxer and poet! She refuses to believe he is dead, and has returned to Mexico for one more search. She turns momentarily away, as though in contemplation or poetic reverie. Or is it to display the beauty of her face seen from the side, with the chin lifted in soft defiance? I have seen that particular pose, that ivory complexion, that indeterminate age, in Sargent's portraits of society matrons. But this woman is no society matron.

Monica Swift, I have seen the name somewhere. A poem in the *Atlantic* or the *Transcript*? Her lost husband, Brian Desmond, was evidently well known in Paris, London, Greenwich Village.

At first she greeted me with the casual courtesy of Papa Jack, he the great man who gives you a minute's half-attention, she the reclusive Artist. But then she looked at me more intently, as if to wonder if some communication might exist between us. Her long fingers closed around her glass slowly, one by one, as though taking a sensuous pleasure in the touch. Then lifted the glass in a friendly salute.

I momentarily forgot my seventy-two years.

Marita would be sixty-five or sixty-six. I tell myself this. Yet I persist in picturing a woman in her early forties. The child, if there was a child, would be fifty-one.

March 29. Waiting for Monica at a table overlooking the spring, the village, and the five Indians who wait there night and day, never moving, only staring up at the third floor where, it seems, something sacred to them exists. "I am willing to believe anything," Monica Swift said last night. "That will be an enterprise for you and me, to gain access to the third floor secret!" Papa Jack thinks some stolen Indian relic is kept up there, or perhaps the body of a dead revolutionary leader. The headless corpse of Zapata has been rumored buried in various places. Why not here? Papa Jack claims to have met a number of the important revolutionaries, and shows a photograph of himself with Carranza. He is full of stories of the past and rumors of what goes on today.

I have walked twice through the village, so deliberately that it would be impossible to ignore me. But the village is asleep. No more lithe young maidens beating corn, naked to the waist. The cockney boxer Jimmy Wilding says they are to be seen at the river, washing clothes. Are there still Isthmus groves where on days of idleness women congregate in the hot afternoons, bathing naked, smoking their black cigars? In 1870 I heard of these feminine rites in Minatitlán, in Suchyl, in Chivela, and here, but was never afforded such a spectacle. Yet in several books travelers reported seeing them.

The bartender says the women dress most elaborately on feast days, though even then they do much of the men's work. But now there are few middle-aged women at all, or few to be seen. The ageless wrinkled crone in the miserable little store paid no attention to me as she broke open packs of cigarettes and arranged them on a tray to be sold one by one. Her pinta scars are smaller than I remember such scars, and there are men and women quite free of them. Nor do the men seem to be as drunk as before. But I see little sign of work being done. The village is no larger than I remember it, but one church is much decayed, and another apparently abandoned. The jungle seems to be conquering the cracked adobe structure, but from within. A sturdy palm protrudes from a break in the roof where the tiles have fallen away. Two orange trees grow where its front door must have been.

The bartender says there are about five hundred in the village, but I have not seen more than thirty. No doubt the most attractive women are working in the hotel, but my glimpses have been fugitive. The maid cleaning my room fled when I appeared, leaving her rags and pail behind. Bowlegged, but with a handsome rounded Mayan face, good breasts, hair parted in the middle and stringy braids. Will I be able to make her smile?

Two small boys, grinning, tried to tempt me to cross the petroleum pit where I had my mishap fifty-two year ago! For an absurd moment I fancied one of the boys to be a native son of mine. Odd that the pit has not been covered over. The ground has been cleared around the spring, and in the unchanged warm waters the gold and silvery fishes still dart. There is a filthy brass cup on a chain with the name of the hotel imprinted.

I scoop up mouthfuls, with most of the water escaping through my fingers. It is a fountain not of youth but of age.

Waiting for Monica Swift, I feel as young and innocent and gauche as the twenty-year-old who accompanied Rosellen on the *Allegheny Belle*.

The Disappeared

HE WAS STILL MEDITATING on the slender fish, oddly luminous in the morning light, when he became aware of her
approach, wearing a jaunty hat, and in a silk dress of pastel
oranges and blues, such a dress, he imagined, as a demimondaine might wear for afternoon tea in a novel of Anatole
France, her stockings a shade lighter than her legs would be.
The silk would be soft to the touch, with her body another
breathing softness beneath it. For a moment she brought back
to him Rosellen all in white, and the long muslin sleeves that
covered her wrists.

"Let's sit down by the famous spring, Mr Stanfield. I saw
you just now, taking a surreptitious taste. Not even using the
hotel's cup."

She sat down on the rough bench, and indicated with a
playful wave a place beside her. Just so, he imagined, the
Parisian demimondaine would try to put a shy New Englander
at ease. Not in all his Cambridge years had one of the severe
Kirkland Street ladies made such a commanding gesture. And
now the hand, also soft as silk, touched the back of his. An
artist's hand, long slender fingers and the nails painted light
blue.

"I don't think I really remembered the water's taste. Very
medicinal. But I do believe the fish have not changed. Can

they have been here all these years?"

She removed her hat so slowly that it was like an act of sensual undressing, then ran the fingers of both hands through her fine black hair.

"And you came back all the way to find out? I know you are joking, Mr Stanfield, but it is true that some fish live hundreds of years." Again she put her hand on the back of his and for exciting moments left it there. "Do tell me why you came back."

He tried to explain why he had returned after the fifty-two years. He was conscious that two Indian children were now watching them from the other side of the spring. One, a girl of five or six, had a stuffed iguana she doubtless hoped to sell. A boy of the same age was crouched beside her, sitting on his heels, staring without expression. Beyond them a small gray horse, lean and old, was grazing.

"Curiosity of course. I found it hard to believe there could be a hotel here, ever, let alone a resort hotel and casino. I was almost the only outsider then, living in a hut with a thatched roof, just like the ones today. I got sick, and a young girl took care of me. I have remembered very clearly my days here, and my few weeks in Mexico. I often daydreamed of coming back. A young boy watched us, just as that one is watching us now. Maybe it was the girl's brother."

"You and the young girl? What was there to watch?"

"Not much. I got sick and she took care of me."

"And?"

"That's all." But he was quite aware she knew he was lying. "I got well and went back to Chivela, where I learned that Rosellen had disappeared. I told you, didn't I, last night? Rosellen Maurepas, how she went off by herself and up the Rio Corte with only two Zoque guides, looking for traces of William Walker. And didn't come back, although her guides did. But they didn't rob her. Because they brought back her money and a diary."

"Which I trust you read?"

"Of course, because I wanted to know what happened. But the diary broke off abruptly. She spoke of her 'old dream of wandering alone in uncharted regions.' Maybe she didn't really believe the Walker stories, but wanted the adventure anyway. She was braver than I. Or at least more persistent."

"Braver than you? Tell me."

"I was here in Santa Rosalia at the same time, only a mile from the river. I tried to get Indians to take me up the river. But maybe I didn't try hard enough."

He kept to himself a sentence in the diary that from time to time would come to him, even as he talked to a classroom of bored students. *'In another life, if another life could be, I would pray for such a lover.'* But Monica Swift with her teasing poet's intuition might have read his thoughts.

"So you had a young love and an older one? Is that why you came back?"

The child with the stuffed iguana had come closer, and was holding it very close, like a precious doll. The boy hung back. But the old horse was watching them now.

"Rosellen was a young man's fantasy. And then in time became an old man's daydream. I never even kissed her."

"But the young girl of course you did." She was gently amused by his reticence, and touched the back of his hand again, ran a finger along one of his old man's protruding veins, up to the wrist and back. "You must not be embarrassed. I have had many lovers old and young, and someday I will tell you about them if you ask. Women as well as men. So there was also the young girl, in this village, and that was not so innocent? Please believe me I'm not trying to embarrass you. You thought if you came back you might find her?"

"More that I was afraid to find her, a dull ugly brutalized creature instead of the teasing young girl I knew. Yes, I thought she might still be here. Yesterday I found myself looking for a woman your age or even younger, whereas my little Zoque would be in her mid-sixties. And the older women look like mummies. How can one tell with Indians? Except for children there is no way to tell their age."

She raised her hand as to brush a lock of hair, but instead gently stroked his cheek, once, twice. The child was now directly in front of them, holding the stuffed iguana by the neck. It stared at them balefully. Stanfield shook his head, but gave her a few centavos. He pointed to the boy, still across the pond, and gave another coin for him. They moved away some distance, but continued to watch.

"You have asked about her?"

"How can I ask? Ask whether there is some woman of the village who fifty years ago took care of a very young American engineer. I don't even know her name, never did. Besides it is the other one I would like to understand at last. Rosellen Maurepas."

"Entranced by the notorious William Walker? You wonder how she could be?"

"How could she—gentle, kind, gracious like you, even a sort of poet like you—be attracted to a brutal megalomaniac? I have read her Journal many times. Still I can't understand her obsession. Do you know much about Walker?"

"Next to nothing. You told me he became dictator in Nicaragua."

"Self-proclaimed President. He liked to kill. Not in battle, not in the heat of things, but deliberately, through a farce of judicial proceedings. He would order executions gratuitously. He had entirely changed from the man Rosellen had her crush on at fourteen. It was twenty-two years after that when I met her, and ten years after Walker's execution in Honduras. So by then, by 1870, she should have had no illusions. She would have known all the terrible things there were to know."

"Entirely changed?

"Rosellen saw him first with his fiancée who was a deaf-mute. She was dazzled by his kindness and by their romantic love. I wager Rosellen dreamed of being a deaf-mute herself. She watched Walker read the fiancée's lips. The beautiful, intelligent fiancée who also used a notebook and gold pencil for conversations. Then the fiancée died and Walker was grief-stricken. He had, moreover, been devoted to his mother's care. Had studied medicine in Philadelphia and in Paris too, to learn how to help the mother who was mortally ill. But still this kind man, who had opposed slavery in newspaper editorials, reinstituted slavery in Nicaragua by presidential decree. He had changed that much."

"Of course there's much you're not telling me, because maybe she didn't tell you."

"You mean?"

"I mean you have much to learn about women if you think the William Walker kind to his mother and romantically generous to a pretty but mute girl is more interesting than a cold and ruthless conqueror. Your William Walker, her William Walker rather, wanted to leave some indelible mark on his passage through life. He wanted to escape mediocrity."

"Rosellen was gentle and kind, as I think you are. Adventurous too. But she was also a little crazy. She made me take her to the Malinche's burial place because she had read somewhere that the Indians believed she, Dona Marina the Malinche, would return to save her people. Which is what the Indians thought of William Walker too. We went there at night, a moonlit night. She swore she saw the dirt move on the hill that is over the Malinche's tomb. Yes, in Nicaragua the Indians thought Walker was a supernatural being who would return to lead them and restore their greatness. The savior was to be a white man, a 'gray-eyed man of destiny.' Rosellen must have half-believed those Indians and later she half-believed a Walker veteran who was sure he had escaped to Mexico. And so she came on to Minatitlán where I met her. Not even half-believing, maybe. But still she came."

"I can understand her," Monica Swift said. "I might be listening to my own story. I too was committed to a powerful man society called a brute. And he was a brute. A megalomaniac, a comedian, a thief and a forger, a destroyer. Brian

Desmond would not accept the commonplace destiny. He would not accept the "patriotic" wars of fools. Nor would he accept the quiet hypocrisy that society calls good manners. A life force, a pulsing energy. A giant, looking much larger than his six feet three, his two hundred and twenty pounds. His hands were as large, almost, as my head. Surely you have heard of Brian Desmond?"

"You mentioned him last night. Yes, I did read some strange stories of his doings in New York. He was arrested, wasn't he, for creating some kind of disturbance at a meeting? He insulted an audience, threw things at them?"

"More than once. He was already quite well known in certain circles in Paris, with his own magazine and his boxing and his defiant gestures, and he had been arrested in Berlin too. Probably also in Spain, where he had his famous fight with Papa Jack. Then he came to New York and we met in 1918."

He tried to imagine this slender woman, whose features were as delicate as Rosellen's, in the arms of a boxer strong enough to face Papa Jack in the ring.

"So it was the fighter not the poet who attracted you? The 'life force?' Maybe you were tired of the weakness of other men you knew. Their effeminacy."

He was astonished by the intimacy that already existed between them. To say such things to a woman he had met only the night before!

"That too. Yes, certainly that. And I admired his strength that could demolish stupid laws and timidities. He resisted all that wanted to hold him down, all self-proclaimed authorities. All that demeaned."

The words came to her effortlessly. She must have said these things many times.

"Are you writing about him? It sounds a bit like it. Or maybe you should be a teacher too, though not a timid one like me."

She seemed to be looking deeply within him. Mischievously too.

"I don't think you are as timid as you say." Her long fingers again stroked the back of his hand. "I think I will count on you to help me."

"But here? Do you really believe your husband would, if he were alive and a fugitive, come here? To a resort hotel?"

"If he is still pursued by the police, this might be a safer place than most. One could always drop off into the jungle. There is that abandoned town, Casas Grandes, where people have been said to hide out. Fugitives, men who were on the wrong side. After all, the revolution hasn't really ended."

"Casas Grandes, it's where Rosellen wanted to go, where maybe she went. And if he is alive, and reads about Papa Jack coming here, and the talk of an Academy of Boxing?"

"Exactly. Brian Desmond started the Academy in Mexico City, that was the spring of 1918, and it was doing well and would do better when Papa Jack joined us. But there was trouble. First, Brian lost a fight to a rather mediocre Mexican boxer, and after that his prestige was gone. To have fought Papa Jack in Barcelona, then lose to a local fighter, it was too much! So after that we went into the country and we nearly starved. A terrible year, and people dying around us from the influenza, and no money. Yes, Brian fought in smaller places. Even in circuses, fighting or putting on a lion skin and being the Strong Man. Then I was to have a baby and I left for Argentina on a hospital ship from Vera Cruz, the only berth left, and Brian Desmond was to follow me. But he didn't come. Then the stories, the several stories of how he had been murdered. It is because there are such very different stories that I don't believe any story and know he is still alive. And if he read about Papa Jack and the Academia de Boxeo in Santa Rosalia he would come here. Might come."

"Would come," he said. "Yes, you believe he is still alive."

"Yes, I do. Want to believe, anyway. Like your Rosellen and her General William Walker."

"No, I don't know what Rosellen believed. I don't think

she herself knew."

"So then we are an absurd triad, Mr Stanfield, and here our trajectories intersect, pursuing phantoms we think we won't find. Your Rosellen in pursuit of William Walker, and I of Brian Desmond, and you...of what? I think it is your destiny to help obsessed women find their lost brutes. How old was your Rosellen?"

"I didn't know then, but it turns out she was thirty-eight. I thought she was younger. I at twenty was a child."

"I am forty."

"And I at seventy-two still feel myself a child as I talk to you. You have had so much experience, have been so many places. Or maybe it's your hat and your earrings and your beautiful voice."

"Only the voice?"

She drummed her fingers comically, waiting for his reply. Her eyes measured him, aware she had made another conquest.

"I was a child with Rosellen Maurepas, now I am a child with you."

"And you will help me, won't you, as you wanted to help her?"

"No doubt. But now that you're here, what do you expect to do?"

"We've only been here a week. We were outsiders last Saturday and Sunday, I was not ready to ask questions of strangers. There will be many more coming this weekend. Besides, I have not yet made a real friend among the hotel staff. But I will. I hope to make lamp shades for the hotel. My very modern lamp shades have been exhibited in Paris and New York. That will bring money. And I do believe Brian, if he is alive, will read about Jack coming here."

"He may be in prison. If he is really such a violent person..."

"Of course. I have scoured the prisons, not an easy thing to do. I have been in all prisons along the border, and in

Guatemala too. Juarez, Matamoros, Nuevo Laredo. San Blas, where I met a French actress looking for her lost husband, though she dreaded to find him alive. And yet I never really believed Brian was in prison, not for more than days. I thought no ordinary prison could hold him."

"So for the moment you're just going to wait?"

"Yes. And ask questions. Artemio is something of a comic, don't you think? But he does get through to people. They laugh at him but they listen. And this weekend there will be many more coming."

"Well," Stanfield said, "I too will listen. I will even ask questions."

But secretly he did not believe Brian Desmond would be found. And he suspected Monica Swift did not believe it either.

The next morning Stanfield and the other guests found a typed page of dates and events had been slipped under their doors. Further copies were distributed with breakfast. Some of the carbon copies were almost illegible.

History of Pueblo and Gran Hotel Balneario
by Antonio Vinalva

1737 Plague of Casas Grandes. All die except some move to Santa Rosalia.

1865 Birth day of Ramón Vinalva, father of Antonio Vinalva.

1871 Three engineers for U.S.A. navy canal survey visit pueblo. Explorations of river. Kidnap young girl of village. Skeletons in cave.

1875 Gringo miner again seen on raft on Rio Corte.

(All above from ESCRITURAS DEL PUEBLO, written 1883 by Ramón Vinalva)

1890 First Hotel Balneario opens. Some visitors from

Europe.

1891 Hotel destroyed by earthquake and flood as predicted.

1893 Birth day of Antonio Vinalva. Gringo miner floats past Labarta on raft.

1900 Prisoners hanged from two orange trees in front of church ruin.

1902 Ashes cover everything in pueblo.

1904 Arrival of my teacher Nabor Ruiz, who becomes alcohólico. Eats earth.

1906 Centenario of Benito Juarez. Antonio Vinalva works with railroad construction in Rincón Antonio.

1907 Grand opening of railroad.

1908 Grand opening of new Gran Hotel Balneario. Ramón Vinalva, concierge.

1910 Dona Juana Cata visits hotel, plays billiards. Death of Nabor Ruiz.

1914 Birth of Jaime Vinalva, son of Antonio Vinalva.

1915 Hotel closed because of revolution. Gringo miner seen on raft.

1916 General Felix Díaz, General Almazán and many soldiers and horses in pueblo looking for secret road to Chiapas. Maria Zarate gives false information. Ramón Vinalva taken by Generals. Never comes back.

1917 Maria Zarate widow of Nabor Ruiz is hanged from orange tree.

1919 Reconstruction of Gran Hotel Balneario begins.

1922 Reopening of Gran Hotel Balneario, Antonio Vinalva manager. Hotel with casino advertised in newspapers of New York, Chicago, New Orleans.

That afternoon Stanfield was able to talk with Vinalva in his office. It was a small windowless room off the lobby, not readily accessible to guests. To reach it Vinalva led him behind the concierge's desk, then through a storeroom cluttered with furniture needing repair. Stanfield saw at once that the room was far more than an office. It was the private place where the young manager could discard his professional charm and relax. A pair of worn slippers with gilt embroidery awaited him beside a wine-dark lounge chair, a silk bathrobe was folded beside it. Above the chair a stained bullfighter's costume hung like a trophy. An Atwater Kent radio and small phonograph were within reach of the chair, also a bottle of tequila and two glasses. On the Empire desk was a brass paperweight, a bull staring at the torero's upraised sword. The slippers he now recognized as a bullfighter's small shoes. There was another lounge chair for his guest.

The room was dimly lit by an overhead bulb and a reading lamp of Tiffany glass. Against one wall was a large safe and above it several guest registers bound in good red leather, with *Huéspedes* in raised gold letters. Two bound books, actually filing cases, overflowed with the frayed edges of newspapers and magazines, and were identified as *Toreo y Boxeo* and *Teatro*.

"My official records," Antonio explained. "I am an amateur of boxing, bullfighting and the theater. The careers of all the champions and how often the great bullfighters fought, both Mexican and Spanish. Also a record of those who were gored. The intimate lives of the great actresses."

The walls of the office were covered with glossy publicity portraits of actresses, ballet and nightclub dancers, boxers, bullfighters and men in uniform, some of them on horseback. The photographs had elegant signatures and sentiments. Several of the actresses had very similar handwriting, not wholly unlike the bolder scrawl of the bullfighters, who greeted Vinalva as a true aficionado. Two of the generals congratulated him on the reopening of the luxury hotel.

A ceiling fan turned slowly.

"I never see the hotel guests in this room," Vinalva said. "There is another room for that purpose. But you are truly an exception, a teacher who was in Santa Rosalia even before I was born."

"Twenty-three years before, Mr Vinalva. You were born after the earthquake, but before the ashes. So you see I have studied your 'History of the Pueblo.' I brought it along to remind me of things I want to ask."

Vinalva looked at the one page with a deprecatory smile.

"Of necessity the history is very brief. Our guests wouldn't read more than one page. Think of all the great events and celebrities I have omitted!" He indicated with nods some of those who had visited the hotel. "Conchita Carmel, the most sensual of our Mexican dancers, star of the revue *Ba-ta-clan*. Rafael Gaona, lucid and courageous yet traditional, the greatest of our toreros. Cecilia Padilla, both idealistic and sensual. The divine Lupe Velez, who sent a photograph though unable to visit the hotel."

Side by side in gold filigreed frames were Emiliano Zapata, the martyred hero of the revolution and Dona Juana Cata, the saint of Tehuantepec, mistress of Porfirio Díaz.

"The hotel's two most eminent guests."

"Why saint of Tehuantepec?"

"She endowed schools, a church, a hospital. Whatever the city needed she provided through repeated telegrams to the dictator in the capital, long after they had parted. She also left money for the statue honoring herself."

"I'm fascinated by the history of the pueblo. There are so many mysteries. The prisoners hanged from the two orange trees."

"The same orange trees you see today."

"What had they done?"

"They were thieves who stole cattle from Señor Vazquez. Their bodies hung in the moonlight. All night I crept out to see that they were still there. The bodies became darker with the passage of the moon. I was a child of seven and I was terrified they would come down or be transformed into the bodies of dogs. The evil dead are sometimes transformed into animals. There is also the animal spirit that follows you through your life. The print of its feet are found on the ashes near the mat on which you are born and that animal will be with you in the hour of your death. All night I crept to the door to look. Were the bodies still there? Once the bodies moved. Both bodies, although there was no wind. And once in the darkness the shining eyes of an animal looked down at me."

"And the ashes that covered the pueblo?"

"For that everyone was terrified, not only children. The ashes fell for three days and the ground was covered, our bodies were covered, the spring water was filthy. We could hardly see the sun at noon, the sun was an orange ball of dust. The cura came, in those days he came perhaps once a month, almost never now. He told us the ashes were punishment for some crime and for three days we thought the ashes would never stop. The school was closed. Today those who have forgotten their age can say, 'I was in my first year of school when the ashes fell.' Later we learned the ashes were from a volcano in Guatemala, October 1902."

"And your poor teacher?"

"He was my guide, even more than my father Ramón. He was a man who had lived only in cities. Oaxaca, Puebla, Tehuantepec. In the first year of his teaching he came to the school in a white shirt of many pleats and a wide black tie. But he was not prepared for the simplicity of our life in those days when there was no hotel. He was a Ladino like me, not a Zoque, and he was not familiar with their ways. And he was lonely, that is the greatest sadness. So he married a woman of the pueblo, Maria Zarate, a woman who could not read or write. I loved my teacher, and I do not want to think of what troubles there were in the darkness of their hut. We heard their shouts and cries. He was disappointed with his life. The council of the ancients was unjust with him. They did not always pay him his twenty pesos a month. So he began to drink aguardiente instead of coffee, and then one day I found him eating clay like the most backward of the children. He had gone to the ravine and was eating clay. I pleaded with him to stop but he only waved me off. It is a cursed habit of the most unfortunate of the pueblo to eat earth."

"I know. They were eating earth fifty-two years ago."

"You think so?"

"Yes. I saw them."

"So my poor teacher got sick and died from drunkenness and the eating of earth. He could not even enjoy the pleasures of the hotel when it opened. He lay drunk in his hut. He was no longer the teacher. He lay in his hut while the rest of us welcomed Dona Juana Cata, the friend of Porfirio Díaz and first lady of Tehuantepec. At the age of eighty she defeated everyone in billiards, here in the hotel. An old lady in the finery of a queen, but with the burning eyes of youth, and a hand as sure as mine. That is how she met the General sixty years before, when he was governor of the Province. She came to the billiard room of the soldiers to sell her coconut candies and she defeated all his men in billiards and so it was she came to the attention of General Porfirio Díaz. Some said she was a witch. But she was the most beautiful Indian he had ever seen."

"And Porfirio Díaz. Did you ever see him?"

"Of course. In Rincón Antonio at the dedication of the railroad." He pointed to a framed commemorative photograph. In it the dictator stands erect and austere near a locomotive with many flags, while other dignitaries form a semicircle in the foreground. The faces of many onlookers are blurred. "You see me here? I was only fourteen, already I had worked on the railroad."

"So then you came back to Santa Rosalia?"

"Of course. For the grand opening of the hotel. 1908. But I was telling you of Nabor Ruiz who taught me so much and who died. I learned the English language from the engineers in Rincón Antonio when I worked on the railroad. Nabor Ruiz taught me everything else. Then he was gone and the troubles fell on his widow Maria Zarate. She was enraged because the council of the ancients would not give her the money that was owed Nabor Ruiz for his teaching before he died. She lived in misery."

"And she was killed?"

"It is not a simple story. For my part I need refreshment." He poured tequila into the two glasses. "We will drink to the memory of Nabor Ruiz."

They touched glasses.

"To the memory of your teacher," Stanfield said. He was eager to ask about the village of today, and thus move to his difficult question. Could his Marita still be alive and living in Santa Rosalia? But the story of Nabor Ruiz had released a flow of memory.

"And now I explain one of the great events in the history of our pueblo. In the rain and in the dark afternoon and without warning the first of a band of soldiers arrived to ask for help. They needed men to help them cross the Rio Milagro. This was the band of General Felix Díaz and General Almazán who could not accept the revolution. They came with their men and their horses and their women, also with three large guns on wagons and a great roll of wire for telephones. Never had we seen such a gathering. They were in flight. They had read in the writings of some Spanish historian of the Conquest of a route from here to the Zoque pueblos in Chiapas that would go across the mountains. 'El camino secreto del Andes,' that is what they asked for. They hoped to escape with this road. They spent two days and two nights in the village."

"In the hotel?"

"The hotel was closed. The rains had ruined everything,

143

there were rats swimming in the lounge. I saw them myself. In eighteen months since the earthquake the hotel was becoming a ruin. No, the generals slept in the Municipal office with their women and their men slept in the huts. We who lived in the huts were driven outside. Much of the two days and nights we spent looking for provisions for them.

"But no one could tell them of a road to Chiapas. So the next day there was a meeting of the generals and the Council of the Ancients, and at this meeting the widow Maria Zarate said two brothers named Arbona knew the secret road and had taken it all the way to San Cristobal in Chiapas. That was a lie."

"Why did she lie?"

"In revenge against the Council of the Ancients and perhaps for some fault of the brothers Arbona. But the brothers Arbona said they knew no secret road. The farthest they had gone was three hours from the village. The Generals Felix Díaz and Almazán were furious. So they tied up the brothers Arbona on a single horse, and they commanded all the men of the village to accompany them in search of the secret road. This was the last I ever saw of my father Ramón Vinalva. In the darkness of the jungle when they were still not far from the village there was much confusion, and one by one the men of the village dropped off and hid. But my father did not get away. In the night the chief lieutenant of General Felix Díaz buried the treasure they had brought with them, and it is my belief the treasure is still there in a cave in the jungle. After that I cannot tell you much. But everyone knows the generals were lost, and could not care for themselves in the jungle and in time they were obliged to eat their horses, also monkey meat. Many died. Not long after this they were defeated by the troops of Carranza. A good thing, too. If not they would have returned to burn Santa Rosalia to the ground."

"And Maria Zarate?"

"She was killed at the order of the Council of the Ancients because she betrayed the brothers Arbona and caused our people much distress. She was hanged from one of the orange trees." He filled the small glasses. "Let us drink to the sadness of the times and to those who have suffered."

"To all those who have suffered," Stanfield said.

They touched glasses. Antonio looked at him intently.

"You are the first of our guests to ask questions about our history. Perhaps this is because you too have been a teacher?"

"Yes."

He did not know where to begin.

"You are also the first of our guests to have come to Santa Rosalia in the old days. Long before I was born."

"That's true. In fact I was here two months before the three engineers in your 'history.' I was sent ahead to survey the volume of water and see what labor was available. So you shouldn't have left me out of your 'history'!"

"It is my father Ramón who is responsible for the history until I began to keep the guest records."

"Did he ever speak of an American who came earlier that year?"

"He was only a child of six. He did not remember much of those days. But one of the engineers gave him a present and that kind engineer he never forgot. I will show it to you."

He went to a closet and returned with a large wooden box. In it was a fine toy ship, perhaps a foot long with a high funnel and a large brass cylinder on its deck. Much of its green paint remained, with red below the water line.

"This is the 'Kensington Screw Steamer,' purchased in England, and operated by steam. Nothing like this was ever seen in Santa Rosalia. My father took it to the Rio Corte and played with it and sometimes the kind engineer went with him. Later I too took it to the river."

In the corner of the box was a small green felt bag.

"What is that?"

"That is a music instrument called a harmonica."

145

Antonio took it out of the bag and put it to his lips. It was rusted and several teeth were missing. A thin wailing interspersed by whistles brought back the boy 'Mon' who had watched them. Stanfield knew that harmonica, he had held it in his own hand fifty-two years before. So the boy 'Mon' was almost certainly Antonio's father, Ramón Vinalva, in due time the hotel concierge, in 1916 taken hostage by the counterrevolutionary generals. And who never returned.

He did not want to hold the harmonica now. He wished Antonio would put it back in the green bag. There was something obscene about that rusted thing. But he plunged ahead:

"There was a young boy who followed us about. Followed me. He could have been about six. He stared at me with his big eyes and he never said a word. I gave him a harmonica, it was certainly this one. It must have been your father."

Antonio Vinalva stared.

"So you knew my father as a child!" He made a sign of the cross. "That is very wonderful. And you too kindly made him a present!"

"Do you have any pictures of your father as a young man? Of his friends?"

"The first picture I have is of all the employees of the hotel at the first opening in 1890."

He took the picture down from the wall and pointed to a sturdy clean shaven man in the center of the group, his arms crossed, looking uncomfortable in frock coat, high collar and bow tie. There were eight ageless and unsmiling women in the picture. They would be the cooks, waitresses and maids. Marita would have been thirty-four in 1890. In the blurred picture all the women looked alike. Only the man in the frock coat wore shoes.

"That is my father Ramón in the center. He was the concierge and from the first he kept the book of the guests and he would comment on them. I put his words into English. It is a tradition I have followed, to comment on the guests and

146

ask for their remarks. Unfortunately the first guest book was lost in the flood. Nearly everything was lost. But I have all books from the new hotel of 1908.ʺ

He took down one of the large guest registers, and opened it to an early page.

ʺHere is our first American guest, entirely written by me in the English language I learned from the engineers of the railroad. *Mr Turner Hallowell, New Bedford, USA, room 14. Hydraulic construction expert, kind to Antonio Vinalva at the railroad.'* And here is Mr Turner next to my writing: *'Magnificent hotel. I remember with appreciation Antonio as faithful and skilled employee.'*ʺ

Stanfield found Antonio strangely incurious about his own stay in the village in 1870, and even about the gift of the harmonica.

ʺI was here nearly two weeks. There was a young Zoque girl of fourteen who brought me my food. I called her 'Marita.' I think your father liked her. I often wondered what happened to her. Could she even be here now?ʺ

Antonio became more attentive. His shrewd eyes looked amused.

ʺShe would be an old woman now, Mr Stanfield, most likely underground. You don't remember her full name?ʺ

ʺI don't think I ever knew it. I simply called her 'Marita' and both of us left it at that. I will tell you why I ask. Your history says of the three engineers: 'Kidnap young girl of the village.' So of course I wonder whether this wasn't the girl who worked for me and who might well have worked for them, bringing food to their hut. What does 'kidnap' really mean?ʺ

ʺI too wondered about that. Perhaps it meant that she chose to go with them to make her fortune in the great world, and the Council of Ancients permitted her to go.ʺ

ʺWould somebody know? Would there be some record kept by the Council of Ancients?ʺ

ʺMy father's was the best record.ʺ

Stanfield persisted. He had come this far in his questioning, it was too late to stop.

"Did your father have a sister? Maybe Marita was his sister."

In the stillness of the room the ceiling fan turned and turned. The silence, which seemed very long, was perhaps seconds only.

"Three, who were all dead before I was born. Maria, there is in every family a Maria so there are also many Maritas. One went away and died somewhere else. But my aunts were not Zoques. They were Ladinos like me and my father Ramón. So your Marita was not his sister." He gently took the harmonica from Stanfield and filled the two glasses. "All that is long ago, Mr Stanfield. Do you really want to find this old woman?"

The small office cluttered with Vinalva's souvenirs had become suffocating. But he could not give up.

"She could have gone away to the ends of the earth. Or she could be dead. Probably she is dead. But also she could be living in the village now, not a stone's throw from us."

"Your Marita? Is there an old woman of the village who babbles at her work about her handsome American lover from the north? I will ask the maids."

He was sickened by the idea of a kitchen discussion among the maids.

"Aren't there older friends you could ask? Even someone who was here in 1870? I'd rather you didn't ask the maids."

"There is a degenerate gringo who has lived forever in a hut near the cemetery. Excuse my language, Mr Stanfield, I would never speak of you as a gringo. An old drunkard named O'Brien who almost never leaves his hut. He may still be alive."

Stanfield knew that name. But the world was full of O'Briens, it could not be the same. A shadowy presence nevertheless moved ineluctably toward consciousness. A face twisted with greed, an eye screwed shut then opening and shutting obscenely. He did not want to see O'Brien. He refused to believe it was the same man. And yet he knew it was.

"There wasn't just the girl Marita. In Minatitlán I met an American woman who was looking for some trace of a famous general she had known. You have heard of William Walker?"

"Of course."

"She was following a rumor that he survived the firing squad and disappeared in Mexico and had even gone into hiding near here. This woman reached San Miguel and went up the Rio Corte with two Zoque guides from San Miguel. She thought he might be in Casas Grandes."

"Casas Grandes!"

"The guides came back without her."

"I am not surprised. It was foolish to go to Casas Grandes. A terrible place, with many disagreeable reptiles, not to mention the plague that destroyed our ancestors. In the old times it was a place of refuge for outcasts. I am surprised to hear Zoque guides would take her there."

"The guides brought back her things, even her money. They left them at the house of a Frenchman in San Miguel who hired them to be her guides. But then the guides disappeared, they were afraid of an investigation. Did your father ever mention this incident? Her two guides might have come from Santa Rosalia."

"Nothing, Mr Stanfield. If two men of our village were accused of killing a white woman, even fifty years ago, this would be remembered. We are a very small place, not much has happened here, our history has only one page. And San Miguel is far away. I think she must have died of an accident and they buried her. But she should never have gone to Casas Grandes. There have always been bandits up the Rio Corte, gringo bandits as well as Mexican. Also those who fled from their officers in the time of the Conquistadors. Not to mention the gringo miner who never gives up, and who floats down the river on his raft."

"Will you ask some of the ancients if they have heard about this incident?"

"I will, I will, but with little hope of success. An American woman killed by men of our village, that I would have heard about."

Gala Weekend

WITH THE WEEKEND the hotel awoke from its long sleep hardly disturbed by the click of roulette balls or the lazy guitarist and hula dancers who rarely left their chairs on the stage. The first visitors arrived early Friday afternoon, most of them with reservations. The fame of the former champion, embellished by a poster photograph in which he appeared gigantic, brought boxing enthusiasts and gamblers from as far as Mérida, Tampico, Vera Cruz. There were prostitutes from Rincón Antonio, where they roomed across from the station, and from Tehuantepec and Juchitán, these latter with coin-studded necklaces. Two from Vera Cruz had the glittering headbands and slinky satins of big city cabarets. The city folk arrived by the Stanley Steamer, which met the train in La Chivela, by the two Ford pickup trucks of San Miguel that called themselves taxis, and on horseback. On Saturday, after the devastating rains, some would even come by oxcart.

There were licenciados in bowler hats and borsalinos, clean-shaven lawyers and railroad union officials, some with silken girl friends. There were even a number of forest people in rags, with muzzle-loading shotguns who came on foot, guns which they crammed with nails and metal scraps, and Indians from small unnamed settlements carrying only machetes. They were seeing Santa Rosalia and the hotel for the first time, and would sleep outdoors or on hammocks in village huts, and barter worthless stones flecked with mica for food. The reports of the champion had reached them by word-of-mouth: a black giant with shining bald head who bare-handed fought bulls as well as men, wrestled bears in a circus, and confronted face to face a jaguar without recoiling. For the Indians who had come from a distance Santa Rosalia was already a place of mythical powers, since it was known the hotel utterly destroyed by flood had reappeared as though nothing had happened. It was also a place of pilgrimage for one small group of Zoques, who camped in front of it year after year and would look up at the dark third floor with patience and reverence.

For the big-time gamblers from Vera Cruz and Tampico, however, and the lawyers and other licenciados, and the girl friends and prostitutes looking for sidewalk bars and boutiques, Santa Rosalia was even more primitive than expected. The shouts from the one cantina were discouraging, and there was nothing worth having in the small store. They were not prepared for the sullen secrecy of the villagers, or for their pinta scars and the ugly shaved crowns of the men. After one look around, and one glass of the spring's pungent water, and one amused look at its darting fish, they stayed in the hotel and had drinks on the terrace or beside the pool.

The quiet life of the village, where people were born and sometimes married and died, and nothing ever happened, was nevertheless shattered by the plans for the weekend. New waitresses and maids were enlisted from girls of the village as young as twelve, those with the fewest scars and least stupefied expression. They remained barefoot, but wriggled uncomfortably in crisp green hotel uniforms and wiped their hands on them in embarrassment. Some learned to make beds for the first time and to clean the strange tubs where gringos and other *ricos* bathed. Other villagers prepared to sell stuffed iguanas, candy, hammocks and rope baskets from carts which they would push back and forth between the spring and the hotel terrace. Two cooks from the Chinese hotel in Rincón Antonio had come in the middle of the week, and bickered unceasingly with the two native cooks and the waitresses.

At the hotel reception desk there was confusion and anger from early Friday afternoon until the last room had been assigned on Saturday. Those without reservations assumed that a small mordida would assure them a room, and were dismayed to be told to return on Sunday. Habitués who had demanded rooms by number were enraged to be put in rooms with ceiling fans that didn't turn or bathrooms whose toilets didn't flush. There was also much confusion concerning admission to the Salon Oaxaca that combined casino, dining room and theater. Antonio Vinalva's original plan was to sell reserved seats for the Saturday evening Papa Jack exhibition, but the gamblers who had been in the hotel before did not see why they should pay to enter the room where they regularly lost their money. Thus some of the newcomers paid for sheets of Gran Hotel Balneario stationery with handwritten seat numbers whereas others paid nothing. The actual numbering of chairs, some taken from bedrooms, was put off until it was too late. To Vinalva the receipts of this weekend were unimportant, and the hotel was prepared to accept a sizeable loss. What mattered was the presence of the great black champion, and publicity to attract investors and gamblers and those seeking pleasures not available in the great resorts. There had been an enticing notice in a New York travel page, and one tourist, Stanfield, had come all the way from Boston.

On Friday morning at breakfast, before any of the newcomers had come, the waitress distributed two typed list of guests who had been offered complimentary weekend stays. The longer list gave the names of distinguished leaders and famous entertainers who had been invited, but who had been obliged to decline or who had not answered. Antonio had a few words of identification for each. Even the fact that they had been invited had publicity value. Pro forma invitations went to the district governor and the archbishops of Tabasco and Oaxaca, and to General Francisco Pancho Villa and several other retired heroes of the revolution. Next came Rudolfo Gaona, "maximum torero of Mexico," and three who had gone to Hollywood: Dolores del Rio, "the sacred mother of Mexican film," Lupe Velez "the sex lanza-bomba" and Ramón Navarro, "suave and seductive." Esperanza Iris, "worthy of her own Theater Iris," was unavailable because on European tour. Mimi Derba, Nelly Fernandez and Emmy Padilla were grouped as "exquisite stars of stage and screen," whereas Lupe Rivas Cacho "dared to imitate Tortola Valencia." From the circus and vaudeville stage the famous clown Ricardo Bell had been invited, with his wife Francisca Peyres and their twenty performing children, and Francisco Carreno and his twenty-four dwarfs ("not all one family"), and Encarnita Duval, dominator of pony and bull. Vinalva chose from the society pages two young women whose clipped photographs had a place of honor above his desk: Señorita Emilia Chulia, dark glasses pertly raised above her forehead: "loveliest woman automovilista of Mexico," and Señorita Rosalia Elena Sierra, black stockings and skirt, white blouse and shoes, noted for her tennis backhand.

The second list included those who had accepted, or who were already on the ground. First "the unique world champion, dancer, actor, singer" Papa Jack, then the poet and artiste Monica Swift, Jimmy Wilding ("small but a man of steel"), the entrepreneur Artemio de la Cruz, Angelita Braciano gracious danseuse, Charles Stanfield, veteran explorer and man of science. After them came Alicia Zobrana, sexy lanza-bomba of review *Ba-ta-clan*; Nicanor Díaz, hero of the province; El Trio Garnica-Matalba, superior chanteuses; Rafael Melillo, successful businessman; Colonel Alvaro Obrero, district chief Policía Rural; Joaquin Noriega, supreme entrepreneur, gambler; Colonel Ramón Pedruza, chief of mounted Gendarmería; Genero Sarabia, supreme entrepreneur, gambler; Licenciado Raúl Toledano, district chief of union CMOM.

Antonio Vinalva hovered benevolently over the breakfast table by the pool, where Stanfield and Monica Swift, the first to arrive, were joined by Papa Jack, Jimmy Wilding and Artemio Cruz. They pondered the lists.

"You are wrong to call Dolores del Rio the sacred mother," Artemio complained. "Nelly Fernandez and Mimi Derba were the first stars, in the movie *In Defensa Propia.*"

"Perhaps. But it is Dolores del Rio who put Mexico on the map. Besides, there is a religious spirituality even in her most sensual scenes. Her gentle eyes repudiate the fiery demands of her body. She would be at home in the convent for the rest of her life."

"I doubt it! However, my point is that Dolores del Rio will betray us by going to Hollywood rather than make films here in the capital. The title 'sacred mother of Mexican films' must go to one who stays."

"It's a matter of opinion."

"What does lanza-bomba mean?" Monica Swift asked.

"It is a phrase from the military. A machine that drops bombs."

"Why is Mimi Derba not a lanza-bomba? Or Nelly Fernandez?"

"They are more spiritual. They are sexy but less so."

"Like Dolores del Rio?"

"Not exactly."

"And your other bomb machine: Alicia Zobrana?"

"She sent a postcard promising to come."

"I'm looking forward so much to your famous bandit Nicanor Díaz," Monica Swift said. "But won't there be trouble with this colonel Pedruza? Or with the Rurales? Brian and I had many problems with the Rurales in 1918. They regularly took half of whatever we had. Though sometimes the bandits got half of the Rurales' half."

"You are speaking of the old days," Artemio said. "Glorious days when even professors rebelling against injustice became bandits."

"The greatest of the bandits stayed in the Hotel Gran Balneario soon after its opening."

"Chavez Garcia was here! The rapist repudiated even by Villa! Don't forget the virgins of Tucumbaro."

"Not Chavez Garcia, Santonón. Santonón was the greatest."

"Who were the virgins of Tucumbaro?" Papa Jack asked.

"Chavez Garcia and his men raped all virgins they found," Artemio explained. "All. In Tucumbaro they chased the virgins into a theater with a balcony. The virgins heroically threw themselves from the balcony. They are honored in Tucumbaro like the boy heroes of Chapultapec."

"Santonón was the greatest bandit, or the greatest after Herculio Bernal, who died before I was born. He held up the train near Rincón Antonio, where I learned the English language. Later he came to the hotel but did not rob. I remember his piercing eye and his handshake. Santanón was a mestizo who rebelled against the men who chained him to his labor, he rebelled against those who beat his mother to death. He was the enemy of the gringo sugar planters, and the millionaire exploiters of the poor Indios cutting wood. In fact he killed one of the millionaires. Moreover, he was one of our own, his home was in San Juan Evangelista. I do not justify his acts. On the contrary. But what do you think of a bandit who had no firearms, though his followers had many? He was armed only with his machete. Sometimes dressed as a Tehuana woman with a basket on the head he would rob small banks. Once he and his men were nuns but with machetes under their robes. They went from car to car on the train from Vera Cruz asking alms for the poor but with the machetes ready if refused. Even in the capital Santanón was feared. Ask Nicanor Díaz what he thinks of Santanón. The Rurales caught him at last, in 1910, only months after he had visited the hotel.

"Today the greatest is Nicanor Díaz. He is the true Robin Hood master of the Isthmus. He will never be arrested. His spies are everywhere. They need only raise a hand in warning, or at night light a match and wave it back and forth. If some corrupt politico in the capital with enough money demands his arrest he can retire to one of the ruins in the jungle. For some months he and his men camped in Casas Grandes. At another time a fortress in the ruins of Guiengola. That was two years ago. Today he can attend a luncheon in his honor in a cafe across the street from the prison, the police hear the speeches and the music. No one would dare touch him. He takes from those who are too rich and gives to the poor, Indians and Ladinos alike. His great pride is in his informants, as far as Juchitán and Tehuantepec to the west and Minatitlán to the east and San Juan Evangelista his birthplace to the north. As far as Yacaba in Chiapas he defended the poor Mayas from the depredations of evil bandits and liberals."

"Even in the capital I heard of Nicanor Díaz," Artemio said. "He recovers monies stolen from the treasuries of Oaxaca and Chiapas by corrupt politicians. He distributes the money and keeps nothing for himself. Next to nothing. He is a friend of the poor, also of orphans." He turned to Papa Jack with a smile. "Do not, however, speak to him of Carranza."

"You are right," Antonio Vinalva agreed. "Carranza and Limantour were the friends of the rich. For Nicanor Díaz the great hero is Emiliano Zapata. When he comes to the Balneario he demands the room once occupied by Zapata. Room 47."

"Zapata came here!"

"Incognito. Now that he is dead his true name has been entered in the guest book."

"I would like to see that guest book," Artemio said.

"Later. Perhaps Monday when calm is restored."

"Why wouldn't the Rurales arrest Díaz here?" Monica

Swift asked. "Or that other one, the mounted policeman. Mounted on what? a mule? a motorcycle? Why wouldn't he arrest Nicanor Díaz?"

"They have an understanding for great occasions: live and let live. From the point of view of the hotel it was necessary to invite all three. I anticipate no problems unless everyone gets drunk. Or Obrero brings too many of the Rurales. They are, anyway, the same kind of men, the Rurales and the conscientious bandits. During the truce they will drink together."

"Please be sure that I get a chance to talk to Díaz," Monica said. "If he knows everything and everybody he's the man I want."

"Of course. If Brian Desmond is to be found, Nicanor Díaz will find him."

"And Casas Grandes," Stanfield said. "I want to talk to him about that. Maybe I too can get there. Fifty-two years late."

The hotel was no more than two hundred yards from the first huts of the village, but it might as well have been two miles. The hotel customers and the villagers frequented the spring at different hours, and outsiders rarely visited the plaza a second time. They felt unwelcome at the tables in front of the cantina and in the small stores where only shiny stuffed iguanas might pass as souvenirs. The two hotel cooks and the barefoot maids and waitresses came and went between the hotel and village, silent and even furtive, telling no stories because they understood so little of what they saw and heard in the hotel. Only Antonio Vinalva and the bartender Luís had a secure place in both societies, although Antonio as a Ladino could not serve in the Zoque councils.

Jimmy Wilding, only days after their arrival, crossed the invisible barrier, thanks to his boxer's expertness at skipping rope. *Oranges and lemons say the bells of St. Clements*, he would skip, past the visiting Indians crouched in front of the terrace, bent over their weaving. They did not look up. *Here we go round the mulberry bush, mulberry bush, mulberry bush*, circling the spring where some of last night's gamblers were taking their first restorative glass of the day. The rope whistled tirelessly as he danced in his boxer's shorts, a British lion and unicorn on the hip, naked to the waist, tattoos splendid in the sun. On he went to the village, past the school, past the ruined church and the two orange trees where prisoners were hanged, past the new church and three, four, five times around the plaza, his high topped boxer's shoes moving delicately in the dust, the rope turning slow and silent, then whistling very fast. Behind him followed a dozen ragged children, who the next day appeared with skipping ropes expertly fashioned from ixtle. The ropes posed no problem, since to work with hemp was the pueblo's one craft. Before the week was out children of the village hovered near the pool, waiting, and greeted him with chirping cries. He would lead them down the two broken streets, picking his way around the roughest places, past the petroleum pit, to the very edge of the jungle and back. He tried in vain to get Papa Jack, forty pounds overweight, to join him.

At the end of his hour with the rope he would disappear into one or another of the villager's huts, or squat at the hut's entrance, gravely accepting a tortilla and cup of coffee or home brewed aguardiente. He knew a few words of Spanish but did not use them, and not a word of Zoque, and did not try to learn. The rope skipping did away with any need for speech, and the rainbow tattoos of coiled serpent and sailing ship in full sail and the grass-skirted hula dancer who wriggled as he flexed his muscles. He had lived his first thirteen years in a slum, prior to his brief career as a fighter in the London streets, and had an instant unspoken rapport with people who had no money and only hammocks or mats to sleep on and a rough table and two or three chairs, and whose small children went naked all the time and whose women were naked to the waist inside their homes and sometimes even outside as they ground corn hour after hour before shaping and slapping the tortillas that appeared at every meal. At their silent invitation he followed some of the men to their milpas, one afternoon, and joined them in picking coffee.

So he was not only accepted; he was admired. Soon he was the lithe darling of the hotel maids, a guileless child who liked to be tickled, yet a child with the rippling muscles and hard stomach of a jungle cat. They came to his room unannounced, giggling, sometimes two or even three at a time, bringing dainties smuggled from the kitchen. He in turn would ply them with colored sugar candies, of which he had bought a large supply in Vera Cruz, and sometimes cervezas from the bar. They liked to feel his muscles, see the green serpent swell as though swallowing a mouse, and the hula dancer dance.

Papa Jack, who was bored with greedy actresses, and with the prostitutes at the bar and roulette tables, looked on with envy.

So too did Stanfield.

On Friday afternoon the bright Stanley Steamer made two trips, full, bringing the first professional gamblers, prostitutes and small town businessmen and their girlfriends. Some were weekend habitués who asked for rooms by number. They made the usual token visit to the spring, where hotel waitresses were stationed with additional cups. They knew there was nothing of interest to be found in the village, no entertainment, only the one cantina. But there were also men who were coming from the first time, drawn by the announcement that the incomparable champion would box an exhibition and that another boxer, an English bantamweight, would take on all comers. They looked around in dismay.

Nicanor Díaz, who disdained the title of "General," arrived Friday evening on horseback, with six of his followers. One of these was a woman and she wore her polished cartridge belt around the waist, whereas the men wore them

strung over the left shoulder and across the chest like a decoration. Díaz himself came unarmed, wearing the sombrero,
trousers and jewel embroidered jacket of a charro horseman.
A silver-studded velvet stripe shone from thigh to boot. The
horses milled about at the front entrance of the hotel, their
hoofs clattering on the pavement in which the marble words
GRAN HOTEL were imbedded. The hotel personnel rushed
to greet him.

Later in the evening, with four roulette tables at work,
and the flowery and ruffled Trio Garnica-Matalba singing its
first songs, Díaz was escorted by Antonio Vinalva to the table
where the gringos were finishing a late supper. Everyone at
the adjoining tables fell silent as Díaz moved past them with
the quiet smiling assurance of the public man who knows he
is being watched. Each person might fancy the hero's beautiful brown eyes paused for a moment as in recognition. The
white welt of the famous scar on the forehead was exactly as
the newspapers reported, and as referred to in a popular bal-
lad. He bowed to Monica Swift and Angelita Braciano, holding their hands as though balancing the finest crystal, and
brushed them with his lips, which were rosy and sensual beneath a fine moustache as dark as the eyes. He turned to
Papa Jack and Wilding with a friendly smile, while seeming
at the same time to honor Stanfield and his gray hairs. His
English was studied and musical.

"The superb Champion! The young bantamweight who
will fight all comers! We are honored." He raised his fists
goodhumoredly and hunched forward in a boxer's crouch.
"Perhaps I myself will challenge the young bantamweight.
My weight is eighty kilos. I have the advantage of weight,
but you have the advantage of age. My age is thirty-two."

Monica Swift was charmed.

"Won't you join us? I think you look like the young Benito
Juarez!"

"I am only partly Indian," he said, patting his cheeks.
"However, I am flattered by your comment. Indian, Ladino:

we are all Mexicans, hijos de la chingada."

"In my opinion you resemble the provisional President Adolfo de la Huerta," Artemio offered. "The narrow jaw, the intensity of the expression."

Díaz acknowledged this remark with the attention one might give a fly landing on his cheek. It was as though the right eye moved while the left remained still. Still standing, he bowed to Stanfield, and with the mere flexing of an index finger indicated to a hovering waitress that a round of drinks should be brought.

"My good friend Antonio Vinalva tells me you visited Santa Rosalia long before any of us were born. We honor all engineers and men of science and explorers from the north. Only the exploiters disgust us."

"I was only twenty," Stanfield said. "I couldn't do much exploiting."

"And now you revisit the scenes of youthful adventure? Perhaps here in Santa Rosalia your dreams of adventure will be realized once more? Do you find anything the same?"

"The petroleum pit where I got stuck, fifty-two years ago. Just the other day a child tried to tempt me to wade. The mysterious silver fish in the spring are the same. The beautiful jungle, the Rio Corte, the Cerro de Ocotal with its splendid trees."

"The petroleum pit! Yes, it is a tradition to trap the unprepared visitor, tempting him to the pit. Even the sombre Zoques play their games. However, the oil is of benefit for many ailments, as well as for the pockets of the millionaires."

"Please do sit down, " Monica Swift urged. "None of us at this table are millionaires. Not even Jack. In 1918 my husband and I nearly starved in Mexico."

"I will join you with pleasure but only for a moment." With another flick of the finger, and while drawing up his chair, he indicated to Antonio Vinalva that he was free to leave. "And now, señora, you do not starve. Your dress is without doubt the most beautiful in this room."

"I designed it myself," she said.

"Antonio Vinalva told me of your search for your lost husband the English poet and boxer. In the next life I will hope to be both boxer and poet. In this life it will be my pleasure to help you in any way I can. There are many who disappear into the wilderness of our country. But some of them are found. I believe your husband will be found." He turned again to Stanfield. "And you too, sir! Antonio tells me you would like at least to know what happened to your dead loved ones!"

"Not exactly loved ones, it was only for a few days."

"I understand, I understand. People say the Yankees are cold and without romantic thoughts. But I know better. The unthinking embrace of one moonlit night can be remembered for a lifetime. Please believe I am at your service." He turned to Papa Jack, who for once was not the center of attention, with a benevolence that seemed to include the open-mouthed Jimmy Wilding. "I and my men would have ridden through fire for the pleasure of seeing the greatest champion. And you, Mr Young Bantamweight, someday you will be a great champion!"

He stood up, bowing again. "But now I must leave you with much regret. Tomorrow we will meet again."

"What a wonderful man!" Monica Swift said.

The six Rurales police on horseback arrived very late, with many of the gamblers and prostitutes already in their rooms. Their chief Colonel Obrero went at once to the bar, where he drank three beers rapidly while conferring with José, who signaled for one of the hula dancers to follow him to his room. The others Rurales, who had only fragments of uniform, as though they had divided two or three uniforms among them, occupied a table near the stage, where workmen were hammering and tightening the ropes of the boxing ring. The chief of the gendarmería Colonel Pedruza did not come at all.

The next morning all was chaos, thanks to a heavy rain

that began about midnight and continued until dawn, leaving the road from San Miguel a morass. Yoked oxen and two teams of mules from a ranchería near San Miguel preceded the hotel Stanley Steamer and the San Miguel taxis, with new bargains struck each time it was necessary to be pulled out of the ditch. The passengers, who at strategic moments were obliged to help by pushing, slipped and slid, cursing. They arrived exhausted and spattered with mud. Their clothes, hastily washed by the maids, then dried over kitchen fires, were wrinkled and stiff. The second trip of the bus from Chivela did not reach the hotel until long after dark, with the gala entertainment underway and the dinner service over.

The boxers' exhibition was to go on at ten o'clock, and for the first time since breakfast the roulette tables would be closed down, as Jack had insisted. The ring had been repaired, the ropes were taut, greased and shining, and British and American flags had been added to the Mexican flag on the wall behind the stage. All the tables had been moved closer to the stage, which was raised about four feet above the dance floor. Antonio Vinalva rushed about, trying to placate those who could not find the reserved chairs for which they had paid. Waitresses protected the three tables nearest the stage. Antonio put Nicanor Díaz at one with Monica Swift, Angelita Braciano, Artemio and Stanfield. At the next table was the union leader Licenciado Raúl Toledano and the three newspaper men, each with camera and flash, along with the chanteuses of the Garnica-Matalba Trio, who had changed to transparent white skirts over glittering satin pants.

Antonio had little chance to sit down, but he left a place for himself with the two big time gamblers Noriega and Sarabia, and the businessman Elizón, since the success of the boxing enterprise, and perhaps even the survival of the hotel, depended on them. Every few minutes he returned to them apologetically. Tonight was only a kind of dress rehearsal for future triumphs, he explained, but at least they would see the famous champion in boxing trunks and with gloves. They would be the first to see him in action since his release from prison the previous year. He had "paid his debt to society," even though there had been no crime. And still it was impossible in the United States, even in Nevada, to arrange a fight for him. A fight in the Balneario with a great South American heavyweight, Firpo for instance, would certainly draw millionaires. Then the casino could be expanded to rival the best European ones, and the great wagerings of Monte Carlo would be possible, and perhaps an enlarged hotel. The owner living in seclusion in Cuernevaca would listen to reasonable offers.

Monica Swift had remodeled last night's dress, creating new sleeves to give the effect of a cape flung open over a satin bust that now seemed more inviting than before. She held out her hand to Nicanor Díaz.

"Tell us where you have been, Mister Bandit. There has not been a sign of you all day, and not a sign of your men. I looked, I did so want to continue our conversation. Were you despoiling some rich plantation owner? Or perhaps a bank. Was it a bank? And whose poor will you give the money to? On our way down from Vera Cruz some nice bandits who said they were ferrocarilleros held us up. Could they have been your nice bandits?"

"Where was this?"

"The train stopped on a long bridge. I thought we would never leave the bridge. Papalo...."

"Papaloapam" Artemio put in. "The men were very pleased to be photographed with the champion."

Nicanor Díaz ignored him.

"I am poor. My followers are also poor, though not quite as poor as the Rurales. So we have every right to 'despoil.' But no, we did not hold up your train. Today too we were not despoiling. Today I attended a wedding in San Miguel, my men joined in the feast. On this occasion the money contributed last week by a filthy and fraudulent licenciado in San Juan Evangelista was transferred to the pockets of this young couple for a wedding trip to Tampico."

"Surely you are joking!"

"Were you joking when you asked if my men held you up at Papaloapam? Not a peso, not one real of the licenciado's money remained in our own pockets. On our return from the wedding we helped the poor city people on the bus, which was lying in the ditch with a back wheel spinning. Santa Rosalia needs a railroad, Mr Stanfield. Why don't you gringos build one?"

"A wedding in San Miguel? It was from San Miguel my friend from New Orleans set out with two Zoque guides to go up the river. A Frenchman in San Miguel provided her with the guides and they went up the Rio Corte to the ruins of Casas Grandes. But they came back without her."

"Casas Grandes. A dangerous place at any time. When was this?"

"When I was here before. 1870. I never knew what happened."

"You grieve for her after so many years? It is true, you Yanquis are not as cold as is said."

"Not 'grieve,' no. And yet I feel there was something I should have done."

"You are a good man," Nicanor Díaz said. "Perhaps you will not be satisfied until you too have gone to Casas Grandes. Meanwhile I will enquire from the oldest inhabitants of San Miguel. I have heard of this Frenchman. He died long ago."

"Maybe we all should go to Casas Grandes," Monica Swift said.

The time had come for the show, though Papa Jack was furious when he looked out on the small crowd. Gone were the aristocrats in tuxedo of the Vélodrome d'Hiver in Paris or the aficionados of Barcelona and Havana. Behind the ringside tables the remaining patrons of the hotel were seated at a dozen tables, which they had pushed closer to the stage. The barefoot waitresses, some of them carrying trays for the first time, were demoralized by orders for drinks of which they had never heard. In the end people had to be satisfied with aguardiente, mescal, wine or beer. The large room had three windows giving onto the terrace, pool and village, and here for the first time since the hotel's reopening the faces of villagers appeared, dark heads thrust between and above other heads. Some of them were there less to see Papa Jack than to see Jimmy Wilding, whom they knew.

He was the first to perform, skipping rope with the boxer's shuffle and dance that had enticed the village children to follow him. He held the rope outstretched like a magician showing his wares to the skeptical, drew it in, extended it again, flexing his muscles to make the serpent swell and the tattooed dancer writhe. Skipping rope, he kept time to the musicians at the side of the stage, the rope circling slowly with the steady drumming of a guitar, then whistling faster and faster with the cornet. When he slowed again, Papa Jack skipped onto the stage, and the two circled it like circus ponies, Jack on the inside and skipping rope more slowly, Wilding moving faster and faster. The belt of fat at Papa Jack's waist shook, his breasts seemed to swell with his heavier breathing, which came in little gasps. The sweat on his face was like another skin.

"I think he is in much need of exercise," Díaz said.

The champion then played the guitar, tap-danced, sang "The Roses of Picardy" in a deep bass, and gave the last speeches of Othello, interspersed with long dramatic silences as an imaginary Desdemona moved in her death agony or lay still. The audience, though puzzled, applauded. Several voices called out for the boxing to begin.

Antonio leaped to the stage and called for volunteers to face Jimmy Wilding, who had stepped into the ring. His warmup dance, shadow boxing imaginary opponents, proved intimidating. At last a wiry young mestizo, in tennis shoes and wearing trousers cut off at the knees, appeared. He must have been wearing gloves for the first time, as he seemed puzzled about what to do with his thumbs. But he must have fought his share of street fights and watched a number of professionals. He bobbed and weaved while Wilding circled him goodnaturedly, now and then flicking a jab. Near the end of the third round Wilding threw one hard right, almost apologetically, that sent the mestizo sprawling.

Then Jack and Wilding went through their three-round act of playful sparring, with the diminutive Wilding held at arm's length by the tolerant giant, flattened by what looked like a fatal blow, then leaping onto the giant's shoulders as soon as his back was turned. The crowd, which had hoped for some real boxing, didn't know whether to applaud or howl its disapproval. Jack, still with Wilding on his shoulders, was breathing heavily. He held up his arms as in a gesture of triumph. At this there were a few derisive shouts from the rear tables, even hisses. Papa Jack glared. He left without bowing.

"What do you think?" Antonio said, as soon as he had returned to the table of the gamblers and entrepreneurs.

"He is in terrible condition, twenty kilos overweight if not more," the gambler Noriega said. "Firpo would kill him."

"He has been training on wine and women, not to mention the year in prison. Give him time."

"There would be nothing to bet on, even if he lay down as ordered. The reporters would take one look at Papa Jack and make Firpo a ten-to-one favorite. Your idea, Vinalva, is a bad one."

"What if we match him with some unknown?" the gambler Sarabia suggested. "Maybe Rudy Macias."

"Even Macias would kill him."

"Tonight tells you nothing," Vinalva said. "The great champion is in his prime. Give him a week's training, two weeks rather, and he would cut Macias to ribbons. The little Englishman will make him train. A warmup fight with Macias, then we go to Firpo."

"Let him cut Macias to ribbons," Noriega said. "So long as Macias wins."

"No, no! He lay down for the big fight in Havana. Perhaps he would lie down for Firpo. Never for an unknown. A loss to Macias would ruin the hotel, the odor of the fix would pervade all of Mexico."

"Are you interested in money or not? Get him up to the room and we'll make him a fair proposition."

"You are making a mistake," Vinalva said. "He needs money, yes, but not that badly."

When Papa Jack returned after dressing, he found Nicanor Díaz in animated conversation with several Mexican men who had hotel brochures which they wanted autographed. Artemio and Angelita listened appreciatively. Across the table Stanfield and Monica Swift were speaking so quietly that he could make out nothing. Jimmy Wilding meanwhile had found some admirers at a table near the back of the room, and was conversing with them in sign language. It was as though he, still the greatest champion, did not exist. Through the drumfire of Spanish he finally realized that the men wanted the bandit Nicanor Díaz's autograph not his own, and also wanted brochures signed for two women at a nearby table. Díaz lifted his glass to the women, then blew a kiss.

Papa Jack sat down heavily. The trousers of his white Palm Beach suit pinched, and the coat was too tight at the armpits, which were soaking again. Even the union leader Toledano at the next table was not wearing a coat, and the flowered Garnica-Matalaba girls were fanning themselves with menus. A new young siren had appeared at that table, the *Ba-ta-clan* dancer Alicia Zobrana. She was gazing at Díaz dreamily, the long ivory cigarette holder pointed in his direction, not listening to the union leader's chatter. She was turned half away from the table, long legs of black silk and sequins crossed to invite the admiration of all the men on one side of the room. Not an Indian or mestiza, her skin had a porcelain delicacy accentuated by dark painted circles beneath the eyes. To win the attention of her cigarette holder would be a sign

169

of masculine success.

Papa Jack had not seen her at the table during his performance, and he found this irritating.

Nicanor Díaz complimented him on his rendering of "The Roses of Picardy" and on his recitation of lines from *Othello*.

"You didn't like the exhibition?"

Díaz stiffened his right arm and jerked the thumb toward his shoulder, but said nothing.

"What does that mean?"

"He admires your strength," Artemio offered.

"You Americans slap the chest," Monica Swift said. "It means the same thing."

"Didn't you like my act with Jimmy?"

Díaz held up his hand and shook it wig-wag fashion, an honest reaction.

"Amusing. But I enjoyed the singing more. You sing with true passion of the sadness of the soldier far from home. You are a man of culture. Is it true in Spain you fought with bulls?"

"Belmonte himself taught me. The greatest."

"I am a provincial," Díaz said, but not in a tone of conviction. "For me Rudolfo Gaona is the greatest."

Another Mexican, who might have been a small town doctor, came over to shake the bandit's hand. A flood of Spanish ensued, with both talking jovially at once. Angelita listened eagerly. The newcomer did not even look at Papa Jack. It occurred to him that the time was approaching for Angelita to go back to Artemio, who had now joined in the drumfire of loud Spanish. Either that or go back to Vera Cruz on her own.

"What are they talking about?" he asked Monica Swift.

"I'm not sure. I think it's about some politician's folly."

"Something about a deputy from Tehuantepec," Stanfield contributed.

Jack nodded to the next table, where the Garnica-Matalba trio were casting glances at men nearby. The newcomer Alicia Zobrana still stared at Díaz, the cigarette holder raised as in subtle promise, while the union leader Toledano talked on and on.

"So that's a lanza-bomba," he said. "She doesn't even look Mexican."

Monica Swift pursed her lips.

"Let's pretend she's a White Russian who is wearied of Shanghai or Paris. The daughter of an archduke who has lost everything. Or maybe the daughter of a priest."

"I wonder how she got here?" Stanfield asked. "Is the *Ba-ta-clan* a good theater?"

"It's a company, a good one. The theater was the Iris. The Rosalia Victoria company used a swimming pool in the orchestra pit. That was even better."

"You amaze me," Stanfield said.

"Brian liked that sort of thing. He had the most degraded taste at times, it was one more repudiation of his heritage."

Papa Jack caught Artemio's attention. He nodded to the adjoining table.

Momentarily the cigarette holder and long unlit cigarette wavered and took him in, then flicked back to its original angle.

"Invite her over," Jack said. "The lanza-bomba with the cigarette holder."

"She is the star Alicia Zobrana. I invite also the licenciado Toledano?"

"Just the lanza-bomba."

Papa Jack watched while appearing not to. Artemio sat down with the union leader and the three restless singers and the lanza-bomba. The discussion went on for several minutes, with occasional glances in his direction. Artemio was making clear that this was the champion's invitation, not Nicanor Díaz's.

Alicia Zobrana stood up, uncoiled rather, not smiling, with much movement of the silken legs. Her shiny white gown, slit to the thigh, was studded with paste jewelry.

At Artemio's urging she sat next to Papa Jack, giving him

a token smile of recognition, then turned to Díaz. She began talking very rapidly. The tone of voice suggested she had been wanting for a long time to meet him. Perhaps this was the reason why she had come to the Balneario.

"What will you have?" Papa Jack asked.

She saw that everyone was drinking a dark liquid, possibly bourbon. With a slight wave of the fingers she said it did not matter, she would have the same. While signalling to the waitress Papa Jack offered her his own glass, which she refused with a look of distaste.

"What kind of dancer are you?" he asked her.

"No habla inglés," she replied. "I do not speak."

"Ask her in Spanish, Artemio."

She replied by a hunching of one shoulder then the other, a wriggle, a kick that left the silken leg almost vertical. Then much wrenching of the torso, this accompanied by many Spanish words.

"She says everything. Spanish flamenco, hula dance, French cancan, Mexican Jarabe Michaocano, La Jarena Yucateca. You ask her, she can do it."

"She'll do it here? Right now?"

Another rapid exchange, during which the porcelain stare and painted eyes examined him coolly.

"Not here," she says, "In the theater."

She turned again to Nicanor Díaz and went on at such length that Jack surmised she was giving him the story of her life.

"I want her to spend the night with me," he said to Artemio. "Arrange it."

Monica Swift and Stanfield looked embarrassed.

"I don't think she's quite ripe to be plucked," Monica Swift said.

"It's sort of a handicap not knowing the language," Stanfield offered.

"I'll pay her of course. Don't tell me she can't be bought. Any woman can be bought."

"Not any woman."

"I mean any woman who looks like this. The lanza-bomba, just to use my new word. Go ahead and arrange it, Artemio."

Artemio shrugged. He waited for a break in the flood of her theatrical reminiscences, then dropped his voice to a whisper. His shoulders were hunched forward as in apology and to indicate that he was a helpless intermediary. Díaz frowned.

Very slowly, like an uncoiling snake, her long neck seemed to grow longer. For only a moment her eyes turned to Johnson's. Their gray turned to a smoky green. The cigarette holder described a small circle in the air, though the fingers guiding it hardly moved.

"No me gustan los negros," she said in a dry and decisive voice.

Artemio started to protest. He looked apologetically at the champion.

"It's all right," he said. "I know that much Spanish."

"I am sorry," Nicanor Díaz. "She is a puta without a soul. For the true Mexican woman the color of the skin has no importance."

"Think nothing of it." He put his hand on Angelita's shoulder, heavily.

"Come along sweetheart, let's hit the hay."

The angry Angelita did not come to his room, but Antonio Vinalva did, accompanied by the gamblers Noriega and Sarabia. They were followed into the room by one of the barefoot waitresses with four glasses, and the bartender José himself, carrying three bottles. The champion could choose between bourbon, tequila and aguardiente. The supply of ice was exhausted, otherwise he could have had champagne. Another waitress appeared bringing two chairs. Everyone sat down except Papa Jack, who watched them sullenly from the door to the bathroom. He was extraordinarily tired.

173

"In the capital of Mexico you will have the finest champagne," Noriega said. "From France. And any women you want."

"I'm not so sure I want to go back there," Papa Jack said. "There was a time I could ring up the President's office and see him the same day. He understood me."

"Alvaro Obregón?"

"No, Carranza," Artemio said. "He shared the champion's views on racial injustice. They were friends."

"There's nothing for me now in Mexico City."

"There will be, there will be. With money anything is possible. You have only to ask. You want a fast car like the Bugatti or an elegant car like the Hispano-Suiza? Or both? A blonde actress from Germany, a dark one from Cuba. Which do you prefer?"

Noriega, who knew far more English, was doing most of the talking, while Sarabia nodded his approval or from time to time shook his head.

Papa Jack turned to Antonio Vinalva.

"What's this all about?"

"They have a proposition for you."

"Money," Noriega said. "Lots of money."

"Tonight was not what I would call a big success," Papa Jack said.

"Nevertheless you will have money. In the capital, of course. We know your love of fast cars. You will race in person at the Autodromo de Chapultepec. Why not win with a Marmon car if not a Bugatti?"

"I'm pretty fed up with Mexico. Cuba too."

"You will travel in style. You name the country."

He finished his drink and poured another. He was drinking very rapidly.

"Let's have your proposition."

"We look forward to a great match next year with Luís Angel Firpo, probably in the Toreo in Mexico City, if not Havana in the race track where you lost to the giant Willard."

Papa Jack did not like discussions of that fight, unless he initiated them himself. He did not want to hear comments on the 26th round and the manner in which he shielded his eyes from the sun while lying on his back. He finished his drink, poured another, and drank it.

"Firpo wouldn't fight me, not even in Buenos Aires. Even now when I'm out of shape. Dempsey won't fight me. Willard won't risk his neck again."

"You name the dancer you want, even two or three, we will produce. You go to the cabarets with us, I guarantee we produce."

The word *cabarets* awoke Sarabia, who had appeared not to be listening.

"La vida nocturna!" he offered enthusiastically. "El cabaret Montecarlo en la avenida 16 Septiembre, el cabaret en la calle de Bucareli, el cabaret Ideal en la calle Isabel la Católica."

"I'm getting tired of the horseshit."

"Yes, yes. I will explain. Our object is the great world-class fight with Firpo. But first we have two warmup fights here in the Gran Hotel Balneario with a courageous but unskilled fighter named Raúl Macias."

"I never heard of him. Why two fights?"

"In the second fight with the movie cameras and the newspapers you cut Macias to ribbons. You knock him out. Of course. So now it is clear you are ready for the world-class fight with Firpo." He paused, a long silence. "The first fight is what will make us rich."

Papa Jack held his glass, which still had a little whiskey, up to the light that hung from the ceiling. He finished the drink and poured himself another.

"I think I understand. I lose the first fight."

"This was not my idea," Antonio Vinalva said hastily.

"What does it matter, since you will win the second fight? You can even cut him to ribbons in the first fight, so long as you lose. We will place bets at twenty to one, even fifty to one."

175

"Nobody will bet on Macias, not even at fifty to one."

"We will bet on him."

"Get them out of here," he said to Antonio. "Before I cut them to ribbons."

"You lie down in Havana before thirty-five thousand? Why not in Santa Rosalia before two hundred? For the first fight there will be no movies."

Papa Jack started to lumber toward Noriega, who stood up quickly. He moved toward the door, followed by Sarabia.

"Think of what you could buy! You are tired of Mexican whores, you call them horseshit. So everyone knows you love cars. The Bugatti, the Marmon, the Hispano-Suiza! How much horsepower do you want? How many cylinders?"

"It was not my idea," Antonio Vinalva said quickly. "For me this idea would ruin the Gran Hotel Balneario. The stink would pervade all Mexico."

"Money!" Noriega almost screamed, courageously making a last stand at the door.

But then closed it hastily behind him.

Toward Casas Grandes

ON MONDAY MORNING, when Stanfield went down to the poolside for breakfast, he found only Antonio Vinalva, who looked exhausted and depressed. The great weekend was over, and Papa Jack, Jimmy Wilding and Angelita Braciano were gone, together with his dreams of tourists and sportsmen rushing to Santa Rosalia from Buenos Aires and New York. Monica Swift remained, but only a handful of gamblers as well as the several prostitutes who had lost all their money at roulette and were stranded. The big money of Noriega and Sarabia, who were as angry as Papa Jack, had slipped through Vinalva's fingers and would not easily return. Empty or broken bottles and crushed cigarettes littered the hallways and the Salon Oaxaca, and the narrow belt of pavement beside the pool.

An Indian woman was sweeping debris toward the hotel terrace as though intending to leave everything there in one great pile. Two or three strokes of her miserable broom, then a pause for rest, or to look through the rubbish for something worth keeping. At the far end of the pool three young Indian girls waited with towels for swimmers who would not come, while others sat on their heels near the spring. Here two of the gamblers, hung over from the night's excesses, were forcing themselves to drink. Overhead the sky pressed down like a sheet of lead. The monkey in the tamarind tree, folded in on itself, was asleep.

"I am ruined," Vinalva said, greeting Stanfield with a limp handshake. "Those men have no understanding of the mentality of a proud black man. I warned them to say nothing of the Willard fight in Havana, they have no subtlety. It is a shameful incident he does not want to remember."

"I understand he has contradicted himself a number of times. Jimmy Wilding swears he was really knocked out. He was exhausted by the heat but would never have thrown a title fight."

"The little Englishman is proud of his hero, but was sad to leave Santa Rosalia. In another week he would have had all the children in the village following him about. Do you know what he asked me, Mr Stanfield? He asked me to tell the people in the village that he loved them and some day will return. What do you make of that?"

Stanfield thought of his own usually silent rapport with a fourteen-year-old inhabitant of the village, fifty-two years before.

"He charmed them with his rope-skipping. And he didn't have to talk. Maybe he was glad to get away from people who talk all the time, and be with people as simple as himself. Besides, they loved his tattoos."

"Will he return to Santa Rosalia? You, Mr Stanfield, have returned. Are you glad you returned?"

"For years on end I didn't give much thought to my few days here, or my two months on the Isthmus. It was at most a daydream I could induce now and then, to be back in Suchyl with my strange companion Rosellen, always in white, or to be here with my wild little Zoque, bringing coffee to my hut. That is how I remember her, as both gentle and wild. It would be only a few minutes of a deliberate waking dream just before going to sleep. But then asleep I would dream of some dull banality. And now my whole life seems to me a long sleep. I shouldn't have had to wait fifty-two years to come

back! Mexico was my one little adventure." He looked beyond Antonio, beyond the nearest huts, and he might have
been talking in a dream, with a quite different voice: "I will
wander alone on winding picaduras. Almost forgotten is my
languid and useless life at home."

"What are you saying, Mr Stanfield? Winding picaduras?"

"Those are the words of Rosellen Maurepas. They are
the lines of her Journal I remember best. Except one other."

"Your life has not been useless."

"Perhaps not, though I think I should have stayed with
my first love and been an engineer building bridges or planning rights of way. Suppose I had come back to work on the
transisthmus railroad as you did? We might have met then."

"I have two loves, Mr Stanfield. The first is the railroad
and my life with the American and English engineers in Rincón
Antonio. The second is the hotel. My true love is the hotel
and its many distinguished guests, who will live forever in
the guest books."

"Think of how much courage she showed, how much
enterprise—she, a well brought-up rich young woman going
where I didn't dare to go! Two or three years ago I began to
think about her more often, going up the Rio Corte to Casas
Grandes. And even think about my little companion who
brought me the coffee. She would reach through the mosquito netting to give it to me."

"The lady should not have gone to Casas Grandes. It was
foolish. She looked for her lover and then she too died."

"Walker was not her lover. It was only curiosity."

"And you too have curiosity, Mr Stanfield. A poet's curiosity, I think, to wonder about a little Indian servant girl after fifty-two years. I have asked some of the oldest of the
ancients. The people of the village now know something of
your history, but only because I have told them. But fifty-two
years! That is beyond their comprehension. They stare at me
when I ask. 'What do you mean? Did your gringo come before or after the sad time when the ashes covered the vil-

lage?' Even before and after is hard for them to understand. However, I will continue to ask."

He was finishing a second cup of coffee when Monica Swift arrived with Nicanor Díaz. She was wearing a bright lemon-yellow dress that made her look taller than usual, but also younger. Her eyes, which were gray-blue, shone with a mischievous gaiety. The poised Díaz seemed almost timid beside her. Stanfield surmised they had spent the night together, and that she had astonished him with her audacious talk. He imagined she would keep talking in the warmest moments of intimacy.

They discussed the departure of Papa Jack and his followers. Monica Swift was sorry for him, yet relieved to be rid of his ponderous and often drunken presence, sometimes buoyant and even euphoric, sometimes darkly brooding and vengeful.

"But it was he and the advertised boxing and the revived Boxing Academy that would have caught Brian's eye, if anything was to catch his eye. He would have come had he seen the posters. Unless, that is, he killed a man or insulted a general, and had to remain deep in hiding."

"If he is in hiding my men will find him," Nicanor Díaz said. "We will protect him against the generals. Even if he insults me I will protect him."

"I won't let him insult you! But what if he wants to box with you. A fifteen-round fight in the Gran Hotel Balneario?"

"Then I will box with him, if you so command me. You can teach me the boxing secrets as you have learned them from the champion and from your husband."

"Perhaps the champion will reconsider," Antonio said. "I assured him there would be matches without conditions, fought only to publicize the hotel. No gamblers from Tampico or Vera Cruz. I told him there could be fights with no decisions and therefore little betting. Or only exhibitions."

Monica Swift shook her head.

"No, I'm rather sure he won't come back. Because there

were the two mortal thrusts, not just one. I despise his masculine contempt for women. But I understand his black man's
scorn. It demands not only white women but white women
he thinks of as degraded. Why else would he marry a prostitute? He could have had others to delight in his famous sexual
prowess. No, he not only takes a white woman, he tramples
on the white man's conception of what to cherish. Well! I too
have scorn for the 'purity' that men pay a price for. So many
dollars or so many years marriage in exchange for virginity.
Virginity should be surgically destroyed at puberty! Then men
might see us as human beings."

Díaz and Antonio Vinalva were astonished by this tirade.
Stanfield too was embarrassed. He had long thought of his
gentle and slightly crazy companion of the *Allegheny Belle*
as a shadowy virginal being, ageless in her white floor-length
dress, as though she had never married. And now after so
many years the fourteen-year-old Marita was only an impish
child who followed him about, not the fierce animal who
had thrashed in his arms. He tried to imagine Monica Swift's
sexual being, her body naked and restless.

She went on in her manner of a woman giving a public
lecture.

"The pride of Papa Jack was a sickness of the spirit and
the nerves, sometimes hidden and twisted. The pride of Brian
Desmond was open and volcanic. Papa Jack needed to insult
the white race through his possession of white women. But
Brian Desmond insulted on a wider range. All the pretentious, certainly including the pretentious writers and artists.
All the established and complacent, all the moralists, all the
hypocrites. He insulted honestly and forthrightly, with his
body more than his tongue. Brian Desmond thought with his
body, he knocked down those he despised." Her rich voice
had risen to a chant. Now she might have been reading one
of her poems. But then she turned to Díaz, as though in
friendly teasing. "And you, Mr Bandit, what is the nature of
your pride?"

"I am proud that I am loved by simple people." He smiled. "They would not understand your thinking, and I also do not understand it."

"But you hate authority, don't you? You will not allow yourself to be commanded. That was Brian Desmond too. Let me tell you of the months when we nearly starved. That was the summer of 1918, in the capital, and people dying of the influenza and no one to listen to Brian's lectures on poetry and few to pay for boxing lessons and no one to buy my dresses or my lampshades. The Americans and English who could have understood the lectures were afraid to leave their houses. So we went out in the country, and Brian thought of the great mines near Guanajuato. There could be mines abandoned by the Spaniards and never worked again. Then an American said, 'Go to Durango, my man in Durango will take care of you.' I stayed in town while Brian went to look over the mine.

"Imagine a silver mine conceived by Dante and painted by Hieronymus Bosch, at the jungle base of a Mexican mountain, a silver mine swarmed over by fleas. At night they rubbed their bodies with aguardiente and gin to rid themselves of the fleas. The foreman of that mine thought to break Brian's pride. And for some days Brian submitted, because he wanted to learn about mining. They made him an *arriero* to bring up the rear of a mule pack train. Well, Pancho Villa had once been an *arriero* too, so he did not rebel at first. Then he was put in charge of the great bath cauldron for the Japanese miners, a wooden tank of water that must be kept hot or the Japanese would quit. One peso a day for common laborers and four pesos for the machine drill miners but only two pesos a day for Brian. For almost a week Brian hung on so he could learn what he could do on his own, working an abandoned mine. Discover what worth there might be in the tailings. Then he had had enough of subservience so he knocked down the foreman and tied his hands and slung him over his shoulder, kicking, and threw him into the tank of hot water.

The Japanese chattered and screamed like monkeys and clambered out of the tank while the foreman kicked and kicked to keep his head above the water.

"So then he came back to me in the city and we went to a place near Taxco where the working mines were so good that people didn't bother about the old abandoned mines of the Spaniards. It was Brian's idea that a strong man by himself could pick and scrabble in the tailings of an abandoned silver mine and pan in the mountain stream nearby and make enough money to keep us. But we nearly starved. So after that we worked with a small circus with Brian to box all comers and me to dance. But Brian still dreamed of a mine that would be all our own and no one to give him orders."

"It was a dream of many yanquis in the old times," Antonio Vinalva said. "They did not make their fortune in California but also they did not want to go back to their homes in the snow. So they stopped. I am told some made true fortunes on the Rio Usumacinta. Here on the Rio Corte there were two that are part of our history. One of these I find hard to believe. This began before I was born but I have met Indians who saw him not long ago. He floats down the Rio Corte on a good raft, and there is a chair on the raft, and he sits, smoking. He does not look to right or left. Once or twice a year he floats down the river, but no one ever sees him go back up."

"What a lovely story!" Monica Swift said.

"Perhaps it is only a story."

"There was another in the old times," Nicanor Díaz said. "He too came back disillusioned from California, though still a young man. And his dream was that of your Brian Desmond. He would find an old Spanish mine and he would live on what silver he found in the refuse while looking for a true vein. He expected to find a new vein, even a *veta madre,* a great mother vein. Yes, he was a young man with shining hopes, returning from California. He knew a little Spanish and he would joke with the girls and with the men in the cantina. Two, three times a year he came down to San Miguel or Rincón Antonio with some miserable fragments which he exchanged for food and other things he needed, maybe tools. He got old. He forgot his little Spanish and then he did not even speak English. He pointed to what he wanted."

"Yes," Antonio Vinalva said. "Once I saw this man in Rincón Antonio, when I was working on the railroad. His hair was long, his teeth were black, everyone laughed at his long hair and his teeth."

"And died?" Stanfield said.

Nicanor Díaz spread his hands out, then turned the palms down.

"Who knows? Perhaps he died in Casas Grandes. He must have died somewhere."

"Casas Grandes," Monica Swift said. "Why is everyone afraid of Casas Grandes?"

"For the Indians it is a place haunted by the dead," Antonio Vinalva said. "Those of the evil dead who have not been changed into animals."

"You sound as though you believe this!" She turned to Díaz. "And you, Mister Bandit, do you think it is inhabited by the evil dead?"

"It has been inhabited by the evil living, that much I know. It is a safe place for the hunted, unless they die from the plague. Some say the plague still lies under the stones or in a closed cave that when opened gives off the diseases that killed all the people of Casas Grandes. Except those that fled to Santa Rosalia and Santa Maria long ago."

"And that is how your lady friend died, Mr Stanfield? Do you think it was the plague from the stones turned over or from the opened caves?"

"I doubt it. I am only a high school teacher of science. But I am very doubtful about an old plague surviving so."

"Your friend," Díaz said. "Why, really, did she go to Casas Grandes?"

Stanfield told again the story of Rosellen following the

traces of William Walker, and the Frenchman in San Miguel who read Racine, and the two Zoque guides, father and son, who took her up the river and returned without her, though they brought back her belongings. And disappeared themselves.

"Is it true they brought back her money? Why then did they run away like thieves? If they killed her they would have kept the money. I will tell you what I think. I think it was shame because they did not bring her back. But it was a mistake to run away like thieves."

"Had you ever heard this story?" Stanfield asked Díaz. "This would have been long before you were born."

"Here in Santa Rosalia the ancients do not know this story," Antonio said. "It happened too long ago. These people have no memory. Only I know the history of the pueblo and the hotel."

"All the same I will ask," Díaz said. "There is very little in the whole Isthmus of Tehuantepec I cannot know, in the past or in the present. I know the secret places too. I have friends everywhere."

"And you, Nicanor—now I will call you Nicanor if you permit, not Mister Bandit—have you in your many hidings also hidden in Casas Grandes?"

"Only once. I do not want to go again."

"Why not?"

Nicanor Díaz looked away from her, frowning, as to say she was intruding too far on his good nature with her questions.

"At that time I was looking for the secret road to Chiapas. You know of it, Vinalva? El camino secreto de los Andes? It was prudent at that time to go with my men to a hacienda near San Cristobal."

"This road caused much suffering in Santa Rosalia and the death of my father. The generals Juan Andreu Almazán and Felix Díaz were looking for the camino secreto and they took the men of the village. My father did not return. So you too did not find the road?"

"We went for two terrible days beyond Casas Grandes, looking. Twice in the jungle we thought we had found it. We came upon stone pathways broad as a cart and elevated above the ground, and we knew these were made by men. Here men had been in the days of the conquistadors and before them Indians. This we knew. The second pathway, several hundred meters long, led us to the ruins of a small city. Smaller than Casas Grandes. We were astonished to see fruit trees gone wild but planted by men in rows and terraces. Some believed this was the work of buzquitas."

"What are they?" Monica Swift asked.

"The savage dwarfs. Some say they are Indians who would not submit to the conquistadors and who in solitude have returned to the times and customs of the oldest ancestors. Others say they are descendants of Spanish soldiers who deserted and went into the jungle. They wear no clothes, it is possible they no longer speak, they belong to no tribe, they are alone. Some say they are demons."

"There was a giant savage near Petapa," Antonio said. "He hung from the trees and his body was covered with hair."

"I do want to believe in your savages," Monica Swift said, "though perhaps not the one hanging from the tree. Has anyone seen one?"

"Dwarfs, yes. A number have seen a buzquita dwarf at the Rio Milagro. He was cracking snails with a rock, crouched over on the river bank. He did not at once run away. He looked up, still cracking a snail, and his face was the worn face of an old man. Then he got up without fear and walked off into the jungle. There was also, long ago, a weeping savage baby who suckled the tit of a woman from Santa Rosalia. This was also near the Rio Milagro. This woman had compassion for the abandoned naked baby but she was terrified because the baby would not let go, it had the teeth of an animal or savage."

"What happened?"

"They cut the woman free."

"With a machete? These women do not carry small knives."

"With a machete, yes."

"I will tell you of something more terrible than the savages," Nicanor Díaz said. "That is the dead zone of the jungle, also beyond Casas Grandes, where there is no animal life. There are no reptiles underfoot and no birds in the trees, no cries of birds."

"Nothing?"

"The insects. There are always the insects."

"It is true," Vinalva said. "It was at the time when they looked for the fallen airplane 'Flecha de Oro.' We saw a flaming in the sky, we had no idea what it was. Weeks later a party of Yanquis with Mexicans from Ixtepec came through Santa Rosalia to search for the airplane 'Flecha de Oro.' Two men from Santa Rosalia went with them. They came to this zone of the jungle in the afternoon of the second day. 'We were surrounded by a terrible silence,' they said, 'the silence of the trees was like the cloak of death.' Even the butterflies and the lizards were not there, there was no sound. Only the ants and other insects."

"Yes," Nicanor Díaz said. "Everyone has heard of the 'Flecha de Oro.'"

"What do you think, Mr Stanfield? You are a man of science."

Stanfield raised his hands in the Mexican way.

"Es una región solitaria y silenciosa y misteriosa. When I listen to your stories I want to think in Spanish. Did they find the plane?"

"No. From several hilltops far apart they saw a shining they believed to be metal from the plane. But they did not find it. Whatever is left of the plane is still there."

There was a long silence. They reflected on the silence of the jungle and the silence of the 'Flecha de Oro.'

"Well," Monica Swift said at last.

"Well?"

"I don't want to look for the 'Flecha de Oro' or the secret road. But I do want to go to Casas Grandes."

"That would be a mistake," Vinalva said.

"I must trust my intuitions. I think Brian Desmond has been there, if it is such a very good place for a fugitive to go, such a solitary place. Perhaps he is there even now."

"I too think it would be a mistake to go," Nicanor Díaz. "As for your husband I promise you I will ask my friends and I will show them his photograph. I have friends everywhere."

"Thank you. But I still want to go to Casas Grandes. Don't you, Mr Stanfield?"

"Yes."

And it was true. It was as though Casas Grandes were an obligation he had not met, and that still patiently awaited him.

It was on this day that he felt for the first time he was being watched by the natives, both in the hotel and in the village, and so knew Antonio had made the promised inquiries. The young Indian maid who cleaned his room started to back out when she found him writing at the table, and shook her head when he tried to make conversation, as though to say she understood not a word of Spanish. Yet they had exchanged greetings a number of times. She was sixteen, she had two brothers, her father went every day to the milpa. No she did not know how to swim but looked forward to the fiesta.

He stared at the new blank page of his Journal, acutely conscious that the young girl was working more rapidly than usual, yet was now and then looking over at him secretly. He wrote:

At breakfast I was aware with an old man's sadness of the unseen flow of energy between Monica and Díaz, though their hands did not touch. It is a chemistry of bodies that have known each other intimately, and which extends unaware to subtle tones of voice, though they be speaking of quite neutral things. So it was once with me, on the *Allegheny Belle*, or in the stifling "hotel" dormitory in Suchyl. No, could have been, not was. Was it truly an opportunity lost? Would she, twice my age, have accepted a serious caress? Or what if, disobeying orders or inventing new ones, I had gone with her to Casas Grandes? And my teasing little savage Marita, not much younger than this terrified maid cleaning my room? It is now my long life in Cambridge that seems quite gone and without reality. So near the end of my life I find myself ready to begin again. With Monica, who is so friendly yet such a woman of the world I have the shyness of one too young and the weakness of one too old. I am both twenty and seventy-two.

Nicanor Díaz left with a flourish before lunch, superb on horseback in his shiny charro costume, waving his white sombrero in a grand sweep and bending far over to kiss Monica Swift's hand. A youthful all-embracing smile for the others: for Stanfield and Vinalva, for the three shy prostitutes who had not won his affection, for the adoring employees of the hotel. His men made their horses wheel and prance, preparing for a romantic departure at full gallop. Nothing was missing but a guitar and soulful farewell song. Instead Díaz announced he would return in a few days, or would send a messenger with whatever he had learned.

Stanfield had lunch with Monica on the terrace, not far from the never-changing huddle of pilgrim Indians bent over their weaving. He was at once aware that the barefoot young waitress was looking at him in a new way. It was as though she did not want to meet his eyes yet felt compelled to. She took a rag from the pocket of her smock and wiped the table attentively, waiting for their order. He put his hand over her hand moving in circles on the table, gently, in what he thought of as a reassuring and fatherly way.

"Do you know who I am, chica?"

She stared.

"El maestro gringo."

"Algo mas?"

"Mande?"

"Do you know I have been here in Santa Rosalia before now?"

She looked past him, distressed.

"Yesterday."

"I was here before anyone," he said, picking his way carefully through the simplest Spanish words, "I was here in Santa Rosalia before you were born." With a sweep of the hand, one he might have learned from Díaz, he included the others on the terrace, the cluster of miserable Indians, the spring, the village. "Before you, before your mother and father, before anyone."

The young waitress appealed to Monica Swift with a scared look, crossed herself, tried to tear herself away, and at last did. Another waitress presently replaced her.

"You terrified her, Charles. The poor girl thinks you're a demon. A devil maybe. Who but a demon or devil was in Santa Rosalia before any of them were born?"

"I'll get Antonio to explain."

"Besides, it isn't true. Antonio likes to talk about the 'Council of the Ancients' and you're certainly not an ancient. Someone was here, and is here now, who watched you with fascination in that old time. In one of the huts there is an Ancient lying on his deathbed, no in his hammock. Do they die in their hammocks? Someone who has vivid and doubtless mythical memories of a young blond Yanqui God arriving in the village, you. You were blond, weren't you? And proposing single-handed to build the canal or perhaps throw up a dam on the river. And incidentally, though that wouldn't seem so important, running off with a girl of the village."

"Except I didn't run off with one. That was the engineers

who came two months later, if it was she they 'kidnapped.'"

"Who is now a housewife in Pasadena or maybe Chicago? Why don't you advertise in a newspaper?"

"You think I'm childish, wondering what happened to a girl I spent a few days with, long before even you were born?"

"No, I think you are romantic. And who am I to throw stones at a romantic? Except you have two lost loves and I only one."

After lunch they walked through the village, stopping first at the spring, where two young girls looked at them shyly, offering the cup with the hotel's name, letting the long chain trail to the ground. The girl wiped it with the hem of her skirt, and gently slid it into the warm water so as not to disturb the fish. In France there were carp hundreds of years old, in the pond of a royal palace, where they had learned to tug a bell for food, handing on this knowledge from generation to generation. Here, mysteriously, there were still conduits from some hidden spring or even from the Rio Corte. And here too, more mysterious still, the petroleum pit that defied time.

"You look like Marcel tasting his madeleine dipped in tea."

"Marcel?"

"A man in a wonderful novel by a writer who was also named Marcel. Marcel Proust."

"I guess I've heard of him."

"He too was a romantic. And Thomas Hardy. Surely you've read Hardy?"

"*The Return of the Native*. Only I'm not a native."

"He wrote a poem about a man who lost something in the course of a picnic. It had slipped into a small pond or perhaps a spring like this one, I think it was a silver drinking cup, and he could not find it. Then fifty years later he happened by that place, and there was the drinking cup in the water, shining in the reflected sunlight. Nothing had changed."

"Here in 1870 there was no cup with the hotel's name.

And horses and cows would come to drink, I loved to see that. More of the Indians of the village too."

They walked on to the ruined church with its two orange trees where men had been hanged, and also Maria Zarate the wife of Antonio's teacher, who had reverted in despair to eating earth. Just beyond it, and beyond the cantina where two men were arguing while a third sang drunkenly, the proprietress of the small village store was standing in its doorway.

"Buenos dias," he said. "Como está?"

She stared, at Monica not at him, and muttered something he could not hear, then turned into the darkness of the one-room store, which had only the door for light.

They went down a first row of huts. A few had thatched roofs and walls of adobe mixed with grass. Beyond them was a row of poorer huts whose wattled walls were vertical sticks. Several of them had been damaged by Friday night's torrential rain, and a number of men had remained home from the milpas to make repairs. They did not look up from their work. At the end of the village they reached the sloping field which contained the two cemeteries, one for the Zoques and one for the Ladinos. At its far end, and at the edge of a steep barranca, a small limestone chapel was all but hidden by a dense grove.

Just beneath it, and seeming to cling to the red earth of a hillside that had washed away, a number of men and women were silently at work, digging. Among them were bones that had been unearthed by the violent rain. These people too, though doubtless aware of the two mysterious gringos looking down, pretended not to notice them.

That night Charles had already turned off the light and was about to get in bed when he heard a timid knock, then saw the door slowly open. Evidently he had forgotten to lock it. A young Indian woman in a shapeless smock, rather than the uniform of a hotel maid or waitress, stood framed by the doorway. The dim light from the hall caught something shining in her black hair, possibly a comb, but her face remained obscure. He wanted to turn on the light, but this meant going very close to the woman, even touching her perhaps, and he did not want to frighten her away. "Buenas noches," he said, very quietly. He tiptoed to the bathroom and turned on the light there. The woman had not moved, she was still standing in the doorway, but now he saw that she was much older than he had thought. She had the smooth features of a young woman yet there was about her an aura of sadness or perhaps immense fatigue. He was sure she had heard of his earlier visit to the village, and was coming to him for help. He thought of the many troubled students, over his long years as a teacher, who had come to his office and been unable to say what they wanted.

"Can I help you? Puedo ayudarle?"

She did not move. The uneven whirring of the ceiling fan was the only sound, except for his own breathing. He could not hear hers. She seemed to become older as he watched.

"Qué quiere, señorita?" he asked gently, almost whispering. He took a few coins from his pocket. "Necesita dinero? Dinero para comer?"

She shook her head slowly, almost imperceptibly, as though she existed in a penumbra of deprivation where money and food were no longer relevant. So he decided he would, but more gently than with the morning's waitress, ask her if she knew him.

"Me conoce?"

She did not move for what seemed to him an interminable interval, then began to turn away.

"Perdone me," she whispered, as though contrite, and not merely asking him to excuse her.

There she was, a real person perhaps thirty years old, or at most forty, a woman of the village who had her own name. Yet he felt compelled to say the other name, as though only this could reach the source of her trouble.

"Marita?"

But she was already gone.

He dreamed he was awakened by a soft repeated knocking at the door. At once, as though in response to the knocks, the ceiling fan slowed and stopped. Moonlight filled half the room, and in the darker half by his bed he dressed quickly, with the intention of going for a solitary walk, even a walk into the jungle, and to follow whatever path offered itself until he reached the ruins of Casas Grandes.

He could not find his shoes, and understood, in the act of bending far over to grope for them, that he was not dreaming. He was awake, and the ceiling fan had indeed stopped. But still it seemed a good idea to take a night walk, to inspect the spring in the moonlight, even to venture a hundred feet or so into the jungle that began not far from the village.

A young woman in black sequined stockings and a rather worn dress of red silk watched him shyly from where she stood by a half-opened door a short distance down the hall. She looked at his odd American shoes, at his gray hairs, and managed a weary smile that was at once respectful and inviting. So it was doubtless she who had knocked, though this could hardly account for the ceiling fan. The thought of a passkey and of robbery came and went.

"Buenas noches," he said, and went on without stopping.

In the salon, which was almost dark, a single gambler in his undershirt faced a croupier who had unbuttoned his guayabera. They were separated by the length of the roulette carpet and wheel, and the croupier issued his commands in a voice that was almost inaudible. The man at the reception desk had fallen asleep over his dominos.

He went outside into the bright moonlit stillness. The unmoving Indians were there in their usual place, huddled in a circle just beyond the terrace and its tables. They were awake, but pretended not to notice him.

Flecks of mica shone in the circular stone rim of the spring, and the moonlit water was clear and blue, as though a light different from the moon's reflection came from the several conduits a few feet beneath the surface. Nothing had changed since his first visit, except for the stone rim, benches and the cup on a chain. Fish could still swim into the warm water of the spring and back out again, perhaps to reach at last the cold water of the Rio Corte. Tonight, however, the luminous fish were more visible than usual in the almost unmoving water, their lozenge scales and unwinking eyes reflecting both the moonlight that came from above and the blue light from below. They seemed to be swimming in a pattern, the small fish weaving in and out among the several larger ones with the delicate sureness of miniature dolphins, never breaking the rhythm of their circling, never colliding.

He cupped his hands in the warm water, feeling the silvery touch of a fish, and drank what was left in his hands. But the ballet of the luminous fish went on undisturbed. The water darkened, he seemed to hear breathing, and became aware of a dark presence at the other side of the spring, only five or six feet away. One of the horses had come to drink. But instead of drinking the horse watched him fixedly. He could not see the eyes, but he could tell from the position of the head that the horse was watching him. When he stood up the horse moved its head and a silvery eyeball shone. The other eye remained dark. Still the horse did not drink.

He passed the petroleum pit, where the oily scum glittered beneath layers of grass and mould, and approached the first dark huts of the village. It would be amusing to creep silently among them, as though he were a prowling thief, a game he liked to play as a child, tiptoeing past the neighbor's houses. Then the loudest sound was the rapid thumping of his heart. Tonight too the silence was extraordinary. Everyone was sleeping silently, no snores or coughs, not the creaking of a hammock's hinges as a restless sleeper turned.

At the fourth hut, however, the silhouette of a woman appeared in the doorway. He could not see her head, but knew where it was from a large necklace that caught the light, perhaps one of the neckpieces into which coins are woven. Could she possibly wear something as heavy as that at night, or was it intended as a signal to such a passerby as himself? But surely there were few passersby; the hotel people did not come to the village. He could not tell whether she was young or old, was not even sure that she was wearing a blouse, perhaps wore only the neckpiece. But he knew she was watching him. She in turn would have no way of knowing what he looked like, although his gray hairs would be visible in the moonlight. The girl he called 'Marita' would be sixty-four or -five. No doubt she was dead, or had long since moved away. He wanted only to greet this dark shadow politely.

"Buenas noches, señora," he said. "Como está?"

She did not move, but also she did not answer, so he continued on his way toward the first opaque fringe of trees and thick underbrush at the end of the village. He listened to the croaking of the frogs and the shrill clicking of the cicadas.

The path faintly visible in the moonlight disappeared with his first steps into deep darkness, and he almost at once tripped and fell. A spiny fallen branch, with a tip sharpened as by a knife, had pierced his trousers just below the left knee. Oddly he felt no pain, although he was aware of a thread of blood. The jungle around him fell silent and watchful, many eyes were doubtless watching him. He walked on, slowly but confidently, though he had no idea whether he was moving in a straight line. Even by day it was only too easy to lose one's bearings, with the position of the sun constantly changing as it pierced the thick forest ceiling. Yet he groped ahead, breathing easily as though he were again an adventurous twenty, feeling that this experience of dreamlike walking would result in whatever was destined to happen. And as though in acknowledgment the jungle voices resumed. A single frog croaked three times, like a dog suddenly alert, then many frogs joined, and a shrill rhythmic chorus of cicadas. It was now very dark, the moon had disappeared, and he saw com-

ing toward him tiny green lights which appeared to be floating in the still air as in a deep and unruffled sea. These were
the fairy beings the Mexicans called cocuyos, fireflies such as
he had almost never seen since his earlier visit. In dark space
they flashed on as though a spark had been struck from a
stone, briefly glowed and faded. Yet their green eyes still
circled him.

Watching them, pretending as in the old times that he
could catch and hold one, he stumbled over a fallen tree, and
found himself inches away from an unearthly blue glow as
from some small creature peering out at him from a break in
the tree. It came from mould on the fallen tree and would, if
he touched it, crumble in his fingers. The light would die, he
did not reach out. There were other insects about now, their
lights like stars or floating lamps, while what must have been
a very large nocturnal bird rushed by only a few feet above,
then came to a stop much higher with a wild fluttering. He
was overcome by delight. For now there were soft sounds
from all parts of the forest, punctuated by the whistling of
the kinkajous. The silvery tinkle of a bell was followed by a
pleasing rustling sound. The cicadas were quieter now, the
frogs less insistent. On the forest floor, unmenacing although
some were venomous, small reptiles scurried past him and
away, while the mosquitoes and insects that continued to bite
him left no itching or pain. The darkness filled with floating
lights and soft sounds appeared to bring a narcotic numbing
of the senses and of fear. He was breathing easily, moreover,
in spite of his exertions, and the need to break through underbrush and climb over fallen trees. If he were lost in the
woods, which was after all highly probable, he would nevertheless find his way back, if that was what was intended for
him.

As though in response to this thought the almost invisible path opened into a moonlit clearing, in the center of
which stood a small hut, obviously abandoned since there
was a gaping hole in the thatched roof and one bamboo wall

had fallen. He had the impression that he had been in this place before, if only in a dream, but was reluctant to inspect it. Across the clearing a narrow corridor like a man-made firebreak in the jungle revealed a rise of several hundred feet and what appeared to be another clearing at its top. The moonlight glared on its rocky surface. He decided to go up there. But now, although the way was much easier, he had more difficulty in breathing, and for the first time was acutely conscious of the many insect bites on his wrists and ankles.

He reached the top. In almost every direction the unbroken woods made a dark and curiously silent floor, rising to rounded mountains. He recognized with satisfaction El Ocotal, the highest of the mountains. Thus he, though standing on a rise above the jungle, was in another sense at the center of a vast bowl. But far to the north there was a break in the bowl, and at its center was a distinct area of white stone. Massive structures such as one might find in a ruined city cleared of jungle. The white buildings streaked by dark gashes seemed in this glaring moonlight to be five or six miles away. It could only be Casas Grandes, he supposed, yet the distance from Santa Rosalia to the unvisited Casas Grandes was said to be at least fifteen. And there was no instance that he knew of such a city, even one abandoned in the fairly recent past, escaping the invasion of the jungle.

It was an experience, vision or hallucination, it would perhaps be better to keep to himself.

The next morning he woke after a deep sleep to find himself covered with scratches, bruises and bites, and several cuts that had left his trousers caked with blood. But he was unaccountably happy, even though he at once wrote at the top of a new page in his Journal:

Did I come back here to die?

The Frenchman's Legacy

HE WAS SOON to learn all that he was ever likely to know of Rosellen Maurepas's fate.

Nicanor Díaz's network of informants was as efficient as promised. Before the week was out a message came to Vinalva that traces still existed of the small house where a reclusive Frenchman named Dupoint had lived, not far from San Miguel, and that in the village itself was an aged Zoque woman who had known him. This "Dona Serdan" was ridiculed in San Miguel for her public and uncalled-for speechmaking: lengthy and crazed attacks on the Church and all its officials. Yet her memory of events that occurred in her childhood, sixty and seventy years before, was remarkably clear, though she could not read or write. The terrified young priest who from time to time came to San Miguel declared she was possessed both of the native demons and the Christian devil. On the occasion of his visits she would bring a chair to the roadway in front of the church to await him.

Antonio offered to accompany Stanfield on this pious journey into the past, and to act as his interpreter. They went to San Miguel by the mid-morning hotel bus to Chivela, where it would pick up new gamblers. They would board the bus on its return trip to Santa Rosalia some six hours later, assuming there had been no mishaps.

199

On the morning journey the bus paused briefly at the foot of the Cerro Cuyulapa, a steep hill of white and gray limestone and slate. Here Antonio pointed to the dark mouth of a cave. Logs had been laid across the entrance to the height of five or six feet.

"The Gran Cueva de Cuyulapa. There are splendid arrows and knives of ice descending from the ceiling and rising also from the ground."

"Stalagmites and stalactites."

"Precisely. Here too was a tragic history of the Zoque people. I will tell you the story."

Many years ago a young woman of San Miguel, distressed because she could bear no children, was told by the curandero to go into the cave and spend one night there alone. This could perhaps cure her barrenness. The remedy was a desperate one, since the farthest recesses of the cave were inhabited by demons, as well as by the invisible dueño or owner of the cave, not to mention various little known reptiles and the hundreds of bats who flew out of the cave's mouth at sunset and returned to it in the morning. A dog of the village was seen entering the cave a few months before her, pursuing a spotted jungle cat, and had emerged several days later so emaciated that every bone showed. But the barren woman of San Miguel did not emerge, and they feared she was lost in the labyrinth of tunnels if not worse.

The husband and a number of her friends waited at the mouth of the cave, calling her name. They sent for musicians who went to the edge of the darkness to play. They played all day, and at night they built a fire to guide the lost woman to the open air. But to no avail. After that incident no native would enter the cave. Some believed there were dwarfs in the cave, old men with child's faces or children with the faces of old men. In some caves, perhaps also in this one, there lived an enchanted woman who was old and ugly by night, in the morning again young. Demon dwarf or enchanted woman, either could feast on the brains of ordinary human beings.

Some said this must have happened to the lost woman. A year or two later several men from a scientific academy in the capital explored the cave, and promised to look for the remains of the lost woman from San Miguel, but they found nothing, no human or other bones. How could her bones have vanished?

"Since then entrance to the cave is prohibited."

In San Miguel they rented mules, as no horses were available, and engaged their owner to guide them to the Frenchman's abandoned house. No one had occupied it since his suicide, which occurred long before the earliest memories of most of today's villagers, but not before the embittered memory of Dona Serdan, who had been widowed almost in childhood. All semblance of a road or path was gone and the Frenchman's "house" itself was not much larger than the usual thatched-roof hut. But fragments of two sturdy adobe walls remained, barely visible through the thick green wilderness of tall thorny grass and bamboo stalks sharp as knives. Hanging vines of a zapote tree clung in tentacles to the broken places in the walls. The house had once had a real roof of tile, but only broken fragments deep in caked mud had survived the earthquakes and the rains.

They climbed over the rubble and into what remained of the house, Vinalva using the guide's machete to cut a way through. The guide would not go inside. Insect life glowed in a fragment of rotten wood; an iguana hung from a ribbon of green vine, watching him. A small green snake slid into the rubble and out of sight. His companion Rosellen had once stood in this room! Here, as recorded in her diary, she had listened to the Frenchman's recitation of Racine and been offered a glass of brandy in a cup of fine cut glass, and also been offered the reliable Zoque guides Juan and Juanito. He wanted to believe that burrowing beneath the rubble of fallen rock and mossy earth would reveal some object, even a wine bottle or fragment of pottery of European design, to confirm that this was indeed the Frenchman's place, and that he could hold in his hands a fragment of the past.

They returned to San Miguel, and to the small house, a real town house this one, where Dona Serdan had worked for half a century as a servant of the rich man of the village, and where she had her own windowless room. Its only light came from the door giving onto a back yard of ducks and turkeys and pigs.

She had been forewarned of their coming, and was dressed in a yellowed huipil which had doubtless lain folded for years in the long wooden chest that stood next to her hammock, the chest almost as large as a child's coffin or small office safe. The huipil was wrapped around little more than bones. She offered them aguardiente of a pronounced medicinal flavor, which they drank from two wine glasses probably borrowed from the owner of the house.

It occurred to him that Marita, if she were alive, would be only a year or two younger than this withered and crazy woman.

She did indeed know the story of the Frenchman Dupoint, and of the Zoque guides Juan and Juanito, and of the rich woman, a gringo, whom they had unwisely conducted up the Rio Corte, even as far as Casas Grandes.

She told her story sitting in darkness so they could hardly make out the mad eyes shining in a face of darkest crinkled leather. They sat cross-legged at the door, with the sunlight of the sane real world behind them and warming their backs.

"I will translate everything," Antonio said. But in reality he simply summarized the wanderings of her rambling Zoque speech, silently turning these into Spanish words and thoughts and rhythms, then into his own English learned from the railroad workers of Rincón Antonio and refined by his years as hotel manager and historian of the hotel and village. Her voice would change when without warning she resumed her fulminations against the Church and its priests, and in particular one priest skillful in gouging the last peso of the poor, not to mention the many virgins of the village seduced thanks to his silken promises and terrible threats uttered in the confessional.

Antonio omitted these digressions, only notifying Stanfield with a wink or shrug.

Yes, she did indeed know the Frenchman, and the father Juan better, and the son Juanito best of the three. Of those still alive from the far-off past she alone in San Miguel had known well the father Juan and loved the son Juanito and knew the full story of their wanderings.

"They came to me in the night after returning without the young lady, the rich young lady who ruined their lives with her madness of going to forbidden places. They came to me for my counsel, to me still no more than a child, only sixteen, but knowing I would not betray them. They thought I was wise. 'What can we do, what can we say? Even the Frenchman will think we have sinned. He will think we killed her for her money or after taking our pleasure on her body. But here is the money, here is her book and her pencil and her bag of clothes. What will we do with these things? The Frenchman was good to us, he was a friend, but still he will call upon the Rurales to punish us. We will be hung from the great tree in the plaza if not worse.' So I told them, yes, they must fly, the priest if not the Frenchman will destroy them if they stay in San Miguel. The powerful gringos in their faroff places will learn of this lady who did not return and there will be no escaping them. So I told them to leave the money and the book and the pencil and the bag of clothes at the door of the Frenchman, the same night in secret, without knocking. Then the Frenchman can say they brought the money back, at least they did not kill her for her money, that much he can say. They must be gone from San Miguel before the day breaks. Then they embraced me and Juanito embraced me a second time and he said, '*Yoma, will I see you again?*' And we wept."

He asked Antonio to explain that we were consulting her about the fate of the gringo woman.

"I will tell you. But first I tell you of Juan and of Juanito his son, after they left the money and the book and the pencil and the bag at the door of the Frenchman's house. For many moons I knew nothing, the rains came and then the cold winds from the north and again the rains before they returned. They went from San Miguel in the direction of the sea. They walked the roads by night and went into the forest by day. First they ate what they could find and then they ate what they could steal, and whenever they saw the soldiers and the Rurales they would hide. Juan said to his son Juanito: 'We will go to the great cities, to Juchitán and Tehuantepec where no one will know us.' But they were afraid. In the big cities the secret doings of the gringos must be feared, the more so because one of their women was lost. In Juchitán there was a great fire set by soldiers from the north, from the city of Oaxaca, and the houses were in ashes. There were Indians walking in the streets lost and hungry. So for many months Juan and Juanito hid with criminals in the forbidden city of Guiengola in ruins and I do not know what they ate. There were great stones and dark cellars where in the old days the good Indians fought against the evil ones until their city was destroyed. How they lived I cannot say. Juanito said to me only, 'We had to live, we went out at night to the first houses of Mixtequilla, we took what we must have to live.' After that they went far north to work in mines underground and they were paid one real for a day's work in addition to which they were beaten.

"Here in San Miguel we suffered much. The Rurales did come, and a man in a suit with many gold buttons to ask questions, and after he left the Rurales came again and our whole village was punished. The evil priest helped them with information, the priest knows who has money and who has none. The Rurales demanded money for the state but we knew it was money to go into their own pockets. When there was no more money they were angry and they took two men as prisoners, Pedro and Lazaro. They did not come back.

"Then the Frenchman was sick with sadness and his shame and he took his life. He did not consult the priest, he too understood the evil of the priests. But before he died hanging from the tamarind tree in his garden he wrote a letter to the authorities. He said he knew Juan and Juanito were innocent of the gringo lady's death. It was he the Frenchman who was the cause of all the evil that fell on our village and for the shame that came to Juan and Juanito. So he died. In his letter to the authorities he left with me two of his treasures which I will show you. One is a secret book, the other is a stone face. I do not know what they mean, but they will be buried with me when I die."

"Ask her to show us the treasures," Stanfield said. "Maybe it will tell us something."

"She will not be interrupted, she has been going over this story her whole life, she must tell it in her own way. If we are fortunate she will get around at last to the deaths of Juan and Juanito since it is very clear to me that they died and maybe then she will tell us about your friend, how she died."

The woman continued.

"At last they went to the city of Ixtepec to ask to join the army of Remedio Toledo but that army had left to go somewhere else so they walked to the big city of Tehuantepec to join the army of the governor Porfirio Díaz but that army did not want them. Then they returned to San Miguel in the night, six days walking and hiding, because they were sick and did not know what to do and they thought to consult the Frenchman. They did not know the Frenchman had hung himself from the tamarind tree in his garden. In San Miguel they came to the end of their lives. They too hung from a tree. For two days and nights they hung naked in the plaza with the approval of the priest, Juan who I had never seen naked and Juanito not often. They had shame which can bring a sickness but they did not kill the lady. They had shame because they did not bring back the sick rich lady but they did not deserve to die."

How, Antonio asked, did she know that they were innocent of her death?

"You accuse me of lying? You think Juan and Juanito
lied to me? I know the truth of their story which I have lived
in my sleep and awake also and when I am cooking and sew-
ing and sweeping the house. I have forgotten nothing. This
gringo lady who is the cause of all our misfortunes was not
right in her head. Each day she wrote in her book, even on
the balsa on the Rio Corte, and by the fire they made at
night. She looked around her and she wrote down what she
saw in her book. She told the Frenchman she never got sick
of the fevers but this was not true. On the second day already, they were passing the rock that is well known, it is an
alligator turned to stone, they saw her face was burning and
without touching her they knew she was sick. They wanted
her to stop, they wanted to go with her to Santa Maria for
the curandero but she demanded they go on. What did she
think to find in the forbidden regions? Another gringo, the
Frenchman said, her lover who was hiding from the gringo
authorities, who was hiding in the stones of Casas Grandes.
I do not know what crimes this gringo had done, perhaps
like Juan and Juanito he was innocent. No matter, she wanted
to find her hidden lover. But she was ill, she who had never
been ill, she could not eat and then she was vomiting and
going into the trees for her sickness. Still she was writing in
her book, even as she lay sick on the raft first burning then
cold then burning. But she made them go on to Casas Grandes
where no man or woman should go, and still she wrote in
her book.

"She went alone into the ruins, she disappeared from their
sight while they waited on the raft. Once she came back in
the heat of the afternoon to sleep on the raft and to write one
more time in her book, and then she went back into the ruins
though they wanted to stop her. She was possessed of the
demons, she was walking to meet her death. So late in the
afternoon once more she walked across the stone plaza, a

flat place by the waters. And she was gone from their seeing. They waited. All night they waited on the raft, but kept a fire on shore to guide her. Nothing. Then the next morning they found their courage and they too went into the ruins. There were others who had died in that place. Long before our time many people had died in Casas Grandes from the terrible plague, it is well known. The sick were left on the stones where they died. No one would touch them. 'Did you see the bones of the dead?' I asked them. 'Is it true there are bones that not even the demons will take away?' And Juan said, 'Yes, we saw bones, we saw the staring skulls of the dead, although almost hidden in places by bushes that grow out of the stones. Two skulls.'

"They went on with courage. They went past the stone ruins where the old gods played ball, and in the stones was a terrible jaguar, and then they came to a stone roadway and to houses that were grown over by the living grasses and bushes and trees. It was here that they stopped. Ahead of them not far they saw high trees and a pyramid of the ancients and beside the trees was a waterfall. They heard the water and it spoke with the voices of the dead. There they stopped because near the waterfall they saw the spirits of the dead, playing, and with them was the lady. The water and the sunlight shone through their bodies. So then they knew it was time to give up their search and to return to their balsa and to the land of the living. But now they too are dead, Juan the father is dead and my Juanito is dead, they hung from the tree in the plaza, the father from one branch and my sayhaya Juanito from the other."

"What does *sayhaya* mean?"

"It means husband. Juanito was her husband."

In the silence the woman stared past them.

"Now I will show you what the Frenchman gave me that I will take to my grave. He told the authorities they were for me."

She stood up and went to a large candle on a table by her

hammock and lit it. She returned to the wooden chest that was large as a child's coffin or a small safe and opened it.

The two objects were carefully wrapped in tissue paper such as one would not expect to find in such a small town. One was the first volume of Victor Hugo's *Notre Dame de Paris* bound in dark red leather, with marbled pages and the title and author's name in gold.

The other was a small marble bust, some ten inches high, of Voltaire in old age.

The English Demon

"So at last you know, after fifty-two years waiting," Monica said. "And I have waited less than four. Brian disappeared in 1918."

They were having breakfast by the pool, Stanfield and Monica and Vinalva, the morning after the interview in San Miguel. The Indian maid was again at her desultory sweeping, while the bored monkey in the tamarind tree looked down on them contemplatively, scratching himself for want of anything better to do. A waitress hovered nearby.

"Yes, I know. Know at least that her two poor Zoque guides saw her 'among the dead playing.' But I still want to go to Casas Grandes. I want to see for myself where she died. See the ball court and the pyramid, and hear the waterfall, even if that grove of the women and their voices is gone. Surely the waterfall is still there, and of course the pyramid, unless earthquakes have changed everything."

"You too are a poet, Mr Stanfield," Vinalva said. "But you must put Casas Grandes out of mind. Even with Nicanor Díaz and his men to protect you it would not be safe."

"But I too want to go," Monica said, "though not for Brian Desmond. No, Brian Desmond is much too restless to stay more than a day in an abandoned town, unless he still fancies finding an unexhausted old mine. He needs people

209

around him to bedevil and insult."

"Bedevil?" Antonio Vinalva mulled over the word. "Bedevil and insult?"

"Yes, bedevil. Tease and torment people with his flaunting of their decencies. A newspaper called him 'el diablo inglés' after one of his fights and he rather liked that. So then he called himself 'el diablo inglés' in a flea-bitten circus near Zacatecas, not even a tent. He would take on all comers in boxing or wrestling, the opponent could take his choice, fifty pesos if he lasted a round. In one strong man act Brian really was a devil, shiny red suit with horns and a tail, wrestling with an old blind lion. The poor beast didn't know what was happening to him. Almost no teeth."

"For the Indians too the devil is red and has horns and a tail. But for some he lives in the body of an animal, most often a dog. For me..."

He stopped himself, looked at Monica intently, then at Stanfield. Monica was much amused.

"Yes, Mr Vinalva, please tell us. What is the devil for you?"

"I am thinking at this moment of the word 'demon.' Is not the English devil also a 'demon?' I believe there was an American boxer here in Mexico who called himself Arthur Demon."

Monica shook her head.

"Diablo is demon is Desmond? You are ingenious. But no one would ever take Brian Desmond for an American."

"Nevertheless I will look. I will get from my office my book called *Boxeo y Toreo*. There was a story in the newspaper of Tampico where the Americans of the oil companies work."

He returned with the book *Boxeo y Toreo* Stanfield had seen a few days before. It was several inches thick and the edges of many frayed clippings protruded. It fell open at an old copy of the *Police Gazette*, its pink pages faded and water-stained.

"A real *Police Gazette*!" Monica said, picking it up and turning its pages. "The last thing I thought to see here, unless maybe a copy of *Poetry*. And here are some nice bathing beauties."

Three women in baggy but clinging bathingsuits looked over their shoulders with inviting smiles. Their names, unlikely names, were underlined in ink.

"A visitor left this magazine in his room. I have read it with pleasure for the boxing and the crimes."

"But also for these ladies? You have marked their names! Confess, Mr Vinalva. Why have you marked their names?"

"They were beautiful women. I thought one or more might be invited to visit the hotel. However, this has nothing to do with the newspaper from Tampico I wanted to show you. I will find it."

The story was headlined *Arturo Demon es Arthur Dover*.

"I will translate the important moments."

Arthur Dover was an elusive English-speaking heavyweight, over one hundred kilos, who had fought twice in Vera Cruz in the last months of 1919. "Elusive" because he turned up only hours before the fights and disappeared immediately after them, waiting only for his purse. No manager or trainer, seconds supplied by the promoter. None of the usual interviews granted by American boxers, or the noisy post-fight celebrations with Yankee sailors and men from the oil rigs. A blurred photograph showed Dover on the canvas, his back to the camera, and holding the lowest rope with his right hand, the elbow crooked, as though about to pull himself up. A black boxer with trunks that reached almost to the knees was held back by the referee. The white man Arthur Dover had lost that fight, but won a decision in a rematch two weeks later.

"That picture could be anybody," Monica said sadly.

The story of the other elusive heavyweight, "Arturo Demon," was covered in more detail. He had fought twice in border towns in January of 1920, once in Matamoros, once

211

in Nuevo Laredo, across the river from Laredo, Texas. He was thought to be in trouble with the American authorities, since he was much averse to answering questions or talking to reporters at all. There were bars where Yankee drifters and draft dodgers and small-time fugitives felt at home, and the zona where all classes met, even visitors from Texas. But Arturo Demon frequented instead the pulquerias of the poor. A Matamoros sports writer found him drinking even with the pependores who live on garbage, and buying drinks for the swarming men he towered over at one hundred and ten kilos and almost two meters tall.

"I'm afraid that does sound like Brian. He had a consuming need to see for himself the lowest depths. He would have preferred your men living on garbage to the fat and complacent Americans who come across the river for a toss with a Mexican whore."

He left the boxing establishment, only an outdoor ring and a shed that was both dressing room and office, without collecting his purse. Perhaps in that crowd of cigar-smoking Yankees he saw someone who was after him. But the Matamoros reporter got the money to him, the winner's purse of one hundred and twenty-five dollars, after an hour spent combing the bars frequented by Americans. He was, the reporter said, an eccentric. A man of culture. He recited poems which the reporter did not understand. They became friends. A few days later they went to the *campo del dolor* to see *El niño fidencio* perform his marvelous cures.

"The camp of pain? The camp of the sorrowing?" Stanfield asked.

"It is well known," Antonio Vinalva said. "A camp of those sick and in pain. It is a city of tents on the road from Piedras Negras to Saltillo. The paralíticos, the lepers, the many with syphilis. Some sleep in tents, some sleep under the stars. The reporter said Demon like himself had come out of curiosity to see what miracles the young curer could perform. The reporter went back to Piedras Negras but the boxer

Arturo Demon stayed."

"That still could have been Brian. And I understand! I too believe there is a humanity among the wretched. Yes, a sanctity of suffering. So I can well imagine Brian in that *campo del dolor*, walking from tent to tent. But 1920! If it is he, then where was he all of 1919? Is there nothing else? There is something you are not telling me."

"Then his path crosses the path of our lamented friend Papa Jack, now in Mexicali. Somewhere in my book of *Boxeo y Toreo* is another story of Arturo Demon and our friend Papa Jack." He moved through the book of clippings with excessive slowness, running an index finger down each of the columns. "Yes, here we are, a column once a week on the English page, "The Manly Art," April, 1920. The writer gives always his personal opinions, he is allowed to say anything. It is in English, an American writer without doubt, you can read it for yourself:

See "Little Arthur" Papa Jack walking the dusty streets of Mexicali, a black prince with a straw hat, stepping along like a hoofer with a fistful of gold coins, American double eagles no less. Behind him the hangers on, including Tijuana matchmaker Cherokee Bob Jones and a slinky high stepper in a black dress and black legs to match. The Champion's white wife lagging behind. Sad. Champion sits down at a cafe table on the sidewalk and makes pronouncements. Dempsey has no style, just a brawler. Himself? Plans a finish fight in Baja, 20 rounds anyway, with Fred Fulton. A warmup. Then home across the border to settle his little differences with American law. Says how can he violate the Mann Act if the woman he was violating was his own wife? Chinese waiter bows so Jack tosses him a coin. The trainers and the sparring partners at the next table plus the big crazy Englishman Arthur Demon, wearing only boxing trunks that come to his knees, no shirt. Sometimes calls self "Arturo." Demon says Jack has "style and audacity and panache" (pronounced panash, you dope) "and should run for president of the U.S." Jack says his first fight in the U.S. will be with Gorgeous Georges, the Frenchman Carpentier. Admires Carpentier for coming to the U.S. with 75 pairs of shoes. Maybe he thought there weren't any trains in the U.S. so he had better have a change of shoes. How about rumor Arthur Demon knocked him down in a fight over in Europe back during the war when he was in exile? Says Demon couldn't knock him down if he had a brick in each hand. So I ask Demon. And he says we did have a fight in Barcelona. "Wasn't quite at my best, old chap. A little uneven."

Monica Swift was stunned. She reached for the clipping. A corner of the frayed page tore away.

"Yes, yes. It does sound like Brian. I think there is something else you are not telling me, Mr Vinalva."

"I thought it better. Yes, I have a picture. Papa Jack and Arturo Demon."

He opened the folder to the last page, with a large photograph of the two men fully clothed but in a fighting stance, without gloves. The enormous head and profile worthy of a Roman senator, the whites of the eyes as large as Papa Jack's, the hands even larger than the champion's. It is Brian Desmond.

In the background are half a dozen small Mexican men, laughing.

"Yes, of course it's Brian. It really is!"

"I felt I should prepare you for this discovery."

"But where is he?"

"This was April, 1920. Since then I know nothing at all."

But they were to hear of another diablo only days later, with the return of Nicanor Díaz, accompanied by a diminutive and wizened lawyer named Aurelio Esteban. Díaz's network of informants, which included a chief of police, had led him to Esteban's room in a hotel in Tehuantepec, where the lawyer was preparing to defend an American drifter charged with the theft of a radio.

He had made a career of defending impoverished Americans in trouble, soldiers and sailors especially, his experience going back to the Pershing punitive expedition of 1917 and even to the 1914 Navy occupation of Vera Cruz. He was one of a corps of lawyers in Puebla in 1920 defending the American consul, accused of complicity in his own kidnapping, and had arranged the ransom payment for two officials kidnapped by the rebel Pedro Zamora. These were glorious moments which won him respect even in the capital. The ambassador had shaken his hand. But his real vocation, going back to the American companionships and perquisites of 1914, was to intervene with angry policemen and judges, and visit in person the open sewer jails or outdoor compounds to interview the sailors who had demolished bars or bindlestiffs accused of petty theft. The poor and the rich alike, a lawyer with honor. He was almost bilingual and had even written poems in English.

Aurelio Esteban knew well the case of a boxer called *El diablo blanco* in Acapulco, who had been involved in a fracas in the Cafe Paraiso in the red zone, and had knocked down a policeman there. A man called Dinamita Lewis, truly a giant, sometimes affable, sometimes ferocious.

"In a good cause! He was defending an American victim! The policeman should have been helping."

He told his story at a table on the terrace, small as a child between Antonio and Nicanor Díaz, and facing Stanfield and Monica Swift. A bottle of the best bourbon, shrimps on a bed of ice. The lawyer's face, scarred on one side by burns, never looked directly at his interlocutor, but was twisted slightly to the left, as though to hide the corrugated skin. He had visited the hotel once before, knew Antonio and the bartender, and was honored to meet the teacher Stanfield and especially the poet Monica Swift.

"I too am a poet. I intend also to write the history of my

life. I have published a poem. Please let me show you."

He took a long poem entitled "Angelina perdida" from his wallet. It had been clipped from a newspaper and was indeed signed Aurelio Esteban. He stood up to read it aloud, then began to empty the wallet of its contents. Here were letters of commendation from the captain of the U.S. military police in Vera Cruz, a card entitling him to use the Navy commissary, the program of a Fourth of July celebration at the Mexico City embassy, studio photographs of smiling sailors in the company of Mexican female companions.

Nicanor Díaz stood up. He bent over to kiss Monica Swift's hand.

"I will leave you with this good friend of all foreign visitors. I did not hear the end of his story. But he has been recommended to me. He will tell you everything he knows."

"You can't stay?"

"Duty calls me to San Miguel. When I return, tomorrow perhaps, we will talk more of the expedition to Casas Grandes."

Aurelio Esteban settled back in his chair with the contented smile of the professional raconteur. There was plenty of time, the bottle was almost full.

"The boxer Lewis was called *diablo blanco*, not *diablo inglés*. Dinamita Lewis, the same as dynamite. The program said from San Francisco. I cannot myself affirm his nationality."

"But his accent?" Monica Swift said. "You know Americans. Surely you could tell from his voice."

"I never spoke with him, I saw him only in the ring, and only for a few minutes. But now I begin my story, which goes back six years to the unfortunate occupation of Vera Cruz in 1914. April, 1914. In this story are four principals: the capitalist Harry Cochran, owner of the yacht *Minerva*, the fugitive Skip Elmore, once a boyish bluejacket of Admiral Fletcher's fleet, myself the licenciado Aurelio Esteban, the boxer Dinamita Lewis. The fatality that commands our lives brings three to Vera Cruz in 1914, again in Acapulco in September, 1920. In Vera Cruz Elmore was a helpless child of seventeen. Every day I looked in the jails for lost Americans. I found the young Elmore among the murderers waiting execution, stripped of his uniform and his papers gone. His glorious white naked body was soiled with mud and with the excrement of his tormentors. I defended him without pay, I got him out of prison, I got him back to his ship.

"But first I will tell you about Harry Cochran, like me a youthful forty-five, but unlike me an evil and corrupt man of brute strength and boiling temper and the possessor of great fortunes. A henequén ranch in Yucatán, twenty thousand cattle in Chiapas, oil in Minatitlán and Tampico, many shares of the National Railway, a fine villa in Cuernevaca. This Cochran was rich but without prudence. He would dare in all his finery go from the Embassy or a dinner of state to the lowest of bordellos intended for the populace.

"In Vera Cruz I met Harry Cochran for the first time. I confronted him in the bar of the Hotel Diligencias and offered my services. No matter what business we did, it is not part of this story. It disgusted me to sit down with a man who had no soul. But he was an American citizen, it was not for me to judge. Nor for you or me to judge the secret intentions in Washington. The whole world knows of the affair of honor in Vera Cruz, with your fine ships the *Utah* and the *Chester* firing on the Naval Academy not to mention the Vera Cruz ice plant. In time your efficient authorities would so purify the historic squalor of Vera Cruz that even the vultures went elsewhere for their food! But not yet. In the street fighting of April 1914 the young sailor Skip Elmore became separated from his companions. He was struck down in the street but not shot. His uniform, his weapon, his papers, his money, everything was taken from him. He was left naked under the windows where patriots screamed "Viva Mexico!" He came to consciousness in the filthy prison among the murderers and rapists and with no papers to prove his identity. I got him out, I know the ropes, I worked without reward. And the businessman Harry Cochran? Harry Cochran sailed back to the States on the fine yacht *Minerva* in the honored company of the ambassador and his wife. A yacht formerly known as *Le Cléopâtre*. Once owned by the distinguished and famous Sarah Bernhardt, later by the U.S. Government. Don't ask me how Cochran got it."

"But what has all this to do with the diablo blanco who could be my husband? I'm sure he isn't, though, because Brian would knock down anyone who called him an American."

"Please be patient, dear lady. The accent? Poor Elmore heard Lewis speak very few words for reasons you will see. To understand what happened in Acapulco in 1920 you must know the fatality. So we go back to 1914, the young sailor Skip Elmore court-martialed for the crime of selling his uniform and weapon and for attempted desertion from the Navy. I wrote a long letter on his behalf, he is dismissed with dishonor. But in his youthful folly Skip Elmore enlisted in the U.S. army. He goes back to Mexico with the famous General Pershing's expedition, March of 1916. The great Cactus Jack, later to command in old Europe. The U.S. army goes across the border to find and destroy Pancho Villa. And I was there in Chihuahua to intervene, to help the soldiers in trouble. This time the doomed Elmore, unjustly accused of desertion from the navy, actually deserts from the army. Drunk and without leave, because of the brown eyes and bare shoulders of a village siren, in reality one of Villa's faithful lieutenants. The woman who seduced Elmore convinced him the intentions of the Americans were evil. He should join the idealistic forces of Villa. And again I found him in jail, not naked but with only underpants and a serape in shreds. It is one of the gratifying memories of my life. He recognized me, he shrieked my name, I held him in my arms as a father holds his son. I paid with my own money to get him out of that jail. I arranged for him to be safely hidden until the expedition had left Mexico. Then ungratefully he left me and went to

Guaymas."

"Do please get to Acapulco."

"We have reached the fatal closing of the circle, which left two of the four dead."

Charles Stanfield intervened.

"The four? You said Harry Cochran, Skip Elmore, yourself."

"The fourth is the man in question, the boxer Lewis, known as *el diablo blanco*. Understand that the closest I ever came to him was the second row of a small boxing establishment under the stars. And don't ask me how Skip Elmore found his way to Acapulco and on this Saturday night to the zone of the mariachis and the prostitutes. I was not there, but I have heard. In the harbor was the yacht *Minerva*, moored a few hundred yards offshore. Harry Cochran had not lost all his millions. And he loves the zonas, the cheap night places, the sweat and the stink, the mariachis. Here in the zona he is a king who can buy as many bodies as he pleases, on this night in Acapulco he buys two. He loves what you and I despise. The company of the wretched, the bottles smashed in anger. And so they come together: the millionaire, the wretched failure Skip Elmore now employed in the cleaning of shrimp, the American boxer Lewis, known as *el diablo blanco*."

"But what happened? For good heaven's sake please get on with it."

"In the Club Paraiso, then, an Acapulco Saturday night. I tell it to you as the doomed Elmore told it. A dance floor, a bar, and behind the bar the dark corridor of vice, six or eight rooms no more. The mariachis, the smoke, the laughter, the quarrels breaking out and suppressed. The two drunk police near the door, competing for the affection of a whore. The boxer Lewis is at one table with his Mexican companions. Aficionados of his boxing. Skip Elmore stands at the bar. The millionaire Harry Cochran has withdrawn to the corridor of the small rooms, accompanied by two of the whores.

I will be brief. One of the whores comes out onto the floor shrieking curses, and behind her comes the drunk and arrogant Cochran, laughing, in his undertrousers only, holding up one finger to display his scorn of the woman's body. There is an eruption of insults. At once the room is divided. The three outsiders, call them the three gringos, and the roomful of enraged Mexicans. One of the two policemen approaches to push Cochran back into the corridor, his hand is at his revolver. Then everyone is fighting. The unlucky Skip Elmore has struck one policeman, the giant boxer Lewis has knocked down the other. I was not there, I will not pretend to say all that happened. But the three gringos somehow escape: Cochran, the boxer Lewis, the doomed Skip Elmore. Harry Cochran's car and chauffeur are waiting, they get away, Elmore and Lewis with them. Otherwise they are in jail for years. At the dock is the motorboat that will take the three out to the yacht *Minerva*. You know Acapulco?"

Vinalva and Monica Swift nodded, Stanfield shook his head.

"Imagine a splendid bay shaped like a giant mushroom if you consider the land, or like a woman's womb if you consider the sea. On the land, filth. Even the street in front of your American consulate is but a country road of broken stones. On the land is the zona. In winter the streets are choked with excrement, in the summer they are seas of mud. But on the bay in the stillness of the night there is peace, and the soft lapping of waves. The sea is sacred and pure, the stars shine peacefully above. The motorboat of Harry Cochran's yacht waits by the customs house and the Fuerte de San Diego of the Spaniards and their galleons. The motorboat is guarded by two policemen, also drunk, who know nothing of the quarrels in the zona. So the three in safety go out to Harry Cochran's yacht the *Minerva*. On the way no one speaks. No doubt they relish in silence the great peace which comes after danger. In their whole lives the boxer Lewis and the deserter Elmore exchanged no more than twenty words.

"I will be brief. I will not describe the extraordinary elegance of the yacht *Minerva*, which the millionaire Cochran has furnished in the manner of a princely castle. Sporting prints of old England, horses leaping fences and fine dogs with birds in the mouth. The heads of animals looking out from the walls. An elephant tusk. Thick carpets underfoot. A chandelier that glitters as with diamonds. And here occurs the fatal insult, as told to me by the doomed sailor Elmore. Present are Cochran himself, already seated in a fine leather chair, with whiskey and soda at his side. A black man as big as the boxer Lewis, his steward, a man with the broken nose and monstrous swollen ear of a fighter. A young white woman in a bathing suit who called Cochran "Daddy." And still Harry Cochran said nothing by way of gratitude to the two men, Lewis and Elmore, who had fought for him in the Club Paraiso. Instead he addressed the steward.

"'Give these fellows fifty dollars each. Drop them off at Caleta Beach before dawn. I don't want them arrested.'

"Skip Elmore was contented enough to get fifty dollars, and a safe landing on shore. But not the giant Lewis.

"'I'm not sure I understand. You're not offering us a drink?'

"Harry Cochran was surprised. No doubt he was still fuming from his own insults suffered at the Club Paraiso.

"'Take them to the crew's mess and give them whatever they want.'

"The boxer Lewis was in a rage. Even Elmore himself was angry by now, though he never expected to sit down at the tables of the rich.

"'You don't invite us to join you?'

"There was a long silence. Cochran looked only at his black steward, not at the two men who had rescued him, not at the woman in the bathing suit. But she perhaps understood more than Cochran did. She backed away in the direction of the door to the deck.

"'You arrogant bastard,' Lewis said quietly. 'You filthy

son of a bitch.'

"The only sign Cochran made was with his finger, the finger that had given offence in the zona. He flicked it at the steward, as though to give a command, then examined it coolly, flexing it, as though debating whether to insult Lewis in the same manner as the whore.

"Both the woman in the bathing suit and the steward had left the room.

"'I'm afraid you don't know who you're talking to, son. You've just lost yourself fifty dollars. I think you better move out of here rather fast.'

"'It's you who don't know, Mr Cochran. Ever done any boxing?'

"The steward returned with a small revolver, which he handed to Cochran, who held it in his right hand. He slowly raised the left hand, with the second finger extended upward.

"'This is going up your ass, son. Way up. Then you're getting off the boat. Head first.'

"Even the doomed Elmore, who told me all this from his corner of a prison cell shared by the scum swept from the Calzado Costera and the zona, even Elmore could not say all that happened in the next moments. He himself was moving toward the arrogant Cochran, the black steward had raised his hands as though in surrender, Lewis was leaping forward. And Cochran fired, twice. Lewis fell. He was wounded but not dead.

"'Self-defense,' Cochran shrieked. 'You are both witnesses, he had a weapon in his pocket, he attacked me.'

"'Bullshit,' Elmore said.

"The extraordinary calm of Harry Cochran had returned, while the giant Lewis writhed and moaned at his feet. His blood moved slowly across the carpet as though a living thing.

"'You think it's bullshit, do you?'"

Monica Swift stood up. Stanfield also stood up.

"I'm afraid I can't stand any more of this. Will you please tell us the end and then go away? It is not Brian Desmond, this does not concern my husband."

Esteban waved his hands in apology.

"I could not tell you at once, it was necessary to prepare you."

"He is dead?"

Esteban nodded.

"The unfortunate and doomed Elmore threw Lewis overboard, though still he lived, with the black steward helping. He had no choice. The brute Cochran's revolver was at his neck. The blood was soaking them all. Through all this the woman in the bathingsuit, though terrified, was watching. She was made to watch. She knew who killed Lewis, who threw him overboard. She would be a witness, if Elmore's crime ever came to trial."

"And it did?" Vinalva asked.

"No. Before the trial could be called he hung himself in the jail." He held both hands out to Monica Swift, but she stepped back in disgust. "I do not believe this man was your husband. There is a misunderstanding. Lewis was an American. Dinamita Lewis."

"Of course it wasn't Brian. Even if wounded it would take more than two to throw Brian Desmond overboard," Monica Swift said. "It would take a dozen strong men. Besides, Brian was a strong swimmer. He would have swum to shore."

"Of course," the lawyer Esteban said. "Of course it was not your husband. If you will show me a photograph..."

But she knew better, she knew too well who Dinamita Lewis was. She stood up, she had the look of a woman who would never sit down again. Why on earth had Brian said he was from San Francisco?

"I'm afraid that won't be necessary," she said.

Antonio Vinalva turned to his book *Boxeo y Toreo* and found the picture of Desmond, alias Arturo Demon.

"Do you know this man?"

"That is Dinamita Lewis," Aurelio Esteban said.

223

In two dreams she hovered between sleep and waking and revisited desolate places where she had looked for him. He would find his way back to them. In the first dream he swam north and found his way, by shrimp boat, canoe, and at last by swimming again, weeks of solitary journeying while his wound healed, all the way to the silted harbor of San Blas where once the great galleons of the Spanish brought spices and jewels and took away bars of silver from the mines. There he would wade ashore. She had looked for him in the jail there, near the Custom House of the Spaniards, and afterward along the old Spanish road to Tepic and Ixtlan and beyond, first by "taxi" and rutted road crossing and recrossing the dry river bottom, at last on a horse along the old road now fit only for oxcart and mule train. He would find his way back, she would find him at last in the same miserable one-room jail on whose outside wall was painted the proud challenge, Sal Si Puedes, as to say "Get Out If You Can," she would pay the necessary bribe. She had not found him there, but this time she would.

In the other dream he swam steadily south, in spite of his wounds, all the way to Salina Cruz, more than a hundred miles. The salt water and the extraordinary strength of his constitution healed the wounds. The sharks left him alone. In the dark night he swam into the harbor of Salina Cruz, past the rusted derelict and the breakwater, past the desolate tankers resting high out of the water, some with riding lights, others with none. The harbor was an oily bowl of darkness in which, on a darker night, he might not have found his way ashore. His body was quickly dry, though he could not entirely rid himself of the oil and tar. For by then the pebbled and littered beach was underfoot. All was dark. But just then he would have seen the single light in a waterside hut, a small cantina, and would have heard the first voices and the drunken laughter. He entered the hut which had a sign with the single word Comidas. *At the sight of him the drunken men at the bar left hastily, left in fact without a word. Only the bartender remained, transfixed, staring at the new customer, who was naked, his body spattered with oil and sand. But there were no visible wounds, the wounds had healed. Above the bar was a poster advertising the Gran Hotel Balneario in Santa Rosalia, and the imminent appearance of the world champion Papa Jack in a three-round exhibition. Would it not be the most natural thing in the world to go there and join his old though arrogant companion? He sat down, he rested, the bartender served him without a word, then showed him where he could sleep. In the morning he would find his way, even before the railway workers were up, to the station. There on a siding was the elegant old dining car* Boca Chica. *In an hour it would be ready for the journey east and north, and on its way would pause at La Chivela. There he would get off, and by bus or if necessary on foot would find his way to the hotel.*

He is a strong swimmer.

O'Brien

THE TIME HAD COME to face O'Brien, and know whatever was to be known about Marita. He found Vinalva in his office, with one of the old guest books on his desk. He had been writing in it with a long quill pen and obviously regretted the interruption.

"I'll come another time," Stanfield said.

"Do sit down. You are saddened by our trip to San Miguel, we will have a glass of tequila."

"I want to see O'Brien. Can it really be the same O'Brien? Why would he have stayed here all this time? Fifty-two years."

"He has been here all my life, he is bound to us by his obsessions. The camino secreto, his dream of the old Spanish deserters and their treasure. Believe me, Mr Stanfield, there is no reason for you to see O'Brien. He is an old man. A liar, a degenerate, a drunkard. His mind is gone. He is an outcast scorned by the Zoques and the mestizos both. He lies on his bed and makes plans for new expeditions into the jungle, but he will never leave Santa Rosalia."

"I want to see him all the same. He may be the only person who would know what Marita I'm talking about. If she's in the village, O'Brien ought to know."

They found the old man lying on a cot that had been brought near the open door to catch the afternoon sun. The hut had an odor of a sickroom, of vomit, of fried onions. The face and bald head were almost black, protruding from urine-stained long johns that hung slackly as on a scatter of bones. The remains of a beard rested on his chest. The right eye was screwed tightly shut, the left eye closed as calmly as in sleep. But the creature was not sleeping. He began to breathe more heavily, wheezing. And growled out a question that was not English or Spanish. An Indian woman, watching in darkness, replied with a grunt.

"It is I Antonio Vinalva from the hotel."

"What do you want, Vinalva? Get out of here, go back to your hotel."

"I have brought you an old friend for a visit. A Mr Stanfield who knew you fifty-two years ago."

The right eye opened for a moment, scrutinized the two men in the doorway, and closed.

"Don't know him. Take him away."

"He is your friend, O'Brien," Vinalva said. "Now I will leave you with your old friend."

"I was in the village in eighteen-seventy," Stanfield said, "You found a hut for me, and a Zoque girl named Marita to take care of me. You told me about the camino secreto."

"That's a lie. I don't tell nobody, the camino is mine. Everything to be found along it. Nobody sees my map."

"Of course. I just want some information about the girl. A woman named Marita. You brought her to me. She would be around sixty-five."

The right eye again opened, closed, opened and closed again, an obscene winking that was horribly familiar.

"You want to buy a Zoque girl?" He laughed, wheezing. "How much will you pay?"

Stanfield's eyes had begun to adjust to the darkness. Now he could see the woman, who had not moved. Ageless, in a shapeless brown sack, her face an oily mask. She was crouched on the dirt floor, staring at nothing. Behind her a low table held an Atwater Kent radio and a phonograph. Over it hung the water bottle and a cutout portrait of Woodrow Wilson. There was a long steamer trunk nearby.

"Just information about the girl you brought me in eighteen-seventy. Marita. I'd like to know what happened to her. Did she marry and have children? Could she still be here?"

"I don't know you," O'Brien said. "I don't know any Marita."

"You found a hut for me, then you brought the girl. We talked about William Walker, you were one of his men. Do you remember now? You were with him in Baja, then in Nicaragua."

The skeleton stirred and began to scratch its groin. The skull tried to rise from the pillow.

"That devil cheated me out of my share of the loot. Written contract, I can show it to you. One percent of everything. So what do I come back with? Jungle fever and the clap." The winking began again. "So you want a girl and you know where to come. Ever had a Chink? Hula girl? I ain't got any."

"Try to remember, Mr O'Brien. Marita was fourteen, you brought her to me. Maybe she stayed in the village, maybe she went off with some Navy officers that came later that year. You might have fixed them up too."

"Fixed them up? That's right. I am indispensable." He whispered the word softly, remembering from the deep past. "Tell me what you will pay?"

"How much do you want?"

"Five dollars American."

"All right. The money is back in the hotel."

O'Brien held out a claw as to cement an agreement, Stanfield made himself touch it. The long black nails dug into his hand.

"Gentleman's agreement, I will trust you." He went up onto his elbow and addressed the crouching woman at length. The harsh Zoque dialect, with now and then a Spanish word interjected. The woman got up, mumbling, and left the cabin.

"She's gone now, never know what she understands. Tell

228

me what else you want."

"Just the information, Mr O'Brien. About the girl Marita. And I'd like to know about Casas Grandes. I'm sure you've been there."

"Be patient, mister. Plenty of Maritas one place or another. You want information? Listen to this. I've seen one of the conquistador's bastard spawn that went savage. I can prove it to you, I have souvenirs. I'm the only one been that far on the camino, way beyond Casas Grandes." He pointed to a low stool near the door. "Sit down where I can see you. I won't tell you everything."

A long rambling story ensued, which Stanfield found impossible to interrupt. Explorations of the upper river were interspersed with visits to the whores in Rincón Antonio and Minatitlán and trips to sell information and "souvenirs." A prolonged debauch in Vera Cruz, six days and nights of it, "one long toss in the hay, fuck of a lifetime. Niggers, sambos, mestizas, genuine Spanish, farmers' daughters, I had them all." He sold bits of information on the upper river and the camino secreto over many years, each time just enough to keep him in business. Only he had found a legendary causeway all but buried under jungle growth, a stone causeway eight feet wide. Just chanced on it following a stream that branched off the Rio Corte far above Casas Grandes. The causeway led to and across a wide lagoon and on the other side to a still discernible path, as though used not long before. At the end of the path was a small buried city, a pyramid showing above wild jungle growth.

"I fought off the bats and the reptiles with my bare hands. Three weeks I dug in and around the ruin before I found what I wanted."

"I want to hear about it, Mr O'Brien. Everything. I'll buy whatever you want to sell. But right now let's get back to the girl I asked you about. Try to remember. You met me at the edge of the village, you put me up for the night. We talked about William Walker. Then you found me a hut and you brought this girl to help me. Keep house, cook for me. Do you remember me now? Remember the girl?"

"You be quiet," O'Brien barked. He had collected surprising strength. "You have no patience, you sit there and listen. I'm just getting to the story."

It was on a subsequent journey O'Brien encountered a descendant of one of the Spanish deserters. The Indian had found him where he was making camp on a stretch of clean sand near the river, never mind what river. The man stepped out of the jungle and approached so quietly he was unaware of him until he saw his shadow.

"There he was, looked like any forest Indian with the shaved head, no trousers, just rags. Thin as a rail, red skin and all, an old one, carrying a net bag. Down he squatted and moistened his right hand. Touched the ground the old way, then touched his heart. You don't see that much any more, makes you feel like a king. He stood up very tall, flapping his arms, trying to speak. And speak he did, but he had to fight to get it out. 'Mi nombre es Vasco Portalo, mi nombre es Vasco Portalo.' Wasn't clear as that, his tongue got stuck, it was all the Spanish he knew. That's what the bastard had left of the old high and mighty Spaniard ancestor rampaging in the Isthmus. And I tell you there was still something of the high and mighty about him, showing through the savage. Shape of the head maybe, nasty proud look. Just a forest savage, 99% red man except that much come down to him over three hundred years. How to say 'Mi nombre es Vasco Portalo.' Had that from the rebel soldier what ran off into the forest. A deserter. So then this old Indian Vasco Portalo opens up his net with his stuff in it and right there on top is a metal box and inside an old greasy prayer book, all falling apart. Spanish prayer book, pages eaten away except some was left. So he opens up the book for me and there it is in big writing. 'Vasco Portalo, 22 augusto, 1536.' And a lot of ink chicken scratches I couldn't read."

"That's astonishing," Stanfield said, although he didn't

believe a word. "A wonderful story."

O'Brien fumbled under his pillow and came up with a long key.

"Think I'm a liar, do you? Take this key, open the trunk. Extra five dollars unless you want to buy. Then there's no charge for looking. Only don't touch the maps. They're not for sale."

There was nothing for it but to humor the old man. It was probably true, he had no memory of Marita or of his visit. The events of 1870 had been erased long ago from his mind floating among its fantasies.

Stanfield opened the trunk. Lying on top was a thick yellow newspaper with a scare headline from the Spanish-American war. CRUCIAL BATTLE STILL IN DOUBT. He folded the newspaper away, a brittle edge broke off into flakes. At one end of the trunk was the roll of forbidden maps, tied with strong twine. Beside it two small pamphlets, an 1852 guide to the California mining areas and a treatise on codes. A flintlock pistol. A framed portrait of Teddy Roosevelt. A rusted fold-in single blade razor. A stack of postcards bound by twine. A match box with three small Spanish coins black with age, the dates undecipherable. A thick envelope with red sealing wax broken through, and next it an ancient metal box eight or ten inches long.

"What's in the envelope?" he asked, turning to the bed. But O'Brien was out of bed and crawling toward him. He was on his feet, but still it was a crawling. He pushed Stanfield aside and handed him the envelope.

"You think I'm a liar? Take a look. No extra charge."

It was a printed letter from *Headquarters of the General,* with *Hap O'Brien, miner* written in a blank space left for the addressee. The document grandly described a patriotic mission *to free old Nicaragua from the evils of despotic slavery and bring freedom and progress to a land endowed with an ideal climate and brimming with riches to be developed by Yankee knowledge and enterprise.* The rest of the document was filled in by hand and gave details of enlistment and military organization. It promised the bearer *one hundredth of the net profit of said expedition, payable not later than six months after the pacification.* A second hand, a few inches below Walker's signature, noted in small ink letters, as though for his eyes only, *Lots of loot, Hap, enough senoritas for all.*

So that much of it was true, O'Brien had really been with William Walker in Nicaragua, more than sixty years before. He had known the Slipper Burke of Rosellen's journal, he had known the Dr Rush who was terrified to hear "Uncle Billy" might have survived and come to Mexico. Stanfield knew it would be useless to bring up Rosellen. And yet he felt compelled to. Had she at least lived on as a local myth?

"I was with a woman who was looking for Walker. Did you ever hear about an American woman who went up the Rio Corte with two Indians to look for him? She went all the way to Casas Grandes and died there. The Indians came back without her."

"That's all foolishness, Uncle Billy never got to Casas Grandes. I would know if he did. This is my territory, I know what goes on."

"I am sure you do, Mr O'Brien. You know everything. Did you ever hear of this woman?"

"When was all this foolishness?"

"The same year I met you. 1870."

"This is 1920 for Christ's sake."

"1922."

"Of course, 1922. I don't know anything about 1870. I don't know you. Go back to the hotel if you don't want to buy." O'Brien stepped up to the trunk and began to shuffle the objects around. He picked up the roll of maps and held one end up to his eye. He was leaning on Stanfield now, the odors of urine and stale skin were overpowering. "You're waiting for Marita, aren't you? Waiting for a toss in the hay." A sharp elbow nudged him in the ribs once, twice, three times. "Just you be patient. Like to see the maps while you're waiting? You can hold them but you can't look. Nobody sees the maps."

"I don't want to waste your time, Mr O'Brien. If you don't remember my visit in 1870 I might as well be on my way."

O'Brien stepped back as though struck.

"You don't want to buy!" It was like a cry of moral outrage. "You wake a sick man and you don't want to buy! At least take a good look at the souvenirs. No charge for a look if you buy. Ever see the old Spaniards' armor? Had a genuine Conquistador crossbow with the picture of the Virgin on it, could still see the blue and gold on it. Bought that one from the bastard Indian. 'Mi nombre es Vasco Portalo.' So I says 'Mi nombre es Hap O'Brien.' Bought the crossbow for a few cigars and a dollar watch and sold it to a tourist for a fifty. No flies on me." He picked up the roll of maps again, this time he held one end to Stanfield's eye. "Wouldn't you just like to look inside? Ten dollars for a peek, only five if you want to invest. But I keep the maps. I'll be going back to the camino in a week or two."

"I'm glad to hear it," Stanfield said. "What happened to the Indian's prayer book?"

"I took it from him. He had no right to it." He picked up the blackened metal box, let Stanfield weigh it in his hand. "My top souvenir. Only five dollars for a look."

Stanfield was intensely curious to see the prayer book. But the sick odor was making it difficult to breathe. He wanted to be back by the pool, watching the monkey and the iguana.

"All right," Stanfield said. "I'll pay you."

The book was folded in tarpaulin that O'Brien carefully peeled away.

A few fragments of black leather binding remained although the spine was gone. There were deep holes in the thick yellow and gray paper and the edges of the pages were brittle. O'Brien carefully opened the prayer book near the middle and slowly turned the pages back toward the front. Wisps of paper flaked off at his touch. And there it was, the flyleaf, with the royal coat of arms, an image of the Virgin, and the inscription that was still faintly blue after the more than three hundred years. *Vasco Portalo, 22 agosto, 1536.*

He felt suffocated, thinking of the almost four hundred years of descendants living in the jungle, deserters from the expedition of Pedro de Alvarado seeking a better route to the Southern Seas, only two or three deserters at first, exchanging rumors of gold in the mountains and sick of the long marches and the discipline, the weight of helmet and armor, even harquebus perhaps, setting out with only dirk and crossbow and a few coins and prayer books, waiting for the hated expedition to lose itself on its way to the Southern Seas. And themselves near starving soon, no gold found yet, sick from the jungle diet, their bowels water, and so beginning to reconsider. But afraid to come out and at last unable to, casually or perhaps forcefully mating the first time and then accepting the free wild life, gradually losing all sense of time, and near death passing on a few genes and a name and a prayer book and crossbow, handed on generation after generation as the white blood slowly thinned. The crossbow sold in 1922 for cigars and a dollar watch.

The book opening to the deep past had become involved with Stanfield's efforts to breathe. He pulled away from the creature clinging to his elbow, from the cold hand lying on him like the hand of the first dead Vasco Portalo.

"I feel sick. I have to get back to the hotel."

But O'Brien was following him to the door, holding him back, bony fingers clutching his elbow.

"You have no patience!" O'Brien screamed. "You ask me to get you a girl for only five dollars and now you walk out on me? I sent the old nanny to find one and now you try to walk out? Nobody does that to O'Brien."

"Let go of me," Stanfield said, pulling at the fingers. "I'll send five dollars to pay for the look at your 'souvenirs.' You misunderstood, I don't want a girl."

"You'll never get away with this, you son of a bitch, I'll report you to the Council of Ancients. You asked me five six times for a girl and my nanny gone to get you one. Five dollars for a toss in the hay."

He was in sight of the hotel when he saw O'Brien's wife approaching in the company of a limping young Indian in a gingham dress that all but reached her bare feet.

He wanted to go back to O'Brien and strangle him.

Casas Grandes

STANFIELD WAS DEEPLY DEPRESSED after the visit to O'Brien and briefly toyed with the idea of going home without having seen Casas Grandes. And Monica had been keeping to her room much of the time since the catastrophic interview with the lawyer Esteban. "I am writing poems," she said by way of explanation. But Stanfield knew she was lying. He was sure she spent the hot days on her bed staring at the ceiling and its turning fan, reliving the horror of Esteban's narrative. But on the third morning after his talk with O'Brien she appeared at the poolside where Stanfield was having breakfast, wearing a bright orange blouse.

"I am going to Casas Grandes," she said. "I hope you will go with me. I have the strongest conviction that Brian has been there. If I didn't go I would be ashamed all my life."

Stanfield now knew he had never really considered going home without seeing Casas Grandes. For all his fifty-two years of safe routine the buried claim of Casas Grandes had lain uneasily sleeping, now and then flickering to life. He never looked at a map of Mexico without his attention falling on the pinworm line of the Coatzacoalcos and the almost invisible thread of the Rio Corte. Even the best maps in the Harvard College Library didn't show Santa Rosalia and the ruins of Casas Grandes with *Unexplored Zone* beyond. But he could instantly see them on the crude wall map of his schoolroom, where for the whole Isthmus only Tehuantepec and Minatitlán were recorded. Not always but often he had the nagging feeling, lasting only seconds, of something left undone. The unvisited Casas Grandes had been quietly moving toward him down all the years of his adult life and at last was asserting its claim. He had had his great adventure at twenty, the two weeks away from his superiors, free to wander where he pleased. Now that seemed the only time he had been on his own, outside the narrow circle of a placid and safe existence. And even then... He had tried to get villagers to take him up the river, but had not tried hard enough.

"Of course I'll go with you."

Vinalva did his best to dissuade them, but in the end gave in.

"I respect your fidelity to your lost one, Mr Stanfield. But you, Mrs Desmond?"

"I am clairvoyant. Surely you with your share of Indian blood can respect that. I refuse to believe Brian Desmond is gone. But gone or not I have an overpowering sense he has been in Casas Grandes."

"In that case I too will go," Vinalva said. "You are the guests of the hotel. My guests. Moreover, none of the boatmen would go without me."

And so the trip took place that Monica Swift would remember all her life, and that sixty years later the young Tulane scholar Eloise Deslonde found records of. There were fragments of a Journal written by Stanfield during the trip, as in emulation of the lost Rosellen. And there were Vinalva's brief postmortem additions to the hotel history, in English and Spanish.

The expedition was delayed several days because Vinalva had much difficulty engaging two men to pole the balsa raft, strong men who could also cut away brush if the ruins of Casas Grandes were overgrown after all. Any trip up the Rio

Corte aroused ancient fears of dwarf savages and demons lurking in caves, not to mention the ghostly descendants of the Spanish. The spirits of the damned inhabit all ruins.

They were five crowded on the twelve-foot raft, three jointed logs of balsa wood, so light two men could lift it past snags and rapids. The casa near the stern was large enough for Stanfield and Monica to sit side by side, protected from the sun by the canopy of thick palm leaves secured by sturdy vines. Vinalva sat cross-legged at their feet. One of the boatmen was stationed at the front to push at the river bottom with his long pole and to guide the raft past protruding rocks. The other remained behind the casa to steer and do his share of the poling.

They made little progress until they crossed the river to quiet water near the far bank. They had gone less than an hour, but already farther than Stanfield on his earlier trip, when a small crisis occurred. The men stopped poling and pointed ahead to the landmark known as Piedra Labarta, a much feared jagged rock that resembled an alligator and protruded from a low cliff. The jaw was open, an eye of darker stone watched the oncoming raft, the clawed feet hung in space. The men kept looking back until with a bend of the river the alligator rock was out of sight.

The rapids were more frequent as the river narrowed, and limestone cliffs gave way to dense jungle coming down to the river's edge. Stanfield had an increasing sense that he had seen all this before, even the alligator rock, and the first rapids they had to wade past, and now the many strange sounds behind the jungle wall. Parrots chattered in trees that overhung the river. With every hour his waking dream became more real and he felt he was reliving in every detail Rosellen's journey. In the stretches of still water when the polers rested he could see the white bottom, and the darting fish delicate as threads of silk. Later in her journey Rosellen would see dark jasper rock and her own entrails swirling. When the rapids became more frequent she too had to wade, while the Indians carried the raft. She too had climbed over the hard gleaming trunks of fallen trees undecayed after centuries.

They carried their shoes when forced to wade, but put them on when they had to walk on soggy soil swarming with insect life. Slithering creatures the color of the mud looked out at them from holes that dissolved as the reptilian heads withdrew. He was filled with a quiet joy to think of so much life continuing unchanged over that long stretch of time. By midafternoon they had left the rapids behind and were moving in a clear and calm stream, hugging the shore, at times within arm's reach of tree branches and thick ferns. The blue wall of the forest was streaked with greenish yellow, and close at hand pink tree trunks peeled slivers of silky tissue. The staccato cry of a bird appeared to be following them. It had been following them for some time, the sound leaping from tree to tree.

The river narrowed again until they found themselves moving in a dark tunnel of green, hemmed in by towering zapote trees with intricately tangled vines and great ferns and branches thick with orchids. For a few moments as they slid past, with the polers working quietly, there were breaks in the jungle, and long avenues of blue narrowed to cones of darkness. They had lost the bird that was following them, but now the forest was alive with incessant rustlings and the shrill beating of cicadas' wings. A distant wail as of a small animal in the throes of dying was answered by a longer howling from another part of the forest. After another long silence the bird calls resumed. Drowsily in the dream landscape Stanfield felt himself closer than ever to the actual steaming afternoon Rosellen had experienced in that earlier time.

He thought again of the Edenic grove where naked women bathe all day, peacefully smoking their cigars and combing their long black hair. It had appeared many times in his waking dreams since reading of Morillot's discovery of the women, and it would perhaps be his good fortune to come upon such a grove on this journey. He would not do so in the company of Monica Swift and Antonio Vinalva, but alone, and not today but perhaps tomorrow.

They were within four or five miles of Casas Grandes and it was still daylight when they stopped to camp. A cold wind was rising, rain clouds were sweeping down from the mountains. A curve in the river left a small clear pool, and beside it a stretch of clean sand. The Indians built a fire, fixed poles for three hammocks, and set up a tent that would be ready if the rains came. The two Indians would keep the fire going through the night with one always on watch.

Stanfield was tired, with dull aches in both shoulders, although he had done nothing more strenuous than wade through cool water and pick his way along a rocky shore while the Indians carried the raft. He lay in his hammock, eyes half closed against the dying sunlight, while Vinalva and Monica tried their luck at fishing and caught several oddly-colored fish. The fish were spitted on long sticks for cooking and had a charcoal taste and flaky texture. The boatmen withdrew some distance from the fire to eat. They drank aguardiente from vessels shaped from bamboo, lifting the stalks high above their heads to drink.

After supper Monica Swift talked about her months traveling in Mexico with Desmond in 1918, away from the big cities where the influenza raged.

"He was such a dynamic presence, Brian, such a huge glorious man, not one photograph does him justice. Imagine if you will the small town circuses and shows, the dusty San Juans and San Patricios and San Lorenzos and the Santas this and Santas that, the out of the way parched places we hoped would bring a few pesos. And still influenza-free. See us there in the villages, Brian the strong man and I a gypsy with tambourine. What a lark when you think of it now! But not always a lark then. A little circus and its much mended tent, only three wagons. The diminutive Mexican clown, the one scrawny lion and one listless bear. Two or three monkeys in their little military costumes, scratching, holding out their beggars' cups. The threadbare mariachis, the magician always dropping things, the little dancer in pink tights with poorly mended holes. Brian among them in the center of the small ring, a giant among pygmies, his immense body still chalk white for all his bareback sunning. The fifty or so peasants staring open-mouthed at Brian's huge unsmiling Roman face, showing his muscles and swelling his chest, attacking the punching bag and the weights, calling for challengers to stay with him for one round. Such a life force! Such an energy even when he stood stock still. So how can I believe all that energy is gone?"

"It's not gone," Stanfield said. "It exists in you, your memory and your voice. Keep talking and he will always be alive."

"That's not enough! Not enough if he lives in a poem people will read after I die. I want his physical presence, not a disembodied spirit." She glared at him as in rage, then looked away. The life went out of her voice. "Even a spirit would be better than nothing."

"The dead return once," Antonio said quietly. "They are silent, but we can see them and they can make their wishes known. I know. A railroad worker named Prudencio Vargas returned to the hotel several months after he died. He had his favorite room for weekends and his special place at the bar, many times we played dominoes. That is where I found him late one afternoon, sitting at the end of the bar. He was there in the dusty twilight, but I could see he had not changed. There was no wasting of the flesh. He greeted me silently, a friendly wave of the hand. And I knew what he wanted. I knew he wanted to see the guest book in which his name was written. I went to get it, but when I came back he was gone. But still I could feel his presence at the bar. I left the book open to the page where his name is written."

"I believe you, of course I believe in ghosts. But I would

not want Brian to come to the hotel then disappear. Tell us, have you known any who have been given up for dead then been brought back to real conscious life? Pronounced dead after a shooting, no breath or heart beat, were dead for long minutes? I have met several, one in the St. Thomas Hospital in London. Do you know what they experienced while dead for those minutes? At first a great bliss and feeling of freedom. But then they saw their own body lying motionless beneath them. Those who have returned after death speak as though they had been at the height of the ceiling, looking down on their own bodies. And then it was a time of quiet sadness."

"A quiet sadness," Stanfield said. "That is what living people say who have seen their doubles. I have read of several instances. One night coming home late I had a premonition. I quite expected to find myself sitting in a chair, reading. I was disappointed not to."

"In the jungle everything is possible," Antonio said. "In the jungle there is no passing of time and there is no interruption between death and life. No one will ever know how many impossible things have happened in the zona inexplorada. Did I tell you of the jungle beyond Chimalapilla where there is always silence and no animal life? Only the plants and trees and the insects. How can that be explained?"

"I don't want it explained," Monica said.

The darkness fell quickly and the mosquitoes and rodadors attacked. A cold wind was blowing down from the mountains, there was a first spatter of rain. So they went into the tent and closed it behind them with a wall of mosquito netting. Outside the wind kept rising, there was a wild clamor in the trees.

The wind was cold but inside the tent was soon stifling. Their folding camp cots were only inches apart. Stanfield could not sleep, and was finding it more and more difficult to breathe. The pain in his left shoulder had increased, and there was a heaviness in his chest as though a foreign presence, something alive but not himself, had set up residence there. In Suchyl he had lain awake in the heat, excited by the sound of Rosellen's breathing so near, spinning fantasies of a life with her after their return to the United States. But now it was Monica not Rosellen beside him. She turned on her side, half asleep or asleep already, and her perfume still present under the heavy citronella seemed to come and go with her breathing. A heavy foot, Vinalva's, struck his. He felt closed in, though less by their bodies than by the heaviness in his chest.

The light rain stopped and he went outside. The two Indians stared into the fire hugging their knees, their heads not moving as he greeted them softly. One of them murmured in protest when he moved toward the forest wall. On his recent night walk he had gone very far and found his way back unerringly. It now seemed to him the abandoned hut in the clearing, rather than the distant vision of a white city, was the most meaningful part of that solitary excursion, and if he ventured into this other forest he would perhaps come upon another such hut. But he had gone only a few feet into the forest when a bamboo branch struck his face like a burning stick and an animal large as a cat moved under his foot and rushed off squealing. He turned quickly and went back to the tent.

They were awakened by wild wind and lightning and by one of the Indians screaming, "Buzquita! Buzquita!" The terrified man was crouched close to the fire while the other Indian stood over him. "Buzquita!" he cried again, pointing in the direction of the raft. A spatter of cold rain moved across the clearing and in a few seconds was gone. There was another lightning flash, and they could see the raft clearly. Far to the south thunder rolled toward them from the mountains.

Vinalva went over to the Indian and questioned him. The murmuring went on for a long time. One of the men had been dozing. In the first flashes of lightning the one on guard saw the white body and large head of a dwarf perhaps three feet high and very old, standing by the raft. It was looking back at him with an expression of hatred. In the murky darkness that followed the lightning a small shadow slowly moved away from the raft. But with a new flash of lightning the palenquero was terrified to see that the dwarf had not moved. It had a small beard and its teeth were the teeth of a cat. Worse still, the dwarf had raised a small hand and was beckoning. Then darkness again and into it the dwarf disappeared.

"I would love to see a savage dwarf," Monica said.

"It is not a thing to laugh about," Vinalva said. "There are savage dwarfs, everyone knows that. Some say the descendants of the Spanish deserters have been changed into dwarfs to pay for their ancestors' sins."

"You think they really saw something?"

"Why not? In all the unexplored areas of the world there are savage dwarfs, not only in the Isthmus of Tehuantepec. The dwarfs are always little old men. Sometimes the face is a baby's, more often wrinkled and old."

The boatmen spent the rest of the night by the mouth of the tent. The next morning was bright and clear, but the two men did not want to go on, the dwarf had been a warning. While Vinalva was trying to persuade them, and Monica Swift was bathing her legs in the river, Stanfield went over to a break in the thick growth of the forest wall. Whatever mark he might have left would be gone, yet he knew he had found the same place. He brushed aside a branch heavy with sticky leaves, and slid past stalks of bamboo and vines sharp as knives to enter the blue and green world of the jungle. An unseen bird directly above screamed and was answered from a distant tree. A woodpecker silenced by his coming went back to work nearby, and he caught a glimpse of its red head. Blue butterflies swirled and floated indecisively and hummingbirds hovered in a shimmering of green and gold. And now it was a spider monkey swinging quite low from tree to tree, carrying its swollen belly. He looked straight up to where the highest treetops appeared to be waving in sunlight, though all was cool shadow below, and he surmised that today at last he would see a toucan bird, shining with bright yellow and carmine and black.

The ground underfoot slowly gave away, and stepping back he looked down on the vast insect world he had disturbed. The mossy base of the nearest tree trunk was swarming with small creatures and their holes. There was a beehive at the foot of a spongy green and black trunk in which myriad insects had their homes, and under the trunk were holes left by larger creatures. Beetles with long feelers emerged in great number, and momentarily appeared to be inspecting him, then went about their work. In his delight he was not surprised, was even pleased when he felt the first sharp stings. All around him was life that would not die with him but would incessantly be renewed.

The men consented to go on after much grumbling, but said they would stop at the first sight of Casas Grandes. Back on the raft, and gliding easily in the bright morning, Stanfield wrote several entries in his journal, thinking of Rosellen writing in hers. It no longer seemed to him strange she could write so much while on the raft, although suffering from a fever. He again tried to imagine himself in her place, and see the river and the forest exactly as she had seen them, and even a particular heron standing on one delicate leg, the long neck and head unmoving, as though both enchanted heron and silently approaching raft existed outside time, a gliding motion within a stillness.

Shortly after noon they reached the tributary leading to Casas Grandes, and turning into it saw the white stone city immediately ahead. The boatmen at once stopped poling, and turned toward the north shore to beach the raft. The plaza, both marketplace and river port for traders in the old times, sloped gently all the way to the river from the first low tier of buildings. It was indeed surprisingly free of jungle growth, with only small strips and tufts of green in the crevices between immense monoliths of almost white stone. The first row of buildings, about two city blocks long, was also free of the usual wild growth. Behind the first buildings the small dead city rose in dazzling white. At each end of the plaza, however, were ruins almost covered by jungle growth. So it would be, he knew, behind the white ruins. Not far beyond would be the ball court and the pyramid near which her guides had seen Rosellen among the dead playing.

The Indians flatly refused to cross the stream, so they went on without them. Vinalva struggled with the pole at the front, Stanfield pushed from behind. He was out of breath after only a few yards, and a sharp pain in his left shoulder made him stop. But he felt oddly indifferent to these familiar reminders. Rosellen had not really expected to find any traces of the dead, and neither did he now. The blazing stone plaza and the solid white buildings were as she had seen them.

The stones of the plaza burned underfoot. He had a growing sense he was now almost alone in spite of Vinalva and Monica Swift only a few feet away, securing the raft. He might have been watching strangers at work and for a few moments felt quite outside his own body and its difficult breathing.

Vinalva broke the silence.

"There is nothing here, there is nobody. Even the insects have left this place."

Monica Swift pointed to a small lizard that was watching them from a crack between the stones. Its coloring was oddly mottled, and some accident had cut its tail which was now only a stub.

"At least there's a lizard. I am afraid there will also be snakes and bats."

The first house or cave they entered had only one room, not more than twelve feet square, and there was no sign or smell of life. But next to it was a house with two rooms. The front room was littered with the refuse of some fairly recent inhabitant. Corn husks, the pits of fruit crusted with dried and furry mould, even the dried peelings of oranges not yet turned to dust. A large smooth round stone was badly stained and caked as with dried mud or excrement. The back room was quite dark, and going near it they were struck with an intense smell of rotten food, burnt charcoal and human waste.

They went through two more houses that were empty except for fragments of glass and broken crockery. But in the last of the houses fronting the plaza they discovered, in the inner room, a mound of rubbish. The papers and tin boxes and cans had been swept into a corner.

The pictures and fancy lettering on the cans and bottles were still perfectly legible after dusting. They suggested the fastidious life of a miner or explorer who suffered from a variety of ailments.

"Look at this!" Monica Swift said. "I was fed this horrible stuff before I could talk. Only an Englishman would take it with him into the bush."

The can, *Vogeler's Curative Compound*, showed a woman in Grecian robe with arm upraised and one breast bared in front of a fountain. "The Greatest Blood Purifier and Strength Restorer known to pharmacy and medicine." There were tins for *Elliman's Universal Embrocation* and one which had once contained *Senier's Asthma Remedy*. A large tin of *Cadbury's Cocoa* contained advertisements carefully clipped from the thick pages of a magazine. One showed a man in white trousers and shirt and with a jaunty straw hat standing beside a languid woman holding opera glasses.

"I would say turn of the century or even earlier," Monica said. "Though Cadbury's is still with us."

"It could have been an Englishman from the railway company," Vinalva said. "I might have known this man in Rincón Antonio. Those men talked much of returning to their homes in England but also they talked much about gold and silver in the mountains."

They were interrupted by the sound of steps. A slight neat man with short reddish hair, not a Ladino or Indian, appeared at the door. His sandals were remarkably clean. He had a small revolver, but did not look like the kind of man to use one.

"Buenos dias," he said in a German accent. "Que tal, señores?"

At the sight of Monica Swift, still elegant after the day and a half, he put the revolver away. He bowed stiffly to her, then at the others, and looked to Vinalva for enlightenment. "Now I see two of you are perhaps Englishmen? You are inspecting with sympathetic curiosity the belongings of a man who brought the best of English culture with him. Or the worst?"

It was the slow, carefully measured speech of a shy man thinking in one language and speaking in another, and who is more attuned to writing than to speech.

"He was certainly a good hypochondriac," Monica Swift said. "I am sure you are right. A British hypochondriac, not a dyspeptic American."

"And you are certainly British, but with a suspicion of the Yankee accent. You might have stepped this moment from the pages of *Sketch* or the *London Illustrated*." He turned to Stanfield. "You, sir, are the leader of this small expedition? I think you look for the Indian artifacts not gold?"

"We are looking for the dead," Monica Swift said.

"Of course, gracious lady. What educated person does not?"

They introduced themselves, but the German did not give his name.

"I am a bit of an archeologist. An amateur archeologist by avocation. An amateur writer also. I am too much of an amateur to venture into the Uxmals and the Chichen Itzas and Palenques. Here even an amateur can make discoveries. I will, if you wish, show you one of my macabre discoveries."

"Are you alone here?" Monica Swift asked.

"Entirely."

"There have been rumors of an Englishman who disappeared, and who might have found his way here. A man named Brian Desmond."

"There are many disappeared Englishmen." He seemed to be measuring them, one after the other. "I myself could be called a disappeared German."

"This man was my husband."

She showed him a photograph of Desmond, looking uncomfortable in a three-piece suit.

The German shook his head.

"I am chagrined to disappoint you. There has been no one here, no one at all." He turned to Stanfield. "And you, sir, are perhaps a professor?"

"Just a retired high school teacher. But I was in Santa Rosalia fifty-two years ago, before I became a teacher. I too am looking for a lost person. One who died here in Casas Grandes."

"So you are a true romantic! I too am a romantic." He turned to Vinalva. "And you, señor, are the guide for these romantic visitors? I invite you to my humble pied-à-terre. I can offer you water that has been carefully boiled."

He had established himself in a protected place in the second tier of stone dwellings, which were reached by a stairway cut into solid rock. The room with its walls and roof of stone resembled a cave, but a cave cleaned with Germanic thoroughness. The small room had been divided into a sleeping space, with the hammock suspended from pegs driven into the walls, and another part of the room for work. Here he had constructed a rudimentary desk and chair. On the desk were a notebook and two eversharp pencils, a German-Spanish dictionary and a small photograph album with *Ich Liebe Dich* printed in golden scroll. An indentation in the wall provided shelf space for a skillet and small coffee pot, a spoon and fork, and a highly polished hunter's knife with many blades. An army pack and machete rested against the wall. Beside them were highly polished boots.

"How very neat you are!" Monica said. "You have brought a bit of Berlin into the most remote Mexico. How long have you been here?"

"Only two weeks. In three days more I will leave, unless there are more discoveries. You admire my housekeeping? I have order in the mind to combat the disorder and anarchy of the spirit."

"That is wonderfully German," she said. "The mind and the spirit! Well, I too have my masculine anarchies and rebellions. But also I design dresses and lampshades."

"To me you are extraordinarily European and feminine. And a most musical voice, the voice I think of an actress on the stage. Unbelievable!"

She glanced at Stanfield, much amused by her new conquest. She picked up the photograph album, looked at the German as to ask for permission.

"Since you haven't told us your name, perhaps this album will tell us something?"

"I have several names. My real parents are not known. Isn't that a good reason for me not to have a name? Call me Karl, if you wish, in honor of the martyr Karl Liebknecht."

"The communist killed with Rosa Luxemburg?"

"Precisely. You will see here their picture, or more exactly a picture of pictures."

It was a newspaper photograph showing a dozen men in mourning looking at two posters six or seven feet high, one of Liebknecht, the other of Rosa Luxemburg. The ceremony was apparently held in the middle of a snow-covered city plaza, and men were holding the posters upright. Liebknecht is dressed with the tie and high collar of a statesman, but Rosa Luxemburg is looking to one side with a motherly softness. In the bleak background a shadowy church loomed in the mist.

"I am one of these seven men on the left. But you will be unable to say which."

Monica Swift looked at the photograph, then at the man

beside her.

"This one, I think."

"Yes."

"So you are a political exile? My husband Brian Desmond chose exile rather than serve in the British army."

"All that is in another life. I have had several lives, of which amateur archeologist is the most recent but not I think the last." He showed more snapshots. "Here I am an actor in a traveling troupe in the provinces, age sixteen." It was a picture of a Hamlet heavily made up to look older and more haggard. "And here I am a printer producing writings on the regeneration of humanity." The young man in shirt-sleeves was leaning bewildered over a small antiquated press. "And here a zealous but incompetent sailor." A poor snapshot showed the sailor, still looking not more than twenty, standing beneath a lifeboat.

"And never a soldier? Like Brian Desmond you refused to serve."

He closed the book.

"These are all fictitious lives. No life is more fictitious than the one I am leading here. So now I will play the role of the recluse inviting intruders to tea. Unfortunately we will have to sit on the floor, except for you, gracious lady, who will of course preside over us in the chair."

Stanfield's not unpleasant dizziness had increased after some minutes of sitting cross-legged on the floor, and he welcomed the invitation to lie down in the hammock. Its gentle sway took him back to yesterday's nap on the raft during an hour of calm water, with the raft tied to the bank, and the jungle sounds of chattering and screaming birds diminished to a low humming. And perhaps even to some much earlier time when he had lain half awake on a steaming afternoon. He lay back with his eyes closed while the German talked and talked. The foreign voice picking its way through long sentences had an agreeable lulling effect. One moment he was talking of the intoxicating confusion of the Munich republic's first days of triumph, cut off from the outside world, not knowing how things stood in Hamburg or whether the repression in Berlin had failed. But in the next he was describing the destruction of Mayan villages in Tabasco, sometimes by bandits, sometimes by Liberals, although the revolution was supposed to be over. There was nothing he could do about it as a foreigner with no legal existence and an imperfect knowledge of Spanish and only a few words of the dialects. He could only observe. The Indian chicleros of the rubber plantations in Vera Cruz province were slaves, men who could with impunity be beaten to death. The woodcutters in Tabasco and Chiapas were also slaves, and even worse was the plight of those working on the river and always in danger of being crushed between the massive logs they were guiding. The curanderos and their herbs were of little use to a man with a crushed leg and certain to die of gangrene.

Listening, knowing he was lying in the hammock and aware of Monica and Vinalva close by, he nevertheless seemed to be back on the raft, with the frightened boatmen silent as they turned into the tributary and saw Casas Grandes. Yesterday? Or was it only this morning they had seen the white city for the first time, and the single lizard on the plaza.

Waking, he knew he had fallen asleep. Monica was looking down on him, her soft hand was on his forehead. The German too was looking at him appraisingly.

"And now if you desire I will show some of my discoveries. You, herr professor, may rest. You may sleep undisturbed by mosquitoes or rodadors or reptiles. Even the insects have deserted this place during the day."

But he went with them, for he felt quite rested, and the earlier dizziness was now only a feeling of lightness and even gaiety, as though his mind had freed itself from his poor weak body, and could advance independent of the weight on his chest and the throbbing pain, but still a slight pain, first in one shoulder then the other.

He was surprised to see that the sun was much lower in

the sky, and that the mottled lizard was waiting at the door. Perhaps the solitary lizard would feel curiosity, even some attraction to the only living beings beside itself, in this quite like the iguana on a white wall that had watched him in such a friendly fashion on some occasion that for the moment he could not remember.

"Please do not have high expectations," the German was saying. Hadn't he already said this several times? "I will show you a remarkable tomb but it is a tomb without precious jade or necklaces of gold. No god with serpent masks, no tigers with bird headdress or birds with the stripes of tigers. Two centuries of looters have preceded us."

The large cruciform tomb was an isolated one, at the foot of the overgrown fortress wall that enclosed the eastern end of the city like a curving hand. It was perhaps twice the length of the German's apartment, with the roof of the main chamber gone but the two arms of the cross still covered with slabs of unmarked stone. It would have been possible to enter by the roof, but a rough stairway fortunately remained. They descended into the tomb, which was almost bare of decoration. Only an uplifted hand, or claw with human fingers, remained of a bas relief that must have been larger than life size. A small section of mosaic, not more than a foot in length, had been left undisturbed. But in one arm of the cross some broken pottery remained, and what appeared to be skeletal remains. He did not want to inspect these more closely, although he had taken only delight, a fraternal delight so to speak, in the anonymous skeleton that hung from the ceiling of the high school classroom.

He was astonished to see that during their few minutes in the tomb another hour might have passed, with the sun much lower in the sky and swollen to a pale disk of musty orange. The German led them past the second tier of houses. There would be other tombs, though more difficult of access; there would be a cenotes, a well into which victims had been thrown. There would be the ball court and the pyramid.

He was tired, the pain in his left shoulder throbbed more frequently, and on the whole it seemed prudent not to go down into the next tomb. He decided to go ahead to the ball court and wait for them there. He climbed with some effort to the highest tier of houses, stumbling several times, bruising his knees and scraping the heel of the hand that broke his fall. The heat of the declining afternoon was intense, but beyond the last houses the tall trees and the unexplored ruins beckoned.

It would require all his strength to reach the ball court, and he decided to rest for a few minutes in the shade of a dim room in the highest row of stone dwellings. The floor was surprisingly clean, it must surely have been swept fairly recently. There was no reason not to lie down. It was entirely normal in this climate to take a brief siesta in the late afternoon as well as in the middle of the day. Half asleep, he turned on his right side, with his knees curled, and his bruised hand against his cheek. It was now apparent that behind this neatly swept room overlooking the city and plaza was a much darker room, perhaps inhabited. But no, it would be inhabited by the dead. In such a room there might well be the intact standing skeleton of a man, surely a man not a woman, standing because the skull was wedged solidly between rocks. An earthquake more than likely had dislodged the rocks.

He looked into the room, and was astonished to find that the skeleton was indeed there.

He went outside at once, and found the mottled lizard awaiting him. He had been in the house only minutes, he surmised, yet another hour must have passed. Soon the bats would be stirring in the secret niches and recesses of the houses.

He climbed a final stone stairway and looked down on the olive-green overgrown ruins. Some of the buildings were entirely covered, but in others fragments of white wall showed, and even bits of mosaic shining in shafts of sunlight. The mosaic changed into an acrobatic bird in a tree directly ahead. The bird, larger than a toucan but no less gaudy, was trying to catch his attention with its calls. It turned somersaults, dancing and swinging from branch to branch, then hung upside down as though waiting for his applause. The bird waited, interminably it seemed, then swung free as though shot and screaming lit on a mossy tree trunk that must have just fallen. Instantly a cloud of butterflies billowed out from the tree trunk, pink and purple and black and gold, all but indistinguishable from the shafts of sunlight now falling on a gorgeous toucan bird that had paused for rest on a nearby silk-cotton tree.

He heard for the first time the whirring of mosquitoes and saw that a rodador was resting quietly on the back of his hand, but harmless, its bite only the tiny prick of a pin. And he knew the ruins were truly alive all around him and he was sure there would be playful monkeys on the walls of the ball court. In another hour, or perhaps in minutes only, the declining sun would trace on the paving stones of the ball court, thanks to the genius of its builder, the shadowed outline of a jaguar.

But the ball court was already behind him, he had seen the shadow of the jaguar, he had seen the friendly monkeys, there had also been the shadow of a serpent not coiled but outstretched, and all this though no time had passed. He did not need to look at his watch, he knew no time had passed. Ahead the jungle was steaming, and he walked through and out of the last overgrown ruins, and was pleased to find that a path had been cut through the jungle, not a very thick jungle after all, as for the use of the inhabitants on their way to a small stream or perhaps to a fountain or well. For there was certainly water, he could hear the distant sounds of water as though falling through trees. He walked ahead with surprising ease although the pain in his shoulder had moved to his chest and he was breathing with some difficulty. The pain and the weight on his chest were being experienced as by someone else. All the small reptiles and insects and birds were watching him now, but in a friendly way. They were waiting for him without hostility.

He walked on slowly, surrounded by the stirrings of the jungle. An open space appeared, seemed even to be awaiting him, and he saw the small pyramid, not more than thirty feet high, and beyond it a waterfall. Beside the waterfall was a high grove of trees forming a semicircle of sunlit green. He was very tired now, and even sleepy, but sleepy in a most agreeable way. The soft sound of water falling blended with the sound of voices, and he knew there were people there, women apparently, gathered by the pond which the green trees encircled.

It could be they had come to wash clothes, but he rather thought they had come there only to pass the time of day, the whole long day in fact, smoking their black cigars, and talking quietly about whatever such women talk about, and combing their long hair.

He lay down among them.

The Indestructible Hotel: 1908-1982

THE WOODEN GRAN HOTEL BALNEARIO of 1890 lasted less than a year before succumbing to earthquake and flood. But its successor, the limestone hotel of 1908, the hotel of Antonio Vinalva, was built to survive torrential rains and jungle decay, and even long periods when its doors were closed, and the road from San Miguel was again only a mule path. The first long closing was from 1916 to 1922. The white ants and comején termites destroyed cheap chairs and tables, leaving them splintered shells and dust. But mahogany and cedar resisted them, and the staircases of guapaque wood were as durable as the trees lying undecayed in the Rio Corte after centuries. Seeds blown into the crevices of stone sprouted weeds, ferns, even whole trees, but the five stories of white stone stood firm. The hotel existed outside time, watched from above by a broken-winged old vulture peering down from the tallest palm, and by the itinerant Indians staring up at the third floor.

The first months after the Johnson fiasco and the death of Charles Stanfield were lonely and discouraging for Vinalva. The absentee owner did not answer his letters, secretaries hung up on him, the emptiness of the Salon Oaxaca was depressing. A single croupier waited at the bar for gamblers who did not come. But in 1924 a new owner, who found his health restored after only a week of the spring waters, encouraged Vinalva's old ambitions. He went to Mexico City to invite journalists, bullfighters, gamblers and actresses to inspect the hotel, all expenses paid. At thirty-one Vinalva stood as straight as an Indian warrior, and had an unmarred complexion of burnished copper. But his thin lips and long face were aristocratic, so too his courtly manners. He toured the nightclubs and haunted the stage doors of the Lírico and the Teatro Garibaldi and the Iris, sometimes in natty tuxedo, sometimes in a belted tweed jacket, hoping for autographs if not companions for a late supper and the night. Young chorus girls, succumbing, were surprised to find a bottle of tequila and two goblets of cut glass on the bedside table and the bed strewn with flowers. On the wall was an enlarged photograph of the Gran Hotel Balneario he had brought with him, also framed and autographed photographs of Papa Jack and Dolores del Rio. The Eugenia or Graciela or Mimi who had spent the night would herself be asked to autograph a sheet of hotel stationery and, if she chose, to add some affectionate comment. One who signed herself only "La Tigresa" scrawled that the night was not a disappointment. Stripes had been tattooed on her tawny thighs.

Vinalva took notes on the Hotel Genève's famous lobby and its elegant men's room. It was in the men's room of a seafood restaurant that he first grasped the importance of a richly decorated tiled urinal, a communal facility extending the full length of a wall, with a dozen customers standing side by side, smoking meditatively or in quiet conversation. There were glowing tiles of bullfighters standing erect at the moment of truth, conquistadors in full armor, volcanoes in eruption, Mayan warriors throwing sacrificial maidens into wells. In the next days he toured the men's rooms in a number of hotels, restaurants and nightclubs, but always returned to the House of Oysters. Here green mermaids with gold and silver scales and alabaster breasts writhed among spiny lobsters, squid with scaly tentacles, pinching crabs and giant clams opened wide as to provide those urinating with a target. Vinalva was determined to have a replica for Santa Rosalia and six months later one was installed. In its honor the men's room was given a romantic name, *Sobre las Ondas,* as to say *Above the Waves.*

The preoccupied owner gave little attention to his small investment in southern Mexico. But he gave Vinalva the modest credit he asked. Large advertisements appeared in *Excelsior,* with testimonials from doctors. And in the mid-1920's a few of the actresses did visit the hotel, some with rich gamblers in tow. Their names were recorded in the guest books, *Huéspedes,* and they were asked to comment on the hotel. Vinalva would then add a few flattering words, both in Spanish and in the English learned at thirteen from the railroad engineers. *Still superb as leading sensualista dancer in "Mujeres y Flores"* or *Hearts throb with the eternal innocence of Delia Magana* or *Undisputed sinuous queen of tango and fox trot.* He put asterisks and sometimes a number beside the names of the actresses who shared his bed during these visits, a secret code intended only for himself. And there were boxing matches once a month. The sagging ropes of the ring were again drawn taut for 20-round fights between provincial champions, and enthusiasts came from as far as Oaxaca and Mérida. But they usually left the next day.

In his windowless office under the turning fan, with his row of guest books and souvenirs, his father's Kensington Screw Steamer and harmonica, his photographs and testimonials, Vinalva freed himself from time and the burdens of reality. He could live in a past that was always present, one in which dead aviators might come out of the jungle to spend a night in the hotel, and even the immortal Emiliano Zapata. Dona Juana Cata, whose coat he had held while she beat all the men in billiards, was no more real than the sad Zapata, silent because he lived in the land of the dead. In the summer months when visitors were rare Vinalva spent hours in his office, drawing up lists of actresses and political dignitaries to invite for the fall season and the Christmas festivities. One afternoon on a whim he added the dancer Alicia Ortíz to the short list of guests who had arrived for a weekend. She had in fact declined to come but sent a glossy autographed photograph. Her bare right knee was raised so that an ample dark-stockinged thigh emerged from the silks and flounces, while the snowy left arm curled behind the head, holding a fluffy boa that trailed to the floor. She too, he was sure, could write in both English and Spanish. *Much appreciated the pool and the cocktail hour on the beautiful terrace,* Vinalva wrote, imitating the scrawl of her autograph. *Hope to return next year, Antonio.*

The imaginary visit gave him much pleasure. So from time to time he added more names of actresses who had declined to come, and even the names of busy statesmen and generals. There was no harm in this pastime, since the guest books would remain locked in his office. Seated at his desk, eyes half closed and lulled by the slowly turning fan, he dreamed of the great times past and great times still to come, but all happening now, the hotel restored to the glamor of 1922, when even a heavyweight champion of the world had been there.

And yet time did pass, though the face staring back from the mirror was always the same. In 1943 the hotel again had to shut its doors, and Vinalva joined the throngs of Mexican workers enlisted to work on railroads in the United States. The hotel remained closed for three years. The solitary guardian was shot less than a month after Vinalva left. His assassin took with him all the radios his one mule could carry. Later bandits made the hotel a warehouse for goods stolen from Isthmus freight trains. They would dump a share of the cargo at an appointed curve not far from Chivela, and from here mule trains carried the spoils to Santa Rosalia along the ancient *picadura de contrabandistas*. The scared villagers did not interfere. This went on for several months. On their final visit the bandits pried loose the great silver handles and ornaments from the front door. For weeks no one went inside. Then several of the village men did. The legendary urinal adjoining the bar beckoned. They found it cracked apart, with one long segment of crabs and lobsters on the floor, attached to the scaly tail of the mermaid. It was removed to the oldest villager's backyard.

By then the wilderness had reached the second floor, and the hotel swarmed with jungle life. Howler monkeys shared the elevator shafts with trapped birds and playful coatamundi, vampire bats roosted on the top floor. Even alligators, after the worst flood of the century, swam bemused among rats in the lobby and the Salon Oaxaca where Jack Johnson had appeared. Yet the hotel survived, ghostly, an enchanted place, as dreaded by the villagers as the caves and forests inhabited by demons, or the ruins where Stanfield died.

Antonio Vinalva, fifty but looking much younger, still lithe and seductively agreeable, settled into a room next to the railroad switching yards in El Paso. From its window he could see every passing train. The walls were soon covered with pinups and calendars of innocent young Hollywood chorus girls, their long thighs bare and lips parted in anticipation. Jack Johnson and Dolores del Rio were there too, and the enlarged photograph of the hotel. A motherly landlady brought coffee and sugared rolls to his room, and caressed him while he breakfasted. He was ready for the enduring romance that had eluded him in Santa Rosalia and Mexico City. And again he could experience, thirty-seven years after his apprenticeship with the American engineers, the romance of railroads. In the switching yard he rose to a position of authority, a mediator between the lone American army officer and the Mexican workers who knew no English. He entertained the young lieutenant with heroic tales of 1907 and the last months of work on the transisthmus railroad. Once again in El Paso he could listen to the crash of metal couplings and the hissing steam given off by old locomotives.

The exigencies of wartime brought ancient rolling stock
out of retirement, even open platform coaches from before
the turn of the century, each with two wooden stoves. There
were modern Pennsylvania sleeping cars and the yellow par-
lor cars of the Chicago, Milwaukee and St. Paul. Also sleeping cars of the Nacionales de Mexico Even, he was sure, the
very observation car from which Porfirio Díaz and his entourage had emerged at the station of Rincón Antonio in
January 1907. Here was another splendid observation car,
this one from the modern *Sunset Limited*, attached to an
ornate Mexican diner named *Boca Chica*, a beautiful car with
stained glass bordering its wide windows. He had a chance
to look inside. There were shiny cuspidors among the tables.
A large mirror at one end reflected writhing decorations of
silver and brass. Old fashioned luxury for the delectation of
Yankee generals, while the common soldiers ate canned meat
and chocolate bars from C-ration boxes. Vinalva was disturbed to see that his reflection in the mirror appeared to
recede as he watched, as though he were being swallowed by
the dark glass.

He frequented the cantinas and cabarets of Juárez, not
the sullen or noisy bars of El Paso where hostile military police stalked. He was present in the Cabaret Jalisco when his
wife-to-be Rosario Manteca, already "Miss Matamoros,"
competed for the larger honor of "La Bonita Chicana." His
attention was first caught by a jewel in her navel, then by the
furry tassels attached to her breasts. They were married two
weeks later. After the war, he assured her, they would live in
the manager's third floor suite of his luxury resort hotel. She
could dance in the hotel's glamorous nightclub. Or she could
retire to a quiet life basking beside the pool and tasting the
spring waters. For the present, however, she had no taste for
the quiet life, nor for Antonio's single room in a boarding-
house of railroad workers overlooking the switching yards.
She began to dance in less public nightclubs between the
tables, the streamer "La Bonita Chicana" now slung like a

cartridge belt over the left shoulder and between the breasts
left bare. Dancing, she gave the impression she was offering
herself to one spectator after another. Only not to the miserable Vinalva. She was irritated by his old-fashioned courtesy
and the way he held his fork. A laughing animal ferocity
possessed her, a need to torment him. At the end of her act
she fell back exhausted onto the first chair offered her, and
drank from the first glass she could put her hands on.

Two months after the marriage she left for Tijuana, and a
nightclub that was also a brothel, and he never saw her again.

The war ended; in 1946 he was fired, and his mind turned
again to saving his hotel. For $100,000, or perhaps much
less, a rich American could buy the handsomest hotel on the
Isthmus. Looking out on the El Paso railyards from his rented
room, his mind turned to Houston and its millionaires, one
millionaire in particular. The private observation car of the
magnate Cyrus Cranfield had been immobilized for several
hours, a few months before. Vinalva's eyes had met those of
Cranfield, who was standing on the back platform in a mood
of irritation. The millionaire, a man of about his own age,
removed his Stetson hat to wipe his forehead. He wanted to
light his cigar and had neither match nor lighter. Vinalva
stepped forward with a lighter and, leaping up, clung with
one hand to the brass railing of the observation platform
while with the other he produced a flame.

Cranfield must have been impressed by the quickness of
the neatly dressed but doubtless impoverished Mexican. He
reached into a pocket for change and, finding none, offered
his business card instead. *Cranfield Enterprises*, Cyrus
Cranfield, President, apparently had two whole floors of a
large Houston hotel. The rich man's friendly gesture, the card
offered as from one businessman to another, surely meant
that at least an underling of Cranfield Enterprises would listen to a serious proposal.

In fact he got to see Cranfield himself. Armed with the
card, wearing a new suit, and carrying a suitcase full of illus-

trative material, Vinalva talked his way past receptionists and secretaries. He put the suitcase on Cranfield's desk, opened it and took out an album of hotel photographs and clippings, including 1922 advertisements from the *New York Times*, testimonials from doctors on the fortifying spring and soothing petroleum baths, also several framed photographs of Papa Jack shaking hands with Jimmy Wilding, another of him with President Carranza. A hula dancer was caught removing her flowered brassiere, another dancer was entirely nude, many actresses had autographed their portraits. Cranfield, still wearing the Stetson hat, gazed uninterested at the turning pages until he saw a full-page colored photograph of the Gran Hotel Balneario bus in the lacquered sheen of 1921, together with one taken some ten years later, with a front fender bashed in.

"That looks like an old Stanley Steamer," Cranfield said.

"Exactly. You are obviously a man who knows cars."

"How much do you want for it?"

"Unfortunately it no longer runs. The boiler must be replaced."

"What year is it?"

"1921."

"I'll get it fixed. Send a boiler down. So what's your final price?"

Vinalva's mind revolved rapidly about this new turn of fortune.

"The hotel cannot be separated from the car. The present owner who is a rich man in Oaxaca insists on this condition of the sale. He too loves cars. It is a question of sentiment. The hotel must keep its bus."

Cranfield laughed. Not an unfriendly laugh.

"You mean I have to buy the hotel to get the car?"

"Precisely."

"And you, Mr Vinalva?"

"I am the resident manager."

Thus Cyrus Cranfield, who owned large resort hotels in

Havana, Miami, Nassau, Hot Springs, Honolulu came into possession of a thirty-room hotel in southern Mexico that he would not himself see until thirty-six years later, 1982, and whose first two floors were almost hidden by jungle growth. He approved without hesitation the proposals for rehabilitating the hotel. The road from San Miguel was reopened in October 1946 and the log bridges relaid. The cracked pool floor was resurfaced, the jungle growth was cut away, the monkeys and vampire bats were evicted. The stolen half of the tile urinal, for two years a feeding trough for pigs, was reattached to the half still fixed against the *Sobre las Ondas* wall. New brochures advertised health tours offering roulette and floor shows as well as the spring water and the petroleum pit. A photograph in the society pages of the Sunday Mexico City *Excelsior* showed Vinalva all in white, welcoming the chorus of a musical review that had had much success in Vera Cruz. The smiling dancers, they too in white, formed a semicircle beside the suave Vinalva, who had come to look more and more like the heroic and sophisticated Ramon Navarro, but an older Ramon Navarro, slick black hair and small but distinguished moustache.

This time the hotel remained open for twenty-two years, from 1946 to 1968. Cyrus Cranfield spoke from time to time of visiting it, and looked forward to driving the Stanley Steamer bus. But to take one of his own planes to Mérida, then a small rented one to Minatitlán, after that a slow train or car, at last the hotel bus, meant more time than he could afford away from his office and its battery of telephones. His ambitions had widened to include offshore enterprises, the buying and selling of fragile currencies, and a benevolent share in the political stability of several banana republics. Benevolent for the moment, anyway; later he might control the banks. Also, he wanted to make a movie, as it were with his left hand, in emulation of another Houstonian, Howard Hughes. Cranfield was acutely aware of Hughes's more spectacular successes. He aspired to do everything Hughes had done, though in a more modest way. In his daydreams he sometimes thought he *was* Hughes, living out the trajectory of another man's life.

He could give the Gran Hotel Balneario only a few minutes of his attention, every two or three months. The assistant to whom he delegated its budgetary problems rarely had time to talk to Vinalva by telephone, and many letters went unanswered. Once again Vinalva toured the capital in slightly outmoded evening clothes, making his appeals to the gamblers, actresses, bullfighters. But at sixty and sixty-five he was no longer able to snap his heels as briskly when kissing the actresses' hands. The discomforts of Santa Rosalia had become generally known. Fewer and fewer of the ailing came to the hotel on the all-inclusive health tours. They complained of the deteriorating train (often no diner after Santa Lucrecia, sometimes even the sleeping car diverted to the Mérida run) and the hot, jolting jungle ride on a bus that threatened to throw its passengers into the many streams interrupting the road from San Miguel. The bus broke down frequently, and even the backup Ford pickup truck had difficulty negotiating the old road. Its two tracks of scaly dried mud and limestone boulders disappeared under weeds and grass, and the road became impassable after every heavy rain.

The remittances and advice from Houston came less and less frequently, and in the mid-1960's simply ceased. It was possible, Vinalva suspected, that Cranfield (who by now was having multiple problems with the IRS) had simply forgotten his existence. At last there was only one customer. He believed the hotel's facilities were keeping him alive. He drank eight quarts of the spring water a day and every afternoon was carried to the petroleum pit. A number of the Indians of the village were always on hand as the skinny old man, naked and abnormally white, advanced step by step into the pit. A kind of harness fitted under the arms circled his chest where every rib was visible. Thus if he were to slip, or if he stepped into one of the areas that had no bottom, an attendant holding a rope attached to the harness could pull him to safety. After some months of solitude as the only diner in the Salon Oaxaca, the only one to breakfast by the now empty pool, the only one to play roulette with the concierge as crou-pier, it finally occurred to him that the hotel might be in dan-ger of closing for good. So one day he asked the manager if this was likely. "The hotel will close when you leave," Vinalva replied. The remark caused the old invalid much discomfort, since *when you leave* could mean *when you die*. "Very well, then, I will be ready to leave tomorrow."

It was during the closing of the hotel in 1968 that Vinalva himself disappeared. One day he was supervising carpenters and masons brought in from San Miguel to board windows and prepare the hotel for months or even years of invasion by jungle growth and rain. He worked without stopping through his last day, seeing to the storing on the third floor of the most valuable hotel property, and the weather-strip-ping of his own office. Here the precious guest books and documents on the hotel's history would be kept, also his framed photographs and souvenirs. The next morning he was gone. No one saw him go. The Council of Ancients debated their own responsibility toward the hotel. It had long been, though feared, a place of pilgrimage for Indians from afar, and a source of income for cook, waitresses, chambermaids. Since Vinalva was gone, did the village now own it? The Ancients were sure Vinalva was dead. He must have walked into the jungle after dark, ready to die, knowing that at sev-enty-five his time had come. Less than a week later the few pilgrims still camping in front of the hotel also left, as though it had lost its sacred character with the extinguishing of the last lights.

The rains began, the jungle returned. A few tentative thrusts of weeds and wild grass were followed by sturdy green shoots, tangling vines, wild flowers, ferns, small trees. Once again seeds blown into the cracks of stone became angry fists of green, then serpentine tendrils that climbed to the higher floors. The old vulture resumed his place high on the palm tree, sinister and watchful, undisturbed by the monkeys that forced their way back in. A first few vampire bats, then hundreds, found their way to inside rooms on the fifth floor. They emerged every evening at dusk. The villagers with their dread of abandoned places kept their distance. Who could say what spirits might inhabit the dark hotel? Within a month the rains had washed away most of the log bridges on the San Miguel road, and by September nothing was left but a trail for mules and men on foot. The village resumed its immemorial sleep.

In January another ragged group of pilgrim Indians appeared and camped near the terrace. And some time during the winter a large coffin found its way to the third floor. How it got there no one knew. The discovery occurred during one of the drunken debauches that accompany Zoque funerals. A former kitchen employee who had seen bottles emerge from a now padlocked closet ventured there with two companions. They broke down the door and found a large number of unlabeled bottles as well as cases of Mexican brandy. The three were very drunk by the time they staggered out the front door, each carrying two bottles. An apprehensive murmur ran through the crowd of drunk villagers. Was the theft to go unpunished? Several others ventured inside. They raced up to the second floor and gathered tables and chairs, some of which went into a bonfire on the hotel's terrace. Still there was no sign of wrath from the spirits that watch over abandoned places. At last two of the intruders went up to the third floor where Vinalva had lived. They were astonished to see a full-size wooden coffin in the exact center of an empty room. One of the men swore that the coffin, as he watched, changed to dark opaque glass. It gave off a blue glow as from a mirror reflecting a full moon. But there was no moon that night, only the flickering from the bonfire on the terrace. Could a corpse inside it give off such a blue light?

The men did not go into the room.

The next morning, while many of the mourners still lay in drunken sleep, and others discussed the existence of the coffin, whether wood or glass, an earthquake shook the village and left an admonitory crack in the masonry wall of the Oficina Municipal. The earthquake was a warning and a punishment. The Council of Ancients debated. To feed the uninvited Indian pilgrims camped in front of the hotel had been their responsibility for many years All the more now was their responsibility for the coffin placed there by no human hands. The coffin and its resting place should have a guardian. No one in Santa Rosalia was willing to serve, but a pious young woman of San Miguel named Josefina Amor was found. She would have a comfortable room next to the room with the coffin, and her only duty was to be there, and to keep the two rooms clean. The village would supply her with food "perpetually." Moreover, she could visit her family two days a month, and the family would receive good wages. So light again appeared at two third-floor windows, light from a kerosene lamp in one window, the light of candles in the other. In her bedroom other candles were kept lit before a small altar with a photograph of the Virgin. She had a battery radio.

Only she entered the hotel, and only she left it, once a month for the long ride by mule back to San Miguel. Months passed without intrusion. Then two young men talked of venturing to the third floor during her absence. No one had looked into the coffin except the caretaker Josefina Amor, and she would not say what she saw. But instead of going to the third floor they broke down the door to the padlocked manager's office. At first they saw only cobwebs. A kerosene lamp was burning on the desk, and seated behind it was a tall skeleton wrapped in a serape. The skeleton moved. The bony hand arrested in the act of turning the page of a book gave off a blue glow. The other hand resting on the desk still had some flesh, which was defaced by the large spots of old

men who are still alive. The terrified men fled. Both had seen
shining ribs protruding from a fold of the serape. But one
had seen only a skull with empty sockets for eyes, an ordinary face of the dead, while the other had seen eyes that
moved, glowing eyes though fixed in the skull, also a small
and neatly trimmed white beard. The first man had seen no
beard. But they agreed that the ghost, surely the ghost of
Antonio Vinalva, seemed sad rather than threatening, as
though resigned to their invasion of its privacy.

For several years after that no one except Josefina Amor
entered the hotel. The sturdy white building was disappearing from view. And Santa Rosalia itself, the lost village at the
end of a mule path, was all but forgotten.

Forgotten even by Cranfield, who owned the hotel but
had never seen it. In the thirty-six years since his whimsical
purchase he had made many millions and lost all but a few
of them. In the mounting curve of his trajectory he was welcomed by foreign ministers and even presidents in half a dozen
steaming capitals and in the boardrooms of multinationals
and offshore holding companies. *Cranfield Enterprises Guatemala* could hold its own with Del Monte in the production
of bananas, *Cranfield Enterprises Haiti* exported baseballs,
coffee, rum. He was entertained even by the jovial American
ambassadors told to distrust him. He found it prudent to live
abroad. But the time would come when he avoided the em-
bassies and consulates, and the teams of lawyers and Internal Revenue agents bent on his extradition. He had exchanged
pleasantries with the paranoid president in the white palace
in Port-au-Prince but ten years later was turned away at the
airport by officials who even made him stand in line with the
tourists while his private jet baked on the runway.

And paranoids do have real enemies. His life, as he moved
into his late sixties and seventies, came more and more to
resemble the lives of the heroic Howard Hughes and the up-
start Robert Vesco. He still wanted, in emulation of Hughes,
to write, direct and produce a motion picture. He also as-

pired to write an autobiography, if necessary with a ghost-writer to help him. But to accomplish these required peace and quiet. He needed protection from the process servers, lawyers, blackmailers, assassins; from revolutionaries and counterrevolutionaries demanding investments; from the CIA and the FBI and the IRS, not to mention the native Treasury police of several small countries. And from fraudulent doctors bent on destroying him. It seemed to him eerily significant that earthquakes followed within days his arrival in El Salvador, Nicaragua, Guatemala.

Like Hughes he preferred to live on the top floors of luxury hotels. It was important that the hotels have entrances on more than one street, as well as separate service entrances he could use in an emergency. This, more than their opulence, appealed to him in the Negresco, the Meurice, the Maria Isabel, the Copacabana Palace. A business manager, three secretaries, two American doctors traveled with him everywhere, as well as several servants. Eventually, now in his eighties, he settled in Mazatlán, on the west coast of Mexico. He was afraid of Acapulco, where Hughes had spent his last days. His several connecting rooms on the top floor of a hotel for tourists, one room an improvised hospital, looked out on a sinister deserted island. He could walk from his bed or wheelchair to the bathroom, leaving a trail of kleenex, but had a portable toilet at hand for emergencies. One of the two American doctors was always on duty, giving injections and advice, while the other enjoyed the pool and bars downstairs or a stroll on the beach.

A Mexican curandero named Pascualito nevertheless managed to reach him thanks to his friendship with a concierge whose wife he had saved from death by dysentery.

Cyrus Cranfield was immediately impressed by the seriousness of the curandero, who had slipped in while the doctor on duty slept. His soiled gray robe was free from all pretentiousness, his eyes glittered behind glasses with powerful lenses, his long hair had not been recently washed. He brushed

271

aside the patient's questions with an irritated wagging finger, and proceeded to examine his tongue, his eyes and ears and his several pulses. He squeezed the prostate, kneaded the bony arms, struck the matchstick legs beneath the knee until at last a leg responded. He opened his suitcase, which was kept together by a string, and took out a bottle which appeared to contain black living things.

"I am Pascualito," he said. "Your American doctors are killing you."

The curandero was given carte blanche two hours a day, then three, then four, while the American doctors fumed downstairs. The curandero convinced Cranfield it was necessary to move to a modest apartment hotel managed by Mexicans, away from the dangers of the tourist zone. The men in guayaberas pretending to be tourist guides, and the licenciados in suits and ties lurking in the lobbies of the luxury hotels, were undoubtedly secret agents. Even some of the pallid gringos in audacious sweat shirts could be secret agents. The curandero brought his friend the concierge to Cranfield to confirm these suspicions. So the move was made to a decaying but friendly hotel on the curving malecón not far from the beach where the fishermen every morning brought their catch. There was only one elevator, the air conditioning functioned only when struck by the palm of the hand. There was a tap for purified water on each floor. Papers, bottles and cigarette butts accumulated in the halls.

The outraged American doctors quit, but the secretaries stayed, dependent now on a single switchboard and a telephone operator who knew little English. Even with converter their electric typewriters would not work. They were unpacking their files of company reports and confirmation slips and transaction histories when an unthinking maid entered without knocking and rushed across the room to open the glass door to the balcony. A wild gust of wind sent many secret papers flying onto the curving malecón four stories below. IBM, Honeywell, Union Carbide, General Motors, records of the many thousands of shares bought and sold, all were caught in the wind and strewn along the beach of the fishermen.

"Even here you are not safe," the curandero said. "You must live in a hotel in a quiet place with a healthy climate and where they will leave us alone, you the dying man, I who am here to save you."

"I think I own a hotel somewhere in the south, Santa something..."

The curandero had already consulted the files, after intimidating the secretaries. And he knew about the famous spring.

"You own the Gran Hotel Balneario in Santa Rosalia on the Isthmus of Tehuantepec," he said. "A very healthy place."

1982

Eloise Deslonde

WHEN ELOISE DESLONDE, a graduate student in history, chose her subject, "Rosellen Maurepas as Liberated Woman in Antebellum and Postbellum New Orleans," she had never heard of Santa Rosalia or the Gran Hotel Balneario Chimalapa, or of Charles Stanfield for that matter. She knew only that her subject had lost a husband in the war, and had disappeared on a journey in search of the traces of William Walker. She had not yet read either Rosellen's journal or Stanfield's. She had read poems by Monica Swift in an American Lit survey, but was unaware that she had married an eccentric boxer-poet named Brian Desmond, and she had a dim sense that "Papa Jack" was the nickname given a disreputable black boxer, once heavyweight champion of the world, imprisoned because he had married a white woman. She had from time to time read stories about the Cyrus Cranfield who was said to own the jungle hotel. A shady entrepreneur involved in international finance. Or perhaps it was shady politics.

Certainly she had no idea she would, ten months after choosing her subject, find herself alone in the sixteen-section sleeping car *Progreso*, on the way to La Chivela, the small Mexican town where she would take the hotel bus to Santa Rosalia. Perhaps the very car that had transported Charles Stanfield sixty years before, and even, a few weeks before that, Papa Jack, Monica Swift and the young British sparring partner Jimmy Wilding. The very "aged English boxer" said to be still living in the Gran Hotel Balneario. A primary source if there ever was one.

In the hot morning, and lulled by the swaying of the train, Eloise closed her eyes and indulged a waking dream. Time enough for note-taking and further planning of her thesis when she had reached the jungle hotel.

At Tres Valles, where there was a long stop, a Mexican in dark glasses and a hairy brown suit got on and demanded that his section be made up, though it was only two o'clock of a steaming afternoon. This man, who carried a soiled briefcase, disappeared in the direction of the men's washroom. He returned a few minutes later, his face powdered and wearing only pyjama bottoms and an undershirt of faded orange over which hung a shiny silver cross. A heavy jasmine odor emanated from somewhere on his person and hung in the air of the unmoving and stifling car, although he had seated himself two sections away. A sweet odor yet also subtly narcotic, as though she had stepped into a friend's sick room or was herself about to undergo an operation.

Through the long night and the morning the train had given several premonitory jerks before getting underway after each stop. Could she have dozed? For this time she was not aware that the train had moved or that a porter had been at work. But the green curtains of one section were in place, ready for a sleeper, and they were no longer in the Tres Valles station. They were stopped in the middle of a field, with no houses in sight, yet once again the usual crowd of vendors still stared up hopefully at the two persons in the sleeping car, herself and the disreputable Mexican, and tapped at the dusty windows. They offered withered tortillas, pineapples with the tops removed, fruit drinks in plastic cartons, also stuffed iguanas and poor imitations of pre-Columbian masks.

The man of the pyjamas, undershirt and jasmine odor had risen from his place and was approaching. He bowed, hesitated only long enough to raise his eyebrows in friendly enquiry, and sat down facing her.

"Buenas tardes, señora. Señorita?"

"Buenas tardes, señor." She did not commit herself concerning her marital status.

The Mexican, who appeared to be in his forties, was staring at her in a peculiar, even inviting way. His dark brown eyes were friendly, quizzical and amused. Suddenly he produced, as though from the undershirt, a horrible cigar. He addressed her in English.

"You permit me?"

But he had already lit the cigar. He drew deeply on it, exhaled, coughed, then held out the cigar as though asking if she wanted one.

"I don't smoke."

The Mexican gave her a soiled card, *Roberto Rodriguez, E.n.p.n.,* and almost without delay took from inside the undershirt a small silver box with a perforated grille over perfumed cloth. He held it to his own nose, sniffed once, then held it directly under hers. Seaside odors, sweet and sickening, as of a street vendor's cart with slices of rotting pineapples on seaweed, oysters not freshly opened.

"Licenciado Roberto Rodriguez. At your service."

"Me llama Eloise Deslonde," she offered, hoping to practice her Spanish. "Estudiante de historia."

"Please speak English. My English is perfect. Let me see your tourist card."

He said this with such authority that she fished at once in her wallet for the card. Could this joker be one of the innumerable plainclothes police, even one of the dreaded Treasury police, always waiting to be bribed?

"*Turismo y recreo,*" he read. "Where are you going? No tourists ever take this train. If you are a tourist why do you not fly to Mérida and from there take a taxi to see the ruins of Uxmal and Chichen Itza? Or Palenque? Those are the best ruins. I don't think you are a tourist. Are you a young busi-

nesswoman interested in our Mexican oil? If so you should
go to Salina Cruz or Minatitlán."

"I'm going to Santa Rosalia. I'm getting off at Chivela
for the Gran Hotel Balneario."

The Mexican stared.

"Chivela! There is nothing at La Chivela!"

"That's where I get off the train. A hotel bus meets the
trains."

She decided to show the skeptical Mexican the rather worn
brochure. It had not been new when she got it, and since
then she had consulted it often. Which room had been Charles
Stanfield's, which Monica Swift's?

GRAN HOTEL BALNEARIO CHIMALAPA

JUNGLE ADVENTURE AND EXPLORATION

NIGHT CLUB CASINO FREE MOVIES

FAMOUS HOT SPRINGS FOR ARTERITIS ASTHMAS

45 ROUND FIGHTS

ALL MASSAGES INDIANS CURES AND HERBS

SALON DE BELLEZA

"AN EROTIC PARADISE!" TROPICS TRAVEL

Roberto Rodriguez read the brochure aloud, slowly and
without change of expression, yet pausing to reflect on a
number of significant words: "Jungle Adventure...Night
Club...Massages...Erotic Paradise. My English pronunciation
is perfect, no?"

He had, however, some difficulty with *Asthmas.*

"Azzmas," she said. "Keep your tongue inside the teeth. Not Athmas."

"Athmas," he said, smiling with pleasure.

"Besides it's a mistake in the ad. You just say Asthma, never Asthmas."

"What is the meaning of Erotic Paradise?"

Eloise laughed.

"I haven't the faintest idea."

Rodriguez inspected the brochure again, first the text, then the picture of the hotel with its tourists and its friendly Indians unspoiled by civilization.

"I do not think there are women with the bust exposed even in a hotel in the jungle. That is an error. In Mexico there are no nudist beaches."

"I was surprised myself."

"I never heard of this hotel. Why would you go there?"

She embarked on a lengthy yet decidely truncated explanation. She had barely begun the story of Rosellen's search for her General when the Mexican interrupted.

"Do you hope to meet young men at this hotel for social activity? For that purpose I advise you to go to the beaches of Cancún, Cozumel, Acapulco. Or Mazatlán, which is the least expensive. You have no money? Is that why you travel by train to this obscure hotel? You are an attractive young lady, the good hotels will give you a special rate. You can make friends at the best resorts. I Roberto Rodriguez can personally recommend you to the hotel managers. No reason to go to Santa Rosalia."

"People I want to write about were in Santa Rosalia sixty years ago."

"Sixty years ago! That's impossible. You have been misinformed."

She resumed her narrative, skipping many details, and had just reached the point where Charles Stanfield was himself about to reach Chivela when her Mexican interlocutor yawned. He looked at her appraisingly, put a hand on her right knee, gave the knee a quick squeeze.

"Now I use my lower berth. You too? It is the hour for the siesta."

Was he really venturing to suggest they share his lower berth? Only the one section had been made up. The faded green curtains extended over lower and upper berth from the floor almost to the stained-glass ventilation window, which was badly cracked.

"I'm not sleepy."

"Remember to get off at Medias Aguas. There is a separation of the train going to Mérida and the train going to La Chivela on its way to Tapachula."

But at Medias Aguas, where Roberto Rodriguez himself got off, a number of curious changes in equipment occurred. In the last hour she had been vastly disappointed by her first view of the Isthmus of Tehuantepec. The great forests of Rosellen and Charles Stanfield were gone. In their place were drab modern villages, though still a number of thatched roofs remained. From time to time a narrow paved highway came into view across flat fields from which all trees had been burned away. The highway was clogged with barrel trucks presumably carrying oil or gasoline. A heavy smell of oil hung in the hot air and the sky in the direction of Minatitlán was a sickly yellow pall.

A long train of oil cars was stopped next to their own train at Medias Aguas. Here it was necessary for passengers getting off to step between two disconnected oil cars. Between them she could see a disappointingly modern small station. Indian women vendors in billowing flowered dresses swarmed outside her window, chattering, and followed her when she stepped out onto the burning platform. She bought more bananas, postcards, a calendar with photographs of Mexican actors and actresses and a wicker basket for which she had no use.

An hour later her train left with herself the only occupant

of the sleeping car. Behind it were several boxcars and two second class passenger cars more than ever crowded with Mexicans. Ahead, seeming much too small for the purpose, a small steam locomotive pulled them, with an oversized coal car behind.

The tiled and thatched roofs of Medias Aguas slid backward toward Mexico City, New Orleans, her drab life as a graduate student. The engine labored, the wheels spinning, and she found herself breathing in time with its slow rhythmic puffing. After a few minutes it stopped. There was much whistling and a conductor raced past, waving a red flag. He looked very much like the porter who had made up Roberto Rodriguez's berth, but he was wearing a fancier uniform. The train began to move slowly backward, the wheels slipping as though the old locomotive were climbing a grade. The last miserable huts of Medias Aguas reappeared, yet they did not look quite the same. Apparently they had been switched onto a siding. In the darkening afternoon she saw that they were now backing toward another station, also with the name Medias Aguas, but a much older station. Evidently this was an area where the railroad left its abandoned stock. Old rusting engines and ancient passenger cars that had been converted to modest dwelling places. Laundry was strung from window to window. A woman was cooking by candlelight.

Here an old dining car was attached to their train, a car surely as old as Charles Stanfield's *Boca Chica*, the oldest car she had ever seen. She stepped out onto the platform to watch as the small engine pushed and pulled to place it between her sleeping car and the second class cars. The name of the car had quite faded from sight, and its yellow and green paint was scarcely visible. The wheels were badly rusted.

It was almost dark when the train, now pulled by a larger steam engine, left the second of the two Medias Aguas stations. Eloise, who had had nothing substantial to eat since breakfast, decided to go to the old dining car although she would be surprised if a real dinner were available.

283

It was empty. It had once been a beautiful diner, surely worthy of a "luxury train," with still lustrous inlaid mahogany and half moon Tiffany glass windows framed in brass. The furnishings were in remarkably good condition, although there where places where ivory inlay and perhaps even more precious metals had been gouged out. The brass spittoons had received loving care. The strangest feature of the old diner was an enormous mirror beyond the farthest tables, a mirror that extended from floor to ceiling fan, reflecting the whole car, though darkly: the dozen empty tables, the brass spittoons, and herself seated at the third table from the door by which she had entered. She could see herself clearly yet seemed to be very far away from the mirror, as though the car had been extended to three or four times its actual length.

She shuddered; she had read about that mirror. She was, she knew, the sole occupant of the diner *Boca Chica* in which Charles Stanfield had traveled, sixty years before.

The train slowed as the track curved into what seemed, at this dusky hour, to be thick jungle. A large leafy branch scratched the windows, one after the other, at last her own window. The large hanging lamp and the three white globes attached to the ceiling had been turned on, although their light was very faint.

There were voices from the kitchen, arguing in a language that was certainly not Spanish.

An old Indian woman appeared, muttering. She wiped her hands on a filthy apron as she limped toward her with a worn menu which turned out to be useless. There was no food, only drinks.

"Cerveza por favor."

She returned to her seat in the empty sleeping car. For a moment she considered lying down in the lower berth vacated by her departed Mexican acquaintance. But the train was scheduled to reach Chivela in less than two hours.

She fell asleep and dreamed.

It was getting light, a curious foggy light, when she was

awakened, not by the porter but by the old waitress of the dining car. She had brought coffee and a stale bun coated with sugar. It was morning.

"La Chivela," the waitress said, very loud, and repeated the station name several times. It was seven o'clock, the train was nearly ten hours late, many hours had been lost while she slept. Outside, a miserable landscape slid by, a brown plain studded with dead trees. The first huts of the town looked abandoned. Some of the thatched roofs had been damaged as by a hurricane and were open to the gray sky.

She stepped off the train, urged down the steps by the impatient porter, who had thrown her bags onto the dirt platform sprouting with weeds. The train began to move at once, as though eager to leave her at Chivela, where she was in fact the only passenger to descend. Some time during the night the old dining car had been removed, although the waitress remained. A second class car glided by with its many sleeping Mexicans, though a few faces were glued to the window, oddly white, like curious fish in an acquarium.

She was alone with the bleak and quiet sky. The small station, which must have been abandoned many years before, was planted with shredded posters advertising several brands of beer. In one direction was a broad and treeless plain across which the train was silently disappearing. In another was the town: a few miserable huts, a church that had seen better days, and a sprawling two-story stucco building, a decayed hacienda perhaps, or even a small convent.

A cold wind was blowing.

She had seldom felt so alone. But as though in response to this thought she saw an Indian running toward her down a road on which no vehicles could be seen, no cars or bicycles, not even a peasant cart. It was the station porter.

The porter was very small and very old. His left eye was shut tight as though sewn. There were stitch marks both above and below the absent eye. His thready headband had his name in bold letters: PEPE.

"Quiero yo el autobús para el Gran Hotel Balneario Chimalapa."

The porter shook his head. By gestures he indicated that the bus was undergoing repairs. Evidently a wheel had come off. The porter struck himself several times on the back of the knee, grimacing to suggest disaster.

"Un taxí?"

The old porter shook his ahead again. He picked up her bag and backpack, slinging them in a kind of net which he affixed by a thick strap to his forehead. He pointed to the white building and led her to it across a stubbled field, weaving with agility to avoid cow droppings. But there were no cows in sight.

He deposited her bags at the massive door of the dilapidated building and pulled a cord that hung from a second story balcony. The porter grinned, pointing to a faded brass plaque: GRAN HOTEL CASA BLANCA.

Casa Blanca? But this surely was the name of the marquesadas hacienda the naval surveyors used for headquarters in 1870 and that Stanfield revisited in 1922. Already then a decayed hotel. Casa Blanca was a common enough name in Mexico. Yet she knew where she was. First the old dining car, now the hotel.

"No, no," she said, although longing to go inside. "Gran Hotel en Santa Rosalia. No este hotel."

The porter shook his head decisively.

"You wait, lady."

They waited at least three or four minutes, then she pulled the cord herself, although the porter tried to stop her. The bell was louder than before and was followed at once by the clatter of several bolts being drawn, then a heavy key turning.

It was, she surmised, the manager himself, sleepy and unshaven. In a bathrobe suitable for a prince, or a bishop perhaps, but a bishop of an earlier era, with a richly brocaded belt and shiny tassels. He dismissed the porter with an angry tirade as soon as she had given the tip.

"Have the favor to wait in the salon. Please follow me. The criada will serve you breakfast."

The salon was a large and gloomy room that might once have been a convent refectory, although it now had both a billiard table and an antique radio apparently connected to a loudspeaker that hung from near the ceiling. There was one long dining table with two places set, also three small ones. On an otherwise bare wall three dark portraits of Spanish grandees looked down on her scornfully, as they had looked down on Charles Stanfield more than a hundred years before. One of them, like the porter Pepe, had lost an eye.

There was a rack of travel folders and advertisements for cheap tours, but no folder for the Gran Hotel Balneario Chimalapa.

No maid came to take her order for breakfast, but the manager himself reappeared after a long wait, freshly shaven and perfumed. He handed her his card. Manager of the hotel, estate director of what had once been the marquesadas. Land granted in perpetuity to the descendants of Cortés. But in modern times...

"I know," Eloise interrupted. "I know about the Casa Blanca."

Once again, as with Roberto Rodriguez, she embarked on the story of Rosellen and Charles Stanfield. He had been in this very room in 1870 and here received news of the disappearance, somewhere up the Rio Corte, of his friend Rosellen Maurepas. And had returned in 1922, when the Casa Blanca was already a hotel.

But the manager was not listening.

"The Rio Corte. It is impossible to navigate the Rio Corte. Only by bongo canoe or balsa raft."

"He went to Santa Rosalia by the hotel bus. I want to take the hotel bus too. Do you have the guest registers for the year 1922?"

The manager shrugged.

"They were destroyed long ago. Why do you go to Santa Rosalia? Stay here in my hotel. Chivela has the best climate on the Isthmus, therefore the best in Mexico. We have the cooling winds. In Santa Rosalia it steams."

She showed him the flier for the Gran Hotel Balneario. He held it between thumb and index finger, as though it might soil him.

"There have been no forty-five-round fights in Santa Rosalia for many years. Long ago as a youth I myself saw one of those fights. It was a disappointment, a knockout in the first round." He made a move as though to tear the flier in two, then returned it to her. "The only reason to go to Santa Rosalia is for the waters. Unless you have come to see the old millionaire cabrón. Excuse my language, dear lady."

"Mr Cranfield? Yes, that too."

"I am told Mr Cranfield sees no one. Also, the waters of Chivela are better."

Breakfast appeared: two eggs smothered in onions and tomatoes resting on a bed of tortilla. The manager looked down on this dish benevolently.

"But where is the hotel bus for Santa Rosalia? Is it true it has broken down?"

"It is the same every day. The bus waits for three hours, sometimes four. Then the driver goes home to San Miguel. The train is always late."

"Can I rent a car?"

"An amusing idea. You would get lost or buried in the mud. The car would never be seen again. For the hotel bus to Santa Rosalia you must first go to San Miguel where the driver has his lady friend. I will arrange for the public bus to take you to San Miguel."

Almost an hour later, during which the radio blared incessantly, the manager rushed into the room followed by a servant who seized her bag and backpack. The public bus for San Miguel was waiting outside; there was no time to lose. In San Miguel she would, if lucky, find the hotel's bus and driver.

The old bus leaned heavily forward and to the right, as though the right front tire were flat. The horrible diesel engine was running; the bus shuddered with its vibrations; its radio was blaring. The driver waved her to a front seat that a moment before had been occupied by two restless chickens tied together at the feet. The owner of the chickens, a fat Indian woman, covered her mouth with a corner of her skirt. Directly in front of her, at times obscuring the view, an immense crucifix, two Barbi dolls and a stuffed iguana hung on strings from the top of the windshield.

A jolting hour through stubbled fields, into and out of a ravine, a slow climb. The first thatched roofs of San Miguel appeared: the San Miguel where Stanfield learned everything he would ever learn of Rosellen's fate. And where the Indian guides Juan and Juanito had hung naked in the Plaza. What had happened to the widow's bust of Voltaire?

She found Roberto Rodriguez sitting at the one outdoor table of a miserable cantina which also served as the bus station. Diminutive Indian girls were offering Rodriguez pencils, paper flowers, chewing gum. He brushed them away as one might annoying flies, but they immediately returned. The street in front of the cafe was strewn with empty bottles and discarded soft drink cartons.

"Miss Deslonde! What a surprise!"

But surely she, Eloise, was the one to be surprised!

"Mr Rodriguez! What are you doing here?"

"I decided to join you for your holiday. I am my own boss." He looked away from her, grinning. "I too will go to the erotic paradise. As a friend of your country I will protect you from unwanted attentions."

"Thank you. I don't want you to bother."

"No problem, dear lady. Now I offer you a copa. A glass of wine to celebrate our friendship. The hotel bus will leave for Santa Rosalia in less than an hour. The driver personally assured me."

At one o'clock, and although nothing had been ordered, a waitress appeared with two bowls of soup. There were chunks of white fish swirled in a fiery liquid. This was followed by eggs rancheros. They hardly had time to pick up their knives and forks when a slab of pale gray meat was served, quite cold, and moments later a sticky pudding.

Rodriguez excused himelf, pushed through the curtain designed to keep out flies, and lay down on the only couch in the dark room that served as kitchen, bar and dining room for the natives. He fell asleep at once.

She would have liked to explore the small town and make enquiries. But apparently everyone in San Miguel was taking the siesta. Moreover, there was always the risk of missing the bus.

Shortly after four the bus appeared and rumbled to a stop in front of the cafe, only a hissing sound from the engine, but with many sounds of protesting joints and springs. It was open at the sides, with five rows of seats and a fringed canvas top. The hood of the bus was very large, with shiny red paint and polished brass fittings. A banner extended beneath the fringed top the full length of the passenger area: *Gran Hotel Balneario Chimalapa.*

Was she hallucinating? This could only be the "splendid" bus described by Charles Stanfield. She ran inside to wake Rodriguez, although tempted to leave without him.

How old was the bus? The Indian driver did not respond to her question and doubtless did not understand it. He was in tatters, but rather formal tatters, with a policeman's cap and an emblem on his jacket that read *Gran Hotel*. He apparently had nothing under the jacket, which was unbuttoned and much too small. There were blue spots on his chest the size of silver dollars.

He stowed their suitcases on the front seat, covering them with a tarpaulin, and indicated rather firmly they were to sit in the third row of seats, although there were no other passengers.

"Now for the jungle," Rodriguez said.

The peculiar hissing of the engine resumed. The bus shook twice, hard, as though to throw off a restraining hand. They were on their way. Small naked children waved and called to them from the last huts of the village.

A disappointing half hour. Then the road, scarcely more than a widened mule path, plunged into the jungle. The sun disappeared behind a dense green wall of trees and a serpentine mass of coiling lianas and parasite ferns. The leaves of palm trees almost as large as the bus scraped its top. Strange bird sounds welcomed them, shrill and strident, louder than the hissing of the bus. They were entering an ever-narrowing tunnel of green. The lurching of the bus threatened to throw them out. They held tight to the polished brass rails.

Surely the road was not this bad in 1922 when the famous Champion came there, as well as Stanfield and Monica Swift, not to mention the gamblers, the bandits, the prostitutes. How could a resort hotel survive at the end of such a road?

She told Rodriguez about the champion and his little British companion Jimmy Wilding. Surely he was the boxer mentioned in the travel page, returning to Santa Rosalia after sixty years. Or who had been there all the time.

"I do hope we find him there."

Rodriguez reached across her to put a fatherly hand on her hand clutching the rail.

"Dear lady, I think you have been misinformed. No boxer from the ancient time would still be in Santa Rosalia. There are many mistakes in the newspaper articles about travel. The black champion was imprisoned in the United States. Did you know that? I have read the history of boxing. Every page."

The road had begun to climb, yet they could not see hills ahead, only the dense forest. The hissing of the engine became more pronounced. She had a disturbing sense that she was being watched, watched not only by Rodriguez, though that was bad enough. Unseen creatures of the forest were watching her.

The bus stopped. A thatched roof over a table and a soft drink stand had appeared out of the jungle as though dropped from the treetops, with an array of colored bottles and two glasses which even from this distance looked filthy. There was a rapid exchange between the driver and an emaciated Indian wearing only ragged trousers. Rodriguez translated.

"They are speaking Zoque, almost incomprehensible. It is a rest stop."

"But we've been going less than an hour."

"It gives us a chance to enjoy the jungle. In addition the bus is very old. I think there will be many rest stops."

Two hours later there was a much longer pause, while the driver worked on the engine, his head and at times almost his whole body disappearing into a labyrinth of tubes surmounted by a large drum.

"An old Stanley Steamer," Eloise explained. "Almost new in 1922."

"That is ridiculous. Please forgive me for saying so. How can you know that?"

Luckily this mishap occurred within sight of another stand advertising *Bebidas* and *Refrescos*. Or perhaps the car always broke down at this point.

There was a shrill clamor in the trees. Hundreds of tiny eyes peered down at them from the wild green tangle overhead. Flecks of sunlight glittered among showers of orchid.

"This time you cannot refuse me, Miss Deslonde. I offer you a glass of tamarinda, freshly squeezed from the tree."

The fruit drink had obviously been watered; she hoped it was from a fresh mountain stream.

"Look!" Rodriguez said. "A ruin."

An overgrown path led to a barbed wire fence and gate. Behind it a small pyramid and a tall stone slab were almost covered by grass. An old Indian with an aristocratic but skeletal profile was sleeping with his head thrown back. He had a small pad of tickets on his lap. Beside him were two crutches painted white, suggesting he was blind. The trouser of his left leg hung slack; the other leg ended in a tennis shoe.

Was she hallucinating again? Charles Stanfield had seen such a cripple near a small ruin.

Beside the gate a sign gave the price of admission. Less than an American penny. A second sign said the ruin was closed.

"I will wake him," Rodriguez said. "I will explain the difference between the Zoques and the Zapotecas while we inspect this small ruin."

The afternoon was darkening; a cold wind had begun to blow. There was a spatter of rain, though the dry season had begun long since. A hard nut, what looked like a miniature coconut, grazed Rodriguez's cheek.

"I think we shouldn't delay."

"Very well. There will be more ruins. I can still tell you about the history of the Zoques and the migration from Chiapas and in what ways they differ from the noble and resourceful Zapotecs."

Another hard object struck Rodriguez, but one that did not fall from a tree. Between them and the hotel bus a monkey no larger than a cat was grimacing angrily. It picked up another stone and threw it with some accuracy, but Rodriguez was able to get out of the way. The monkey chattered in rage.

It was nearly dark when the old bus broke down again. This time there was a sound of scraping, then shattering metal, as though a truly vital part had expired. Luckily they were not far from Santa Rosalia, and completed their journey on foot. The Indian carried all the bags. Eloise wore her backpack.

A last awful climb, sliding in mud where the rain must have fallen more heavily, then a tortuous descent. A sudden downpour greeted them, and abruptly ceased. A cloud of insects, as though released by the rain, bore down.

"Santa Rosalia," the driver said, pointing to the first thatched roofs. Three horses, as though pursued by the insects, galloped out of the twilight and back into it.

Something large and black swooped viciously past, vicious yet silent.

"A vampire bat," Rodriguez said. "Very unpleasant. They suck the unwary, especially the horse."

The driver was pointing in another direction.

Out of the gloom of a thick grove of trees a white building rose darkly. There were almost no lights at its base, but the top floor had many.

"Gran Hotel Balneario," the driver said. "Luxury hotel."

At the Bar

SO HERE SHE WAS! Marble lettering almost effaced by time and the trudge of visitors extended across the entrance floor: *GRAN HOTEL BALNEARIO*. Several Indians crouched nearby, exactly as in Stanfield's time, huddled under serapes although the night was warm. The small and shabby lobby was poorly lit by an ornate chandelier, all but two of its bulbs dark. One white wall had the look and smell of fresh paint, but plaster was peeling from the others. Only three keys were missing from the long rows of mail boxes behind the desk and no one had any mail. The hotel was almost empty.

A mestizo at the desk was reading a comic book. He put it down reluctantly.

"You are very late. Were there problems with the bus?"

"There certainly were."

"There are always problems with the bus."

"The bus is a disgrace," Rodriguez said. "It should be retired."

He reached over the desk to shake hands and addressed the mestizo in a torrent of Spanish Eloise couldn't follow. She caught the words *aire-acondicionado* and *matrimonio*, which she knew meant double bed. From time to time the mestizo scrutinized her suspiciously. Perhaps a gringo visitor was now a rarity, because of the atrocious road and "luxury train." The harangue went on and on, interrupted only by the mestizo's brief replies.

"What was all that?" she asked.

"I told him who I was and of my influential friends in the hotel industry. I asked for a special rate. In reply he offered us a double room for the price of a single. Also he said the single rooms are not renovated and have a fan on the ceiling. The double rooms are air-conditioned. So of course we will share a room."

Eloise laughed.

"I want a single room."

"Why throw money away? I asked for two beds of course, not a matrimonio, no cause for alarm. Moreover, I am old enough to be your father. For me you are an untouchable virgin."

She addressed the concierge, trying not to laugh again.

"A single room, please."

"No problem. First give me your passport."

"Only a formality," Rodriguez said.

There were two elevators, one marked *Private* and the other *Out of Order*, so they were obliged to use the winding stairs, separated from the elevators by cinder blocks, Rodriguez and a diminutive Indian maid went ahead. There were several piles of empty bottles and stacked papers in the upstairs hall that might have been there for months. The barefoot young Indian maid who carried her bag kicked one of the bottles as they passed. She had the shreds of a uniform with *Gran Hotel Balneario* printed across the chest.

Eloise gave her a tip after she opened the door, but still the maid remained standing in it. She could hear Rodriguez lecturing the other maid in the next room. *So*, she thought, *adjoining rooms. The man is irrepressible.*

"Como se llama?" she asked her own maid. "Me llama Eloise." But in reply the maid merely put a hand over her mouth. "Muchas gracias," Eloise added, but the maid still did not move. There were faint white and blue patches on her face.

The room was dominated by a mosquito netting that covered the large four-poster bed and hung to the tile floor. Beside it was a five-gallon bottle of slightly cloudy water turned upside down, *Agua Purificada,* also two smaller bottles. These were empty and had pasted handwritten labels: *Spring Water* and *Aguardiente.* Beside them were two upturned glasses, in one of which was a large spider. A sturdy table, two chairs with leather seats but hard backs. The high walls were white. On one wall there was only a crucifix. On the wall opposite two slender green lizards watched her, pencil thin and no doubt very young.

She was delighted. Charles Stanfield's friendly lizard multiplied by two in the intervening sixty years! It was as though no time had passed. She fancied she had been given Stanfield's room. She could feel his presence.

The maid was still there. She held up a finger as in admonition, pointed to a switch near the door, and tried it several times. Finally it clicked, and a scraping sound came from overhead followed by a low whine. A ceiling fan had begun to revolve very slowly. At last the maid withdrew, but not before pointing to a badly printed list of *Rules and Services* in English and Spanish. There were admonitions to call *Room Service,* but the room had no telephone. *Free welcome cocktail and free welcome liqueur.* Instructions to Call Bartender Luís to arrange for *Native Masseuse, Jungle Walk, Aguardiente Rubdown, Hostess Service, Moyaquil extraction* and *Horses for rent.* Was hostess service the "erotic paradise?" The rules admonished her not to take towels to the river, since the native girls dry you for a small tip. *No loud noises after midnight.* Handwritten additions noted that the iguanas were friendly and the pinta disease was not contagious. Clients were permitted to pick the hotel oranges, the best in Mexico.

The room appeared to get hotter with the slow turning of the fan. She ran a cold bath to cool off and rid herself of the caked mud of the journey, then put on white slacks and a light blue blouse and went down to the bar. It occupied a corner of a dark high-ceilinged room with a raised stage at one end. She knew that room from the Blue Notebook, still called the Salon Oaxaca. The great Papa Jack had pranced on that stage. It was like walking into the past, but a past that was itself outside time, enchanted, sleeping in dust and cobwebs. The large windowless room was evidently still the dining room as well as nightclub. Several tables were set for dinner. A much larger number were empty and many chairs had been piled against a wall. An open space at the center of the room was presumably a dance floor. But on the stage there was no sign of a boxing ring for the 45 round fights. Near it a billiard table had been turned on its side and was resting against the back wall.

The bar too was surely unchanged, with its long mirror and array of bottles and its numerous photographs, some framed, some pasted to the glass. She found Roberto Rodriguez in earnest conversation with the bartender, a young Mexican who played with his stubbled moustache as he listened. At the far end of the long bar, almost in darkness, a small man was hunched over, staring in the mirror. Near him four florid young women were seated at a table as though waiting for something to happen. They had similar bouffant hairdos and their shoulders were bare over tight black silk dresses. Were they a floor show? In Stanfield's time there were only three, in hula skirts and with leis over their brassieres. The Garnica something.

Rodriguez stood up to introduce her to the bartender.

"Meet my friend Luís, Miss Deslonde. Ask him for anything."

But she was already behind the bar and had gone directly to a large inscribed portrait of Papa Jack in tightly fitting trunks that extended almost to his knees. He was leaning against a crude photographer's prop of an open cockpit plane. *Salud y pesetas a mis amigos del Balneario! 4 novembre 1922.*

298

Papa Jack.

"Yes! Here he is. And 1922! I can't believe I found him like that, right away."

"That is Papa Jack," Rodriguez said, "He was once the heavyweight champion of the world, who boxed in this hotel and also danced in the nightclub."

"I know, I know. Papa Jack was here in 1922 to publicize the hotel."

Beside the portrait was a large poster, so faded it might have been a distant reflection in the mirror, advertising the 1916 fight between Papa Jack and Brian Desmond. Barcelona, Plaza Monumental. She moved down the row of photographs and stopped in front of a group picture. Papa Jack in a tuxedo that was much too small, with sleeves that showed several inches of starched white, towered goodnaturedly over a slender and intense woman who had her arms around two small uniformed barefoot maids or waitresses.

"And this is the poet Monica Swift," Eloise said, "the wife of the poet and boxer Brian Desmond, who disappeared in Mexico. She was often photographed in profile. I think she was very proud of her nose, she would turn her face to the side. Here she looks less aloof than usual."

Rodriguez was again astonished.

"How can you know all this?"

"I tried to tell you about my research but we didn't get much beyond 1870. I want to know everything about the hotel, particularly 1922. For the lover of poetry her face is more familiar than Papa Jack's. She was a fine poet, quite well known. She had many lovers, but the boxer Brian Desmond was her true love."

Rodriguez stared.

"Your voice is very pleasing and musical, but you say these things with the confidence of a politician. Well, Miss Deslonde, I too am a lover of poetry. I intend to write poems while in the Hotel Gran Balneario. It's never too late to begin, all that is needed is talent. After I have written mine, we will read our poems to each other, both English and Spanish."

The bartender was pouring a milky liquid from a tall glass pitcher. But before he could offer it to her, Rodriguez took the cocktail from him.

"Allow me as Miss Deslonde's guide and interpreter to offer the welcome cocktail. No charge, the hotel will pay."

She took a sip of the milky cocktail, which was thick and with a bitter medicinal taste. She put it down on the bar.

"Thank you, Luís. Thank you both. I'll finish it later."

"Look at all the famous actresses," Luís said, pointing to the photographs on the wall. "Also famous revolutionaries. Guests of the hotel."

At a glance the many actresses with their bare shoulders and billowing silks looked very much alike. So too their scrawled wavy signatures ending in curlicues.

"But where is the very old boxer who was here in 1922?" She scrutinized the man in the darkness at the end of the bar. He looked very small and old. There he was! He was wearing a faded, much mended sweat shirt with the words *Papa Jack* still faintly visible.

"That is Jimmy Wilding, an English boxer in retirement," the bartender Luís said. "Very old but still he offers to give boxing lessons. A bantamweight, one hundred-eighteen pounds, a permanent resident of the hotel."

She approached Wilding, smiling, and slid onto the bar stool next to his. Rodriguez followed, and seated himself on the other side of the wiry old man. He might have been an aged jockey, skin lined and drawn by years of racing and fasting to make weight. Only his bright blue eyes looked alive.

"Papa Jack," she said dramatically. "Monica Swift! Brian Desmond! Jimmy Wilding!"

His mouth fell open. He had very few teeth.

"I'm Jimmy Wilding."

"I know, I know. I really want to give you a big kiss. May I? You were here in 1922, you knew the young engineer

Charles Stanfield. No, I mean the old engineer. He was old when he came back in 1922."

Wilding blinked.

"The Havana fight was 1915. I was in Jack's corner. He didn't throw the fight, the newspapers had it wrong."

"No, no. I mean here in the Gran Hotel Balneario in 1922. You knew them, Mr Wilding! You knew them all! Charles Stanfield was over seventy when he came back. But only twenty his first time in Santa Rosalia." She tugged at his patched elbow. "Please look at the pictures with me."

"They're not for sale."

"Of course not. But I must pick your brains. Ask you to identify people."

He hobbled after her as she moved from picture to picture. Papa Jack as Othello, with deep white smudges beneath the eyes, as though he were a white actor in black face. Papa Jack in bullfighter's costume, grinning, the jacket much too small, the bulging trousers about to split at the waist. Another in business suit, shaking hands with a scholarly looking man with an ample bushy beard and many medals.

"That is Venustiano Carranza, the President of Mexico until shot," Rodriguez said.

"Think of that! Carranza himself!"

"You have heard of Carranza! You know our history? The history of the Mexican revolution?"

"A little bit."

"The body of Carranza was exhumed from the Panteón de Dolores and conducted to the Monument of the Revolution. I have seen pictures of the skull. The head of Pancho Villa has never been found. The head of one revolutionary is preserved in oil."

Eloise glanced at Rodriguez, not sure whether to laugh at these non sequiturs. She stopped next before a group picture, taken in a ring raised on a stage. Papa Jack was having his gloves laced. Beside him was a very small and youthful boxer, bare to the waist and ribs showing, slim legs in dark training

301

tights with a sash made from a British flag. His arms were heavily tattooed and on his chest was the outline of a small boxing glove. Stanfield's 1922 journal had mentioned that odd tattoo.

"I think I know who that is," Wilding said, pointing to the tattoo.

"It's you."

"Right here in this room, miss. Salon Oaxaca. Every night there was a show. Jack did a soft-shoe number and played the banjo and sometimes he talked about his life. I was part of the show. We tap-danced. Or maybe that was at the World's Fair in Chicago. New York too, I've been there. Often, I have. Jack did his act at Herman's Museum on 42nd Street. I lived at the Dixie, 42nd Street too. Later in the Bowery with Monica, that's where I lived."

"You don't look a day over eighteen."

"More like eighty." He began to count on his fingers.

"No, I mean in the picture. And to think you lived with Monica Swift!"

"That I did. Three floors we walked up and many a night there were drunks on the stairs."

"You must tell me all about Monica. Maybe tomorrow, just the two of us."

In the next picture Wilding was in long tight-fitting bathing trunks that clung like a racing cyclist's pants. Beside him Papa Jack, wearing an embroidered bathrobe, had his arm around a diminutive Mexican woman in a flamenco costume. Eloise put a finger on a pleasant looking gray-haired man standing a little to the side, as though reluctant to be photographed. He was in a loose guayabera. Charles Stanfield, the young engineer grown old. She knew that wistful smile, those thin arms and wrists, that aristocratic nose from the twenty photographs the grandson had given her. "And this man, Mr Wilding?"

"That's not my picture, no, not at all. This is me here." He unbuttoned his shirt to reveal the boxing glove, almost invisible now on the leathery skin. "I got it in Havana, the first time we were there. A girl I picked up paid for it. She watched the man put in on, wanted everything just right. Very proud of it she was."

She pointed to Stanfield.

"Of course it isn't you. It's Charles Stanfield. Don't you remember him."

"It couldn't have been last year, miss."

"No, no. It says at the bottom. 1922."

"I think so, Monica was there too."

In another picture, apparently taken near the spring, with Indians in the background, the slender Stanfield seemed to be staring at the Indians and beyond them. It was as though he did not know he was in the picture. Papa Jack was shaking hands with a shabby Mexican in a soiled Palm Beach suit, with a bow tie that was slightly askew.

"Here he is again, Mr Wilding. Please try to remember. His name is Charles Stanfield. He died long ago. Near here in Casas Grandes."

"Casas Grandes!" It was the bartender Luís.

"Yes, I want to go there, where they went. Where they died."

"No one goes to Casas Grandes," Luís said. "It is a terrible place."

"That's the spring in the picture," Wilding said. "You should try the spring water, miss. It tastes nasty but is very good for the liver, that it is."

"Yes, yes. Tomorrow I'll try it, I can't wait to taste it. But I wish you would try to remember this man. An engineer who came here to Santa Rosalia long ago, even before there was a hotel."

"I can't say I remember him. Not for sure. Face looks like somebody."

Luís, as in honor of someone who knew of the hotel's glamorous past, brought a new bottle of the best tequila and a tray with small glasses.

"The manager will be pleased to hear you are interested in the history of Santa Rosalia."

He showed her the bottle with a devil and pitchfork on the label. But before he could proceed Rodriguez seized the bottle and was preparing to pour.

"Allow me, as the oldest Mexican guest, to do the honors and welcome one more friend from the north. The free welcome liqueur. Aguardiente of the region, better than any brandy."

Luís frowned but said nothing. He reached under the bar and brought out a large leather book with gold lettering, also a thin pen much chewed at the top.

Huéspedes.

"Please sign your name and add any comments you wish to make. 'Huéspedes' means guests. Mr Rodriguez has already signed."

The Guest Register appeared to be fairly new, extending only to the start of the year, with not more than fifty names. It included information taken from passports, age and weight and even the color of the eyes. And brief personal comments on the guests. What an idea, to comment on the guests! All this in addition to the room number. The comments had been made by Luís or some other hotel employee, and most of them were in English. Her own name had already been entered in a laborious blocked handwriting, but she was nevertheless expected to sign and add a few words. Had the bartender forgotten that he had already recorded, as for no other eyes, his initial impression of her? He had seen her only for a moment before she went up to her room.

"*Deslonde, Eloise. U.S.A. pasaporte. New Orleans, USA, age 23. 110 pounds. Eyes brown, also hair. Una profesora. Room 23 con balcón.* Another sentence had been added in a different handwriting. *Pretty young lady muy simpática.* By whom and when? All very strange.

She looked up from the book to find that several pairs of eyes were fixed upon her, including those of the bartender

Luís. His were friendly and amused. He handed her the chewed pen.

"Now you write."

"*Look forward to tasting the famous spring waters,*" she wrote. "*Hotel personnel muy simpático.*"

"Thank you, Miss Deslonde, the manager will be pleased. He is not well but asks me to welcome you. He hopes you will enjoy your stay at the Balneario."

"I hope he's well soon. I'd really like to talk to him."

Luís started to take the book out of her hands, but she held to it firmly.

"Do you mind if I see who is here?"

"Of course not."

Roberto Rodriguez pointed to the top of the page and his own name. He was 38, was born in Guadalajara. Brown eyes, black hair, small scar over eye. He was assigned to room 24 with balcony and jungle view. *Amigo de la casa,* Luís had written tersely, to which Rodriguez responded in English: *At the Balneario anything is possible. Roberto Rodriguez, businessman, licenciado, sportsman.* Very odd. Already a 'friend of the house,' yet she was sure Rodriguez had not lied to her. He was in Santa Rosalia for the first time.

Next came the four young actresses, who had moved to a table closer to the bar, and were much interested in the proceedings. Their black sheaths were so tight they were like a second skin. They exchanged whispers and much laughter when Rodriguez introduced them. The two youngest, Suzy and Lupita, had evidently already attracted the interest of Roberto Rodriguez. They in turn were ready to tease him. As with common accord they went up to him, each offering a cheek to kiss, but pulled away at the last moment. They went off into peals of laughter.

How much the irrepressible Rodriguez had accomplished while she was taking her bath! Already he had learned of their ambition to be in a film to be made by the hotel owner Cyrus Cranfield.

"Read what it says about Dolores Inocencia," Suzy said, nuzzling close to Jimmy Wilding and fondling an ear. The old man turned his other ear for another caress. A twisting of the shoulders, then an exaggerated rocking, caused her breasts to swell and push upward precariously.

Eloise read the book. Dolores Inocencia, had acted on the stage in the capital, though not yet twenty, and been in two films. *Mundana, sensualista, hermana, espiritual.* A few words had been added for foreign eyes: *Intelligent woman of the world.* Suzy was eighteen, worthy of a city where the most beautiful women of the district were born, except for those of Tehuantepec. Lupita, formerly Miss Juchitán, was sensually alluring when she danced: *serpentina, agíl.* When not dancing a lover of healthy pleasures. Consuela was the intellectual of the group, a student of human nature, although she too danced in nightclubs and had been honored as Miss Tehuantepec.

Two of the girls had already written Mr Cranfield asking for auditions, while the others were still composing their letters. The four shared a double room on the fourth floor, but this had no direct access to the fifth. It was necessary to take a special elevator from the lobby to reach the Cranfield apartment. The special elevator was kept locked.

"You must have fun writing about your guests," Eloise said. "Don't they ever mind?"

"The comments are the manager's. He dictates, I write."

"I have read about Mr Cranfield. Where is he in the book?"

"He is in a different book. With the manager."

"Can I see it? I'd love to read the registers with the descriptions of the guests."

Luís looked uncomfortable.

"Some of the information is confidential."

"How far back do the books go?"

"I have no idea. There is a great accumulation of books from the old days. Before my time."

306

"I would so like to see them. I'm interested in everything that went on here in the old days. I want to know the whole history of the hotel, but especially 1922."

Luís began to show signs of irritation.

"Some other time."

"I too would like to see the book about Mr Cranfield," Rodriguez said. "He is a famous millionaire. Why does a famous millionaire live in a place like this? You say he makes a movie. Why make a movie in a jungle? Miss Deslonde and I wish to meet him."

"No one sees Mr Cranfield. He has his own elevator but he never takes it, only the curandero Pascualito. The other elevator, which is out of order, is for you. It serves the second floor and the fourth."

"He's very old, isn't he?" Eloise asked.

"Very. I will show you a confidential photograph."

Luís took a thick wallet from his hip pocket. It was full of cards, newspaper clippings and flaky currency. There were also two Polaroid photographs. He held the first under the light. The second, which he slipped back among the cards, was a dim picture of a coffin in an empty room. How odd to have a photograph of a coffin. But it would be rude to ask about it. Probably a family member.

Cyrus Cranfield. The ravaged face was swathed in rumpled toweling and almost covered by gray hair hanging in matted strings. The picture had caught its subject asleep; the fixity of expression might be that of someone who had died. The lines of the face were hard to distinguish from the hair. There were dark swellings below the closed eyes.

"I, Luís, guarantee this picture is authentic. I took it."

For the moment there were no other guests. An American journalist named Chappell had hung around for two weeks, hoping for an interview. *Age 40, 145 pounds, 5 feet 8 inches, brown hair, gray eyes. A serious man who keeps his plans to himself. Hopes to see Mr Cranfield.* Two very old Americans, Barbara Swenson and Charles Murphree, had recently left. They spent most of their time in their fourth floor suite, attended by two black Haitian servants who knew very little Spanish and traveled with them. Hippolyte Dieuaimé and Jasmine his wife. They too were in the guest book, which attempted French. *Homme soit gentils y grand. La femme joly, elegant.* The ancient lady Barbara Swenson liked to tell her story whenever she had several drinks, always in the same words. Long ago, 1963 to be exact, Barbara Swenson wanted to finance an invasion somewhere in the Caribbean, both to help a worthy poet and statesman named Villamayor return to his homeland and to give her "adventurous companion" Murphree a chance to use his experience in guerilla tactics. An old soldier who as a young man had participated in many idealistic invasions. That was all Luís remembered. They too, Barbara Swenson and Charles Murphree, had hoped to see Cranfield, but in vain. And had come, of course, for the waters. Without the waters the hotel would not exist.

Barbara Swenson, age 82, 95 pounds, five feet, red hair, blue eyes. Three glasses morning and night. Requires two gallons every day from the petroleum pit to mix with morning bath. Must be warm. "I have come to the Balneario for a second youth. A second youth also for my friend."

Charles Murphree, age 80, had ordered six massages a week. *The insects do not touch him. While his friend sleeps he visits the bar and talks with the journalist Chappell of his many wars. A true viejo verde, admirable, who enjoys visiting the kitchen and has a sparkling eye for young girls of the village.* Murphree had written in response: *Nice hotel but deteriorating. A restful pause to catch our breath between actions. STILL WANT TO SEE THE COFFIN. How about a group visit?"*

"'I still want to see the coffin,'" Eloise read aloud. "What is that about?"

Luís told them about the occult appearance of the coffin during the years when the hotel was closed. The Council of

Ancients had employed a young woman, Josefina Amor, to guard it. It was on the third floor which could be reached only by stairway from the cellar.

"But who is in the coffin?"

"The coffin is a mystery," Luís said. "This happened before my time, I have not seen it myself. Will you have another cocktail?"

"Thanks, no."

"No one knows who is in the coffin. Maybe even the maid Josefina Amor who cleans its room doesn't know."

"But why keep it then?"

"It is sacred. Indians come from far away to sit in front of the hotel and stare up at the third floor which is closed to the public. At the moment there are four out there. The suite has been paid for in advance to assure the perpetual rest of the coffin which is of glass. Room, bath and balcony. Also the wages of the maid."

"In Guanajuato the corpses stand in a corridor," said Rodriguez. They are preserved by the quality of the clay in which for many years they slept. Perhaps here the corpse sleeps in oil. That is only a guess."

"What does the maid say?"

"She says nothing. Once a month she goes for three days to her parents' home in San Juan Evangelista and there she is allowed to talk. But not about the coffin."

"I know San Juan Evangelista well," Rodriguez said. "I would like to talk to this young woman, if only about her home and her parents."

"Is there really no one else on the third floor?" Eloise asked. "I mean there must be a number of rooms."

"In the hotel are thirty rooms, all with bath, some with air conditioning, some with ceiling fan. However, the third and fifth floors are not open to the public."

"Of course," Rodriguez said, "Third floor for the coffin and its maid. Fifth floor for Cranfield and the curandero. You still have many empty rooms. I think you need a new manager."

"It's not the season," Luís said, "There have been problems with transportation."

"In the old days the hotel was often full," Eloise said. "In 1922 they came all the way from Mexico City to see Papa Jack box."

"How do you know that?" Luís asked.

"I'm getting a Ph.D. in history," she said. "I've read a lot about the history of the hotel, but I'd like to know more." Her brown eyes widened. "You said he dictates the comments and you write them down. Does he say it in Spanish and you put it in English? There are two different handwritings."

"It is all the manager, both English and Spanish. His knowledge of English is perfect."

She was still rather puzzled.

"Where is he?"

"He is in seclusion, also on the third floor."

Someone in a nearby room was ringing a bell over and over, a loud bell. It might have been the bell from a small church.

"Time for dinner," Luís said. "This is the dining room. Also the ballroom, boxing club and theater. We eat at one table, one big family."

"Terrific," Eloise said. "May we see the menu?"

"There is no menu," Rodriguez said. "Put yourself in the chef's hands."

The Guest Book

SHE WAS WAKENED TWICE during the night, the first time by dogs barking and a sound of rolling thunder, then the distinct shaking of her bed, later by high winds and torrential rain. She was too tired to get up, but the next morning found the earthquake had left a long crack in the ceiling and in one place plaster had broken off to reveal rotted boards. There was a puddle of water near the window. But the sun was shining and the terrace beneath her window had been washed clean. The four Indians had not moved from their place of vigil, although several serapes had been laid over terrace chairs to dry. But even as she watched, one of the Indians raised his eyes to the third floor, to the room directly above hers, as though wary of some alarming development. Perhaps a ghostly fleshless countenance, or at least the face of the maid deputized to watch over the coffin.

Slipped under her door was a curious badly-typed document.

History of Pueblo and Gran Hotel Balneario

1922 Visit and boxing exhibition of heavyweight champion Papa Jack, poet & actress Monica Swift, boxer Jimmy Wilding. Death in Casas Grandes of teacher Charles Stanfield (cardiaca).

1924 Secret visit for cure of President Calles.

1925 Death in Belgium of romantic Empress Carlota (crazy).

1928 Cristeros assassins of President Obregon shot, including Padre Miguel Pro.

1931 Big earthquake. Death of Jaime Vinalva in Tampico. Shot by police.

1933 Airplane "Quatro Vientos" falls in inexplorada jungle.

1943 Hotel closed. Antonio Vinalva goes to El Paso USA to work on U.S. army railroad. Marries Rosario Manteca, "La Bonita Chicana" (Miss Matamoros, 1942). She leaves him.

1946 Death in auto crash of champion Papa Jack. Cyrus Cranfield of Houston, Texas buys hotel. Hotel opens. Antonio Vinalva, manager.

1953 Friend of pueblo Jimmy Wilding living Bowery U.S.A. Also poet Monica Swift. Jimmy sends many photos of Papa Jack.

1968 Hotel closed. Last road (San Miguel-Cofradia-Santa Maria) closed. Only paths for mulas, people by foot. Antonio Vinalva disappears.

1973 More dwarfs in inexplorada jungle. La divinadora Alicia arrives in pueblo. Predicts end of world.

1982 Gran Hotel Balneario opens again. Road also. Owner Cyrus Cranfield arrives with famous curandero Pascualito for cure of spring water and oil baths. Will make movies. Boxer friend of pueblo Jimmy Wilding returns to live in Gran Hotel Balneario. Old hotel bus discovered in garage Salina Cruz. She still runs.

After breakfast she set out to explore the village alone, but found Rodriguez and Jimmy Wilding at the spring, seated on benches. This morning Jimmy looked alert and younger. His blue eyes were friendly, even mischievous. Near them were several young girls who were barefoot and wearing cheap cotton dresses. They greeted her with sharp chirping cries and much giggling.

"Jimmy instructs me two glasses before lunch is recommended," Rodriguez said briskly. "I'm afraid you will not like the taste. Think of some pleasant experience as you drink."

"This is a pleasant experience for me! A young American engineer drank from this spring more than a hundred years ago. Charles Stanfield. He was surprised to see fish in the water. Are there any fish today?"

She was almost reluctant to look into the water, which gave off a strong smell of steamed cabbage. There were bubbles in one place near the rim, and here the water swirled gently as from a conduit a few feet below the surface. Small silver and yellow fish hovered there, struggling against the current, but deeper still a fish lay unmoving.

She took a sip and felt the nausea rising in her throat.

"Drink the first glass rapidly," Rodriguez said. "It is a mistake to look into the water as you drink. Think of the pleasure of a lover's embrace."

"I'm thinking about Charles Stanfield drinking from this spring. And you too, Mr Wilding, fifty years ago!"

Wilding stared at the water, frowning.

"There were brass cups with the name of the hotel on them, very shiny they were. What happened to all the cups?"

"Do you remember Charles Stanfield this morning, Jimmy? It tells about his death on this thing I found under my door. He died of a heart attack."

"Of course I remember him. He was my friend. An American he was, a lovely man at that. Bought me beer more than once. Sat at the bar and told me about the old days. Told me he saw Tom Sharkey and old Jeffries in a circus. They were fat. Mr Stanfield liked to look at my tattoos."

"Did he tell you about Rosellen, the woman who died in Casas Grandes? Please try to remember."

"Can't say I remember about that. I will tell you this. He came from Boston, Massachusetts and he saw John L. Sullivan in a theater show. The Boston Strong Boy they called him. He danced and sang in a show but Jack did it better. John L. was champion until Jim Corbett beat him flicking away with his jabs. But John L. couldn't touch Jack for fighting. Papa Jack cut him to ribbons. Knocked him out."

"I don't believe they ever fought," Rodriguez said gently. "Were you there?"

"I believe Papa Jack came later in the history of boxing. I have a great memory for historical events."

"Have you now? Just tell me please when the Willard fight was."

"1915. It ended in the 26th round."

"That's right!"

"In my father's house in Guadalajara there were many books of history, both of the Mexican revolution and of world events. And a book called the Everlast Boxing Record. I too am an aficionado. I can tell you when the last fight of your friend Papa Jack was. 1926 in Juarez, Mexico, across the river from El Paso, Texas. He was knocked out."

"He was fouled. Not a true knockout, I can tell you that. I was there. Only time Jack was knocked out was Willard in Havana. Heat exhaustion that was, not the blows, he lay there under the terrible lights they had for the pictures, the heat drained away his great noble body so he couldn't get up. Wasn't out from the blows, never fear that. Never believe anyone tells you he threw the fight. Not Papa Jack."

Eloise was eager to pursue Jimmy Wilding's reminiscences, but was afraid they would pertain only to boxing, now that his mind was on that track. She would return another time to his memories of Charles Stanfield and 1922. She showed the page of village history to Rodriguez.

"Did you find one of these things under your door?"

"I found it in disorder, like everything else. Bad typewriting. Why include the death of the Empress Carlota? That is worthy of a history of Mexico but not the history of this hotel. The hotel is a disgrace to the Mexican hotel industry."

Jimmy Wilding was puzzled.

"It's a nice hotel," he said. "I like it."

"I would like to take a tour of the village, Mr Wilding. I'm sure you know it better than anyone else. Wouldn't you like to see the village, Mr Rodriguez?"

"I can't walk very fast," Wilding said. He was obviously much pleased. "First we'll go to the Oficina Municipal on the plaza. After that the school and the San Sebastian Church. How would you like that for a tour?"

She was disappointed by the village. A rutted dirt road climbed to the small plaza past huts that looked deserted. Only weeds and straggling hibiscus and tamarind trees to relieve the brown monotony. There had been no monkey in the tamarind tree by the empty and cracked swimming pool where Stanfield and Monica Swift had been welcomed by the dapper and courtly Antonio Vinalva. Lean dogs looked out of dark doorways. In one a burro stood as though on guard, in another a small pig, in a third an old woman who was obviously both blind and deaf. A young woman in a shapeless sack was sitting on the ground in front of another hut, mending a basket. She waved her hand at Wilding but did not smile. Her face was marked by pinta. From inside came the sound of a hand-turned mill. A scrawny turkey appeared at the door, gave the ground a few desultory pecks, and went back inside.

A rickety wooden bandstand sagged above the field of mud left by the night's rain. In the small Oficina Municipal an old man was sleeping while a young girl much scarred by pinta read a comic book. Next door was a prison cage without a roof. A solitary Indian was asleep on the dirt floor, snoring.

Wilding led them to the ruins of a small church. Its one standing wall was almost hidden by wild growth. In front of it were two old orange trees. They still bore fruit.

"They hanged people here."

"Yes, yes. Charles Stanfield wrote about that. The teacher's widow was hanged there for some reason. Some terrible story of betrayal. The teacher was unhappy and went to pieces and even ate clay."

"Some of the children do that," Jimmy Wilding said. "It makes you sick. If you see them you must make them stop."

There were two cantinas at the far end of the plaza, with swinging doors and metal banners advertising *Carta Blanca* and *Modelo* beer. The rooms were dark. In one cantina two men were arguing drunkenly, while from the other came the sounds of raucous singing.

"It's only ten o'clock. They seem to have a good head start."

"Luís says the men drink every day all day," Rodriguez said. "Unless they are working in the fields. They load the coffee on the mules to go to San Miguel Chimalapa. Then they get drunk. To get drunk is the principal entertainment for the men of Santa Rosalia. There is also the discoteca with jukebox."

"They work hard," Jimmy Wilding said. The sounds of canned music came from a hut at the far end of the plaza. "That is the discoteca. Sundays the young people of the village listen to the Mexican football games and the music."

"Doesn't the hotel have anything for them?" Eloise asked. "No entertainment?"

"They used to come to my hotel room for boxing lessons. I thought I'd find a champion in the village but it didn't happen. Back in the good times they looked in the windows when there were fights in the hotel. Forty-five-round fights."

"I don't believe there were ever forty-five-round fights here," Rodriguez said.

"Maybe next week," Wilding said vaguely.

"But where are all the people?" Eloise wondered.

"Some are in the milpas working, some are asleep. The women are probably washing clothes in the creek."

Rodriguez put his arm around Wilding in a comradely way.

"In Tehuantepec the women wash themselves in the river, not only their clothes. You can see them from the railroad bridge, the train goes slow for that purpose. Very satisfying."

They continued down a narrowing dirt street too rutted even for an oxcart. Children were playing in a courtyard next to a small adobe house. It was the school. On seeing the visitors they gave up their game and moved toward a hole in the wire fence, laughing and pointing.

"Gringita! Gringita!" several cried, while others clustered around Jimmy Wilding, tugging at his trousers and begging for chewing gum. "Jimmy, Jimmy, Jimmy, Jimmy!" Two of the older boys squared off in the position of boxers at the start of a match and began feinting and throwing punches that were not meant to land. Smaller boys tried to pry open his hands, hoping for gum or a coin. Two of the girls, vying for his attention, began skipping rope deftly, first forward then back in the manner of boxers in training.

"Look, Jimmy, look!" they cried in time with the turning.

He led them down another muddy street to a grove of trees and a small stone building. Behind it the cemetery sloped sharply down to a ravine containing much refuse. Flowers and low mounds without crosses indicated where those recently dead lay.

"I find all this a little depressing," Eloise said. "Don't you, Mr Rodriguez?"

"As a lover of my country I am sorry you came to this place. Too bad you couldn't do your historical studies in a beach hotel in Acapulco or Cancún. Except for the hotel there is nothing in Santa Rosalia. What is there to see? Once there were the ancient Olmecs and the famous Mayans and the ferocious Aztecs and the peaceful Zoques and the Conquistadores. And in time a few gringos. Engineers for the canal

317

that was never built and the railroad that went somewhere else."

Jimmy Wilding looked around him, puzzled.

"It's not so bad."

Eloise wanted to hug him. He looked years older than a few minutes before when he seemed proud to show them the school.

"Why did you come back, Jimmy?" Eloise asked.

"It was cold in New York. The paper said they were going to have fights. Forty-five-round fights. When Jack fought Willard it was a forty-five-round fight but it ended in the twenty-sixth. People were good to me here. I thought I might find a real comer here and train him and take him to Vera Cruz. Make him a champion and bring him back to Santa Rosalia."

"I think this place was more alive sixty years ago," Eloise said. "Maybe even in 1870 when Charles Stanfield came for the first time."

"A taste of tequila will cure your depression," Rodriguez said. "We will go back to the hotel and have a mid-morning tequila. How about you, Mr Wilding?"

"A cerveza for me, please. Only beer when I'm in training."

The hotel depended on the radio for news and an occasional newspaper brought by the bus. But when there were no customers the bus stayed in San Miguel. At the moment the only working telephone in Santa Rosalia, or in all of the Chimalapas for that matter, was in Cranfield's fifth-floor suite. With it he could keep track of his many interests. Another line extended from the concierge's desk and disappeared into the jungle, but had repeatedly been cut, whether by the sharp teeth of animals or by suspicious natives. From time to time Luís picked up the receiver and said "Pronto" in a loud voice, hoping service had been restored. Then a shrug and apologetic smile. Only the radio kept them abreast of what was going on outside. The hotel had a television set but it produced only snow and noise.

On Wednesday, Eloise's third day, the radio reported rumors that an old guerilla leader, Pepe Contreras, was hiding somewhere in the remote Chimalapa mountains with a few desperate followers. He had been seen on successive evenings near San Miguel, Mateus Romero and La Chivela, wearing a kind of uniform, and with long white hair that flowed over the uniform's broad shoulders. A few of his men came into the villages to buy beer and cigarettes and to post proclamations. The old leader remained on the outskirts, glimpsed momentarily on horseback, then disappearing into the trees.

The little band of residents was again at the bar, waiting for the call to dinner. Jimmy Wilding remained at the other end of the bar, dozing, and the four starlets were talking rapidly among themselves. Radio Minatitlán reported the sightings. A small band in Guerrero had recently been operating not far from Acapulco. But even a large group could easily take refuge in the mountain areas still labeled *zona inexplorada* on maps.

"It is probably Pepe Contreras," Luís said.

"That is ridiculous," Rodriguez said. "Pepe Contreras is dead. Everyone knows that. He died in the ruins of Guiengola in 1978."

"Who is Pepe Contreras?" Eloise asked.

"He was a revolutionary of the old school of revolutionaries. An impractical but noble idealist dedicated to the unity of all Spanish-speaking people of the Americas. In 1947 he was with Fidel Castro and the tiger Rolando Masferrer in doomed preparation for the overthrow of the unspeakable Trujillo, dictator of the Dominican Republic. In 1977 he was in Peru, from which he was lucky to escape with his life. There were many attempted revolutions in between."

Eloise felt like snapping her fingers to accompany the rolling flow of his sentences.

"In doomed preparation?"

319

"Your government intervened, Miss Deslonde. They would not permit the invasion of the Dominican Republic."

"But Trujillo was killed by somebody. I distinctly remember."

"That was later. You are a historian, dear lady. A historian should know the order in which events happen. But tell us, Luís, was Pepe Contreras ever a visitor in the Gran Hotel Balneario? He was in the mountains in Guerrero before he met his death in the ruins of Guiengola. Was he here in the 1960's, before the hotel closed?"

"I was at that time a bartender in Mérida at the Hotel Colón. I had never heard of the Gran Hotel Balneario."

"Please consult the books of 'Huéspedes' for the 1960's."

"The old guest books are locked up in the office of the former manager, Antonio Vinalva."

Eloise leaned forward and impulsively reached for Luís' hand.

"Do please ask the manager to let me see the old guest books. The very oldest ones, especially 1922. I must know what they say about Charles Stanfield. And Papa Jack and Monica Swift."

"I will ask the manager. But I do not think he will permit this. Some of the comments on the guests must be kept secret."

"But surely what someone said in 1922 doesn't matter now."

"We were talking about Pepe Contreras," Rodriguez said. "How could you not know he was dead, Luís?"

"He survived. I know what I know."

"For a concierge and assistant manager you are extremely uninformed," Rodriguez said.

"I can't follow this conversation," Eloise complained. "Please tell me about him."

"A noble idealist. However, he was always too late. I will tell you what Pepe Contreras was always in time for. The earthquakes or floods. He arrived to help with the revolutions, in Guatemala, El Salvador, Nicaragua, Peru. The next day there is a catastrophe. Pepe Contreras was a revolutionary before I was born. Even in Tabasco in the time of the mad dictator, when all references to God were forbidden and everyone wore red. Liquor also was forbidden, but no matter since the speeches made people drunk. Every day parades and culture festivals. He was a decamisado in the capital, no shirt no shoes, listening to the orations of Francisco Madero. Then he too joins a union and makes speeches. Land reform, Educación Socialista, equality of the sexes. You know what that means, Miss Deslonde. At first justice for the poor Indios, but soon it is all Latin America. Do you know his famous saying, Luís? *Give me fifty good men in the mountains and I will liberate the Americas.* Instead he dies in the ruins of Guiengola in 1978."

"He didn't die there. He survived. At this moment he is probably in Casas Grandes. A good place to hide."

"You are a good concierge and assistant manager, but you know nothing of the history of Mexico."

"I know what I know. He visited the manager, here in the hotel."

"You saw him?"

"I have said too much already. The visit was secret."

"I gather you think Contreras was something of a fool," Eloise said.

"On the contrary. I honor Pepe Contreras. He was a noble idealist who lived only for others. The history of Mexico is rich in noble idealists who lived only for others and were shot. Pepe Contreras was not shot, however."

The conversation turned to Cyrus Cranfield, the owner of the hotel.

Eloise asked why a rich man would settle in such an isolated place.

"For the health-giving spring waters," Luís said. "The curandero Pascualito who met him in Mazatlán knew the Balneario was the place for him, especially since he already

321

owned the hotel. One look at the thinness and decayed face
of Mr Cranfield was enough. 'For you, sir, it must be your
old hotel in Santa Rosalia in the Chimalapas.' That is what
Pascualito said. He was right. This is a peaceful environment.
The manager guarantees privacy, I too guarantee it. In the
big balnearios there are always people to steal his money.
Here he is a king."

"Why haven't we seen Pascualito?"

"He came down more often when the old ones were here.
Two months ago we had many old ones, ten at least.
Pascualito came to the bar for a bottle of chica for the treat-
ments. One treatment, one bottle, much of the chica he drank.
He spits the chica on the chest of the old ones, some of it he
swallows. Also he went with the old ones to the petroleum
pit to fix the straps. With the straps he could pull the old
ones out if they sink too far in the pit."

"I am ready for the petroleum pit," Rodriguez said. "I
am strong, no need for the straps. I will pull myself out at the
end of the bath. You too, Miss Deslonde. We will go together
into the petroleum pit."

"You first," she said, laughing.

"The movies too," Luís said. "You have heard of the rich
Mr Howard Hughes? He made movies and so Mr Cranfield
wants to make movies. Even here in the Balneario he wants
to make movies." He nodded to the four young women playing cards nearby. "Actresses for the movies."

"Won't we get to see Mr Cranfield?" Eloise asked.

"That is out of the question." He leaned forward to whisper. "Even these beautiful young girls have not seen Mr
Cranfield."

"And the manager? Will we never see the manager?"

"That too is out of the question. The manager is not well."

"I do so want to see the guest books."

"I will let you look at one book," Luís said. "An old one.
But only for a moment."

He left them and returned several minutes later with the

guest book for 1929. The leather cover was badly stained, presumably from rains during a time the hotel was closed. *Huéspedes*, identifying it as a guest register, was in bold silver letters on the cover.

Luís turned the pages quickly. There were newspaper clippings, publicity photographs and typed pages in faded blue ink among the handwritten entries.

"You are going too fast," Rodriguez complained. "We can't see."

He put his hand on a page to stop the turning. It was a list of guests for December, 1929. His eye fell on the name of Padre Miguel Pro, the implacable priest of the Cristeros rebellion.

"That is impossible!" Rodriguez said. "Padre Miguel Pro was shot. Everyone knows that. Your own History of the Pueblo says the Cristeros assassins were shot in 1928. Padre Miguel Pro and Vigil were the most important of the conspirators."

"I wasn't here," Luís said. "I was born in 1952."

"Padre Miguel Pro wasn't here either. He was dead."

"I have no responsibility for the information," Luís said, much irritated. "I will have to put the book back. I should not have let you see even this one book."

The next morning, however, Eloise was surprised to learn that she, but only she, the profesora and historian, would be allowed to look at all the old books. The manager was persuaded, Luís said, by her serious interest in the old times of the hotel, including the famous visitors of 1922. She was taken at once by Luís to a small windowless room which had the musty odor of long disuse. The walls were covered with publicity stills of actresses and bullfighters, some very faded, most of them inscribed. There were formal photographs of men in resplendent uniforms. A number of books with *Huéspedes* on the cover were piled neatly on a small table. On the desk were three framed photographs. A small boy holding a shiny machete nearly as large as himself, a handsome clean-shaven man of perhaps thirty, a young woman in a strapless bathing suit with a banner across the chest, *Miss Matamoros,* and beneath it a second banner, *La Bonita Chicana.* On the desk were a jug of water, a large glass and a small one, a bottle of tequila. Hotel stationery and two pens were neatly ranged. There was also an envelope addressed to herself.

"These are the manager's family?"

"This is the family of Antonio Vinalva, who left eight years ago. This was his office. It has not been changed. Here you see his father Ramón, his son Jaime, his wife the winner of a beauty contest. The son was adopted from an orphan of the village."

"Can't I see the manager now?"

"He is not well. He sends you a letter of explanation and welcome. Now I leave you to your work."

It had apparently been typed with the same old machine that had produced the one page "History." The only signature—*"The Manager"*—was written in large letters with a shaky hand. Why not a name?

Dear Profesora,

My dear friend Antonio Vinalva, many years manager of the Gran Hotel Balneario, has long the great desire to write in the Spanish language and in the English language both the true history of the hotel and of the pueblo Santa Rosalia. He learns the English language from the railroad as a youth in Rincón Antonio later in El Paso, USA. I see my sacred duty to finish this book for my friend but I am not a writer of histories. It is too much. Please write the history of the pueblo and the hotel using the secret documents and books. You have come to Santa Rosalia to write your thesis so please write my thesis also. Ask questions of bartender Luís Carrasco, he will ask me, I will answer, I am too sick to see you. Luís says you are beautiful young lady muy simpática so I regret. If you do this I will give you free room and bath with Jungle View for six months and drinks plus 50% my thesis profit.

Yours respectfully,

THE MANAGER

She was much amused, and began composing in her head a fitting reply. But meanwhile she was curious about the worthies who had given Antonio Vinalva their photographs. Here was the famous comedian Cantinflas in tattered uniform, kneeling before a demoralized bull, with a fond reference to a stay in the hotel. Beside it a newspaper photograph showed the corpses of two men in dark suits, with grinning spectators behind them. There was a handwritten comment in bold letters but faded ink: *La historia juzgará y hará fecunda la sangre de esos venerables martires.* The handwriting was remarkably similar to that of Cantinflas. An enlarged snapshot showed a handsome man on horseback in charro finery, inscribed *Por mi compañero Antonio,* with a sweeping signature, *Nicanor Díaz.* Eloise inspected this one closely, since the name had appeared several times in Stanfield's 1922 journal. Nicanor Díaz was *an attractive bandit and Robin Hood who turns many heads, even I'm afraid Monica's.* Stanfield had recorded his debt to Díaz for the interview that told him all he would ever know of Rosellen Maurepas's fate.

She found no more pictures of Stanfield or Monica Swift. There was a large array of publicity postcards and glossy pictures of dancers and actresses, apparently covering several decades. Some were in the bulky white tights of the early 1900's, with ample busts and soulful stares, others were in skirted bathingsuits that reached the knees, still others were clad in festooned or metallic bras with feathers or spangles at the hips. A Yolanda Montes in grass skirt, affectionately signing *Tongolele,* danced along a burlesque runaway, long black gloves extended to the upturned faces in the audience. "Tongolele" looked forward to visiting the hotel. There were others who wrote intimate messages in hurried handwriting. Carmen Carmin, Mimi Agaglia with a challenging smile, a very youthful Josefina Padilla in flamenco dress, Conchita Carmel. One willowy siren had even contributed a poem in a handwriting strikingly similar to the others. A more modest looking beauty had inscribed, enigmatically, and in quite different handwriting, *Antonio mi muerte te honrará. Adios.* She suspected Antonio Vinalva had written some of these messages himself.

On a table near a second door, which perhaps led to a closet, was a small glass case with several presumably cherished possessions: a box camera, a large Waltham pocket watch and an elaborate metal toy boat that had lost nearly all its paint, although it was still possible to see the water line and there were streaks of red near the small rusted screw. And a harmonica. A harmonica had appeared in Stanfield's two journals. The harmonica given to a young boy, possibly the father of Antonio Vinalva, had come back to remind him of a passionate moment in his youth!

She turned to the guest books, *Huéspedes*, each with its years on the cover. It was at once apparent they were day books for Antonio Vinalva's ideas and speculations as well as a register of hotel guests, and that sometimes he must have reached for the first book at hand when an idea occurred to him. For two or three weeks in *Huéspedes 1922-1924* there were only the names and dates of arrivals, with brief comments by Vinalva, usually in English, and more florid responses by the guests in Spanish or English. But this was followed by several entries on volcanic eruptions that occurred later. Evidently both Popocatepetl and Colima had erupted in the same month, January 1926. But not "our own" El Chichón, which still sleeps. *Y nuestro El Chichón, que todavía duerme.* Some of the commentaries had been written on separate sheets, then pasted in the guest book. There were also clippings of important events and a few newspaper references to the hotel.

On the first page for *Huéspedes 1922-1924* Vinalva had written an admonition to himself: *Faithful to my education in Rincón Antonio I will write every day in English. I must preserve the language for if not the language will die. 15 minutes a day minimum.* Eloise leafed through the pages, many of them water-stained, looking for Stanfield's name. She found first his letter from Cambridge, making a reservation, and a few pages later the record of his arrival. A comment on Stanfield's gentle manner was broken off for elaborate computations concerning a possible fight between Papa Jack and Luís Angel Firpo, the "Wild Bull of the Pampas." *Possible only with help of biggest New York financieros and gamblers. Will the champion demand too much money?* An entry written in small letters: *The teacher's secret. Does he think he will find in the pueblo a son or daughter born of his love for the girl he calls Marita? Is she the girl of pueblo kidnapped later by U.S. engineers also studying water of Rio Corte? The teacher is a spiritual man of romantic feelings. He has compassion for the poor Indios. I honor him also for his sorrow after the visit to the house of the Frenchman Dupoint.* There was nothing more on Stanfield in this first volume. But glancing far ahead she found his name in an entry on *The Lonely Deaths of Heroes* in the volume for 1929-1932:

The arm lost by Obregón in battle and preserved for years by Doctor Enrique Osornio is placed in a niche in the great monument in San Angel in the presence of the authorities. The skull of Venustiano Carranza also receives honors. The head of General Blanquet was in oil for many years. The good & evil are companions in death.

I think piously of the death of General Maycotte, who was bitten by an alligator, and of the mysterious death of Nicanor Díaz, who was a friend of the teacher Stanfield and the poetess Monica Swift. The hero Díaz in the rebellions twice attacked the fortress at Salina Cruz, the last time 1929. Two or three years later history says he dies alone and abandonado in the field from stomach disorder.

He returned once. If he return one more time incognito I will give him a room with the heroes on the third floor. But I think it can be only once.

On the next page Vinalva had copied a page from the autobiography of General Juan Andrew Almazán, published in 1958, and above it had written *The Secret Road of the Andes, The Death of My Father Ramón.*

So much suffering on a page! "El 15 de Septiembre 1916, con fuerte núcleos enemigos en las inmediaciones, nos internamos en la Sierra de Chimalapa." More, in English language: "we obtain information from the Indians we took with us. Without provisions, moving in mountains and at night not able to light fire soon the jungle brings sickness, madness, demoralisations, suicides and many calamaties for the brilliant column in front of which I have had so many victories and defeats." The Indians "we took with us"—only those words for the death of my father and other men of the village!!

Dona Juana Cata *A happy memory is visit of the saint of Tehuantepec Dona Juana Cata the loved one of Porfirio Díaz in his youth. She spends one night in the hotel, plays billiards and always wins. The table is dedicated to her visit with inscription. When she dies I go to La Chivela to wait for her funeral train. I put a peso on the railroad track another for Jaime. Both pesos flat and shiny very beautiful from the train passing over the two pesos.*

Eloise was surprised to find at the end of this volume a bulky envelope containing a smaller notebook from a much later year, perhaps even from quite recently, with entries obviously written at different times, and in handwriting that deteriorated noticeably. At times there were painfully wrought block letters.

The Coffin *The writer from Mérida asks again, 'When did the coffin come?'*

328

*And I say again, 'It came when I was away from the ho-
tel, the hotel was closed at that time.' The coffin was not
there in my childhood, nevertheless the third floor is sacred,
the Indians have always come from far places, sometimes
only three or four.*

*I did not tell this writer from Mérida of my three secret
visits to the room when Josefina Amor was gone with her
family in San Juan Evangelista. Once there was a blue light
from the bathroom. Once only candles. Once the blue light
came from inside the coffin and that time I was afraid to
look. A petrified corpse preserved in clay and oil will shine
the light of fósforo. The preserved corpse of the conqueror
Cortés lay in a coffin of crystal in the Hospital de Jesús then
was stolen. With the blue light from the bathroom I looked.
I saw the face of my father Ramón as a young man concierge
of the hotel dressed in fine clothes long before he was taken
by the generals Almazán and Felix Díaz. I was ashamed, I
told myself, 'This cannot be.' The third time was a general in
uniform but what general I could not say. I will not go into
the room again. The coffin came, money was paid for the
food and care of Josefina, the coffin was there even when the
hotel was closed and water covered the floor and the rats
swam from room to room. In my dreams I have seen rats
devour the corpse in the coffin. I will write no more of this.*

*The airplane Cuatro Vientos 20 June 1933 the aviators
from Spain Barberan and Collar in the airplane Cuatro
Vientos La Habana to Mexico crash in the inexplorada jungle.
Aviators looking for them see a shining in the jungle between
Santa Rosalia and Chiapas near the sleeping volcan El
Chichón. Years later the pieces of the Cuatro Vientos are found
far to the north and the aviators skeletons Barberan and Collar
killed by Indios in the mountains. Maybe, maybe not. Three
weeks after crash two Spaniards come down the Rio Corte
hungry sick one with broken arm to spend one night in hotel.
They refuse to give their name, they have no passport. I think*

it was the aviators. In the morning they are gone before the concierge wakes up. In Mexico their names go on the Monument of the Mártires of Aviación. If Barberan and Collar visited hotel incognito, they should be honored with plaque or urn on the third floor. They were heroes. I believe Barberan and Collar will return one more time.

This was followed by a list of "illustrious men, also women" who had visited the hotel.

General Francisco Villa, Centaur of the North (incognito)
General Emiliano Zapata, Caudillo and Liberator (incognito)
Presidente Calles, Maximum chief of the Revolution (incognito)
Dona Juana Cata Romero, the saint of Tehuantepec
Dolores del Rio, the sacred mother of Mexican movies
Padre Miguel Pro Juarez, dies for the Cristeros (incognito)
Nicanor Díaz, cabecilla, master of the Isthmus
Pepe Contreras, hero guerillero, liberator of Belize, Ecuador, etc.
Papa Jack, world champion

She leafed through several other volumes, with a growing suspicion that whoever wrote the entries had little concern for chronology in spite of the dates on the cover. It seemed to her many hours had passed before she came at last on the entry she had been seeking, in a volume for 1956-1958, it too entitled *Huéspedes* though in those years there was no road open to the village, and the hotel was closed.

And the event remembered was of 1922.

The Death of the Teacher Stanfield *Today I visit in my books Huéspedes my friends from the splendid times of the Gran Hotel Balneario. The walls were white, the chairs were not broken, there was music and dancing, famous actresses and segundo tiples from the Teatro Garibaldi, the great night of Papa Jack and Nicanor Díaz and the small boxer Jimmy Wilding. The kind quiet teacher Stanfield who came back after so many years. His death.*

He should not have gone with us to Casas Grandes, we could have told him what was there. On the trip he was tired, he could not breathe, still he walked into the jungle alone and came back without harm. The teacher Stanfield lay down while the German who would not tell his name talked. We went down into a tomb and here or could it be later in the day we lost the teacher who stays behind to rest. In one house I find his hat, he had rested there and gone on to walk without his hat, a mistake in the hot afternoon. In this house I knew there was something evil in a second room. I did not want to look but I looked. The shadow of a dead man in the corner standing up all his bones there the head everything. Not the dead man, only his shadow on the wall.

I cannot believe what I see. No wonder the teacher left his hat!

So now we look for him in other houses and in the tombs and then the houses away from the river covered with weeds, bushes, trees. There are many birds, I think I see above me a jaguar watching. The ball court of the old times is there where they died who lost the games. I alone go on, Monica Swift and the German writer look for him in the tombs. It is that way with the lady Rosellen the teachers friend she too goes on alone and the guides are afraid and they let her go. The guides say they see her with the dead playing so they do not go on. I think does the teacher hope to find her bones? After the ball court the houses are all covered there are trees growing in the walls and then no more houses. There is a small pyramid, tall trees, a green place, a waterfall.

And I see him, the teacher, I find him at last, lying in the field near this green place, his heart has stopped. Three women are there, poor peasants they stood beside him. They wanted to help him. But they saw me and ran away. Monica Swift says we must bury him in Casas Grandes, not in a tomb but in this place where he died. Not in Santa Rosalia, she says, why not here where he wanted to go. She says a poem.

The Fifth Floor

ROBERTO RODRIGUEZ was waiting for her in the lobby when she left the office. He was all expectation, and proposed a cocktail in the bar, on the terrace, or beside the empty pool. "You choose." But she waved him off, saying she was tired, and wanted to lie down. She would have liked to walk to the Rio Corte, which Stanfield had gone up fifty years before, and Rosellen fifty-two years before that. But she knew Rodriguez would follow her, if only at a distance, like a faithful dog told to go home. So she went to her room and lay down, staring up at the cracked ceiling, and reflected on her two hours with the guest books. She surmised the former manager Antonio Vinalva had forged some of the autographs and flattering inscriptions, and she very much doubted Pancho Villa and Zapata had ever visited the hotel. But the account of Stanfield's last hours and his death had the accent of truth. The pyramid and the small waterfall existed, and would be there still, however overgrown the ball court. Somewhere nearby both Rosellen and Stanfield lay, though perhaps no jaguar still roamed the ruins, and there would be no women in the grove, no spirits of the dead playing. She too, she was now convinced, would go to Casas Grandes.

That evening, when they again assembled at the bar, Luís proposed a novel wager. The hotel had a large number of unlabeled bottles—wines ranging from ordinary Mexican blanco to fine old Bordeaux, tequila but also Martell three-star, even Scotch more than forty years old. The provenance was a freight car shunted onto a La Chivela siding, and relieved of its contents by revolutionary bandits. For many years the bottles lay in an insufficiently protected place and all the labels had been eaten away. Those who years later participated in the private auction did not know what they were bidding on. Now tonight he, Luís, would open any bottle for five dollars U.S. currency. Who would take a chance?

"How do you know the Scotch is more than forty years old?"

"Because this revolutionary theft of the train was forty years ago, during the confusions of the time."

"And the private auction? You were there?"

"It was before my time."

"I will take a chance," Rodriguez said. "I will entertain our American friends. Don't forget, Luís, I am a friend of the hotel. Be fair."

"The bottles are not marked."

He called to Jimmy Wilding at the end of the bar, and the four girls at their usual table.

"Come old champion boxer, come young actresses. There is a taste for everyone."

They gathered at the bar as Luís wiped the dusty old bottle and held it up to the light.

"Allow me to do the honors," Rodriguez said. "It was my five dollars."

The four girls had been in a bad mood all day, and threatened to leave unless word came soon from the fifth floor. But they perked up with the fun of the mysterious bottle being opened. The night before two of the girls had paid a noisy visit to Rodriguez's room with much laughter and ambiguous sounds as of wrestling and sudden movements of the bed. The games were interrupted from time to time for serious conversations in which all three talked at once.

The bottle was a good bourbon, surely a hundred proof, with a rich almost syrupy taste.

"It's quite worthy of New Orleans," Eloise said. "I think the private auction should be part of the hotel history. Won't you ask the manager when it was?"

Luís looked at her warily.

"Please remember only you have read the guest books."

"I won't reveal any secrets. But do tell me this about the guest book we all saw. How can the manager comment on new guests when he's sick in bed and doesn't see us?"

"He asks me questions, then tells me what to write. He asks for example the color of your eyes, Miss Deslonde. I tell him they are brown. In Spanish we say 'ojos café.'"

"The handwriting changes a lot, sometimes just a child's block letters, sometimes quite good. But the style doesn't change that much. The manager sounds a bit like Antonio Vinalva, what he wrote long ago. Sometimes he even sounds a lot like you."

"The handwriting of Antonio Vinalva was learned in Rincón Antonio in the English school for the children of the railroad workers. He sat there among small children, learning both the English language and how to write in the English manner. I learned my good writing in Mérida."

"And the manager?"

"I don't know. Maybe in the U.S. If you wish I will ask him."

The evening brought a further surprise. After dinner the curandero Pascualito came to their table but addressed only Eloise in words dropped syllable by syllable. Wilding had seen him before, and Luís of course. But no one else. He was in a soiled gray robe, no trousers apparently. But his steel-rimmed glasses and skeptical expression gave him the look of a medical man. A fanatic medical man, one who lived on roots and herbs. His baked red skin was drawn tight over sharp bones. She thought he looked like a mummy.

"I have come with an invitation from Mr Cranfield. He receives you tomorrow afternoon at five o'clock. Tea."

"Just me?"

"You are the writer. The manager informed Mr Cranfield. You write the history of the hotel."

There was a rapid exchange in very colloquial Spanish between Rodriguez and the curandero. She caught hardly a word.

"What was all that?"

"I told him that I must be included in the tea. I explained I am your assistant."

"Really that's too much! I'm a pretty pliable person, Mr Rodriguez, but you are pushing things rather hard. I don't want any help."

"Whatever you wish, Miss Deslonde. I too am pliable."

The girl Dolores, whose English was quite good, had followed this exchange intently.

"But we must go too! We've been waiting ten days to get to the fifth floor."

"I will represent you," Rodriguez said. "Think of me as a father looking after your interests."

"Some father!" This time it was Suzy. "How about last night?"

"Only Miss Deslonde," the curandero said.

When the time came, however, Rodriguez contrived to come along. The rusted accordion inner door of the elevator moved so slowly that he was able to slip in before the curandero could close it, and once in he was not to be dislodged. He was all smiles, speaking more rapidly than ever, and evidently making promises. Talking all the while, he took out his wallet and showed an array of official-looking cards visible in their many plastic covers. The edge of a large banknote was folded over to suggest many more behind it. He promised to remain in the hallway if Cranfield still wanted to exclude him.

The curandero accepted the banknote.

There was no hallway. The elevator gave immediately onto what was evidently living room, studio, kitchen, medical consultation room and laboratory, with the odors of a poorly-ventilated toilet. At one end of the room was a screen for moving pictures and beside it an array of maps folded over a bamboo rack. On the other side of the screen a life-size printed anatomical chart of a man was pinned to the wall. The map showing was a large one of southern Mexico. Just beyond the screen were a stove and refrigerator, pots were boiling on the stove. The toilet odors, she surmised, came from the stove, although they might also emanate from the patient, who was seated in a high and elaborate wheelchair in the very center of the room. Beside the chair was a table with bottles, one of which appeared to contain black living things. The floor was littered with crumpled tissue.

She had never seen a man so emaciated. The bathrobe was loosely open over a chest that was all ribs, although the nipples were surprisingly pronounced. Tangled gray hair fell in a wild shower that covered the shoulders, but the moustache and stubble of beard had received some crude attention. The arms were thin sticks dotted with bandages. The oddly swollen belly and emaciated legs emerged from gray underpants. Dark toenails curled up obscenely. The patient (for already she thought him as that, not as the "millionaire recluse") was laboriously at work on the wheelchair's levers and wheels, turning slowly to greet them.

He glared. It might have been only his eyes that were still alive. They fell on the interloper Rodriguez.

"Who are you? You look Mex."

"Licenciado Roberto Rodriguez, sir. A lawyer and lover of your country who longs to be helpful to anyone honoring Mexico with art films that reflect truthfully our tragic history."

"What's all this? You weren't invited."

"As a writer myself I have offered to help Miss Deslonde

337

with her history. I go where she goes. As a lawyer I represent
young actresses waiting patiently for interviews and screen
tests. Exquisite actresses."

"They will have to wait longer. Luís says they look like
secretaries."

"Good-natured Mexican girls who only want a chance,
Mr Cranfield. The best of Mexican womanhood. Screen tests
clothed or nude, your choice."

"You sound like a madman. Go back downstairs."

The curandero tiptoed to his patient, cupped his ear with
his hands and whispered something. It seemed to her that of
the three weird men in the room, Cranfield might well be the
madman. What had she got herself into?

"If you don't mind, Mr Cranfield, I would prefer to have
Mr Rodriguez stay. He has been most helpful to me."

"Very well. Sit in those two chairs there. Sit facing me."

There was an awkward silence, which was broken by the
curandero, who had approached quite silently and was now
taking the sick man's pulse.

"Be brief," the curandero said, "Do not waste our time."

"Leave me alone with my guests," Cranfield said petu-
lantly, but without much conviction. Like any patient, he was
somewhat afraid of his doctor.

"I'm glad to meet you," Eloise said at last. "But I rather
wondered why you wanted to see me."

"I need a writer, an honest writer for a change, one who
can see things as they are. The manager says you are a historian."

"Just a graduate student, really. Besides, the manager really doesn't know anything about me. We haven't even met
him."

"He has my full confidence, he knows everything that
goes on."

"What is it you want written, Mr Cranfield? I don't know
anything about screenplay writing."

"Who said anything about a screenplay? What do I call

you, anyway? Professor? You're young for a historian."

"Just Eloise will do."

"All right. First of all I want some decent publicity for my hotel." He reached into a voluminous pocket and pulled out one of the hotel brochures that caught her eye in New Orleans. "Look at this trash! Maybe there were forty-five-round fights long ago but there's nothing like that now. I want more emphasis on health. A brand new brochure with testimonials on the spring and the petroleum pit. Mexican herbs. Know any holistic medicine?"

"Not really."

The curandero looked up from the boiling pots.

"To cure the body one must first eliminate the impurities and pollutions. Then the herbs. Healthy body, healthy soul."

"It's a disgrace I have this fine hotel and the great climate and nobody comes."

"The personnel need a shaking up," Rodriguez offered. "I have experience in hotel management."

"I have a manager."

"The bartender says it's not the season," Eloise said. "And transportation problems."

"Luís is a fool. People like to get away from the paved roads and the pollution. How many people get to ride in a 1921 Stanley Steamer? You can help write some good publicity. If you're a historian you can get the facts straight. Answer all the lies."

"Lies about the hotel?"

"Lies about me." He leaned forward, his bony hands clung to the steel arms of the wheelchair. They dug in like claws. His voice had fallen to a whisper, but an intense, crazed, whisper. "I want to get the record straight, it's a job for a historian. Every damned journalist that's written about me has written some new bullshit. Then that bullshit becomes a source for the next journalist."

He looked at her expectantly.

"Yes, I've heard some of the rumors," Eloise said. "I found

them hard to believe."

"I don't listen to rumors," Rodriguez volunteered.

"Be quiet! Be quiet and listen."

Cranfield looked with some anxiety at the curandero, who was now holding a burning candle inside a large glass cup. He tested the cup on the back of his wrist, then went on heating it.

"I'm not in the best of health," he said. "There may not be much time to get the record straight."

"You're writing an autobiography?"

"Just compiling a record for posterity. Maybe fifty pages, only the facts. You will be well paid for helping me. Everyone knows I pay well."

"I hadn't really intended to stay here that long. But if you'll help me with my work, Mr Cranfield, I'll try to help you. I won't need any money. Or not much."

"Yes, the manager told me what you were up to. You want to see all the guest books."

"Then you see the sick manager? Why does everyone just say 'the manager?' Doesn't anyone use his name?"

"I just call him 'Tex.'"

"Luís says you bought the hotel a long time ago. Did you ever know Mr Vinalva the former manager?"

Cranfield stared.

"Why do you ask me that?"

"There are so many interesting things about the hotel's history. Is there really a coffin on the third floor? Is there anyone in it? Mr Vinalva in the guest books claimed he saw a corpse. Two for that matter, first his father, then a general."

Cranfield laughed harshly.

"Ask Pascualito about the coffin. That's more in his line."

The curandero was again beside the wheelchair, but in no mood for questioning. He pushed aside the bathrobe and affixed the heated cup to Cranfield's left nipple, which could be seen through the glass to rise.

"For the spleen," he said in the tone of a powerful doctor conducting ward rounds for medical students. He pressed the cup more firmly to the patient's flesh.

"Can't you wait till my guests have gone?"

"There is no time to lose."

The curandero removed the cup, inspected the erected nipple and rubbed it with one of the pomades on the bedside table. This went on and on.

"That's enough. Let's leave out the spraying."

"You are ungrateful," the curandero replied. "Say the word and I will return to my village and leave you here to die. If I stay I must be allowed to do my work."

"Of course, Pascualito. Of course."

The curandero went back to his stove and his boiling mixtures.

"I can help with the hotel's publicity," Rodriguez put in. "I know all the advertising managers in Mérida. In the capital too. I can arrange free advertising in the form of travel articles."

"Go downstairs, Rodriguez. Take the elevator and go down." His eyes suddenly took on a paranoid glare. "You're in one of the agencies, aren't you? FBI, right? Aren't any drugs here. Treasury police, is it? I know a plainclothesman when I see one. What are you up to here, really?"

"A writer and lawyer helping an American friend. Also a little archeology, sir. A few ruins."

What next, Eloise thought.

"Are you after Pepe Contreras? Is that why you're here?"

"There is some mistake, sir. Pepe Contreras is dead. He died in the ruins of Guiengola in 1978."

"Keep quiet!" Cranfield roared. "I have information Contreras may be hiding out in the area with some of his men. Reliable information."

"I am not a policeman. However, I know what I know. I have seen photographs of the body." Rodriguez opened his mouth, the tongue protruding thickly, and with thumbs and

341

index fingers held his eyes wide open so that much white showed. "The face was like this."

"Get in the elevator. Go downstairs."

"Let's get back to the actresses, please. Only an interview, not even the screen test."

They were interrupted by the curandero, who seized Cranfield's left wrist and hunted for his pulse, then dug his fingers in hard. After a long interval he dropped the hand in disgust.

"These people are tiring you. Finish your business."

"I'll get to the point, Rodriguez. You too, Eloise, you will be a witness. I am just an old man who wants to make movies. There is a great story here, Pepe Contreras getting terminated more than once but surviving. And turning up here in the mountains for a last stand. I want to do a real life documentary. You think he's dead? Let me tell you something, these Mex guerillas have nine lives. Zapata himself was here in the hotel even after all the newspapers had him dead."

"Zapata is immortal in the spirit," Rodriguez offered. "But not in the flesh. The same with Contreras."

Cranfield ignored him.

"If Pepe Contreras is in this area, I want to know about it. If he's up the river or in the jungle or in one of those ruined cities."

"In Casas Grandes?" Eloise put in.

"You know about Casas Grandes? What else do you know?"

"People have hidden out there in the past."

"Exactly. That's the story line. Contreras's last stand here in a ruined city. Torture and confession, then termination. Another Che Guevara! If the Mex FBI is coming here for Contreras, an interrogation and all the rest, I want to be there. And have exclusive rights to the execution. What wouldn't the world give to see the interrogation and death of Guevara! Termination with extreme prejudice, right?" Cranfield's expression had changed in what seemed to her a most alarming way. "I have money," he finished lamely.

"I don't know what you're talking about," Eloise said. "I think we'd better go. We can come back another time."

"Turn that map over, Eloise. We'll look at the next one."

It was an enlarged map of the Chimalapa region, with the Rio Corte curling up into the mountains and the unexplored areas. San Miguel, Santa Maria Chimalapa, Santa Rosalia, and, designated as ruins with clusters of dots, Chimalapilla and Casas Grandes. At the extreme southern rim of the map was the dormant volcano El Chichón.

"Imagine old Pepe Contreras somewhere up here in this accursed jungle, maybe in one of these ruined cities the Indians won't go to. Yes, Casas Grandes." Cranfield's voice had changed again, it was almost a chant, the voice of a veteran moviemaker musing aloud with a mad eloquence. "We have Contreras worn out, old as I am, sick, diarrhea no doubt, fever. Hanging on with just a few last diehards, maybe veterans of the '68 uprising in Mexico City. Already old then, even then worn out, the old revolutionary surrounded by crazy children smoking dope and making speeches? Think of that for a scene. Fifty years of useless rebellion, even sixty. What a picture Eisenstein would have made! Pepe Contreras—all the way from a shirtless kid in the capital, listening to Madero and the rest of the fools, all the way to this godforsaken jungle!"

"Sounds very exciting," Eloise managed.

Roberto Rodriguez had moved his chair closer and closer to the sick man.

"You misunderstand our history, sir. You get everything wrong. Make a romantic movie instead about love and sex in the jungle. There are young actresses downstairs waiting to serve you. Forget about Pepe Contreras, who is dead anyway. Make a good love movie on a low budget, you have in your hotel an ideal background."

"Get out of my sight!" Cranfield shouted.

He pulled himself up as though about to stand, then fell

back. His breath came in gasps. The curandero looked up from his boiling pots, rushed over to his patient, and began to massage his chest. He raised the matchstick arms above the head, then resumed the massaging. This was followed by the spraying that Cranfield had hoped to deter. The curandero took several long swallows from an unmarked bottle, filled his mouth with the liquid and swirled it noisily, then sprayed the chest and its protruding ribs. Cranfield's fierce eyes were closed.

"You have tired him too much," the curandero said. "You have sucked away some of his life. You leave at once."

"Wait!" Rodriguez said. "We must wait while Mr Cranfield rests and gets the curandero's treatment. Miss Deslonde, Miss Deslonde! If we leave him now we may never have another chance. At least think of the actresses."

Rodriguez's voice woke Cranfield from his stupor. He opened his cold yet bloodshot eyes.

"What's this? What's this? I sent you downstairs."

"Only interviews. Ten minutes for each actress."

"Get back," Cranfield shouted. "Get back downstairs. Otherwise I will have you thrashed and caned."

"I think we'd all better leave," Eloise said.

One of the first results of that visit so suddenly broken off was the angry departure of the four starlets. They had waited in the bar, watching the forbidden elevator, fishnet stockings taut and blouses discreetly unbuttoned, for a summons from the fifth floor. Screen tests fully dressed or nude, as the ancient gringo filmmaker preferred.

But nothing! Last night Mr Rodriguez had been full of promises. Soon there would be screen tests for all! Suzy pointed a carmine finger sharp as a nail file.

"You put your mouth to my breast like a child to its mother's tit. I permitted that, Mr Rodriguez. I rocked you like a baby in my arms. I did even more. So did Dolores. And what did we get for it? Not even an interview."

"Be fair," Consuela said. "We asked for the insults. Nobody told us to come to the Balneario."

"I was not insulted," Lupita said. "I did not go to Mr Rodriguez's room."

"The newspapers said there would be dancing every night in the hotel discoteca Salon Oaxaca. There is no discoteca in the hotel, only this bar and empty dining room. The swimming pool also is empty, the air condition does not work, nobody plays roulette. The water of the spring is disgusting."

"Where are all the rich gringo tourists and the licenciados from Mérida and the gamblers from Vera Cruz?"

"It is not the season," Luís said. "People worry about the earthquakes which in fact are small and harmless. The hotel bus is disabled. Next weekend will be more exciting."

"It will be exciting without us."

They flounced to the farthest table, chattering.

"Give them one of the five-dollar bottles," Rodriguez instructed Luís. "It is true they have a right to be disappointed. I will pay half, that is no more than fair, the hotel pays the other half."

Jimmy Wilding was at his usual place at the end of the bar. Eloise beckoned to him to join them. But he was off somewhere, probably reliving a Papa Jack fight.

"What are we to make of Mr Cranfield? First he wants me to write publicity for the hotel, then it's publicity for himself, a fifty-page résumé, maybe a short autobiography. But then he got off on his movie scenario about the life and death of Pepe Contreras. His last days and his execution, as though it were going to happen in front of the camera."

"His last days occurred four years ago," Rodriguez said. "Pepe Contreras is dead. Mr Cranfield would need to use somebody else's execution from the files. There are fine newsreels of executions during our Mexican revolution with blindfolds. He has only to pick up the telephone, the Cineteca can provide executions for the asking. For a fee."

Luís had stopped polishing glasses, but remained with his back to them, facing the mirror and the framed photographs. But now he turned to them.

"As a bartender I do not join conversations unless asked. But this time I must speak. Pepe Contreras is alive. In fact he visited the hotel very recently."

Rodriguez was dumbfounded.

"How recently?"

"Pepe Contreras is an old friend of the manager. He visited the manager in his room. He came after dark and left before dawn, that much I know. No doubt they talked of old times and the revolutions."

"I saw the body myself," Rodriguez said, "Newspaper photographs of the tongue sticking out. There were black and white pictures the first day, then beautiful color in the gráfico magazines. Only Pepe Contreras had such long white hair and the famous gap between the teeth. You saw the man yourself, Luís?"

"I was in San Miguel. You can ask Jorge the night watchman. He took him to the manager's room. Or ask the manager."

"How can we ask the manager?" Eloise asked. "No one gets to see him."

But the next morning she did receive an invitation. The bedridden manager wanted to see her "at her convenience." But it was evident from Luís's manner that she should go at once.

"He sleeps much of the day in a room that is kept dark. Often he forgets whether it is morning or night. Sometimes he forgets who he is. But today his voice is strong. He says to me, 'Bring the beautiful historian with the ojos café.' So we must go right away, before he goes back to sleep."

"I am also invited," Rodriguez said. "That goes without saying."

"No, only Miss Deslonde."

So she was to see the forbidden third floor. Luís led her

through the kitchen, past two maids who did not look up from their work, down to a cellar full of rusted pipes and discarded furniture, then up stairs lit only at every turn by a single feeble bulb. The stairway looked and smelled as though it had never been cleaned. It ended in a locked door that Luís opened after much fumbling with the key.

"The third floor," he said. "Please do not repeat to your friends anything you see or hear."

The poorly lit hallway was identical in design with that of her own floor, and ran as in any hotel between rows of numbered rooms. But at its farthest end, in the direction of the river, a scared Indian woman stood by a closed door as though protecting it. She was wearing a shapeless white sack over a dark skirt. The woman crossed herself while holding tight to the doorknob. It could only be Josefina Amor.

Luís knocked very softly on the manager's door, then opened it a few inches. The room was dark, with lowered blinds, and had the smell of a sickroom. At first she could make out only the glitter of a brass bedstead, then a table with a glass and small bottles. She saw the head of the sick man, a darker shadow, the shine of spectacles caught by the light from the door. His frail body seemed no more than a rumpling of the blanket.

"You must stand here. A little more this way, Miss Deslonde, so the manager can see you. Here, with your back to the light. Now I will leave you with him."

A surprisingly strong voice came out of the darkness.

"You are kind to write the history of the hotel and the pueblo and you are also kind to pay a visit to an old man."

She was sure he had been pondering his English sentences while awaiting her, dredging them up from a deep past when he had occasion to use the language often. She was at once certain the man in the bed was Antonio Vinalva, who would be eighty-eight or eighty-nine. He had disappeared in 1968, the one page "history" said. That was the year the hotel closed. When had he returned?

"I am not quite sure what you want me to write. So many strange things have happened. There are so many fascinating events in your Guest Books. Such interesting people."

"Exactly, that is the reason for the history. They must not be forgotten. Dona Juana Cata must not be forgotten. Or the secret visit of Emiliano Zapata, or President Plutarco Calles incognito, or the great boxing champion Papa Jack or the noble Nicanor Díaz. There have been many beautiful Mexican actresses and many heroes of the people, also magnificent bullfighters. Luís Carrasco tells me at the bar you talk of the old hero Pepe Contreras. Contreras was my soul brother. Only two visits to the hotel, but I will not forget him. The last time he stood where you are standing. His hair is as white as mine. You can not see my hair but it is white."

"Mr Cranfield seems very interested in Pepe Contreras."

With great effort the man in the bed propped himself up on one elbow.

"I tell you in confidence a secret. Mr Cranfield is crazy. Once in Texas he was a millionaire with thick arms and a great hairy chest. He owned many hotels. But now he is crazy. You must believe nothing he says."

She decided to move ahead without caution, knowing the visit might end abruptly.

"Is Pepe Contreras alive? Some people think he is dead."

"That is foolish nonsense. Pepe Contreras escaped from prison, I have forgotten what prison. And now he is hiding in the mountains. He wanted to take the camino secreto where my father died and the generals ate their horses, also the meat of monkeys. I advised Cases Grandes. Pepe Contreras has known many prisons but always he escapes. He comes out of prison rubbing his hands, no enemy is too powerful. The brutal chicleros and the Yankee oil companies and the Germans of the coffee plantations. The dictators in Guatemala, the evil ones in Surinam and Belize, also the corrupt thieves in the federal district. Pepe Contreras fights them all."

"When was he in the hotel? Was it long ago?"

There was a long silence. When he spoke again, it was in a quieter voice, like the voice of one hypnotized or drugged.

"Not long ago. It was after the fall of the airplane Cuatro Vientos, maybe last month. But we must talk of your own history book, Miss Deslonde. You want to know about the kind teacher Stanfield, who came back to the pueblo after many years. The young boxer also returned but not the lady poet or the champion. Papa Jack was insulted by an actress."

"Yes, I read about that."

"The teacher Stanfield was a good man. He made mistakes, I do not remember exactly what mistakes, we all make mistakes. He came back to Santa Rosalia to learn about the young Indian girl and about the woman from New Orleans. I forget her name. Think of that, you too are from New Orleans."

"Rosellen Maurepas. My great-great-grandmother Delphine Deslonde was her good friend."

"You want to honor the people who came before you. With your history you reach across all the terrible things that have happened. So that is why you are a young historian, young and beautiful. Please move a little back so I can see you."

"Wouldn't you like me to turn on the light?"

"I do not want you to see me."

Again she felt a need to push ahead. At any moment he might fall asleep.

"Mr Stanfield died in Casas Grandes. Was he buried there?"

"There is a small pyramid of the ancients, also a waterfall and beautiful trees. That is where we buried him, near the small pyramid. A jaguar lives there, sometimes in the ball court, sometimes by the pyramid. There are women who live in the trees near the waterfall. Your grandmother Rosellen is buried with the teacher, they died in the same place. Let me tell you a secret that you must put in your history. The dead are permitted to return once. Only once. Some have returned

349

to the place where they died, others to the place of their birth. A few have returned to the Gran Balneario where they spent happy times in the great days of the hotel when there was dancing every weekend. The Spanish aviators of the Cuatro Vientos spent a night in the hotel, after they died, but that was their only visit."

"And Emiliano Zapata?"

"Of course. He came to us from the camino secreto, but incognito. Look on the table, you will find the Golden Book. Luís put it there for you. Open it where I have put the knife and read to me."

She found the book.

"It's too dark, I can't read without the light."

He stirred in the bed, a feeble overhead light came on.

"Please read aloud but do not look at me."

The handwriting of the first entries was firm, but the final one was in childish block letters that wandered over the page. The words, however, had been chosen with care.

General Emiliano Zapata, April 12, 1920. Room 31 with Jungle View. *He asks for spring water to be brought to his room. Three bottles. Without hesitation I know him but he puts a finger to his lips above which larger than in life is the famous moustache. His left hand graciously rests on his hip, the hypnotic eyeballs with much white gaze past me to inquire if we are alone. There is no sign of the terrible wounds, the beautiful vest is unspoiled, the silver stripes on the trousers shine even in the poor light of the lobby. There is to be no speech between us, I lead him silently to his room. Only two words as we enter:* Está bien.

Padre Miguel Pro, March 20, 1929. Room 36, with fine gold crucifix. *He has come on foot through the heaviest rain, the inexplorada jungle, his beautiful black shoes are covered with mud. It is the first time I have waited behind the desk of the concierge so in my heart I knew some great visitor would come. He stands at the entrance, on the stone letters* GRAN HOTEL BALNEARIO, *waiting for me to speak. I have no love for the Cristeros, I honor the dead president, but I know my hotel is honored by this brave mistaken man. I kneel, I kiss his hand which has no ring, the hand is cold. But no blood anywhere. He shakes his head when I ask if supper should be brought to his room. I know without asking that he too will be in the hotel for only one night before going on his way. He will go from here to Casas Grandes.*

Dona Juana Cata, August 6, 1965. *Slowly she unbuttons her beautiful cloak of white fur. Her face is hidden by a veil yet I see the burning eyes of a young sensualista girl. In my youth I thought she was a witch, now I know she is a saint. And she speaks, she calls me by my name. 'Antonio, take me to the billiard room.'*

Nicanor Díaz, 2 octobre 1938. 36 con balcón. *My old friend the cabecilla embraces me! I long to ask him of all his great adventures which end so sadly, but he wants to go to his room. To think this noble hero and handsome man died alone in a field, even no horse, with terrible pains of the stomach. In the morning he will be gone on his road into the inexplorada jungle.*

Pepe Contreras. 1 mai 1982. Room 31. *He sleeps in the room of the great hero of the revolution. His white hair hangs like moss from the trees, he is very tired. Too tired for a supper or bath. Josefina Amor gives me a bath she could give a bath to Pepe Contreras. Tomorrow he will look for the camino secreto where the brave Ramón and so many of our village died captured by the evil generals. There was also a Spanish knight on a horse, with a rusty sword. He looked like one of the Conquistadores but very old. He had a servant with him who rode on a mule. They must have come from San Cristobal.*

She put down the book. She went to the old man's bed-side and took his hand.

"I understand," she said gently. The Spanish knight loved one of the kitchen maids."

"How did you know that?"

"I am a historian. I know many things. I even know where you learned to speak English so well. "

She listened to his breathing in the dark room smelling of sickness and age.

"It was from the railroad workers," he said at last. "They gave me a watch. My name is Antonio Vinalva, my father was named Ramón. You will find it all in the history."

"Yes, Antonio, I will call you Antonio, and none of it will be forgotten. You knew Charles Stanfield, who knew Rosellen Maurepas. And she knew William Walker who conquered Nicaragua and Jefferson Davis who was President of the Confederacy and General Beauregard who married Mathilde Deslonde! How far we go into the past!"

"Don't forget Porfirio Díaz at the ceremony of the open-ing of the railroad, and Dona Juana Cata the saint of Tehuantepec. She defeated us all in billiards. As a young woman she was a witch."

"Yes, yes. You put a peso on the tracks that was flattened by her funeral train."

"And Tongolele, also the beautiful Conchita Carmel. Tell me, dear historian, did all these beautiful stars of the theater and movies really come to the hotel? Are they in the Guest Books?"

"Of course they are there. I saw the names myself. And you knew Nicanor Díaz the bandit who liked Monica Swift. And Pepe Contreras. Did you ever talk with Mr Cranfield about Pepe Contreras? Did you tell him of his visit? Did you tell him Pepe Contreras was going into the mountains?"

There was a long silence. Again Vinalva was making an effort to sit up.

"Mr Cranfield is crazy." There was another long silence, his voice seemed much weaker, it was time for her to leave. "I advised him to go to Casas Grandes, not to the camino secreto."

"I want to go to Casas Grandes," she said. "I want to see where the teacher died."

"No," he said. "Not yet. You are young and beautiful and must stay here in the Gran Hotel Balneario to write the history."

"Yes," she said. "May I come to see you again tomorrow?"

There was no answer, only his heavier breathing.

She returned to her room feeling inexplicably tired and at once lay down, too tired even to turn on the ceiling fan. It was as though many hours had passed. A shaft of sunlight falling on the cracked wall had the uncertain quality of late afternoon, and at its farthest reach a small lizard was watching her, only its head in pale yellow light, the body and tail in shadow. Hours later, many hours it must have been, she woke to find the room all but dark, but with the metal railing of her balcony glittering from an almost full moon. The ceiling fan was turning, a slight metallic snap at the end of each slow turn. She remembered distinctly not turning it on, and was at once aware, quite calmly aware, there was someone in the room, standing in the deeper darkness near the door she had doubtless failed to lock. Yet not "someone," rather an insubstantial presence, an emanation of the darkness itself, one that might or not take on human shape, even possibly her own. It seemed altogether acceptable that she could be standing solidly by her bed, but also be waiting quietly in the darkness by the door.

It would not be Monica, certainly not Rosellen who had never been in the hotel, it could only be Stanfield. Her intuition on that first night had been correct. Now she was sure the room she was occupying had been Charles Stanfield's, and that she was reliving an incident of his life, one that had been recorded in his Journal for the night on which he took his solitary jungle walk. She was both herself and her not unwelcome visitor, who would be gone yet not gone when she turned on the light. It was waiting for her by the door. And now she too longed to venture out into the night, though not necessarily for a jungle walk. It might be to find her way to the Rio Milagro where a white dwarf had been seen, looking for snails and cracking them against rocks.

Only Luís was in the bar, he and a woman on her knees scrubbing. Neither of them noticed her. So too for the sleeping Indians, huddled as though against winter cold, not one was keeping vigil although she could see flickering blue light in the third floor room where there was supposed to be a coffin. She decided to take a quiet walk around the sleeping village, first the plaza and the open-air jail where the single prisoner would be curled on the ground, then to the edge of the jungle a few hundred feet beyond the cemetery. Time enough then to decide whether to proceed a short distance into it, if only to see the green lights of the cocuyos floating in the forest darkness, or to set out in some quite different direction, perhaps even to the Rio Milagro. She was sure she would be able to find it, if it became apparent that this was where she was supposed to go. For still it lingered, the calm sense that she was both herself and a silent companion guiding her.

She heard the faint bubbling of the spring before she came upon it, then saw the silver ripples and a brighter shine where it caught some floating object, a piece of wood with a metallic strip if not the scales of a dead fish. No, she would certainly not kneel to cup her hands and drink the disgusting water, once was enough for any reasonable visitor to Santa Rosalia. And yet here she was on her knees, the water was warm on her hands, only a sip would do no harm. At the far end of the silent village a man had begun to sing drunkenly and two others were shouting him down. This lasted less than a minute, followed by an eerie silence. She was aware of the horse even before she heard the first rustling of its quiet approach to the spring. She did not have to look up to know that a horse was watching her with curiosity and that a silver eyeball would shine in the ever more intense moonlight. Soon there would be other animals coming to the spring to drink as in the very old times when even Charles Stanfield would have watched them, he too sleepless on the warm night. The teacher would be there.

The dwarf of the Rio Milagro would have to wait, since she had already decided to return to the hotel, not to her own room, but rather to the third floor. The decision had apparently been made for her by her silent companion, who was still both outside her and within. On the way, it was after all only a small detour, she paused to look at the petroleum pit. No wild hogs tonight or other animals to bathe in the moonlight shining on the oily surface and its silver and turquoise froth. Tonight too there would again be water in the hotel's empty pool, an old frog on a floating lily pad, the friendly monkey sleeping in the tamarind tree.

The woman was still scrubbing the floor in the Salon Oaxaca, Luís was still cleaning glasses behind the bar, it was as though no time had passed.

"I want the key," she said firmly. "The manager is expecting me back."

He studied her for a few minutes, frowning, then took the key from a trousers pocket.

"Why not? For days now he has talked about the 'beautiful historian.' Soon he will be dictating his thoughts to you not to me. Give me a moment, then I will escort you."

"No need for that," she said, again with a firmness that surprised them both. "I know the way."

Once again the two maids in the kitchen did not look up from their work and she found without difficulty the stairs to the cellar, then the much narrower stairs to the third floor. This time the climb seemed endless, and she had to catch her breath before trying the key to the locked door. No problem, the key turned instantly as though the lock had been oiled since their earlier visit. This time the young Indian woman was sitting hunched over on a straight chair asleep, a comic book on her lap. Eloise knocked very quietly on the door to the manager's room, so as not to wake the woman yet give the man in the bed due notice of her arrival. A pro forma knock, so to speak, otherwise he would have reason to complain.

The room was lit only from the bathroom but now she could see better than before the ravaged yet still handsome face of the sleeping man and the long white hair curled neatly above it like a halo. How handsome he must have been when courting all those actresses! Even as she watched, a few of the dark folds beneath his closed eyes seemed to be changing, and she now saw that his small moustache had been neatly trimmed.

She brought a straight chair to the bedside and settled down for a long but not disagreeable wait. Time to reflect on the events of the evening and her sense that she was being quietly guided through them, living in an unmoving present time yet also in some earlier and more exciting existence. How nice it would have been, might still be, to find Stanfield and Monica Swift waiting for her in the Salon Oaxaca!

Vinalva's quiet voice from the bed interrupted her reverie.

"You have come back. You want to hear about the old times."

"Yes, always that."

"I am very tired, I cannot answer many questions."

"I am happy just to sit by you," she said. "Just to think about your wonderful life and how handsome you were when the actresses were here. Conchita Carmel and the others."

"Don't forget Mimi Agaglia and Josefina Padilla. And Tongolele, who came from the South Seas and danced in a grass skirt."

"I'll think about them all."

It was pleasant to sit in the room faintly lit thanks to the bathroom door left ajar. On the walls there seemed to be more pictures than earlier in the evening and she noticed for the first time an old gramophone with a large conical speaker. Antonio Vinalva had again fallen asleep, and she was tempted to open the Golden Book, which was almost within reach, and to read again about the death of Stanfield. Perhaps she would find there whether he had in fact lived in the same room.

He was not asleep.

"Do not be afraid, dear lady," he said in a quiet voice, almost a whisper. "I have something surprising to tell you."

"I won't be afraid."

"There is someone in the room with us."

Of course, she thought with delight. *I have brought the presence with me. It is standing in the darkness beside the old gramophone.*

"I am not surprised, Antonio. Please tell me who it is."

"I don't know," he said. "The visitor has not yet made himself known."

"Is it the teacher?"

"Be patient, dear historian. Sometimes the visitors can be seen, sometimes they only speak. With Dona Juana Cata we played billiards, she defeated us all. The hero Emiliano Zapata spoke only two words. Está bien. The most memorable words of my life."

She stared fixedly into the darkness, suddenly aware of her own heartbeat. Her heart went on beating though she was quite sure no time was passing.

"All evening I have been aware of a presence. I seemed to be guided by it. At times it was within me, more often nearby. Tell me, Antonio, have you ever the illusion that you are living here and now but also in the past?"

"Every day I experience this. This morning I lay helpless on my bed but I was also conversing with the black champion at the bar. It was a terrible thing the actress said to him, I am afraid he will never forgive her. *No me gustan los negros. What a thing to say to a famous guest!"*

"He will forgive her," she said. She peered into the darkness by the gramophone, it was already less intense. "Is he still there, the visitor? At the moment I feel nothing."

"I am not sure. It is possible this was an intruder, one who never stayed in the hotel during life. That has happened more than once. The intruders do not know me, they become discouraged and go away."

"It could be Rosellen," she said. "She died in Casas Grandes in 1870."

"The loved one of the teacher? That is possible."

"Or Monica Swift, who came here in 1922 with the champion. Please try to remember, Antonio. Did Monica Swift stay in my room number 23 con balcón and with jungle view?"

"No," he said very quietly. "Your room was occupied by the teacher."

Of course, she thought, the lizard on the wall was his. Vinalva turned toward her slowly, his thin right hand reached for hers, his fingers were hard and cold.

"I think the visitor has left us and now I am very tired. Promise me you will come again and we will talk about the teacher and his friends. He too loved the actresses. Also the bullfighters, we mustn't forget them. Rafael Gaona was the greatest."

She held the hand against her cheek, willing her warmth to pass into him.

"I will come whenever you ask, Antonio. Nobody will be forgotten."

At the far end of the hall the Indian woman Josefina Amor was stirring in her sleep, her comic book had fallen to the floor. Directly behind her the door to the forbidden room was slightly ajar, as though inviting her to have a look. It had been closed before. She had again an uncanny feeling, almost a shadow of dread. Once again the expected obstacle had disappeared, as though removed by her unseen companion. Josefina Amor asleep and the door open.

She picked up the comic book and put it on the young Indian's lap, sliding it under her fingers. It was a life of Christ, folded open to a dramatic picture of a young hero with up-lifted sword and a number of frightened old men, probably Christ driving the money-changers from the temple.

She went into the room. The only light came from a Tiffany glass kerosene lamp near the window. It cast a blue glow as from a phosphorescent source floating under water.

The small open coffin was of dark wood not glass, and inside it were what appeared to be only rumpled clothing and discarded rags seen from a considerable height, floating in a substance that was both water and air. But moments later all was changing, the dresses were moving, a woman's figure was quietly taking shape. The rags and discarded clothing had become a white muslin dress of an earlier era, a cameo brooch near the heart. A slender human face without distinct eyes or mouth, still floating in a watery atmosphere, the face of someone who had died quite young, the face of a woman who had drowned. But even as she watched the lines of the face were becoming more distinct. The face had changed again and was becoming distinctly familiar. She knew that face too well.

Now she could see clearly the eyes, her own large eyes, her regrettable slightly twisted corner of the mouth, her good nose. She knew them as her own although still the woman in white muslin appeared to be underwater, dead yet stirring, the body slightly swaying as from the gentle shimmering motion of unseen waves.

Casas Grandes: The Last Journey

ELOISE DID NOT GET TO TALK with Cranfield or Vinalva again, but a bouquet of flowers was waiting for her at lunch the next day, with an affectionate message from Vinalva: *For the pretty historian with ojos café*. The two old men had been exhausted by the brief visits, though Cranfield was more angry than tired. Another such intrusion, the curandero warned, and the unspeakable Rodriguez would be ejected from the hotel by force and turned over to the rural police for a beating.

Of her visit to Vinalva Eloise said almost nothing.

"He is a dear old man. His mind wanders all over the place. He wants me to write about the hotel, and Mr Cranfield wants me to write about himself and the hotel too. What wouldn't my thesis adviser say! At this rate I'll be making a career of Santa Rosalia."

"I will help you," Rodriguez said. "I volunteer my services. Take me with you on your next visit to the old manager."

"I doubt if there'll be another visit. He seemed very tired."

They were the only nonpermanent guests of the hotel left, but were usually joined by Luís and Jimmy Wilding. So today they were four at lunch, although Wilding was far away, his child's blue eyes vacant. The curandero came to them as they were having lunch on the terrace, not far from the four Indians exercising their hereditary right to camp in front of the hotel. This apparently included a right to any scraps from the kitchen. One of the crouching Indians stood up on seeing the curandero, but Pascualito waved him off.

He stood above the diners, tall and austere in a robe much stained by his concoctions.

"I will not tolerate interference with my patient. He for his part will see only those he invites and who have my permission." He pointed a scornful finger at Rodriguez. "You would be wise to leave by the next bus. Mr Cranfield is a powerful man."

"I too am a powerful man," Rodriguez said. "I am respected by the police. Ask anyone in Mérida."

"You are nothing."

Eloise was the peacemaker.

"Please sit down and join us, sir. We are all sorry if Mr Cranfield has been disturbed."

"I will accept a glass of brandy but remain standing."

"The best," Luís said to the scared waitress, who could not make herself look at the curandero. "The best Mexican."

"What exactly is wrong with Mr Cranfield?" Eloise asked.

"He suffers from many things but most of all from the Evil Winds. The lungs, the intestine, the heart, the bladder. Especially the bladder. He keeps me busy day and night."

"The mind too," Rodriguez said. "The mind is gone. Does he truly think he will make a movie about Pepe Contreras?"

"There will be no movie until the body is restored, also the spirit. I want three months, after that he can do as he wishes. He who cannot even get himself to the sanitario speaks of going to Casas Grandes. That I will not permit."

"I am sure you are right, sir," she said. "He looks much too weak to travel."

The waitress arrived with the brandy. She poured a glass and put it in front of the curandero, but without looking at him.

"Won't you sit down with us?"

"That is out of the question."

The curandero swished the brandy in his mouth, then quickly finished it. He glanced at the hovering waitress, and pointed to his empty glass. He was tempted to sit down but did not.

"Guerillas," Jimmy Wilding said brightly. "Nicanor Díaz is a bandit guerilla. He is in Casas Grandes."

"Nicanor Díaz is dead," Rodriguez said. "Long ago."

"I don't think so."

The curandero looked at the old man with a professional interest. He drank his second glass of brandy at one gulp, and seized Wilding's wrist.

"The pulses." His fingers explored the wrist for its several pulses. "I would be happy to treat the English boxer for almost nothing. Only a bottle of chica once or twice a week."

"I don't want to be treated," Wilding said. "When are we going to Casas Grandes? I want to see where Monica died."

Eloise put her hand over the other slender wrist. Beneath it were the protruding veins of age; above it, two tattooed feet, all that could be seen of the dancing girl and her grass skirt.

"Not in Casas Grandes, dear Jimmy. Monica Swift died in Colorado. You're thinking of the nice teacher Mr Stanfield. He died in Casas Grandes."

"That's right, Miss. I didn't get to go."

"It wasn't that you didn't get to go. You and Papa Jack had left the hotel by then."

The curandero continued to explore Wilding's wrist.

"The English boxer truly belongs to the pueblo. He knows the dead return, the good dead and the evil also. The dead are here now, possibly at this table. Time is a gringo illusion."

"Perhaps you are right," Rodriguez said. "Our ancestors, however, made the greatest calendars known to man. Consider the pyramid of Papantla with its 366 niches. What do you say to that? Not to mention the Toltec calendar."

"You dare tell me about the ancestors!"

"You are a victim of superstition," Rodriguez replied. "You think to cure the old man by spitting chica on his chest? You would do better to give him the chica to drink."

"I want to go to Casas Grandes," Wilding said.

The curandero held him by the chin and gazed into the old man's eyes.

"If you go there you will not return."

She went up to her room and lay down to stare at the ceiling. Odd, there was a new long crack that had not been there this morning. Had there been a small earthquake while she slept? She was not at all tired, but experienced rather a pervasive, almost physical sadness, as though weighed down by premonitions of an illness. Loneliness too, for the first time since leaving home. Who was there to talk to? Not Luís, after all, nor Rodriguez really, amusing though he was with his irrelevant rejoinders. A half hour of Rodriguez was enough.

Saddest of all, not to be able to communicate with Jimmy Wilding. He had known Charles Stanfield, had been with Monica Swift in New York after Mexico, apparently had even shared an apartment in the Bowery, though surely not as her lover. But he had hardly a word to say of that New York time, although he remembered so much of his years with Papa Jack. He would come out of his solitude at the end of the bar to bring up some vivid moment in the London or Paris of seventy years before. A gymnasium in Earl's Court where The Champion had watched him shadow boxing and punching a bag. The men in tuxedos at ringside for the great twenty round Paris fight with Frank Moran, the women in glittering gowns. "Imagine that, Miss Deslonde! Dress up like that for a fight, that's Paris for you!" Always Papa Jack this, The Champion that, the hero who could do no wrong.

His memories were so vivid, yet the words so halting that she began to feel herself drawn into his wandering narrative and expanding on it, helping him to get it out, herself creating from a sharp memory of a Havana hotel room or a dark stairway in the Bowery or the sounds of 42nd Street in New York, Herman's Gymnasium just down the street, the living feel of his life at the time. But so little about Monica Swift here in the hotel, next to nothing about Charles Stanfield, a "nice man from Boston."

The afternoon was sultry and oppressive, and she twice fell asleep over the Guest Books. Once she was awakened by the barking of dogs, the second time by a gentle shaking, and the staccato rattling of the framed photographs above the desk. Another earthquake? Or was it only a dream in which the light canoe carrying her and Rosellen Maurepas was rocked by the turbulent Rio Corte? Rosellen's flowing white dress reached her ankles, long sleeves covered her wrists.

She decided it would be prudent to go outside. The faint sulphur smell of these last days had become more intense, and the sullen gray sky was turning brown. The huddled Indians had not moved from their station and the village was quiet, with everyone either asleep or working in the fields. The silence was broken by a long mournful howl. A dog at the far end of the village, then more dogs nearby. Two of the horses that so often appeared at dusk, tormented by the first night predators, rushed silently toward her down the rutted street, then abruptly wheeled and disappeared behind the first thick trees in the direction of San Miguel. The Indians by the terrace seemed to be conferring. She could see their lips move. The stillness pressed down.

She found the others in the bar.

"Was there an earthquake or did I dream it?"

"A small one," Rodriguez said. "Only one of hundreds that each year rock the Sierra Madre Occidental. Our country is rich in earthquakes and valuable sulphur and the hot *manantiales* that bubble from the earth. Nature rocks us gently on her warm breast. With the earthquakes come our beautiful volcanoes, of which Orizaba is the highest. Nearest to us is the sleeping volcano called El Chichón which means in Spanish the breast. It emits solfateras and bubbling springs but does not erupt. Nature's breast sits upon the hot caldera."

He pointed to the large faded poster of the Papa Jack-Brian Desmond 1916 fight in Barcelona. It had slid far to the right, so that the stylized image of the black body appeared to be falling toward the white one. However, no glasses were broken, and they decided the earthquake was too small to worry about.

Jimmy Wilding slipped off his stool and went behind the bar. He stood on tiptoe to straighten the poster.

"I was there. The bull ring in Barcelona."

"Tell us about Brian Desmond," Eloise said. "I still find it hard to believe Monica Swift was so in love with him."

"Mr Desmond was a bit out of things, not all there. Stopped listening I did, he talked so much. Had a good left hook, you have to admit the hook. But shouldn't have been in the ring with Jack. Those Spaniards thought they were cheated. They threw bottles at us. Thought Desmond was drunk, had to have six or seven to get up his courage. Newspaper said he was so drunk he could hardly climb into the ring. He just danced around and clinched and held on for dear life. Can't say I blame him."

"Did you like him, Jimmy?"

"Monica loved him. She came here to find him. That was some time ago."

"But you didn't like him?"

"Jack was my friend, not Mr Desmond. Jack was Lucille's daddy and he was my daddy too. I didn't know Mr Desmond that much. Didn't know what he was talking about. Talk talk. He swaggered into that night spot in Paris, the naked savages dance show. 'Sauvage nue.' That was where they met. Lucille said we'll all get arrested. Mr Desmond took one of the naked savages and picked her up, just one hand, and then he said to Jack, 'Let's see you do it, Mr Champion!' And Jack did. Lucille said to me, 'Try to break it up, Jimmy!' But Jack wasn't insulted. He liked Mr Desmond. He was there in Barcelona and Mexico City too. In Barcelona I didn't know what was going on, Jack drank so much. He got out of shape, couldn't even get into the bullfight pants. Mr Desmond took that Barcelona fight just for money. Jack was taking it easy but he still could have killed him without trying."

"Do you remember when she was here with you, Jimmy? Did she really still expect to find Brian Desmond?"

"Sure she did. She called him a God. Mex promoter called him a devil. El diablo inglés." He turned to Eloise with a puzzled look.

"Maybe he's in Casas Grandes."

"He is dead," Luís said. "Long ago. If he fought in Barcelona in 1916 he is now under the earth. Certainly."

"You don't know that. No one could kill Mr Desmond. He was a giant."

"People just die," Rodriguez said.

Jimmy Wilding ignored him.

"Let's all go to Casas Grandes. You too, miss."

"Of course I'll go, Jimmy. If anybody goes."

"Maybe Mr Desmond is there, maybe not." He turned his innocent blue eyes on Rodriguez. "You don't have to go, you can stay here in the hotel."

"I am Miss Deslonde's assistant. I go where she goes."

"This conversation is ridiculous," Luís said. "Even I have never been to Casas Grandes. No one goes there. The palenqueros will refuse. They are the men who pole the raft. How would you get there without them? Walk through the jungle?"

They were interrupted by another and much larger earthquake. A rumbling of thunder in the mountains rolled toward them, then went underground and moments later the floor was pounded as by drums, loud then diminishing. The four of them seated at the bar were pitched forward as the earthquake struck. Several glasses fell and the bottle from which Luís was pouring dropped from his hand. A long crack in the wall appeared just above the mirror and the photographs of boxers and actresses and distinguished guests. Two of the photographs fell.

They went outside.

The odor of sulphur was more intense than ever. The browning but still cloudless sky, a dull copper sky, had become an inverted bowl that closed them in. All the dogs of the village were barking.

Three men were running toward them, waving their arms. They surrounded Luís, and all three were talking.

"What are they saying?"

"They say the earth is spitting. In one place near the cemetery the earth smokes, in another place the earth spits." He pointed to the oldest of the three Indians. "This one says it is the end of the world."

Several other Indians were at the spring, pointing. One of them beckoned.

The delicate beads that usually sparkled on the surface had given way to throbbing jets and clouds of sulphurous steam. The water beneath was yellow and opaque and even as they watched two dead fish floated up. Their bellies flopped and twisted with each rhythmic thrust as from pistons beneath the surface.

The water of the spring burned their hands.

One of the Indians made the sign of the cross, the others at once followed suit.

"It is a warning," Luís said. "You talk of the forbidden Casas Grandes and see what happens."

"That it is ridiculous," Rodriguez said. "Is our conversation to bring on fumaroles and geysers? There are earthquakes in Mexico every day."

Far to the south, in the direction of Chiapas and the volcano El Chichón, perhaps about to follow the secret road of the Andes, the rumbling began again.

"It is nothing," Rodriguez said. "Nature rocks us on her warm breast. Mexico has survived many earthquakes."

Two days later the quiet life of the village was disrupted by the arrival of a small circus, a family of five nearly starved Indians, Guatemalan refugees with one mule, two monkeys whose frequent fights alternated with sudden violent copulations and a trained dog that liked to shake hands while standing on its hind feet. The oldest of the refugees arrived dressed as a clown, one of the youngest was a dancing girl beating a drum. A short and stocky child, evidently retarded, was kept on a leash. The circus equipment and a few personal belongings were carried by a mule that was on its last legs. Within minutes of their arrival there was talk among the Zoques that the child on leash was a savage dwarf, captured as they walked through the jungle. His head, half hidden by a sombrero, was abnormally large.

More disturbing still, they were led by the adivina Alicia, who had visited the village in 1973 while the hotel was closed, and had then predicted the end of the world. A large black hound stayed close to her side and would have nothing to do with the others. The refugees set up camp in the plaza, next to the rickety bandstand, driving poles into the ground. In only minutes a sizeable tent was in place. It might have been done by sleight of hand.

The villagers gave them food, aguardiente and water, but after that kept their distance. So too the four Indians regularly camped near the hotel terrace. The refugees knew Spanish, but their Quiche dialect was incomprehensible to the Zoques. The adivina Alicia knew many languages, even English, and served as interpreter and guide.

"The Zoques remember the terrible predictions of the adivina, some of which came true," Luís explained. "The world was about to end, although she did not say when. Also everyone is terrified by the dog. A black dog carries the souls of the dead across wide water on the journey to the Underworld."

"That is ridiculous," Rodriguez said. "Mexico is ruined by superstition."

"Nevertheless that is what they believe. Also they are afraid of the child that looks like a dwarf."

The refugees were among the many thousands who fled the oppression in the Petén district of Guatemala in 1982, crossing into Chiapas and setting up numerous camps along the border. The Mexican government, appalled by this influx, had begun to push refugees back across the border. The five refugees had lost friends and family, tortured and killed by the death squads in Guatemala. Hence they wanted to put as much distance as possible between themselves and the oppressors, and Chiapas was too close. So they made their way north across the mountains into the Chimalapas and Santa Rosalia was their first village.

"What does that mean, across the mountains?" Rodriguez asked. "Did they take the famous camino secreto?"

"No one takes the camino secreto," Luís replied. "They must have come by Tapachula near the ocean, not across the mountains. But the adivina says they came across the mountains. She was their guide."

Once Alicia was famous throughout the Isthmus and her renown had taken her to the capital and even to Guatemala and Honduras. Her honesty was her financial ruin. In village after village she accurately predicted foreclosures and the ruin of crops, earthquakes and other natural disasters, the infidelity of loved ones, deaths by cancer, the erosion of house foundations. The lost ring would never be found, the stolen horse would not be recovered.

She would return after five or ten years to the same villages and be greeted by sullen silence. The predictions were correct but no one wanted to hear any more. One year a fiery young priest followed her for weeks on end denouncing her to her face. "You bring on the disasters you predict." Long ago she had a fine Buick Roadmaster, now she traveled on foot with the Indian refugees, accepting defeat like one who had taken a vow of poverty. She too was a fugitive from Guatemala.

Later in the afternoon the manager sent Luís with an invitation to the adivina to stay in the hotel free of charge. She arrived barefoot as they were having drinks on the terrace, wearing a jaunty crown hat with yellow plumage and carrying a suitcase, a small green bag and high-button black shoes. The black dog came with her. Tangled threads of gray hair fell over her aristocratic Spanish face baked by the sun and lined by exhaustion and disillusion. And by over forty years of invoking the cosmic deities and opening her body to them, by 260-day calendar calculations and the sorting of the seeds and crystals, interpreting them and responding to questions.

She sat down with them after putting on the high-button shoes.

"I offer you the free welcome cocktail," Luís said. "Then tell us why you left Guatemala."

"It is a moral story," she said. "Also a sad story. I would like a chica, preferably in a tall glass."

She would not begin until the waitress had served her.

"I was sixty years old, I had buried all my loved ones. Once I was honored in Juchitán and Vera Cruz and Mérida. Now there were only the villages and even they didn't want me. 'Go on to San Juan Evangelista or San Geronimo,' they would say. 'We don't need you, no one here has any problems.' So I went to Guatemala and made my fatal mistake. The seeds unerringly warned me. But I was tired of poverty, I longed for a few luxuries."

The luxuries were provided by a provincial governor who was also an entrepreneur on a grand scale. Stock markets and markets in commodities, the buying and selling of businesses, loans made to other entrepreneurs. Here she had her own room and private bath in the governor's house, dinners were served on a terrace overlooking the sea, cocktails every afternoon, wines and liqueurs every night. The rich men and their ladies who came for dinner had stories of vacations in Miami and New York and wore garments that came from France. All this luxury in exchange for formal divinations and informal consultations done with cards. She met with this great man four or five times a week.

"This continued for two happy years, while the seeds and crystals always came out in his favor. He was a genius, his instincts were nearly always right. 'Yes,' the seeds would say, 'buy the hotel,' and he would buy it at a good price. 'Yes, do buy the Brazilian cruzeiros and the Colombian pesos,' the seeds confirmed, and the prices would rise the next day. He consulted me on every enterprise. He even asked me to be present in his meetings with the rich men in their guayaberas, smoking their Cuban cigars, scattering ashes on the beautiful table. 'Alicia is my mistress and my wife,' he said to the rich men, 'Don't try to take her from me.'

"He was a man of genius. He always made the right decisions, the seeds and crystals confirmed them. But all this ended when he decided to buy a chain of resort hotels. His heart was in this, it was to be the greatest enterprise of his life. Unfortunately the seeds were against him. I said the prayers, I invoked the deities, the mountains and the elements, I shook my bag, I held crystals to the light, I sorted the seeds many times. And always the same result. So I went to him and I said, 'Abandon this enterprise. Buy the hotels and you are ruined.' He was enraged. 'You know how much I want these hotels, Alicia! For two years I have fed and clothed you and now you turn against me. You are a monster of ingratitude.' I made the mistake of insisting. 'The seeds can't lie,' I said, 'No one interprets the seeds as well as I. Don't buy the hotels.' There were more words. He begged me to change my advice. I refused. Then he slapped me. Believe me, there is nothing like a slap delivered by a rich man. 'Get out of my house, take your accursed little bag, leave behind the jewels and fine clothes I gave you.' I lost my temper and slapped him back. An hour later I was in jail, accused of insulting the governor. I was in jail many months waiting for my trial."

"What happened at this trial?"

"There was no trial. I made predictions of marriage for one of the guards who was grateful and let me escape. Then I made my way to the border and it was there I came upon many refugees running from the death squads and I met this small circus. I knew at once I had to lead them across the mountains into the province of Oaxaca. They were helpless innocents, it was my duty, fate put them in my way. I consulted my seeds and crystals and they replied, 'Yes, these are your brothers and sisters, take care of them.'"

"Where did you cross the mountains?" Luís asked. "I think you came through Tapachula beside the ocean. Nobody crosses the mountains. The last places you saw were San Miguel and Santa Maria. That's the way you came."

"Not this time. I know them well, San Miguel and Santa Maria, I was here nine years ago. This time I crossed the mountains from Chiapas, no villages since Chiapas. The only villages we saw were dead ones. Ruins left by the old Gods. One day we walked on stone paths cut through the forest. The paths were buried in the growth of the forest but we found them and they were as good as new. Also there was a place of silence in the jungle, no life, no sound of birds, nothing. A dead place, even the ancestors would not visit there."

Luís persisted.

"Maybe you took the picadura de contrabandistas from the east, that is the only other way, through the mountains perhaps but not across them. Unless you took the camino secreto, which is impossible."

"I don't care what men call the pathways. We came across the mountains. We nearly starved but we came across. Ten days since the last village where there were living people. Behind us was a smoking volcano, the volcano was following us. Every night we saw its fires, pointed in our direction."

"The Volcan de Tuxtla," Rodriguez said. "El Chichón is

the nearest but El Chichón is a dead volcano."

"There was much lightning. Inside the body there was lightning. It was awakened by the lightning from the Gods."

"There is always lightning in the mountains," Rodriguez said. "Nothing unnatural about that."

"Tell us about the dwarf," Luís said. "The villagers are all afraid of the dwarf."

"He is not a dwarf. He is an unfortunate little man who didn't grow, not in body, not in the mind, that is why he has the leash. His name is César and he is the brother of the dancer Annabella. In the circus he beats a little drum for the dog that dances, also for his sister when she dances."

"Your story is fascinating," Eloise said. "And beautiful, really. You are a good woman. Do you think you saw Casas Grandes along the way? You have heard of Casas Grandes?"

"Of course I have heard of Casas Grandes but no we did not see it." She looked at Eloise intently. The adivina's tired eyes seemed to come from far away. Then they were intensely present, the black pupils enormous, almost no white. "I know why you ask about Casas Grandes."

"I'm going there."

Alicia opened her large canvas bag and took out a leather bag and shook it, a sound of marbles and of seashells clicking.

"My seeds and crystals. Do you want a divination for one American dollar? I think not, you would be throwing your money away. Because I know you will take this trip, even if the seeds advise against it."

"I would love to have a consultation," Eloise said. "Do you believe in reincarnation?"

"Of course I believe."

"I would love to talk to you about that."

"Gladly. Just to talk there is no charge. But not today, and not with these men listening. Tomorrow we will talk about the dead who live again."

But the promised talk never took place. Just before sunset the five refugees of the circus had a parade through the village to announce a performance that would be held that evening in the schoolhouse. The old clown led the way with his comic antics, trying to do somersaults and always falling. The dog walked on his hind feet and now and then did a little dance. The monkeys fought and copulated. The dancer Annabella did pirouettes in the dust, the child Cesar beat his small drum. The two others straggled behind. They had just reached the plaza and bandstand, followed at a distance by thirty or so villagers when one of them cried out, 'That is not a child, that is not the brother of the dancer, that is a dwarf!" The other villagers took up the cry.

"Take your dog and your monkeys and your dwarf and go somewhere else. Take them to San Miguel or Chivela. Take the adivina with you."

The next morning they were gone.

They were able to make the trip, after all, and much sooner than expected. In spite of his misgivings Luís engaged two balsas and four palenqueros without difficulty, once it was known Jimmy Wilding would be on the expedition. His presence assured the safety of the Zoque palenqueros who would pole the raft. He was the venerable and loved boxer who had chosen to return to the village in his old age, although he could have ended his days in Oaxaca or some other world capital. He had, moreover, taught the children to skip rope in the manner of professional boxers, listened to the villagers' complaints, and attended their marriage and funeral celebrations. Wherever Jimmy went, the palenqueros would be safe.

They set out on the eighth day after the visits to Cranfield and Vinalva, watched by a sizeable silent company of natives, and under a sullen copper sky. Eloise and Jimmy Wilding were on one balsa raft, Rodriguez and Luís on the other, each raft with two palenqueros and carrying provisions for several days. For Luís had changed his mind and decided to go, in spite of his dark predictions and those of the curandero, and the ancient tales of dwarfs and demons and jaguars, and the bones left unburied since the time of the plague. He felt a certain obligation as bartender and director of the hotel's social activities. Without him his friends would be unable to communicate with the palenqueros. Even Rodriguez, though a licenciado and man of learning, had only a smattering of Zoque and mispronounced everything.

Antonio Vinalva had urged him to go. "They are my guests, in my absence they are now your guests. You must guide them to the place where the teacher died, you must protect them from any harm." To Luís this had the force of a dying man's last wish. Or not far from the last. The old man had lost much strength in the last weeks, his fingers moved almost imperceptibly as he waited for the words to come. "You will find the ball court with the shadow of the jaguar and not more than one hundred meters beyond is a pyramid and a waterfall. A small pyramid. It is there the teacher died, also his lady friend from the old times. Make no mistake, show this place to the historian."

They left shortly after ten o'clock. The two rafts moved upriver slowly under a sullen copper sky, at times almost touching. They were scarcely underway before Eloise found herself drowsing, with Jimmy curled at her feet, already asleep. She leaned far back under the roof of the little casa, a canopy of woven palm leaves. The Indians worked in silence, keeping the rafts close to one river bank or the other. Here were the limestone cliffs of Stanfield's journal and the Navy report, with only the tips of trees showing above them. She trailed a hand in the water, which was surprisingly warm. Odd, even the calm waters near the shore swirled silkily about her fingers as though tame living things were there, translucent fish darting and vanishing. Sleepily and through almost closed eyes she watched the movements of the palenquero poling in the front, whose loose white cotton garment was like a shroud. Hours and hours seemed to pass as soothingly she descended into a waking dream. What an effort of will, to raise her arm from the water and look at her watch! Only twenty minutes had passed.

Two oppressive hours went sleepily by. Even Rodriguez had fallen silent and the stillness was interrupted only by the rapids where it was necessary to go ashore or wade, with the Indians carrying the light rafts. Presently the narrowing river was closed in on both sides by blue-green jungle walls teeming with unseen life. Fantastic flowers emerged from intricately twining vines and creepers. How nice it would have been to have Charles Stanfield there beside her to tell all their names! By early afternoon the sky was again overcast, a misty yellow permeated by swirling gray ash. The silence was broken, at first intermittently then unceasingly, by jungle sounds. With the chattering parrots, and the wild cries of birds she had never heard before, Eloise closed her eyes and in a drifting daydream saw herself as the adventurous Rosellen alone under just such a palm-roofed casa as this one, trailing her hand in the water so surprisingly warm, and with the two Zoque guides as palenqueros, the father and the son not dressed in the coarse cottons of today but almost naked as they must have been in Rosellen's time.

Increasingly through the long afternoon the hallucinatory sense continued of experiencing the river and the jungle through another's eyes, although nothing in what she had read of those earlier journeys prepared her for this sinister sky and the pervasive sulphur smell. Here were the fallen trees that had lain for centuries without rotting, and the insects swarming on the soggy riverbank, and behind the forest wall the chatter of parrots and the shrill bird calls and wailing cries of a life they could not see. Long straight corridors of green forest ran off into dissolving depths of blue. Nothing but the clouded water and the sullen sky had changed in the century of silence since the dying Rosellen, not knowing she was dying, stared at the dream landscape gliding past.

Even the loquacious Rodriguez, after several attempts to

converse from raft to raft, had succumbed to the drowsing afternoon. But suddenly Jimmy Wilding, who had been sleeping with only his head protected by the casa's shade, sat up.

"When will we get there?"

"Not until tomorrow, Jimmy. We'll camp out tonight. Luís brought a big tent for us."

"Tomorrow morning we get there," Luís said. "Or early afternoon."

"Do you think we'll find him?"

"Find who?"

"Mr Desmond. He has been hiding from the police. He is a fine one for getting in trouble with the police."

"I'm afraid we won't find him. It's been a very long time. I think we just want to see the place where Mr Stanfield went, after you and Papa Jack left. See where he died."

"He wasn't in Havana. Lucille and I were in Havana, not Mr Desmond. We had enough trouble in Cuba without him to insult people. The newspaper reporters and their lies."

"Lies?"

"They said Jack threw the fight. They saw Lucille leave her seat at the end of the 25th and go outside so they said she went to collect the payoff. They said Jack wouldn't lay down until she had the money in her hand. That's lies. I'll tell you the truth, miss, this is how it was. Jack had me tell her to go. Jack wanted Lucille to go outside because he was all but gone, he couldn't stand the heat. He knew he was finished. He didn't want her to see it." He shook his head, perplexed. "Monica Swift wasn't in Havana either."

"I know. Monica didn't meet Papa Jack until Mexico."

"You knew Monica!"

"No, I was only a child when she died. But I know a lot about her. About her coming here to the hotel, and Casas Grandes, and later how she went to New York and lived in the Bowery with you. She wrote many poems and people read her poems in the schools. She became quite famous."

"I know all about New York. I was there. There was this

377

narrow stairway, up three floors you went, and the drunks slept on the stairs. Sometimes we dragged the drunks inside and fed them."

"What are you talking about, Jimmy?" Luís called from the other raft. "I never heard you talk so much."

And later, after dark, around the fire when the tent had been pitched for the night and they were eating the fish that Luís cooked on spits and thrust into the earth, a spitted fish stuck in the earth for each of them, Jimmy continued to talk. It seemed to her now he was talking to keep alive, talking against the nearby sounds in the forest where Stanfield had wandered alone, and the sounds of the night animals in the jungle, the soft whistlings and the cries of birds she had never heard. And he talked until presently she drowsing was living within his words, she too seeing the things he had seen, looking for instance at the splendid gilt and ribboned uniform of a doorman in the Hotel Dixie. And the 42nd Street Museum of Oddities where Papa Jack Johnson gave his last performances, a shuffling dance, a few chords of the guitar, Othello's dying speech and Hamlet's last one, and he Jimmy sometimes stepping up to say Kipling's poem "If" or a bit of the "Charge of the Light Brigade." And Jack telling stories of his life, not all of them true, because he Jimmy was there and knew, he had seen it all. And the glorious Hotel Dixie where for two years he lived in a room next to an elevator that whistled and howled while the ambulances shrieked and the fire engines in the long canyon avenues wailed and he was always welcome backstage at the burlesque house across the street where the naked girls teased and hugged him and sent him out for sandwiches and beer, the young strippers and the kind older ones, Betty and Hinda and Georgia and June and Rosita with her snakes, and Marcia too, winking at him when he slipped into a vacant seat and he would wave back, and the walk-up apartment on the Bowery where Monica was kind to the drunks and the crazies in the doorways, the old drunk professor who talked about the poets, and long before that the Chicago World's Fair where Jack did his thing and sometimes sparred with the children of the customers not far from where Sally Rand waved her fans, and he Jimmy was there, watching to keep Jack out of trouble, and to run for sandwiches, and sometimes himself sparring with Jack, and stripping to show his tattoos.

"Just like here where the kids want to see the tattoos. See, first the neck swells up, then the rest. Like the serpent swallowed a mouse."

He held his arm up to the fire, then went over to show the tattoos to the palenqueros who had strung their hammocks in the open between trees at the river's edge, indifferent to the rodadors and mosquitoes. He made the serpent swell for them and the dancing girl writhe.

"When did you meet Jack?" she asked, hoping he would go on talking, and Rodriguez would continue to be still. "It was London, wasn't it?"

"I was streetfighting for pennies with the buskers outside the theater."

"Tell us, Jimmy. Tell us everything."

"I was fourteen, natural flyweight, eight stone give or take a pound." In the Balneario nearly seventy years later he must have weighed twenty pounds less. For again she was within his words, but also within everything she had read about Papa Jack and Monica Swift, seeing it all and perhaps seeing more, her eyes closed and the fire burning her cheeks, listening to him talk as for the last time in his life, honoring that great time: a light rain falling in the London street outside the theater and he stripped to the waist, no tattoos then, bleeding at the mouth but a winner, fighting for pennies and sometimes even sixpence, tolerated by the buskers, a runaway from home, family and coal mine, and staring at the Champion, seeing him for the first time, splendid in a toff's gray coat and flowing tie on which glittered many diamonds, tall and huge and black towering above the white wife Lucille

Cameron who in time he Jimmy would shepherd and protect and play cards with. And here in the London street was the great Champion about to enter the theater with wife, chauffeur, manager, trainer, hangers-on: the Champion turning at the top of the theater steps to light his cigar and actually seeing him, their eyes meeting, and a flicker of understanding between them, as though Papa Jack too might have fought for pennies, still looking and the cigar not yet lit, until Lucille Cameron said (eighteen, gentle, a little full at the waist, following Papa Jack into exile): "What's the matter, Daddy? What are you looking at?" And the Champion grinning, a smile as wide as the theater marquee, "That kid, he won his fight. Give him a pound."

"A pound note it was!" The next time was the gym at Earl's Court where he Jimmy a real boxer now was training and Papa Jack came to look the place over and saw him punching the bag, with real boxing shoes now, and trunks, and hair cut short almost bald like Papa Jack himself, the Champion in snappy checked suit, straw hat, cane with a silver tip, and the proprietor pointed out the good ring with its clean ropes, the four rows of chairs for spectators, the shiny weights and pulleys, the six punching bags beside the one where he Jimmy now stood, staring. And again the Champion saw him, the enormous eyes rolling in their survey. Then they stopped, and the big right eye winked. But secretly, as though only the two of them should know. And the Champion turned to give the proprietor a nod of approval, one that included himself Jimmy Wilding, and said "It'll do." So after that he stopped what he was doing whenever Papa Jack came and offered to help. And soon after that he was on the payroll not that there was really a payroll and when he carried water to the ring he was carrying it for the Champion.

"Then Jack had to go to France, he was fed up with England where they wouldn't let him fight. I went to the station to see them off. The platform crowded with the sportswriters and the gamblers and the preachers and politicians who wanted to be on hand when the Champion and the rest left for Paris. *Good riddance!* a big headline screamed, a paper sold right under the Champion's nose, who had a fine bowler hat now and bright red four-in-hand like for the races and spats and cane, as though to tell off all the preachers and hypocrites who wanted him out of the country. So he Jimmy pushed his way until he was not twenty feet from the fancy first-class car where Lucille and the rest were already seated at little tables with glasses and flowers and crimson lamps. But Jack was still in the door to the car with his manager, looking over the crowd and the reporter. "How did you find our British hospitality, Mr Johnson?" It was a scornful aristocrat's voice, rubbing it in. The Champion didn't smile. "I was bitterly disappointed by my reception. I expected I would experience fair play in the home of the manly art. I was led to understand the British would allow any man black or white to marry the woman of his choice. I have broken no English laws. I am disappointed I was not allowed to encounter your champion." His gaze swept haughtily over the crowd of reporters and scorners and the few who wished him well. And one of these was himself, wearing the splendid coat Lucille Cameron bought for him at the shop where they also had tea and cakes, and he was wearing his best to see the Champion go. Then the Champion saw him and did not look away. And turned to his manager and said, smiling, "Let's take the boy along."

"So I was with him every day for six years. I was one of the team, Paris and Brussels and Madrid. Barcelona and Mexico City and his Cafe de Champion in Tijuana. I was there till he stepped across the border to take his punishment in Leavenworth. Should not have been punished because that law wasn't even on the books when he took her across the state line and besides by then she was his wife. So he stepped across and was arrested and the marshal was proud to shake his hand."

"When was that?" Eloise asked.

"July 20, 1920. Everyone knows that."

It was stifling in the tent, with the men's bodies almost touching hers, and she thought she would never fall asleep. But she did because she woke shaking as from cold, then knew it was the earth shaking, as Luís scrambled to his feet and tore at the muslin covering the tent's mouth. But before he could go outside, with Jimmy also now on his feet, there was a great thunderclap far away yet incredibly loud, much as she imagined a wartime bomb would sound, or a heavy gun from one of the old wars, then the staccato firing of smaller guns subsiding to an intermittent rumbling as of waves at sea. The guns firing were more and more distant.

They went outside and the Indians were huddled together and on their knees, crossing themselves. One of them pointed to the river and a break in the forest where far to the south fiery arrows darted and died above a widening arc of crimson sky. It was not yet midnight.

Luís spoke some words of reassurance in Zoque, but the men stayed on their knees.

"Only another earthquake. Nothing to be afraid of."

"But also a volcano," Rodriguez said. "At this distance it can do us no harm. Nature again shakes us on her warm breast." He crossed his arms and rocked from side to side in a cradling gesture. "Sometimes she must spit to relieve herself of the internal pressure, then it is a volcano. The earthquake comes first, sometimes the volcano. Mexico is rich in volcanoes. This eruption is without doubt the Volcan de Tuxtla named after the capital of Chiapas."

"Why not El Chichón?" Luís asked. "That is the nearest volcano."

"El Chichón never erupts," Rodriguez said. "Let me tell you about volcanoes. The roar of a volcano in the Pacific Ocean was heard eight hundred kilometers away. That is five hundred miles in the U.S. measurement. The volcano Paricutín in Mexico rose out of the earth while a farmer watched. His good land became a volcano. The superstitious Indians say the volcanoes are inhabited by Gods. Some female, some male. I think this volcano is the Volcan de Tuxtla."

There were several small earthquakes during the night, but no more sounds of eruption. By morning the sky was a sullen brown and the sun was screened by opaque and milky dust, glaring and a pale yellow. The sulphur smell had become more oppressive. A fine layer of ash and pumice had settled on the rafts and on the ground, and the water was even warmer than the day before. But there was no reason to give up the expedition, since in an earthquake they would be safer on the river and at the edge of the jungle than under cover, even the sturdy cover of the hotel.

They had been on the river about an hour when the Indians on both rafts showed signs of agitation. They continued to pole, but more urgently while conferring from raft to raft. They looked back repeatedly.

"What are they saying?" she asked.

"They say we are being followed."

Behind them the curving river was quite empty. They could see for almost half a mile before a bend in the river took it behind the wall of trees.

"There's nothing there," Rodriguez said.

"Indians do not need to see," Luís said. "They hear."

"Who would follow us?" Eloise asked. "It was hard enough to get the palenqueros to come."

"The men say they saw something," Luís said. "Also they hear. One says a raft, another says a bongo. If a bongo it could not have come from the village. The bongo is too heavy to carry past the rapids. So I think it is in their imagination. I who was born in Mérida cannot see demons and witches, but the ignorant Zoques can see anything. They are demoralized by the eruption and the earthquake. There is no cura in the village, but when there is a flood or earthquake they become good Catholics and want a priest."

There were several more delays as the palenqueros con-

tinued to insist a raft was following them. First they wanted
to beach the rafts and hide behind the thick wall of trees,
then they wanted to push on. Shortly after two o'clock the
two rafts, now only a few feet apart, turned into a narrow
stream, and there was Casas Grandes. It was smaller than
she had been led to expect from the journals, smaller than
she had dreamed, but still remarkably free from encroaching
wilderness. Under the brown ashen sky the sloping plaza rising from the river to the first buildings was drab and yellow-
ish gray under a thin layer of ash. Her eyes were smarting, a
film had formed over them, or over what she was watching.
The stone which moments before was thinly covered with
ash appeared to be slowly changing to a very light and certainly evanescent green and from green to white. A dull ache
had begun to throb behind her eyes. Now she could see the
plaza was indeed a single immense monolith descending
evenly from the row of stone houses to and under the water
of the stream. She could see the white bottom. At the end of
the plaza tufts of green were visible in the larger crevices and
a single scrawny tree had broken through near one of the
gaping black doors. The two terraced rows of houses were
smaller than she had surmised from the Journals and from
this distance she could see no fallen statues.

She felt both exhilarated and depressed, it was as though
a terminal point had been reached. Here from the spinning
raft, spinning though tethered and still, Rosellen had seen
the naked man holding a gun above his head, and from here
Stanfield and his companions had gone to take refuge from
the heat and in one of these stone rooms encountered the
German archeologist. In the more than hundred years the
ruins had hardly changed. She thought of the Biblical rock
city of Edom and the deserted city of the camino secreto,
with the dead jungle near it where no animal life existed,
only the eternal insects.

They landed. The palenqueros remained behind. In the
terrible heat the stone of the plaza burned underfoot, although

it was dusted over with a soft coating of ash. They took cover in the house with the largest door cut out of the stone. It was a single square room with no other door. The blackened walls were bare except for pegs for two hammocks. This was the only sign that anyone had been there before them.

A lizard watched fixedly, so fixedly he might be dead.

"I will remain awake for the first hour," Rodriguez said. "Then Luís will be on guard. However, I am convinced this place is deserted and without danger, except for hidden diseases."

"What diseases?" she asked. "Where there are no people there are no diseases."

"The germs sleep for centuries in the tombs," Luís said. "Why did the ancestors leave this place except for the mysterious disease? Why did they leave the city on the camino secreto of the Andes? Why were the great cities Uxmal and Chichen Itza abandoned by the ancestors?"

"Nobody knows," Rodriguez said. "As for the mysterious disease of Casas Grandes, I think it is a superstition for old women and curanderos. Nobody would want to live in this place, that is why they left."

"Why did the gringo teacher die here not in the hotel?" Luís asked.

"It was the heat," Eloise said. "He should not have walked alone in the heat. But now I've begun to think he felt the time had come for him to die. There is a very beautiful moment in his Journal, only one line, where he asks whether he had come to Santa Rosalia to die. I think his life had been rather a disappointment, a drab and ordinary life, after his great adventure as a young man. But then at the end of his life he came back to the place of his adventure and was reconciled with all that had happened."

"A beautiful thought," Rodriguez said. "You are a poet, Miss Deslonde, not only a historian. But your young woman Rosellen, was she reconciled and ready to die?"

"I wish I knew."

"This is a famous mystery," Rodriguez said. "Some die when they are not ready, others are ready but cannot die."

The men were soon asleep, even Luís was asleep. Jimmy slept curled up and with his mouth open. Was he who lived in a timeless past now ready to die? Rodriguez too had dozed off with the revolver held loosely in his lap. But she could not sleep. She was lying in a hammock for the first time in her life, and whenever she closed her eyes felt herself enveloped by the netting and suspended as in airless space. She got up with some difficulty, the hammock swinging off as she groped to get one foot on the ground. There would be time, later, to explore the ruins of the city in the company of her friends. But now she felt a need to venture alone into the other houses facing the plaza, and even go beyond that, as Charles Stanfield and Rosellen did before her. She tiptoed past the sleeping Rodriguez and went outside. He had fallen asleep while on guard.

The sultry afternoon and odor of sulphur had become more oppressive. She was inside less than an hour, yet the sickly gray and yellow sky was distinctly lower, an inverted bowl from which the clean air had some time since been withdrawn. She tried to breathe more deeply, but the taste of sulphur was disgusting, like an exhalation of rotten lungs. A fleck of ash fell on her hand soft as a moth, another lay on her cheek.

She went inside the next house, but there was nothing there, nothing at all. She longed to come upon some form of life, even an anthill and procession of ants, even a lizard with a broken tail. The stone room might have been swept clean by some ghostly inhabitant long dead, and been miraculously preserved. Or visited only today by the tidy reclusive German who in three years had moved from the turbulence of revolutionary Munich to this solitary place. There was even none of the insect detritus to be found in any long-deserted place. But in the third house there were many faintly visible graffiti on the walls, with names and dates and exhortations, some in chalk, others only charcoal smudges. The dates went back many years, but a few were quite recent. Here long ago a first band of bandits, idealists, dreamers had left their mark, and later other men in hiding had added their signatures and slogans. *Viva Zapata Viva Santibañez Viva Nicanor Díaz Brigado Caballero Batallón Rojo de Juchitecos.* Some admirer of the romantic Nicanor Díaz, if not Díaz himself, had spent time hiding here! *Independencia Rectificación Revolución.*

She went outside in the darkening afternoon, darkening though it was not yet four o'clock. Now she could actually see ash falling, the sky thickening with ash. The ash was soft, touching her almost soothingly, warm and harmless although the half-hidden copper sky still burned. She came to the end of the row of houses, peered for moments only down into a long dark place, a stone stairway to what was surely a tomb. The tomb could wait. For she was climbing now, anxious to see what she could see before her companions joined her, feeling that she was herself Eloise yet was also loyally living within the minds of her dead friends of the Guest Book and the Journal. Rosellen's Journal ended with her strange vision of a naked man holding a gun. Yet after that she had gone ashore and ventured alone beyond the plaza and its houses, even beyond the ball court where the jaguar watched, at last to the grove where her Zoque guides saw her among the dead playing.

The second row of houses had smaller doors, but the rooms were large, they appeared to be cut deeper into the stone hillside. She was astonished, glancing in the high-silled doorway of the second house, to hear voices, then to see the moving shadow of a small man, not his features, only the moving shadow. She was sure it was a man. "Hola!" she called, but it was no more than a whisper, "Buenos dias, señor." A soft tentative animal growl responded. She wanted to run. She longed both to enter the room and to be back in the safe place where her friends were sleeping. But she stood her ground until her eyes became accustomed to the darkness of the room, and now she saw that it was unfurnished. The people if there were any, or only the one man, or the animal she had mistaken for a man, would be hiding in a back room, if there was a back room. But she could see no door or other opening in the blackened wall.

She went up a stone stairway to the second row of houses.

The sickening sulphur smell pressing down from the inverted bowl of sky now seemed to rise from within her, and she thought of Rosellen's vomiting. Rosellen had gone on, though her Journal was finished and her life was behind her. The naked man with the gun had disappeared, so too in her own life the shadow of the growling or whining animal. But there was much else still to be discovered, and she boldly entered another stone house. In the center of the small room was a roughly hewn table of some very light wood which on closer inspection proved to be stone. A narrow door led to a room that was utterly dark. Had there been a chair, even an uncomfortable stone chair, she would have sat down at the table, which could certainly be used for a desk. Here it would have been possible to rest and perhaps to add belatedly certain explanations to her Journal. Only she had not really kept a Journal, in that she had failed, she had only notes.

She closed her eyes and was instantly aware that a man, or the statue of a man, a very tall man, perhaps the skeleton of a man, was watching her from the dark room. He was standing in the narrow door.

She found herself outside, wanting to run but also needing to vomit, intending to lean far over with arms resting on her bent knees, a most uncomfortable position, waiting for the nausea to subside. She vomited. Or rather, to be precise, it seemed to her important to be precise, she had vomited some time ago, and had apparently scrambled up an overgrown stone stairway, since she was now standing at its top. The plaza and the river were far beneath and behind her. She was looking down instead on a wilderness of grays and greens, and on a stone avenue that cut through it. The narrow way was almost hidden by creeping plants and bushes, but she knew it would lead to the ball court and beyond it to the pyramid and waterfall. She knew this even before, moments later, she saw the elevated stands of the ball court covered with ferns and coiling lianas. The silence lay around her like an invisible barrier thrown up by the sullen heat of the declining afternoon. No birds, no alert and watching reptiles, none of the butterflies and dragonflies she had hoped for upon leaving the dead stones of the houses. But just then, as in response to this thought, a cloud of gnats flew out of a nearby thicket. And she herself set out to see whatever she was intended to see, and first of all the ball court.

She was already there. She stood in the very center of the ball court where so many players had died, hoping to see the figure of a jaguar carved in the stone floor or even, thanks to the architect's design, the shadow of a jaguar that would be thrown on only this day of the year, at this hour of the afternoon. The ball court was not, as she had expected, bare. Bright green plants and several small trees had grown through cracks in the stone. Ferns sprouted from the walls and serpentine festoons flourished near the stone hoop high above the ground. Beneath the hoop was the bas-relief of a dancer almost life-size, wearing only a thick belt, and near him a man with the same belt, kicking a large ball, a much larger ball than could have gone through the hoop. On closer inspection she saw that the dancer, but not the ballplayer, had the large stubby ears of a great cat, a jaguar, and a brutal mouth turned down at the corners. But the eyes and nose were those of a man.

There was no shadow of a jaguar on the ball court, it would be the wrong time of day. But then she knew, even before looking up, that a living jaguar was watching her. It was at the far end of the ball court, at the top of the wall, motionless as a statue, not spotted but sleek and black, the great shoulders bulging, the stubby tail unmoving, the front paws and claws at rest, the small ears shaped like triangular leaves. The jaguar, though at first seeming no larger than a great hound, appeared to grow as she watched.

Then the tail did move, and the jaguar looked away. Its brutal face had turned aside and could no longer be clearly seen. But the lovely body still for a few moments continued to glide in her thoughts, even after the animal was gone.

It was as though she was not the person the jaguar had expected. Reluctantly she decided it would be proper to wait for the others before proceeding to the pyramid, the waterfall and the grove.

When she got back to the plaza they were standing in front of the house where they had taken their siesta. They did not see her where she stood near the steps to the second tier of houses. They were looking across the empty plaza at the river where a young Indian was wading toward them with a man on his back. He was carrying Antonio Vinalva. His thin arms hung slack over the Indian's shoulders, his head had fallen to one side and his long white hair covered his face. It was apparent that he was either dead or about to die and in any event was unaware of his surroundings. But she knew he would, before losing consciousness, have given directions on how to reach their destination.

The young Indian carrying Vinalva slowly approached, but took no notice of them. She was pleased to see that her companions, even the irrepressible Roberto Rodriguez, had not moved. They too had become part of the afternoon's stillness. The Indian carrying Vinalva climbed sturdily past the second tier of houses and would soon be out of sight. They would move from the dead ruins to the living ruins beyond, where the cloud of gnats had flown out of a thicket, past the ball court and the jaguar, and at last to the pyramid, the waterfall, the grove. Presently she and the others would go there too, but for the moment it seemed proper to wait.

In the interval she would ponder the meaning of the several journeys of which she had become the last historian.

Surely Rosellen had known all along that William Walker lay still and dead in the Trujillo grave, and all his brutalities at rest. But the dream of survival allowed her to wander at last along winding picaduras and even as far as Casas Grandes. Stanfield as well must have known that Rosellen and Marita were not to be found, yet they had achieved a second life outside time in his imagination, as Brian Desmond the strong swimmer in Monica Swift's journeys and poems. Stanfield too, in his solitary death, was reconciled. But now it seemed to her Antonio Vinalva more than any of the others had freed himself from time, in the guest books and commemorative photographs, and even in the forged greetings and autographs of the great. In his dreaming mind they were all immortal, and in Casas Grandes he would join them.

Author's Note

William Walker belongs to history, as do Dona Juana Cata, Nicanor Díaz and the various Mexican generals and bandit revolutionaries mentioned. The story of Papa Jack is a fictional recasting of Jack Johnson's life in Mexico after his release from prison. The story of Monica Swift was suggested by the wanderings of the poet Mina Loy, who married the eccentric boxer-poet Arthur Cravan in Mexico in 1918. Cravan, who fought Jack Johnson in Barcelona in 1916, disappeared in Mexico. There were continuing rumors of his survival, but his body was never found. Mina Loy long refused to believe he was dead, and was said to have looked for him in a number of Mexican prisons. She wrote an unpublished novel, *Colossus*, about her life with Cravan. She died in Aspen, Colorado in 1966.

The isolated Zoque village of Santa Maria Chimalapa was known even to the conquerors. In 1853 it was connected to the outside world by one of the worst roads on the Isthmus, but in 1970 could be reached only by difficult mule paths. It is more accessible today. Santa Rosalia must have been totally destroyed by the 1982 eruption of El Chichón. It is not to be found on any map.

A. J. G.